JASMINE CRESSWELL
Marriage on the Run

Muriel Jensen
The Little Matchmaker

TORONTO • NEW YORK • LONDON
AMSTERDAM • PARIS • SYDNEY • HAMBURG
STOCKHOLM • ATHENS • TOKYO • MILAN • MADRID
PRAGUE • WARSAW • BUDAPEST • AUCKLAND

If you purchased this book without a cover you should be aware that this book is stolen property. It was reported as "unsold and destroyed" to the publisher, and neither the author nor the publisher has received any payment for this "stripped book."

ISBN 0-373-83522-1

HARLEQUIN SPECIAL Vol. 2

Copyright © 2002 by Harlequin Books S.A.

The publisher acknowledges the copyright holders of the individual works as follows:

MARRIAGE ON THE RUN
Copyright © 1994 by Jasmine Cresswell

THE LITTLE MATCHMAKER
Copyright © 1997 by Muriel Jensen

All rights reserved. Except for use in any review, the reproduction or utilization of this work in whole or in part in any form by any electronic, mechanical or other means, now known or hereafter invented, including xerography, photocopying and recording, or in any information storage or retrieval system, is forbidden without the written permission of the publisher, Harlequin Enterprises Limited, 225 Duncan Mill Road, Don Mills, Ontario, Canada M3B 3K9.

All characters in this book have no existence outside the imagination of the author and have no relation whatsoever to anyone bearing the same name or names. They are not even distantly inspired by any individual known or unknown to the author, and all incidents are pure invention.

This edition published by arrangement with Harlequin Books S.A.

® and ™ are trademarks of the publisher. Trademarks indicated with ® are registered in the United States Patent and Trademark Office, the Canadian Trade Marks Office and in other countries.

Visit us at www.eHarlequin.com

Printed in U.S.A.

CONTENTS

MARRIAGE ON THE RUN   9
by Jasmine Cresswell

THE LITTLE MATCHMAKER   125
by Muriel Jensen

Marriage on the Run
Jasmine Cresswell

Marriage on the Run

Jasmine Cresswell

Chapter One

OTHER PEOPLE had eccentric great-aunts who kept too many cats, or wore funny hats, or always ate TV dinners. Great-Aunt Bette blew up garages. She didn't mean to, of course, but her chemical experiments had a disastrous tendency to go explosively wrong. Consequently, when Laura checked her answering machine and heard Great-Aunt Bette proclaiming an emergency and asking her to come to Columbus at once, Laura called the airline and booked the first available flight. She considered the chances no better than fifty-fifty that her aunt's newest garage would still be standing by the time the plane landed in Ohio.

But for once it seemed she'd been too pessimistic, Laura thought, paying off the cab that had driven her from Columbus airport to the quiet, tree-lined suburb of Arlington, Ohio. Aunt Bette's house and garage were both still standing, and the latest roof looked unscathed. No smoke belched with chemical fury from any of the windows. Most astonishing of all, the grass in the small front yard was neatly mowed, a concession to suburban order that Aunt Bette usually ignored as beneath the dignity of a scientific genius such as herself.

Laura jumped nervously when a feminine voice sounded behind her, calling her name. She spun around and saw one of Aunt Bette's neighbors waving across the garden fence.

"Hello, Renée." Laura spoke cautiously, preparing herself to hear the worst, despite the neighbor's cheery smile.

"Laura, how nice to see you, and looking so calm, too!"

Her stomach clenched. "Should I be looking, um, worried?"

Renée chuckled. "I guess not, with Stefano waiting for you. Bette wasn't sure when you'd arrive! All set for the big day?"

What big day? And who was Stefano? Laura started to sweat, but long experience had taught her it was much better to confront Aunt Bette directly, not get garbled versions of the current calamity from friends and neighbors. Somehow, she managed to return Renée's beaming smile.

"We're all set," she said, just as if she knew exactly what she was talking about. "Isn't it a lovely evening?"

Renée rolled her eyes. "Well, the humidity has been driving me crazy, but I can understand how you feel, I was just the same— Oops, there's my phone. See you tomorrow, my dear."

Glad to escape, Laura waved goodbye and continued up the path to the front door. Renée and Aunt Bette had always been good friends, so if Renée was cheerful, perhaps the situation wasn't too serious. Ringing the doorbell, Laura allowed herself a faint glimmer of hope. Maybe Aunt Bette simply wanted Laura to write a rude letter to the United States government. Aunt Bette conducted running battles with various government departments, including the IRS and the FBI. Her animosity toward the IRS rose and fell according to the season and the status of her tax return, but her dislike of the FBI had been unwavering ever since the occasion, some twenty years earlier, when the bureau had chosen to investigate one of her exploding garages. Bette had despised the FBI special agents assigned to the case.

"They were even more dim-witted and boring than Walter Willis," she would say in recounting the story. "Good grief, they thought that the mere existence of some absurd local ordinance was a valid reason to stop the march of scientific progress." Walter Willis was Aunt Bette's ex-husband, the man she had dropped out of college to marry. To accuse someone of being more boring than Walter was Bette's greatest insult.

Laura knew better than to get embroiled in a discussion about Walter Willis. Instead, she concentrated her efforts on writing placating letters to government officials and doing her best to keep Bette out of jail. She loved Aunt Bette and was anxious to keep her a free woman, if at all possible.

But where was Aunt Bette? Shifting uneasily, Laura peered in through the leaded-glass panel set into the door. All she could see was a stretch of empty hallway. The house remained ominously silent. Why hadn't her aunt answered the door? Laura's brief moment of optimism vanished, gobbled up by dread. Visualizing her aunt either pacing the concrete floor of a prison cell or stretched out unconscious over a rack of poisonous test tubes, she rang the doorbell again, longer this time, and banged the old-fashioned door knocker for good measure.

To her relief, the response this time was immediate. She heard the sound of footsteps coming from inside the house, and after another ten seconds or so, the door was finally opened, although not by Aunt Bette. A tall dark handsome man, with a pair of spectacular smoldering brown eyes, stood framed in the doorway. As soon as he saw Laura, his mouth quirked into a devastatingly sexy smile that displayed perfect white teeth and an entrancing mischievous dimple in his right cheek.

Laura took one look at the man, and her heart plummeted right to the soles of her sensible summer sandals. Aunt Bette, she decided grimly, was in even worse trouble than she'd feared.

"Hello, you must be Laura. Your aunt has been so anxious for your arrival." The man took her hand in a firm warm handshake. "I am most sorry to keep you waiting, but Bette and I were in the basement."

Every one of Laura's alarm systems jangled in immediate red alert. "In the basement?" she said, in a voice slightly cooler than an Arctic ice floe. "Doing what?"

"We were...experimenting." If she hadn't known better, she'd have sworn the man was being deliberately provocative. He held her gaze, his eyes twinkling with what many women would no doubt have considered lethal charm.

"I am Stefano Corelli," he said. "I am your aunt's friend and also her colleague. Please do come in. Bette has been waiting for your arrival with much eagerness."

This must be the Stefano Aunt Bette's neighbor had mentioned. He not only looked like a cross between Rudolph Valentino and a young Marlon Brando, but he also spoke with a beguiling hint of an Italian accent. The hairs on the back of Laura's neck prickled, and her palms started to sweat. This man meant serious trouble, she knew it beyond any possibility of doubt.

Aunt Bette's foibles weren't limited to blowing up garages and writing rude letters to the lawfully appointed agencies of the government. She also suffered from a disastrous tendency to pick unsuitable friends who turned out to be charlatans at best, or outright criminals at worst. This man was too darned handsome and too darned sure of himself to be honest. What could a six-foot hunk of sexy Italian manhood find interesting about seventy-two-year-old Aunt Bette?

Laura had well-honed instincts for sniffing out fakes. Having grown up in Manhattan, with parents almost as eccentric as her great-aunt, she prided herself on possessing all the practical worldly wisdom the rest of her family lacked. She knew from experience that men with melting eyes, sensual smiles and cute dimples were *always* too good to be true. When you got to know such men a little better, you discovered that they were frauds who wore tinted contact lenses and spent hours practicing their smiles in front of the bathroom mirror. Nine times out of ten, they even had their dimples surgically implanted.

The man—Stefano—smiled at her again, and Laura's stomach gave an odd little jump. Of warning, no doubt. When she realized he was still holding her hand, she pulled away from his clasp, her movements jerky and uncoordinated.

"Stefano Corelli? My aunt has never mentioned your name. You must be a new acquaintance." She spoke with the cool courteous formality she had found most effective in dealing with Aunt Bette's retinue of no-hopers and entered the familiar hallway of her aunt's home without waiting for him to issue a invitation.

Stefano stepped aside, gesturing with European flair

to indicate that she should precede him. "Yes, that is true. I am a very new friend of your aunt, but I hope also a good one."

Laura looked up at him, meeting his gaze but refusing to respond to the friendly welcome she saw in his eyes. Charm, for most of the con men Aunt Bette collected, was an even more necessary quality than good looks, and Laura dismissed his overtures for what they were worth—precisely nothing.

"How did the two of you meet?" she asked, putting down her overnight bag and leading the way into the comfortable cluttered living room. She looked around anxiously for subtle signs of whatever her aunt's current problem might be. On the surface everything seemed to be normal—at least for Aunt Bette—but Laura's stomach was already performing a jig of anxiety. Her instincts were infallible where her aunt was concerned, and she was beginning to suspect that she had walked into the midst of a major problem.

"How did your aunt and I meet? We found each other at a university cocktail party." Stefano gave another of his devastating smiles. "As a newcomer to the department of chemical engineering, I was feeling most alone. Your aunt was kind enough to tuck me under her wing, and we have spent much time together ever since."

That figured. Stefano had obviously spotted a gullible victim and latched on like a leech. Poor Aunt Bette hadn't stood a chance. "My aunt is an exceptionally generous woman," Laura said.

"She is indeed." Stefano showed not a hint of guilt. "It was a privilege to meet her. She is a woman of...astonishing intellect."

Laura heard the tiny hesitation before he spoke the

last couple of words, and she smothered a quick flare of defensive anger. It was all right for her to question Aunt Bette's achievements, but she resented this outsider's obvious sarcasm.

"Are you sure you're qualified to judge my aunt's intelligence?" she snapped.

He looked taken aback, but any response he might have made was lost in a flurry of air and the bounce of sneaker-clad footsteps. Aunt Bette erupted from the basement, perennially innocent blue eyes sparkling and hair spiking around her head in a silver halo of excitement.

"Laura, dearest, you've come!" Her aunt enveloped her in a bear hug that smelled of equal parts Giorgio perfume and something sulfurous. After giving her niece a kiss, she pushed her away and examined her critically. "You're looking better than usual. Your clothes are still hopeless, but you've changed your hair. Being blond suits you."

Laura blushed. Trust Aunt Bette to notice the change in her hair color and to comment on it with Stefano listening. Laura's hair was thick and wavy, but it's natural color was a boring nondescript brown. A couple of months ago she'd been seized by a burst of spring fever. On the spur of the moment, she had walked into her local salon and asked the hairdresser to highlight the mousy strands with streaks of bright apricot gold. Laura was self-conscious about the dramatic result, which she realized was totally unsuited to her life-style. As a senior accountant working in the tax department of Peabody Foreman, a giant New York law firm, she needed to dress soberly.

But somehow, despite her doubts about the new hair color and the outspoken disapproval of Brett Hotchkiss, her boyfriend, she had gone back to the salon three weeks ago to have the golden streaks renewed. Laura was alarmed at what this desire for flamboyance indicated about her character. It seemed as if some secret part of her bore a disturbing resemblance to Aunt Bette. The truth was that she felt a tiny kick of pleasure each morning as she stepped out of the shower and blow-dried her hair into a dazzling cloud.

Bette gave her another hug. "You must be thirsty after your plane journey. We must all have a drink," she said, a declaration that could produce anything from carrot juice to coffee to vintage burgundy. "No, no, Laura, you've had a long flight. Sit down and get acquainted with Stefano while I make the tea. I know you two are going to like each other a lot. I'm just sure of it." With a beaming smile at both of them, Bette disappeared into the kitchen.

Stefano sat down, leaning back against the sofa cushions and looking thoroughly at home. "I have noticed a funny thing," he said, giving Laura a smile that was considerably less warm than the one he'd greeted her with. "Whenever a friend of mine introduces me to someone and tells me I'm going to like that person, it never seems to work out."

"In Aunt Bette's case that isn't surprising," Laura said. "Her judgment about people is terrible."

Stefano's smile tightened still further. "Do you find it so?" he inquired blandly. "For myself, until I met you, I would have said her judgment was excellent."

Until I met you... During the course of her work, Laura often found herself trading barbs with corporate financial sharks who used words as a form of unarmed combat. Under the circumstances, it was strange that Stefano's mild gibe hurt. Quelling an impulse to apologize, she sat down in a snug old armchair and sent him a stern assessing look. "You were about to tell me some more about the circumstances under which you and my aunt met, Mr. Corelli."

"No, I wasn't," he said softly. "You were conducting an inquisition on that subject. I had expressed no intentions at all. But now I will do so. The prickles of dislike coming from you are making me uncomfortable, so I believe I will go into the kitchen and help my good friend, Bette. I can rely on her to provide company that is always most enjoyable. Excuse me, if you please."

He rose to his feet, shoved his hands into the pockets of his slacks—a piece of clothing that accomplished the amazing feat of being both fashionably baggy and yet skintight across his hips—and strolled with casual nonchalance toward the kitchen.

Ill-mannered lout! Laura fumed silently for a couple of minutes, but by the time Bette returned, she'd mellowed enough to realize she was being ridiculous. Stefano's only crime so far was to exude an aura of blatant sexuality that left Laura feeling uneasy. Which, when you got right down to it, was her problem, not his. She watched almost enviously as Bette and Stefano sauntered into the living room, chuckling over some private joke. Stefano was carrying a large tray laden with a teapot, cups, saucers and a plate of warm muffins wafting delicious smells of apple and cinnamon. He set the tray on the table and bowed over Bette's hand.

"All ready for you to do the honors, signora."

Laura's stomach muscles clenched in suspicion. Why the heck was Stefano being so nice to Bette? What did he stand to gain? Then she told herself to stop being ridiculous and give Stefano the benefit of the doubt. Maybe he was just exceptionally gallant and bowed over old ladies' hands all the time. She forced herself to smile at him as she went to the table, sniffing appreciatively. "Those muffins look wonderful, don't they, Stefano? I didn't know you'd taken up baking, Aunt Bette."

"I haven't. Stefano made them." Bette beamed at her new protégé with maternal pride. "Wait until you taste his zabaglione. He's a great cook."

"How...unexpected," Laura murmured, her suspicions returning with the speed of light.

"Not at all," Stefano said, offering Bette the plate of muffins and grinning at her affectionately. "These days, every smart bachelor realizes that the way to a woman's heart is through his kitchen."

"True," Bette said. "Your cooking would have won my heart a hundred times over, even if you'd been a dud as a scientist. These muffins are scrumptious." She sat down and sighed contentedly. "Now, Laura, you must tell me how everything is at home. And at work, of course." Bette turned to Stefano. "Have I told you that Laura is likely to be the youngest woman her firm has made partner? And the first partner ever who isn't a lawyer."

Stefano squeezed Bette's hand and grinned affectionately. "I think you may have mentioned it once or twice, *cara*. In between telling me how beautiful she is and how sweet-tempered."

Bette flicked away a crumb. "Well, was I right?"

Stefano looked up, his gaze locking with Laura's. "Your niece is most exceptionally beautiful," he said.

Laura felt heat flare deep inside and rush upward into her cheeks. She glanced down and found herself staring at Stefano's strong brown fingers curled over Aunt Bette's tiny blue-veined hand. She blinked and hurriedly focused her thoughts on her aunt's original question.

"Everyone is fine at home," she said briskly. "Dad likes the new director of the orchestra, and he's been teaching a master class at the Juilliard, which gives him a lot of satisfaction. And Mother is working on a new story line for her soap, which she thinks will be a surefire ratings winner. She's combined a missing heir, a baby who needs a lifesaving transplant and a love triangle involving a woman, a man and a person who could be either."

"Either of what?" Bette asked, looking puzzled.

"Either a man or a woman. Mother plans to decide later in the season when she has a few more plot twists laid down."

For once Aunt Bette seemed at a loss for words. "It sounds spectacular," Stefano said. "Your mother needs only to make her man/woman into an Elvis reincarnation, and I'd say she was on to a ratings blockbuster."

Laura laughed. "Good point. I'll suggest that to her."

"I'm not going to ask you to explain what you're talking about," Bette said. "Let's change the subject to something I can understand. How is Brett? Still working hard?"

"Very hard, and he's fine, thank you. Hoping for a promotion next month."

"That's good, dear. He seems such a nice solid young man."

"He's very reliable," Laura agreed, giving her aunt a grateful smile. Bette was always willing to accept other people's life-style choices, which was one of the reasons Laura loved her so much. Unlike Laura's parents, who had taken a totally unreasonable dislike to Brett, Aunt Bette never said he was a stick-in-the-mud or attempted to persuade Laura to end the relationship.

"Brett is Laura's boyfriend, as well as her boss," Bette explained to Stefano. "He's just finished writing a book. What's the book about, Laura, dear?"

"The tax implications of profit repatriation for American corporations."

"How...fascinating." Stefano reached for another muffin.

Bette smiled brightly. "Brett is an exceptionally well-informed young man, and he's always anxious to share everything he knows with anyone willing to listen. Have you two gotten any further in settling on a wedding date?" she asked Laura, pouring more tea all around.

"Er, no. Actually we aren't even officially engaged," Laura mumbled, taking her cup back from Bette.

Now why had she felt compelled to produce that piece of information? Laura wondered. Brett had asked her to marry him more than two months ago. And last month he'd produced a tasteful diamond solitaire ring, which he politely asked to slip on her finger. She had stuttered and hesitated and finally refused, although she was quite sure that one day soon—very soon—she would accept his proposal. In fact, the more she thought about it, the more difficult it was to understand why she hadn't agreed to marry Brett the moment he asked. He was everything she wanted in a man: calm, organized, thoughtful, conservative. And a crashing bore. She quickly pushed the disloyal thought away. It was surely a mark of her erratic upbringing, and her own lingering immaturity, that she couldn't distinguish between a well-ordered life and a boring one. Brett was a man who had the details of his life under firm control. That didn't make him dull or tedious or any of the other adjectives her parents constantly used to describe him.

"Brett and I are both so busy at work," she said. "Sometimes our personal lives just have to take a back seat."

"To corporate taxes," Aunt Bette said, with suspicious blandness. "Well, you know I've never quite been able to understand your mutual devotion to IRS form 1040."

Laura had long since given up trying to convince her aunt that counseling corporations on their tax liabilities involved more complex and far more interesting decisions than how to fill in the blanks on a standard tax-return form. She decided it was time, past time, to get the subject away from her relationship with Brett and back to basics. Such as why Aunt Bette had summoned her from New York with a frantic telephone message.

"Well, boring forms or not, I'm terribly busy at work, Aunt Bette, so maybe we should get right down to business. What exactly is the problem you need me to help you with? Why did you ask me to fly out here to visit you?"

For the first time, Aunt Bette began to look a little nervous. "It's just a small favor," she said. "Nothing that would inconvenience you in a major way."

Laura sighed. "Out with it, Auntie. The more you protest like that, the more nervous I get. What is this 'small' favor you want me to do?"

"Absolutely nothing to get excited about."
"Then tell me."

Aunt Bette drew a deep breath. "I need you to marry Stefano," she said. "Tomorrow morning, if you wouldn't mind."

Chapter Two

LAURA STARED at her aunt in shocked silence. Then she laughed. "All right, Aunt Bette, now please tell me the real reason you sent me that frantic message."

"But that *is* the reason," Bette said. "I need you to marry Stefano as soon as possible."

"B-but why? Wh-what for?"

"I'm not suggesting a real marriage, of course. Just the sort of union they used to call a 'marriage of convenience' in my mother's day." Bette seemed to think this explanation made her proposal entirely reasonable. She smiled brightly. "I can quite see that you wouldn't want to enter into a real marriage with a man you didn't know. Besides, I daresay Brett wouldn't be at all happy with the idea of your marrying Stefano. Not if it was going to be permanent."

Laura recovered the use of her voice. "He certainly wouldn't! What's more, *I'm* not at all happy with the idea. In fact, I couldn't possibly consider it. It's crazy!"

Bette leaned forward and took her niece's hand. "You have to understand the problem, dear, before you can leap to conclusions about whether my solution is crazy. The point is that if Stefano doesn't get married soon, he's going to be arrested and thrown into jail. You wouldn't want that, would you?"

"Don't bet on it," Laura muttered. All her doubts about Stefano rushed back in a tidal wave of disapproval. She had no difficulty believing he was in trouble with the law, but how matrimony would help his plight, she couldn't imagine. Whatever the details, he was clearly using Aunt Bette for his own ends. Any desire to laugh or treat her aunt's suggestion as a joke vanished. "Aunt Bette, if Stefano's committed a crime, marrying me isn't going to keep him out of trouble."

"Actually I have not committed a crime," Stefano said. "Not even a very small one."

Laura swung around, her expression severe. "The police don't usually waste their time and energy pursuing innocent people."

"They are overworked and understaffed. They are also human." He shrugged. "Sometimes they make mistakes."

"And in your case, they've made a mistake?"

Stefano didn't seem to hear her sarcasm. He smiled cheerfully. "But of course. In my case they have made a most terrible mistake. Besides, it is not precisely the police who are chasing me. It is the enforcement officers of the Immigration and Naturalization Service. They wish to deport me as an illegal alien. They have threatened to fly me out of the country on the next available plane." Stefano looked hurt at the mere thought that anyone, least of all the INS, might want to get rid of him.

"Precisely how have these INS agents made a mistake?" Laura asked. "If you're not an illegal immigrant, why do they think you are?"

"Well, it is just possible that—technically speaking—I may be an illegal resident. Under a strict interpretation of the rules, you understand." Stefano gave another charming self-deprecating shrug. "But it is all one big mix-up, you know? Unfortunately I cannot convince the Immigration and Naturalization Service to stop chasing me long enough to listen while I make my explanations. They say that I have entered the country without legal papers, and now they wish to make an example of me by deporting me. It seems there have been too many foreigners entering the United States on student visas and then disappearing into the criminal underground when it is time for them to go home.''

"And that's what you've done?" Laura asked.

"How can you ask that when I am here with Bette? Of course I am not disappearing into the criminal underground." Stefano sounded wounded that she could even suggest such a thing. "Nor did I enter America on a student visa. At least, I did not do so intentionally. I came here under a quota that grants special residence status for experts and scholars."

Laura knew better than to judge people purely by their outward appearance, but it was very difficult to imagine Stefano, with his athletic body, melting brown eyes and sexy dimple, fitting into the category of "expert and scholar."

"And what, precisely, are you an expert on?" she asked, barely bothering to conceal her sarcasm. *Women* was the answer that flashed into Laura's mind.

For the first time Stefano looked embarrassed. "I would not claim that I am an expert on anything."

"Nonsense," Aunt Bette interrupted. "He's a professor at the University of Bologna, in Italy, and he's also this year's visiting professor in chemical engineering at Ohio State, a position that entitles him—"

Laura blinked at Stefano in amazement. "You're a

professor of chemical engineering?" The question tumbled out with an embarrassing lack of tact.

"Why, yes." Stefano appeared amused. "Is there some reason I should not be a professor?"

She swallowed hard. "No. No, of course not. It's just that you look so, um, young...." That wasn't quite what she'd intended to say, but it was better than telling him he looked too damn sexy to be a chemist.

"I am thirty-five," he said. "Nearly thirty-six. Even in Italy, that is quite old enough to have accumulated several college degrees. And once you have enough fancy letters after your name, there is always some university that feels obliged to hire you."

Laura didn't think it was quite as simple as he made it sound to attain a full professorship by the age of thirty-five, but she didn't allow herself to be sidetracked. After years of dealing with Aunt Bette, she had learned how important it was to stick to the main subject. "But if you're a member of the faculty at Ohio State, I don't understand the problem. Why hasn't the university's legal department taken care of your visa mix-up?"

His shrug was eloquent. "They have tried, but it is one of those horrific bureaucratic muddles that are everyone's fault—and nobody's. Alas, the clerk who processed my paperwork seems not to have filled out the correct forms, but she no longer works for the university, so nobody knows why she failed to complete the proper paperwork. And nobody, of course, has any explanation as to why the error was not spotted until now, when it is too late to make the necessary applications for a correction."

The knowledge that Stefano was simply the victim of a paperwork snafu filled Laura with relief. The man's ethical standards were no business of hers, except as they affected Aunt Bette; but oddly enough she was rather glad he hadn't committed a real crime. For some reason she wasn't at all anxious to see him clapped in jail. She risked giving him a cautious smile.

"Look, Stefano, I think you're worrying too much about your visa situation. Bette has a jaundiced view of the government, and she's probably scared you more than she should. I deal with the Internal Revenue Service every day, and the folks over there make the INS look like Sunday school teachers." She leaned forward, stressing her point. "Reason will get you much further than emotion, Stefano. Just tell the INS they've made a mistake. Be polite, but firm—"

Stefano sighed. "I wish it were so simple! But, alas, the INS doesn't wish to be reasonable and accept a correct revised application. The university lawyers are working on my behalf, but naturally they cannot permit me to remain in the employ of the Chemical Engineering Department when my status is not legal. Their hands are tied. My lawyers are, however, confident that when my case comes up for official review, I will certainly be given permission to remain and teach my courses."

"Then I don't see why you have a problem."

Stefano smiled wryly. "Unfortunately the INS insists that I must return to Italy to await the outcome of the court hearing they plan to hold."

"That must be frustrating for you and for everyone," Laura said. "But it seems quite fair and reasonable, given the problems this country has with illegal immigrants."

Aunt Bette snorted. "Fair, you say? *Reasonable?* I suppose it might be, except that the INS estimates it will take five years for Stefano's case to come to trial."

"Five years!" Laura was appalled. "But that's outrageous!"

"It could be even longer than five years," Stefano said gloomily. "Or a few months less, of course, although even the INS does not hold out such a hope." He spread his hands wide in a helpless gesture. "For the university it is frustrating that I cannot fulfill my contract and deliver a series of lectures during the fall semester, but they have given up hope of—how do you say?—fighting city hall. But for your aunt, and now for me, it is vital that I stay in the country. Our work together has reached a critical point—"

"An extremely critical point," Aunt Bette asserted. "I can't possibly go on without him."

"Actually, *cara*, I'm not at all sure that is true. You learn so fast.... Anyway, suffice to say that Bette has become my champion against the raiders of the INS. A most fierce and noble champion, I should add. She was very excited when she came up with this plan for a marriage with you as a way to salvage my right to live and work in the United States. I told her we could not hope that you would say yes, but Bette..." Stefano glanced at Bette, his gaze almost tender. "Your aunt—she is most persuasive."

"I believe you. Aunt Bette's a scrappy fighter." Laura sighed. Her aunt's heart was as wide and generous as the Mississippi, but she had no grasp on practicalities. Laura didn't doubt for a moment that it was Aunt Bette who'd come up with the crazy idea of marrying her off to Stefano. The scheme was vintage Aunt Bette. Realizing there was no way to convince the woman that the idea was unreasonable, Laura turned to Stefano again in the hope he would have a better understanding of reality.

"Stefano, I'm sorry. I can see this is a rotten situation for you. I've read some of the stories in the newspapers about the activities of the INS, and I realize the whole agency is overworked and backed up in their paperwork to a point that's a national scandal. But you can surely understand that I can't marry you just because you're having visa problems." She shook her head. "I'm sorry, but the whole idea is crazy! Not to mention illegal. The truth is, we could both end up in jail if anyone found out what we'd done."

She should have known better than to add those final sentences. Aunt Bette took up the charge at once. "Illegal!" she exclaimed, jumping to her feet. "Hah! In this country it will soon be illegal to blow your nose without asking for permission from the government! We citizens have got to stand up for our rights—"

"But that's the whole point." Laura cut off her aunt before Bette could launch into one of her impassioned lectures on America's vanishing liberties. "Stefano *isn't* a citizen of the United States. He is an illegal alien."

Her aunt was not to be bested. "But if you marry him, he won't be illegal anymore, and certainly not an alien. Ridiculous phrase, 'illegal alien.' It sounds as though the INS expects him to jump aboard his spaceship the moment their backs are turned." Bette wriggled on her chair cushion, smiling triumphantly. "So you see, Laura, you must marry him right away—it solves all our problems."

Long experience warned Laura that direct arguments would be useless. "Why are you so anxious to have Stefano remain in the United States?" She turned to Stefano. "For that matter, why are you so anxious to stay?"

Stefano hesitated, exchanging a secretive glance with Bette. "There are several reasons," Bette said vaguely. Laura had the strangest impression that her aunt looked momentarily scared.

"Aunt Bette?" she said. "Has something happened to frighten you?"

"Good heavens, no." Bette's smile returned at once. "I was worried about Stefano of course, but nothing else. I really need him here, Laura."

"Why?"

Stefano gave Laura another of his suspiciously sexy smiles. "As you've probably gathered, your aunt and I are nearing completion of a very important project," he said. "Bette has achieved a major breakthrough in the technology of fabric manufacture. She has provided the scientific insights and most of the hard work, but I have been able to offer her some good advice on how to take commercial advantage of her discoveries and also how to streamline the process of production."

"We've patented everything," Bette said smugly. "Three major companies are negotiating with us to buy our formula."

"It is amazing to me what extraordinary success your aunt has achieved with such limited laboratory equipment," Stefano said, glancing at Bette with every appearance of genuine admiration. "Frankly, it reminds me once again that in the field of science it is ideas and brainpower that count, not the splendor of the work setting."

Stefano wasn't telling her more than half the truth, Laura was sure of it. Her suspicions about him returned in full force. Too many of her aunt's previous partners had rhapsodized about Bette's amazing achievements, usually only days before they took off with the contents of her bank account. Bette had no formal scientific training, and years of exploding garage "laboratories" had left Laura unable to believe that her aunt really hovered on the verge of a major scientific discovery. Walter Willis, Bette's ex-husband, had a lot to answer for, Laura thought wryly. He had been a chemical engineer, and he was the person who had set Bette off on her lifetime hobby of scientific experimentation. And as far as Stefano was concerned, if he was truly a trained scientist, a professor as he claimed, he would be in an excellent position to know that although Bette was a wonderful kind bright person, she was a rank amateur in the field of experimental chemistry.

"Explain to me some more," Laura said, unable to keep a renewed chill from entering her voice. "I don't understand exactly what it is you've discovered, Aunt Bette."

"In layman's terms, it's hard to say more than that we've developed a process for manufacturing a completely new sort of fabric," she said promptly. "We're very excited about the potential, aren't we, Stefano?"

"Very excited," he agreed, giving her another fond smile.

"What's different this time, Aunt Bette?" Laura asked with more than a touch of weariness. "You've been working on this project for years. I distinctly remember that new-fabric development was the cause of exploding garages numbers two and three."

"And now all my years of work have finally paid off," Bette said. "At long last we'll be able to recoup the cost of all those exploding garages you keep on about, Laura. Maybe we can even charge them off as a development expense on my next income tax return."

"Wouldn't that be great?" Stefano grinned at Bette before turning to face Laura. "Your aunt has taken a giant step forward in technology," he said. "We are working on the last few minor kinks in a process that will enable us to manufacture a fiber that is made of natural cellulose, like rayon, but with the strength and durability of fibers made from artificial polymers, like nylon. The combination produces a yarn that's soft and pliable, but nearly indestructible."

"Think of it, Laura!" Bette's baby blue eyes shone with enthusiasm. "Once my new fabrics are in production, companies will be able to manufacture a cloth that drapes and breathes like a natural fiber but washes and wears like polyester."

"It sounds wonderful," Laura said. "Almost too good to be true, in fact."

"But your aunt has made the impossible dream a reality," Stefano said.

Bette leaned forward in her chair. "There's so little work left to be done," she said. "And Stefano has all the training and the expertise I lack. Alone, we both have good skills. But together, we create a synergy. With his skills and mine, we can reach an answer to these last few problems in a matter of weeks—maybe even days—I know we can. By myself, it would take me another year at least. In fact, I might never resolve the final problems. I've reached the point where my lack of formal training in chemistry is really a handicap."

"You're too modest, *cara*." Stefano patted Bette

on the hand. "You are a genius. You would succeed sooner than you believe."

Laura's temper snapped. She couldn't bear the idea of Bette being taken advantage of yet again. "For heaven's sake!" she burst out, directing her anger toward Stefano. "The pair of you don't seriously expect me to believe that you've cooked up a product in my aunt's garage that's going to revolutionize cloth manufacturing in this country!"

"Not in the garage," Bette explained patiently, "in the basement. I have my laboratory in the basement nowadays. So much more room, and we avoid the problem of all those gasoline fumes."

Laura gritted her teeth. "That's not the point, Aunt Bette. How could you and Stefano achieve a breakthrough that's eluded everyone else, including giant chemical corporations like Dow and Monsanto? They've spent millions of dollars on research and development, and you're claiming that the two of you beat them to the punch—with test-tube experiments in your basement, no less!"

Stefano looked at her coolly. "You misunderstand the situation," he said. "*The two of us* haven't discovered anything. It is your aunt who has made the breakthrough. Your aunt alone. And she has achieved this amazing feat because she has one of the most creative and brilliant scientific minds I have ever encountered."

Bette blushed. "You were a big help, Stefano. You know you were."

"Yes, sure," he said, giving her another friendly grin. "I was great at washing test tubes and keying your experimental data into the computer, while you produced the ideas."

Aunt Bette waved her hands in a dismissive gesture. "Stefano, you're much too modest, but we don't have time to argue right now. We have to get you married so that we can see this project through to the end."

His mouth twisted ruefully. "A most excellent idea, *cara,* but it seems that I lack a bride."

"Nonsense. Laura takes a while to shake loose from her inhibitions, but she always sees the point in the end, don't you, dear?"

Laura was struck speechless by this novel view of her behavior patterns. Aunt Bette took advantage of the silence. "You see? She's not protesting anymore. She's beginning to see reason."

Laura stuttered, but Aunt Bette gave her no chance to become coherent. "Well, then, dear, now that you understand the situation, I take it that everything's settled, at least in principle? Laura, I don't want you to think that this marriage to Stefano is going to be a major imposition or anything like that—"

"Heaven's no! What's a wedding or two between friends? Do you want us to have the ceremony before lunch or afterward?"

She should never have risked being sarcastic. Aunt Bette beamed her approval. "Oh, definitely before lunch. The sooner the better. I'm sure that weasely little INS agent is going to track Stefano down any minute now."

"Which INS agent is this?" Laura asked.

Bette, of course, totally ignored the question. "I'd better go and call Judge Waterman right away to confirm our appointment for tomorrow morning." Jumping to her feet with an agility that would have done a woman of thirty proud, Bette enveloped Stefano in a bear hug. "You see, Stefano? I told you she always behaves sensibly in the end."

"Sensibly!" Laura finally recovered her voice. "Look, Aunt Bette, I wasn't serious—"

"Dearest, your problem is that you're always much too serious. But I admit we do need to discuss a few practical details. However, everything can wait until I have Judge Waterman all lined up and ready. Now, where did I put his phone number?" Aunt Bette peered around, pulled out a notepad from under the teapot and glanced at the chicken scratches that passed for her handwriting. "Ah! Here it is! I knew I'd written it down somewhere." She waved the pad with a triumphant flourish and bounded from the room.

An ominous silence followed her departure. Stefano cleared his throat. "I have a most strong feeling that the wedding Bette is arranging will not take place."

His quiet statement pierced the bubble of Laura's anger. Ridiculous, but she almost felt guilty for not agreeing to get married at twelve hours' notice to a man she'd just met. A man she didn't trust and suspected of lying. At the moment, however, Stefano didn't look like a con man. He looked like a handsome intelligent man, struggling to find a way out of a difficult situation. She tried to stop reacting emotionally to the situation and point out to him calmly why Bette's scheme was so impossible.

"Look, I'm sorry, Stefano. I truly wish I could help you out of this tricky visa situation, but getting married is out of the question. The concept of marriage means something special to me...."

"I quite understand," he said quickly. "In fact, I blame myself for allowing Bette to summon you here. Selfishly I did not try very hard to dissuade her from her grand idea. I thought only of Bette's work and how a stupid legalistic tangle will prevent me from helping her to achieve something that will benefit people everywhere."

"I don't understand what you mean."

"An easy-care fabric that is strong and yet attractive would make life easier for many people. Mothers who must wash their children's clothes, organizations that must provide uniforms, furniture manufacturers that would like hard-wearing attractive upholstery fabric at low prices. The list goes on and on."

The guilt feelings were growing. Laura clung to the threads of her common sense. "Stefano, even if Aunt Bette's project is as terrific as you say—"

"Why do you doubt it?" he asked. "Is that not insulting to your aunt? To doubt her ability to produce a great work?"

"Of course not," she said, horrified by his accusation. "For heaven's sake, I love Aunt Bette—"

"Love her—and patronize her," he said. "The quaint old lady in tennis shoes, who can never quite remember where she left her umbrella. Naturally she could not have developed anything genuinely important."

"No. Good God, no!" The denial was heartfelt, but Laura flushed, appalled to recognize a smidgen of truth in Stefano's accusation. But only a smidgen. She might have doubts about Bette's chemical experiments—and heaven knew, she had some justification for her doubts in view of the many past failures—but she loved her aunt without reservation. Laura not only recognized Bette's insightful original perspective on the world, she genuinely valued it. Ever since she'd been a toddler, Bette had wrapped Laura in a blanket of warm affection and unstinting praise, closing the emotional gap left by her parents' absorption in their own marriage and careers. The truth was that she owed Aunt Bette. Big time.

She got up and paced the living room. "Aunt Bette is very important to me," she said. "I would do almost anything to help her."

"Except sign your name next to mine on a marriage certificate."

"Unfortunately I can't just sign my name and walk away. Once we go through the ceremony, we'll be married. Husband and wife. Joined at the hip and so on and so on."

"We would be married only in strictly legal terms. You would surely agree that a true marriage consists of something more than two names on a government form." Stefano caught and held her gaze. "In fact," he said softly, "even in legal terms, a marriage requires more than two signatures on a piece of paper to be considered complete. There is the little matter of consummation, the physical union of the husband and wife."

Laura was beset by a vivid image of Stefano and herself in bed together, her hair floating in a golden cloud across the tanned skin of his chest, while his legs twined intimately around hers. The picture set her pulses racing and her skin burning with sudden heat. She forced the intrusive picture away, struggling to speak coolly. "Naturally even Aunt Bette isn't suggesting we should go that far to save you from the INS." She was rather proud of the sophisticated way she managed to toss off that comment.

"Naturally not," Stefano agreed pleasantly. "I am

sure that she knows you feel as I do about having sex. I never do it, not since I was eighteen or nineteen."

"Never?" Laura squeaked, shocked into indiscretion. "In fifteen years!"

Stefano grinned, brown eyes darkening with hidden laughter. "Ah," he said, "I am pleased that at last I have caught your full attention. No, in fifteen years I believe I have never *had sex*. Personally I prefer to make love with a woman, not simply to perform sexually. And to make love, it is necessary for both partners to feel at least some measure of liking and affection, not to mention a certain amount of mutual trust. And in our case that does not seem to be possible, no?"

"No." Laura cleared her throat. "Definitely not," she said more firmly. "So our marriage would certainly remain unconsummated in every way."

"However, when we apply for the divorce, we should say only that we have irreconcilable differences," Stefano suggested. "The legal process might become more complex if we point out that the marriage has never been consummated, and we certainly don't want to arouse any gossip if we can help it."

"No, we sure don't." Laura gulped. How in the world had they progressed to the point of discussing the terms of their divorce? she wondered. A couple of minutes ago, they'd both been agreeing that the whole idea of a marriage was unreasonable.

Aunt Bette chose this inopportune moment to pop back into the living room. "Everything has been settled with Judge Waterman," she said cheerily. "He'll be here at ten sharp. You know, I'm beginning to feel positively excited. Have you got something pretty to wear, Laura?"

"I have a pale peach cotton dress." She replied automatically, then sat bolt upright in her chair, horrified at how her adamant refusal even to consider the idea of marriage had somehow transformed itself into a discussion of whether or not the union was to be sexually consummated and what she ought to wear for the ceremony. "Wait! I haven't even agreed to go through with this marriage yet. I mean, it's absurd. I'm expected back at work after the weekend."

"That's no problem," Bette said. "You must call Brett right away and explain to him that you need to take a couple of weeks' vacation."

"Two weeks! Aunt Bette, that's impossible! Besides, what am I supposed to say? By the way, Brett, I'm getting married?"

"Are you getting married?" Stefano asked quietly.

"No, of course not!" Her denial was loud with anxiety.

Bette's forehead crumpled in thought. "I'll explain everything to Brett," she said. "But you must agree to stay with Stefano for a couple of weeks at least—no signing the marriage certificate and taking off for New York on the next flight. You know what government officials are like, always suspecting innocent citizens of committing a crime—"

"You're forgetting something," Laura said dryly.

"What's that, dear?"

"We *are* planning to commit a crime. We're aiding and abetting Stefano's attempt to remain illegally in this country."

"Oh, that!" Bette sniffed. "That's not a crime, dear. That's just taking care of straightening out one of the government's more illogical spasms."

For once Stefano seemed to be paying no attention

to Bette. He looked across at Laura, his gaze hypnotically intent. "Have I understood you correctly?" he asked. "Have you decided, after all, that you are willing to marry me?"

Laura's stomach dived into a roller-coaster loop-the-loop. She swallowed hard. "Yes," she said, wondering at what point during the afternoon she'd taken total leave of her senses. "Yes, I guess I've agreed to marry you."

Chapter Three

IN THE CAUSE of getting Laura married to Stefano, Aunt Bette transformed herself into a model of swift-moving efficiency. Like a conjurer pulling successively larger rabbits out of a hat, the same lady who had never yet balanced her bank account or been able to find the claim stub for her dry cleaning overcame each and every hurdle with airy aplomb.

Laura's efficiency seemed to decline in direct proportion to her aunt's amazing accomplishments. She stumbled and bumbled through a phone call to Brett, quickly discovering there was no good way to explain to someone you'd been dating for a year that you planned to marry another man. She was weak with cowardly relief when he finally lost his temper and slammed down the phone.

Fortunately she was spared the horror of explaining the impossible to her parents, since they weren't home when she called. Bette seemed crestfallen, as she hung up after leaving a message on their answering machine. "I'm so sorry, Laura. I was hoping they might catch a late plane out here tonight and attend the ceremony tomorrow."

Laura's mouth fell open, either from shock or horror, she wasn't sure which. Before she could recover her voice, Bette—a tornado in sneakers—had moved on to the next item on her list.

By ten o'clock the following morning, when Judge

Waterman arrived to perform the ceremony, Laura was worn to a frazzle. Even Stefano, resplendent in a navy blue Italian silk suit, appeared a touch frayed around his magnificent edges. Bette, however, looked fresh as a daisy in her green linen dress and perky high-heeled sandals. Indefatigable in the cause of giving this marriage a gloss of romance, she sent Stefano into the dining room to entertain the judge with champagne and orange-juice cocktails, while she took charge of putting the finishing touches to Laura's bridal outfit.

"Try to smile, dear." Aunt Bette pushed Laura onto the stool in front of her dressing table. "You look as if the IRS has just turned down your claim for a tax rebate."

Laura grimaced. "In the grand scheme of things, that's beginning to seem like a minor problem."

"You're right, dear. We should always try to keep life's problems in perspective. Who cares about the IRS? Or the INS for that matter?" Humming to herself, Bette took out all the pins with which Laura had fastened her hair into a neat French knot and brushed vigorously. When her niece's hair was billowing around her face in a cloud of soft waves, she beamed with delight. "There, now, that's more like it."

"Like what?" Laura asked, although she couldn't help sneaking a sideways look in the triple mirror. Her great-aunt's unexpected talents included considerable skill as a hairdresser.

"Like a bride. We have to keep up appearances, don't we? Now, sit still for another minute. I have to find you a necklace." Bette trotted across to her closet.

Laura picked up the silver-framed photo that had sat on Bette's dressing table ever since she could remember. The picture showed a young, plump and sweetly pretty Bette gazing adoringly from beneath the brim of a white straw hat into the eyes of a handsome man with bright blue eyes and sandy hair. "This is Walter Willis, isn't it?" Laura said, when her aunt returned carrying a black leather box. "Your ex-husband."

"Yes." Bette didn't even glance at the picture. "That was taken on our wedding day."

"Why have you kept it on your dressing table all these years?" Laura asked, suddenly curious. She'd seen the picture a hundred times and never questioned its presence. Today, for the first time, it occurred to her that not many women would choose to display a constant reminder of a marriage that had failed almost forty years earlier.

"Walter Willis took my dreams and trampled on them so completely that it was ten years after the divorce before I could believe in myself again." Bette sounded matter-of-fact rather than bitter. "When I could look at that photo without feeling ugly and stupid, I knew I was cured. I keep it there to remind me that an intelligent woman can easily fall in love with a destructive mean-spirited man. But that's enough about Walter. He's really not worth discussing." She flicked open the lid of the jewelry box and drew out a strand of lustrous pink-tinged pearls. "These were my sister's," she said. "Your grandmother's. She looked a lot like you, you know, tall and fine-boned, not short and squidgy like me." Bette fastened the glowing pearls around Laura's neck and smiled with evident satisfaction. "Mmm...they're perfect. You must have them as a wedding gift." She hummed a few bars of a melody. Wagner's "Wedding March," Laura realized, feeling cold with sudden fright.

"Aunt Bette, come down out of the clouds!" she said. "Listen to me. This setup is a fraud, an illusion. I am not really getting married, and Stefano isn't my genuine husband-to-be. He's an illegal immigrant, and I'm marrying him to keep him out of jail, no other reason."

"Shh!" Bette glanced nervously toward the door. "Sol Waterman may be seventy years old, but he has ears like a hunting hound. Stop worrying so much. Remember you're doing this for a good cause."

Laura's stomach performed its hundredth somersault of the morning. "That's what all the mad dictators say. However immoral the action, they always claim it's for a good cause."

Bette picked up the posy of pink roses lying on the dresser, but she hesitated, not handing the flowers to Laura. "If you have genuine moral objections, you can call this off, you know. Stefano might be jailed for a few hours, even a day or two, but the university lawyers will soon get him released. After all, he's considered one of Italy's most outstanding scientists. Some high-paid lawyer should be willing to hit the INS over the head hard enough to make them sit up and notice that they've made a mistake."

Aunt Bette spoke briskly, but behind her bravado Laura heard the disturbing throb of something that sounded almost like fear. She remembered the furtive exchange of glances she'd noticed earlier between Stefano and her great-aunt. Was Bette scared, Laura wondered, and if so, what could be scaring her? Come to that, why did she need to finish this research project so quickly when she'd been working on developing a miracle fiber for years?

The answer flashed into her mind as soon as she

formulated the question, and her hands turned icy. "Aunt Bette, you're not sick, are you?"

"Sick?" Bette seemed genuinely amazed at the question. "Laura dear, I'm healthy as a horse. Can't you see that?"

"Promise me? You wouldn't lie?"

"I promise I'm not lying," Bette said. Her eyes twinkled. "All those years of munching on raw vegetables because I was too lazy to cook seems to have paid off. According to the doctor, my heart's thumping away with more oomph than a teenager's."

"You certainly look kind of sprightly," Laura said, her entire body flooding with relief. She reached out and squeezed Bette's hand, taking the little bouquet of garden roses and burying her face in their delicate pink blossoms. "Well, what are we waiting for?" she said. "I'm all gussied up, so isn't it time for us to get this wedding over with?"

Bette remained silent for another long moment, then she leaned forward and gave Laura a quick kiss. "Thank you, sweetheart. I'm sure you won't regret this."

The doorbell rang and Bette straightened, shrugging off her momentary seriousness. "That will be the Hortons. You remember Nick and Renée, don't you? My neighbors from across the way? They're coming over to act as witnesses for you and Stefano."

"You have this wedding amazingly well organized, Auntie. Anyone would think you'd been planning it for weeks!" Laura spoke teasingly, wanting to lighten the slight tension that lingered between them. She was surprised when her aunt's cheek flushed with guilty color.

"I haven't been planning anything," Aunt Bette

said, trotting toward the door. "You just underestimate how efficient I can be when I set my mind to it. Now come along, dear. You don't want to keep Stefano and the judge waiting."

"That," Laura said dryly, "is debatable."

STEFANO WAS WAITING for her by the window in the living room, framed by the dramatic crimson of Aunt Bette's favorite velvet draperies. Oddly enough, he looked almost as nervous as Laura felt. Their eyes met as she walked toward him, and she sensed a momentary bonding, a twinge of empathy that must have had its roots in the fraud they were jointly perpetrating. Laura looked away, burying her nose in her bouquet of roses, trying to think of something—anything—other than the fact that her stomach clenched tight with desire every time he looked at her.

Stefano stepped forward and took her hand. He carried it to his lips, brushing a graceful kiss across her knuckles. Infuriatingly, she felt her heart speed up, so she scowled at the top of his head and told herself that by the time he was middle-aged, he would undoubtedly develop a paunch and grow a bald spot.

He bent his head low over her hand, pulling her toward him, speaking only to her. "You are so beautiful that I have no breath," he said.

Laura's knees buckled, and he steadied her with an arm around her waist. She reminded herself that he was Italian, and his national honor required him to make American women weak-kneed as a matter of principle. The reminder didn't help. She stared at her shoes, because she was afraid of what he might read in her eyes if she risked looking up at him.

The judge, thank goodness, chose that moment to

speak. "Hello, Laura. It's nice to see you again, and on such a happy occasion, too."

She managed to find her voice. "H-hello, Judge Waterman."

The judge beamed with paternal reassurance. He was of the old school and obviously approved of brides who blushed and lowered their gaze. He wouldn't be so benevolent if he suspected the truth, Laura knew, and the thought of the deception she and Stefano were perpetrating was enough to stiffen her backbone. She gave her groom another scowl. Trust Stefano to carry his portrayal of the lovesick swain to excess! *She* at least had the decency to keep their pretense of affection within reasonable bounds.

"This is a very happy occasion," the judge declared again, in a tone of voice that permitted no dissent. "Now, my dear, are you ready for me to marry you to this fine young man?"

"Yes." She stared straight ahead, fuming. *Fine young man, indeed. Huh!*

"Stefano, do you wish to marry Laura? To take her as your wife until death separates you?"

Stefano had the audacity to take both her hands and hold them against his cheek before replying. She couldn't make up her mind if she was impressed or infuriated that he managed this feat without crushing her bouquet. He smiled at her with every appearance of exquisite tenderness. "Yes, it is very much my wish that Laura should become my wife."

At least that was true, she reflected, clinging to the remnants of her common sense. Stefano managed to sound so sincere because he was desperate to marry her, even if it was for all the wrong reasons. She thought wistfully that if Brett had shown half Stefano's eagerness, she'd have accepted his proposal long ago. It wasn't that she'd wanted Brett to sweep her off her feet and carry her to his bed while showering her with kisses, but in an entire year of dating, he'd shown no real passion at all. She at least wanted to feel that her husband looked forward to taking her to bed, and Brett simply hadn't seemed to care. She was sure Stefano would never leave his bride wondering whether or not he desired her. When Stefano chose his *real* wife, she would know he loved and wanted her more than any other woman on earth. Laura sighed, admitting to just the faintest tinge of envy.

"Who has the wedding rings?" the judge asked.

"I have them." Aunt Bette stepped forward, holding out a neat little velvet tray with two rings nestled within its folds. After the past several hours, Laura accepted her aunt's efficiency as a matter of course. Stefano took the smaller of the two rings, a thin gold band that gleamed with the patina of age. "It was my mother's," he said to the judge, and Laura had a horrible conviction that, for once, he was telling the truth.

"Do you promise to be faithful to Laura and to support her through the difficult times, as well as the good?" the judge asked.

"I do." Stefano took the ring and, without waiting for the judge to prompt him, reached for Laura's hand. "I give you this ring as a token of my love and a pledge of my commitment to you." He spoke softly, as if he and Laura were the only people in the room. She felt her eyes prick with tears, and she fought them back. This was ridiculous! If she got carried away like this at a fake wedding, she'd need a mop and bucket to soak up the moisture if she got married to a man she really loved.

Stefano gave her hand a reassuring squeeze, almost as if he knew what she was feeling. "You can count on me, Laura. I will always honor you and I promise to cherish you in good times and bad. Whatever happens, I will always be there for you."

He sounded so sincere she almost believed him. He slipped the ring on her finger. It fit perfectly, but she'd reached a point of unreality where she almost expected that.

"Laura, now it's your turn," the judge said.

She took the ring from the tray held out by Aunt Bette. "I give you this ring as a token of my love." The words were no more than trite formula, and she tried not to think of their meaning. Suddenly she looked up and found herself staring straight into Stefano's eyes. From some source hidden deep inside her, a new spate of words welled up. "I promise you that I will always stand by you, Stefano, and that I will always be your friend, no matter what."

He smiled. "A wonderful promise, *cara*. I thank you."

The judge harrumphed. "Very nice. Now, by the authority vested in me by the state of Ohio, I declare you husband and wife...."

She had no idea if the judge added anything else to his ritual patter, because at that moment Stefano stepped forward and took her into his arms. "At last," he murmured, "I may kiss my bride."

Italian men must take lessons in kissing, Laura thought dazedly, and Stefano had undoubtedly earned an A-plus in all his courses. It was her last semicoherent thought for several minutes. Stefano's mouth moved over hers with masterful possession, leaving her clinging to him, tingling with excitement and craving for more. Absurdly, instead of feeling grateful that he didn't take advantage of the situation to deepen their kiss, she kept wondering how it would feel if he teased apart her lips and thrust his tongue deep into her mouth. Her breasts grew heavy and she felt her lips part, and her body instinctively molded itself to Stefano's.

At that very moment, he ended their kiss with chilling abruptness. Blinking, Laura lifted her head and became aware of a smiling applauding audience. Aunt Bette hugged her. "Congratulations, dear, I know you've done the right thing."

Nick Horton thumped Stefano's shoulder and congratulated him on his pretty bride, and Renée laughingly informed Laura that Italian men made wonderful fathers. Judge Waterman handed them a piece of paper that certified they were legally married, and the entire wedding party headed for their cars and the celebratory luncheon that Aunt Bette had organized in a downtown restaurant.

Laura sat in the back seat of the judge's Lincoln Town Car, taking care not to allow even an inch of her skin to touch Stefano's long muscular legs. In view of that post-wedding kiss, she'd decided it was safer if she and her supposed husband didn't come into physical contact with each other ever again.

After a couple of minutes, it became obvious that her resolution was unnecessary. Her new husband was in no rush to exercise any of his conjugal rights. Stefano, in fact, seemed barely aware of her existence. He leaned forward in his seat, staring out of the car's side window with hypnotic intensity. Laura began to feel somewhat frustrated. She had been looking forward to delivering one of the sharp witty put-downs she had lain in bed last night inventing. It was annoying not to need any of them.

The judge and Aunt Bette kept up an animated conversation as the car inched through heavy lunchtime traffic toward the restaurant. By the time they'd been driving for ten minutes, Stefano's lack of interest in his new wife was becoming so blatant Laura began to develop an entirely fresh set of worries. Dammit, didn't Stefano realize he had responsibilities? He was supposed to be crazy in love with her! In order to justify their hurried marriage, he needed to maintain the illusion of a man swept off his feet by passion. Unfortunately, with his back turned to her face, they didn't look much like a pair of torridly loving newlyweds. Distant cousins who'd just renewed a bitter family feud was more like it.

Laura cleared her throat, but Stefano continued to stare out the window. She cleared her throat again. He didn't twitch a muscle. This is the final absurdity, she thought wryly. Somehow, she had to get his attention. Should she kick him or kiss him?

"Stefano." She tried to sound wifely and devoted, but ended up sounding irritated. She laid her hand on his arm. "Stefano, honey." The endearment nearly choked her. "Honey, what in the world is so fascinating out there?"

He stiffened and turned around at once. "*Carissima*—my darling—forgive me. I...um...er...thought I had seen an old friend from Italy."

"And had you?" she asked sweetly. "He must be a very good friend to keep you staring so long."

"Yes, indeed he was. He is. But I am not sure if it was really my, um, friend. I believe so."

"What a shame you couldn't speak to him. I don't suppose you'll be able to find out where he's staying."

"I believe there is no problem in finding him again," Stefano said wryly. "I am fairly sure that he will follow me."

Laura looked up and Stefano gave a slight almost imperceptible shake of his head. What had he meant? she wondered. Was he being followed by a government agent, and did it matter even if he was? After all, that was the whole point of their marriage. Stefano now had a legal right to claim residence in the United States, so he no longer needed to hide from overzealous INS agents.

Judge Waterman looked at them through his rearview mirror, his gaze more than a little puzzled. Stefano must have sensed the judge's attention and realized at once how out of character his behavior appeared for a new groom.

"Mia cara sposa." He twisted on the seat so that his back blocked Laura from the judge's view. Then he leaned forward, murmuring passionate endearments, mostly Italian, and appearing to burrow his face into her neck. With surprising tact, not to mention skill, he managed to keep at least three or four inches of space between their bodies.

He smelled wonderful, Laura reflected, a mixture of soap, woodsy after-shave and sheer man. He felt pretty good, too, with an impressive set of biceps bulging in his arms as he braced himself against the rear seat cushions, straining to create the appearance of holding her close while actually maintaining a polite distance.

Because of her position vis-à-vis the judge, it was

impossible for Laura to play her part in the illusory embrace without truly hugging Stefano. Reluctantly she curved her arms around his shoulders. She felt him tense, and her stomach tightened in an answering knot. Of anticipation, she realized, not of repugnance.

Stefano shifted on the seat. He gave an inarticulate grunt, perhaps of apology. The gap between the two of them narrowed to less than an inch, then closed completely when the car bumped over a pothole. Laura's skin instantly erupted in goose bumps, but she didn't move away.

Telling herself she despised physical passion that had no roots in emotional harmony, she sought to get a grip on her runaway hormones. Now was the time to whisper a stinging one-liner into Stefano's ear, reminding him that he'd better keep his distance. Unfortunately her mind seemed to be empty of witty one-liners. Her mind, in fact, was fast emptying of all coherent thought. Her fingers, by contrast, seemed to have acquired a will of their own. They were running up and down Stefano's arms with undeniable eagerness and were soon linked behind his head. At the same time, Stefano was rubbing his cheek against hers, while his lips brushed softly against the corner of her mouth.

A coherent thought finally formed in Laura's addled brain. She wanted him to kiss her. She *badly* wanted him to kiss her.

"Stefano..." she whispered.

"Laura..." His mouth hovered over hers for a tantalizing few seconds, then moved on. She heard him draw a shuddering breath. "You are a great actress," he murmured. "Thank you, Laura. You have saved the day. I was careless and the judge was becoming suspicious of my indifference."

"You're welcome." The words came out in a husky murmur. Her fingers, she discovered, had finally unlinked themselves from their clasp around Stefano's neck and were now twined in his hair. Twined *tightly* in his hair, pulling his mouth down toward hers. Several seconds elapsed before she registered that his arms were no longer braced against the back of the seat. Instead, they were wrapped around her waist, and his rib cage was crushed against hers. Her breasts began to ache and her nipples tingled.

Lack of oxygen, she decided. Stefano was much too close and his weight was becoming oppressive. But for some reason, she made not the slightest effort to cure her problems by moving away from him and drawing a refreshing breath of air.

"Laura…" There was a new and urgent note to the way he muttered her name.

"Stefano…" She sounded like a frog croaking on a lily pad. Or a woman whispering to her lover.

"Here we are!" Aunt Bette exclaimed. "The restaurant at last!"

Judge Waterman chuckled. "I think we've arrived just in time. Our newlyweds nearly ignited a three-alarm fire back there."

At the sound of the judge's voice, Laura and Stefano sprang apart. Stefano reknotted his tie—heaven knew when or how it had come undone—and she patted her hair and tugged at the skirt of her dress. She didn't achieve much, since her dress was irretrievably crumpled, and her hair was happily twisting itself into a riot of unkempt curls as the heat and summer humidity intensified. Giving up on her appearance, Laura walked into the restaurant looking neither to the left nor to the right. At that precise moment, there wasn't a single person's gaze she was willing to meet.

The Hortons were already waiting at a corner table, situated with a pleasant view of the tree-lined walled garden that surrounded the restaurant. A magnum of champagne stood frosting in a bucket of ice, and a waiter hovered in readiness.

"Welcome to the happy couple." The waiter bowed and smiled, easing the cork out of the champagne bottle with professional slickness. "We hope you will enjoy your first lunch as a married couple. The champagne is a gift from our manager."

"Thank you." Stefano had completely recovered his poise. He took the glass offered by the waiter and raised it high. "I salute Laura, my beautiful new wife. Thank you, *carissima,* for all you have given me this day. Because of you, I have the chance to fulfill my most heartfelt dreams for happiness."

He was too darn clever with words, Laura thought, admiring the subtlety of his double meaning. He was too darn clever in lots of ways. "You're, um, more than welcome." That sounded so trite as to be almost embarrassing. She raised her glass. "I hope all your dreams will come true, Stefano."

"Our dreams," he corrected. He smiled at her warmly, touching his glass to hers.

"Our dreams," she agreed, her gaze meeting his. She quickly looked away and swallowed several generous gulps of champagne. His eyes looked so full of desire it was unsettling, even though she knew he was simply playing a part.

She hadn't eaten any breakfast, and the champagne bubbles fizzed straight to her head, leaving her instantly tipsy. At least, she told herself, she must be tipsy. She didn't want to think of any other reason why Stefano's melting brown eyes suddenly inspired her with an insane longing to be alone with him in a darkened room, furnished with a king-size bed.

The meal of poached baby salmon was light but delicious. One bottle of champagne quickly became three. Laura drank her share, although she remained sober enough to notice that Stefano drank almost nothing. The meal ended with espresso coffee and a wedding cake, another of Aunt Bette's organizational miracles. The waiter looked positively benevolent as he stepped out of the kitchen carrying a small white-frosted cake, topped with a plastic bride and groom and set on a fancy silver doily.

The waiter handed Laura a silver cake knife. "Would you and your husband like to cut the first slice, Mrs. Corelli?"

The name made her jump. She blinked. "Oh, yes. Yes, of course." She got up and moved around the table to the serving cart, where the waiter had placed the cake. Stefano joined her, resting his hand over hers as she cut the first slice and slipped it onto the waiting plate.

A movement in the bushes outside the window distracted her attention just as Stefano raised his fork to offer her the traditional first bite. When she instinctively turned to look out of the window, Stefano barely managed to prevent the cake from falling off the fork. She ended up with cream smudged all over the side of her mouth.

"Oh, Lord, I'm sorry."

"Don't apologize. You give me the perfect excuse." He glanced at the judge and winked. "I love your American customs," he said, pulling her into his arms. He cupped her face in his hands and licked the cream from her cheek with elaborate care. "Mmm, you taste simply wonderful."

She felt herself sliding into the hazy dreamlike state that seemed to be her permanent condition whenever Stefano touched her. On the verge of closing her eyes and letting the delicious feelings consume her, she remembered she had something to tell him.

With considerable effort, she focused her thoughts and leaned closer so that she could whisper the words right into his ear. "There's a man hiding in the bushes. He's watching us."

Stefano released her with a deft twirl that left him facing the garden and Laura looking into the restaurant. After a second or two, he looped his arm casually around her shoulders and smiled at their wedding guests as if he didn't have a care in the world.

"You know, Laura and I have suddenly discovered the most urgent need to return to my apartment. I wonder if you would be so kind as to excuse us from finishing dessert?"

Renée Horton laughed. "I'm surprised the two of you lasted this long." She held out a set of car keys. "Here, these are yours. We parked your car in the corner under a tree, so it should have stayed cool. We'll drive home with the judge, like we planned."

Nick Horton winked at Bette. "Good thinking on our part, eh? Looks like the pair of them could use some cooling off."

"On the contrary," Stefano said, with an answering grin. "We are just beginning to enjoy the heat, isn't that right, *cara?*"

The man outside the window was still there, staring

at them from between two bushes, his face framed by half-dead lilac blossoms. Laura found herself smothering an acute desire to giggle. He looked like one of the Fruit of the Loom men about to burst into a commercial jingle.

"What? Oh, yes, sure we are." Laura slipped her hand into Stefano's. "Come on," she said, suddenly eager to confront the INS agent with the fact of Stefano's marriage. The guy had a mean-looking face and shifty dishonest eyes. "We must hurry," she said. "We don't want to lose... I mean, we need to get home."

Even the judge smiled at that. Laura was too impatient to feel embarrassed. She covered her edginess as best she could, but it seemed to take them forever to exchange goodbyes and get out of the restaurant.

"Did you recognize him?" she asked Stefano the moment they were outside. "Is that the INS agent who's been harassing you?"

"No," Stefano said.

She stopped in her tracks and swung around to stare at him. "What do you mean, *no?* Do you think they've put a new agent on the case?"

"I do not believe so." Stefano strode toward the garden. "He will be gone by now, but I suppose we must look, just to be sure."

She followed him along a narrow stone path, slippery with moss. The restaurant garden was apparently designed to be viewed from afar, not strolled through. They arrived at the section visible from the table where they'd been seated. As Stefano had predicted, it was empty.

Laura looked around the sunny flower-filled garden. The lilac bushes no longer aroused in her even the faintest desire to laugh. "Stefano, what's going on here? Why has he gone? Doesn't he want to arrest you?"

"I do not think the man who was watching us is from the INS."

Laura rubbed her arms, which were suddenly chilled. "If he wasn't a government agent, then who was he? And why was he spying on us?"

Stefano put his hand beneath her elbow and directed her back toward the parking lot. He hesitated a moment before replying, "I do not know his name, but I have seen him before. I think that he is the burglar who attempted to break into your aunt's basement a couple of weeks ago. Fortunately I happened to spot him as I drove up to pay a visit to Bette. He was caught in the headlights of my car, and I saw him clearly. Unfortunately I was not able to catch him. He ran into a neighbor's backyard as I was getting out of the car, and somehow I lost him."

Laura couldn't believe she had heard right. "And nobody thought it was worth calling to let me know that Aunt Bette had been the victim of an attempted robbery?"

Stefano unlocked the doors of a gray Buick parked beneath the shade of a leafy oak tree. "Your aunt did not wish to worry you."

"Have the police been notified?"

"Yes, but they have taken no action."

"Why not?" Laura demanded.

"If I were a cynic, I might say that they are too busy chasing down illegal aliens. A kinder explanation is that there is no action for them to take. The burglar smashed a basement window, that's all. He was scared off before he could steal anything." Stefano grabbed her arm. "Where are you going?"

"To talk to Aunt Bette, of course. You know she doesn't even remember to lock her back door half the time. I have to get a security system installed right away—"

"It has been done," Stefano said quietly. "You probably didn't notice, but there are now electronic keypads by each door."

"Aunt Bette will never remember to set them."

"She can't avoid setting them. They buzz at her until she does." Stefano broke off almost in midword and ran toward his side of the car. "Get in!" he shouted. "Hurry! We must get out of here! Now, Laura. Now!"

Chapter Four

LAURA BANGED her head getting into the car and spent the first couple of minutes of their getaway seeing stars. Even so, she was aware of a nagging sense of having overlooked something important in the rush to escape. Something about the man she had seen lurking in the lilac bushes was triggering a memory, but she couldn't bring the picture into focus. After a while, she gave up and turned to Stefano. "What was that all about?" she demanded. "Another sighting of Aunt Bette's burglar?"

"That was an INS agent," Stefano said tersely. "Officer Raymond Dennis. I have christened him Dennis the Menace, because he always seems to turn up when I least desire his company. But I think we managed to lose him. I don't see his car, do you?"

"I never saw his car in the first place." Laura rubbed her forehead, which was still throbbing. Maybe it was the blow to her head that was making her so slow-witted. "I don't understand the problem," she said. "Why do we have to run like criminals at the mere sight of an INS agent? We're married. You now have the right to stand firm in the face of invading INS inspectors."

"You are right," Stefano said, "in theory. However, none of my conversations with the INS so far has convinced me that they are anxious to listen to reason. I am afraid that Dennis the Menace would prefer to jail me first, deport me second and apologize later. Much later."

Laura leaned back in her seat and shaded her eyes from the sun. "I wish Aunt Bette would take up rescuing stray dogs or knitting afghans for senior citizens," she muttered.

"What is that supposed to mean?" Stefano asked, sounding amused.

"Let's face it, I'm a wimp. Major-league, big-time wimp. My palms get sweaty if I drive three miles over the speed limit. I'm not cut out to be chasing mysterious prowlers one minute and fleeing from lawfully appointed government officials the next."

Stefano gave her a considering glance. "Bette doesn't call you a wimp. She says you're her first line of defense whenever she has a problem."

Laura's face softened into a smile. "Well, you know Bette. Once she takes you under her wing, you can do no wrong. She always manages to see the world from her own special perspective."

"She told me that you are the most creative and intelligent of all her friends and relatives. According to her, your major problem is that you are afraid to let your tremendous gift of creativity fly free."

Laura laughed, a touch wistfully. "You just proved my point, Stefano. Bette sees in people what she wants to see, not what's really there. I'm a tax accountant, for heaven's sake, and I *enjoy* my work. The horrible truth is that if I ever met the INS agent who's chasing you—"

"Dennis the Menace?"

"Yes. If we ever met, we'd probably discover we're soul mates."

"I am sure you would not." Stefano glanced away

from the road and smiled at her. "I agree with your aunt—you deceive yourself, *cara*. You are not quite the fusty old stick-in-the-mud you would like to pretend. In the first place you agreed to marry me, virtually sight unseen. And in the second place..." His smile deepened. "Well, remember, I have kissed you several times, which was a most enlightening experience. Not to mention...stimulating."

Laura felt her cheeks flame. She really disliked the husky intimate way he called her *cara*. She especially disliked the hot restless feelings he could summon up, seemingly out of nowhere, just by looking at her in a certain quizzical way. She turned and stared out the window. "You're right, we seem to have lost Dennis," she said. "There isn't a sign of anyone following us."

"Great!" Stefano accepted the change of conversation with every appearance of equanimity. "Now we can double back down this street here, make a left at Burger King—you see that I have learned how to give American directions—and go to my apartment."

"Do you have any special plans for how we should spend the rest of the day?" Laura asked, pleased she managed to make the question sound businesslike.

He replied with equal crispness, "Obviously it is better if we remain indoors. We do not want to do anything out of character, and we are newlyweds. On their wedding night, I think most couples prefer to celebrate privately, no?"

"Er, yes, I'm sure they do."

He smiled cheerfully. "So, we shall remain inside my apartment and organize our own wedding-night celebration. We shall do nothing to attract the attention of Dennis the Menace." Stefano turned the car onto a pleasant street of restored older homes, close to the university campus. "Here is where I have my apartment," he said, squeezing the car into a narrow parking alley. "The second floor of this house is all mine, and there is a separate outside staircase leading to my front door. Welcome to my home, Mrs. Corelli."

Mrs. Corelli. The name had an oddly attractive ring to it. Of course when she *really* got married, Laura had every intention of keeping her own name and drawing up a prenuptial agreement that would be very specific about mutual expectations and prospective financial arrangements. She realized she was twisting her wedding band around her finger and she quickly stopped. Her mood today had been downright peculiar, and she resolved to behave more rationally from now on.

"Thank you," she said, unlatching the gate into the tiny but well-tended front yard. "It, um, looks like you have a nice place here. We're in German Village, aren't we?"

"Yes, I like this neighborhood a lot. Great restaurants right around the corner, not too far from campus. In Italy, near a major university, we usually cannot find so much space." He grinned. "Not to mention such terrific modern plumbing—and a garden, too."

She looked at the rosebushes clustered in the corner and the neat borders of impatiens and geraniums. "Did you design this garden?" she asked.

He shrugged. "I like to work outside," he said. "Pulling up weeds and mowing grass is good thinking time."

An image of Bette's amazingly neat garden, with its grass properly mowed for the first time in years, flashed into her mind. "You've been taking care of my aunt's yard, as well as this one," she said.

"You sound so accusing that I must plead guilty." He took her hand. "Come on, we need to get inside before Dennis the Menace comes cruising by and spots us."

"Thank you for helping with Bette's yard," she said, following him up the metal staircase. "You've obviously been a good friend to my aunt."

"As she has been to me." Stefano found his keys and opened the door to his apartment with a flourish. "Come inside, Mrs. Corelli." He grinned companionably. "It will be my pleasure to cook us dinner, and afterward, when we have eaten...well, we can choose our entertainment for the evening. If you like to read, I have many recent bestsellers, which I bought to improve my English. I have movies, too, and CDs, if you prefer to listen to music."

"Where will I sleep?" She blurted out the question and immediately regretted it. Good grief, she sounded gauche! And for no good reason. Stefano was behaving like a perfect gentleman.

"I have two bedrooms," he said. "You shall choose one. I will take the other." For a second, Stefano laid his hand lightly on her arm. "Laura, it is my nature to joke and sometimes to tease, but about this I give you my word. You have done me a great favor by marrying me. I shall certainly not repay your kindness by taking advantage of the situation in which we find ourselves. I understand very well that you do not wish this marriage to be given any physical reality, and of course I respect your wishes."

That was great, and she said so as she followed him into the well-lit, newly refurbished kitchen. Except the problem wasn't so much what *Stefano* might get up to, Laura reflected gloomily. The problem was what *she* might find herself tempted to do during the long dark hours of the night ahead. In laying the ground rules for this marriage of convenience, neither Bette nor Stefano seemed to have considered the possibility that Laura might find herself over-whelmingly attracted to the man who was now her lawfully wedded husband.

Laura, unfortunately, had been considering little else ever since she'd first laid eyes on Stefano.

STEFANO POSSESSED an upbeat nature, and he'd always believed he enjoyed an amicable relationship with God. Watching Laura as she explored his apartment, he realized he'd been horribly mistaken. It was clear that God had decided to punish him for a lifetime of sin. Stefano could think of no other explanation for the horrible twist of fate that had united him with a wife who was both off-limits and everything he'd ever wanted in a woman. Talk about a no-win situation, Stefano thought gloomily. He could indulge his desire and break his solemn promises to Laura. Or he could keep his promises and spend the next several nights sleeping in chaste separation from the most desirable woman he'd ever been privileged to meet.

There was really no choice, and he knew it. So he set out to make himself agreeable, trying to pretend he wasn't constantly holding his breath in case she brushed against him, or fantasizing about how she would look lying naked in his bed, or remembering how she had felt when he kissed her.

Fortunately Laura seemed eager to help him cook dinner, and he breathed a sigh of relief when they fell into an easy camaraderie as they prepared a feast of homemade pasta, with marinara sauce and mushroom caps stuffed with spicy ground beef. Stefano enjoyed good food, and he'd spent some memorable evenings cooking elaborate meals with beautiful women, but he'd never before appreciated how much fun it could be to share a sunny kitchen with a smiling woman, whose eyes sparkled like the Mediterranean on a summer day.

Laura accepted his offer of a glass of Chianti, and they bickered amicably over the exact ingredients for the sauce as they diced pepper, chopped onions, and sautéed ground beef. They managed to combine their two favorite recipes just fine until they got to the point of adding garlic—and that proved to be the end of harmony.

"Two tiny cloves?" Stefano demanded, raising his eyebrows in feigned horror. "How can we make a marinara sauce with only two cloves of garlic?"

"Very easily." Laura clapped the lid on the saucepan. "Everyone knows that garlic should never be more than a subtle undertone."

"I know nothing of the sort," Stefano said. "And I am Italian."

"What's that got to do with anything?" Laura demanded. "Are Italian babies born with cells carrying the recipe for spaghetti sauce encoded in their DNA?"

She tossed her head triumphantly, obviously convinced she'd managed a pretty good comeback. Unwilling to remove her hands from the saucepan lid, she blew at a stray wisp of hair that had fallen over her forehead. Stefano decided she looked adorable.

"Most certainly we Italians are born with special genes," he said, partly to tease her and partly because he had to say something or he would simply sweep her into his arms and kiss her until neither of them gave a damn about the garlic. "And my DNA is telling me that this pathetic excuse for a spaghetti sauce needs at least three more cloves of garlic."

"Hah!" Laura abandoned logic and resorted to brute force. She armed herself with a wooden spoon and barricaded the stove with her body. "Your DNA is obviously scrambled. No more garlic," she said fiercely. "Only the ignorant think marinara sauce has to be loaded with herbs and spices until you can't even taste the tomato."

"Only the ignorant, hey?" Stefano directed her a mock scowl. "Them's fightin' words, lady." He tried hard for a Western drawl, but ended up sounding like Desi Arnez giving a bad imitation of the Lone Ranger.

Laura collapsed in giggles, and Stefano took advantage of her laughter to sneak behind her back and toss the crushed cloves of garlic into the pan.

"Hey!" Laura straightened, pretending outrage. "That's not playing fair!"

"Why? Because I made you laugh?" Before he stopped to consider the wisdom of his actions, Stefano put his arm around her waist and gave a friendly squeeze. "Life is not entirely a grim struggle to do one's duty," he said, smiling down at her and hoping like hell she wouldn't notice he was holding on to his self-control by the merest thread. "Maybe you need to give yourself permission to laugh more often."

He was wrong, Laura thought. If he continued to smile at her like that, what she would need was permission to breathe. His smile faded and his eyes darkened, his gaze fixing on her mouth with fierce intensity. "Do not look at me so," he murmured. "Laura, I beg. You must not."

Her lungs labored to produce enough oxygen. Without success, apparently, because she was beginning to feel hopelessly dizzy. She swayed toward Stefano, and he obligingly removed the wooden spoon from her limp fingers, wrapping his arms more tightly around her waist and drawing her close. Laura's dizziness stopped, but another sensation began—one that flooded her veins with heat and touched her skin with chills at the same time.

"Your aunt told me many times that you are very beautiful," Stefano murmured. "She did not exaggerate."

"Th-thank you."

"You are welcome. But for my sake, I almost wish that Bette had stretched the truth a little bit."

"Wh-why?"

He smiled wryly. "How can you need to ask? It is a most frustrating experience for a red-blooded Italian male to find himself married to so beautiful a woman and know that he must not touch her."

"But you are...touching...me," Laura pointed out, clinging to a vestige of logic in a world swirling with unreasonable emotions. "Y-your arm is around my waist."

Stefano smiled softly. "That is not touching," he said. He drew his hand slowly down the side of her cheek, tracing the outline of her mouth with his forefinger. "*This* is touching," he said huskily. "And... this." He bent his head, seeking out the hollow of her throat and pressing his mouth against the pulse that throbbed there.

The feather-light stroke of his lips against her skin

was far more erotic than a kiss. Laura jammed her palms flat against the counter and resisted the crazy urge to grab Stefano's head and pull his mouth to hers. After a moment or two, his intoxicating caress stopped, but she could feel the frantic race of her pulses even when he straightened and moved away slightly. He still held her loosely in the circle of his arms, looking down at her in a silence fraught with unspoken questions. Her nipples peaked, swelling against the light cotton bodice of her dress—her *wedding dress,* she thought wryly—and her stomach tightened with awareness of her own desire. She recognized that she and Stefano were fast approaching a precipice, but she didn't turn away, and she didn't step back out of the danger zone.

Stefano's cheeks darkened with a trace of color. "I believe we have encountered an unexpected problem," he said thickly.

"What's that?" Her voice emerged half an octave lower than normal.

"You know my problem. I am sure you can feel it." He pulled her against him for a split second, making her aware of his hardness, then let her go. "I want to make love to you, Laura, but I have promised that I will not do so." His mouth twisted in rueful self-mockery. "An honorable man does not break his promises."

She stared at the buttons on his shirt. Anywhere so she could avoid his eyes. "You could always say to hell with honor." She wondered if she had gone terminally crazy. Laura the practical, Laura the cautious, was surely not encouraging a man she barely knew to make love to her!

Stefano held her a little away from him. "No," he

said regretfully. "I could not say that because I made the promise to you. But *you* could."

His words vibrated in the constricted space between the two of them. Small noises sounded loud in the sudden silence of the kitchen: the bubble of simmering sauce, the hum of the refrigerator, the pounding of her heart. Laura looked up, finally discovering the courage to meet his eyes. In one clear sharp instant of self-knowledge, she recognized that she had been attracted to him from the moment he opened Bette's door. Her insistence on a marriage with no physical consummation had been precipitated by a need to shore up her own defenses, not by any need to protect herself from Stefano's unwanted advances.

She swallowed hard. "To hell with honor," she whispered.

Startled, Stefano looked down at her. "Laura? I am not sure that I have heard you correctly."

She cleared her throat. "To hell with honor," she repeated.

His breath expelled on a thick tense sigh. "What a great suggestion." He bent his head and captured her lips in a long searching kiss. When they finally broke apart, Stefano framed her face between his hands and tilted her face upward.

"I would not want you to feel pressured," he murmured, "but I would like to point out that my bedroom is behind the first door on your left."

Laura blinked and stared in the direction he had indicated, but she didn't move, chiefly because her legs seemed to be incapable of motion. Stefano gazed at her with fierce intensity, all trace of laughter wiped clean by desire. Suddenly he bent down, put his hand behind her knees and swept her up into his arms. He strode along the corridor, nudged open the bedroom door with his knee and deposited her triumphantly in the center of his queen-size bed. Her hair spilled over the pillows in a wild tangle, making her feel both wanton and aroused. He slipped off her shoes and tossed them into a corner of the room, then tugged at the buttons of his shirt, stripping it off and dropping it on the floor.

She reached instinctively toward him. A moment later, he was lying beside her, his arms strong and possessive, his body hard and lean—an infinitely desirable contrast to the down-filled softness of the pillows and comforter on which she lay.

He spoke quietly, his voice a husky promise. "We shall make this a wedding night to remember, my heart. You have my word on it." He smiled then, just a little. "And remember, I am a man of honor. I never break my promises."

Not this one at least, Laura thought dazedly. For sure he wasn't breaking this one. He stroked her with caresses as subtle as they were knowing, as arousing as they were tender. Sensations, dazzling as a rainbow in sunlight, tantalized her body and warmed her soul. The searing heat of his mouth burned into her skin until it seemed that every nerve ending shivered with awareness of his touch. She was alive as she had never before been alive, acutely aware of each separate part of her body and yet aware, too, that she would never feel complete until she was joined to Stefano. When his hands moved between her legs, searching and enticing, she cried out, and he swallowed the tiny sounds of her pleasure into his kiss, returning them to her with his own harsh groans of need. And when they climaxed together, she felt a moment of joy so intense she knew she would remember it forever.

Several long minutes later, when they had both stopped panting, Stefano cradled her head on his shoulder. His hand traced slow lazy patterns over her back. "It has never been like that for me before," he said quietly.

"For me, either."

"It was amazing. Do you think it could ever be that good again?"

"I don't know." She stretched drowsily, already half-asleep.

She felt, rather than saw, his smile. "Let's find out, shall we?"

That made her eyes fly wide open. "Stefano, we can't make love again! I'm exhausted."

"I will revive you," he said.

She yawned, eyelids drooping again. "Mission impossible, I'm afraid."

"Never offer an Italian husband such a delightful challenge," he murmured, kissing her.

Against everything she would have believed possible, Laura felt the faint stirring of response, the sudden acceleration of her heartbeat, the tingle of her skin. He kissed her again, then cupped her breast and rasped his tongue gently across her nipple. She shivered, her hands clutching at him involuntarily, and he laughed softly. "You see, *cara*? Signs of life already."

Signs of life that quickly translated into full-blown desire and culminated with astonishing speed in a climax more shattering than the one that had gone before.

What was happening to her? Laura wondered as Stefano finally drew away. She found no answer to her question, but in the silent afterglow of their tumultuous lovemaking, she had plenty of time to realize that her marriage of convenience had just become ominously less than convenient.

THE PHONE RANG the next morning almost before the sun had broken over the horizon. *Aunt Bette,* Laura thought, stretching drowsily. Her great-aunt could never be persuaded that the rest of the world didn't share her delight in having coffee perking by 6 a.m. at the latest.

Stefano groaned and pulled a pillow over his head. "Answering machine," he mumbled. "Let it ring."

The machine picked up after five rings. "This is Stefano Corelli. Please leave a message after the beep."

A rough uneducated voice spoke. "I'm gonna call back in two minutes. If you're there, Dr. Corelli, you'd be real smart to pick up the phone."

Laura and Stefano both sat bolt upright in the bed, and Stefano lunged for the phone. "I am here now," he said. "Who are you, and what do you want?"

"A real simple request, Dr. Corelli." The answering machine was still on, and Laura could hear the conversation quite clearly. "I want the formula for the fiber you and Bette Prendergast have developed, and I want it soon."

"Who are you?" Stefano repeated. "How do you know about this fiber?"

"Word is out all over town that Bette and her fancy new partner have invented themselves a real hot product."

"Then you should know that we are already negotiating with three major companies for the sale of the formula. Do you wish to be included in the list of negotiators?"

The caller laughed. "Yeah, I guess you could say that. And here's my deal. You bring me the info on your new product, and I'll give you a real good price for it."

"You understand that the other interested parties have already made offers of many millions of dollars—"

"My deal's better, Dr. Corelli, and here it is. You give me the formula, and I'll give you Bette Prendergast. I guess that cute new wife of yours would be real sad if she thought her auntie was missing, soon-to-be presumed dead."

"Bette!" Laura exclaimed. "What does he mean? What's he talking ab—"

Stefano gestured for silence. "I do not understand you," he said curtly.

"Having problems understanding simple English, Dr. Corelli?" The caller spoke with sneering contempt. "Then I'll speak real slow and real clear. Don't go to the police or any other law-enforcement agency if you want to see dear old Bette alive again. Got that?"

"I understand your demands, yes. But how do I know that you really have Bette?"

"Call her house. You'll find a message on her answering machine. But before you place that call, I have some instructions for you, Doctor. So listen up, because I'm only saying this one time. You come to the Café International parking lot on the university campus at eight o'clock this morning. Bring with you the six computer disks that contain your research data. In exchange, I'll bring you Bette Prendergast, alive and unharmed."

"How do I know—" Stefano stopped in midsentence.

"What is it?" Laura clutched his arm. "I can't hear him anymore. What's he saying?"

"Nothing," Stefano replied, his voice harsh. "He has hung up."

"Oh, my God!" Laura felt panic swell inside her. "Oh, my God, poor Aunt Bette! What are we going to do?"

Stefano was already dialing a phone number. "No!" she said, grabbing for his hand. "Don't call the police! You heard what he said!"

"I am calling your aunt's house," Stefano said quietly. "He claimed there is a message on Bette's answering machine. We should check it out. It is possible, you know, that the call was a hoax."

"Oh, of course, I'm sorry." Laura felt her panic subside slightly in the face of Stefano's calm. She swallowed over a rush of nausea as the answering machine clicked in after four rings.

"Laura, Stefano, this is Bette. Please do as you have been instructed. Stefano, take the disks to the university. Otherwise, I don't know what will—" The machine cut off abruptly. The buzz of the disconnected call echoed frighteningly through the room, and Stefano gently replaced the receiver.

"It isn't a hoax, is it?" Laura tried hard to keep her voice from shaking.

"Probably not," Stefano said. He glanced at the bedside clock as he strode toward the shower. "Six-forty-five. We will work on the assumption that Bette has been kidnapped. There is no time to chase across town to check out the house in person, and the voice on the answering machine was almost certainly hers. Fortunately we have time to plan a little and still make the eight-o'clock deadline. This early on a Saturday morning, there will be almost no traffic on the roads."

"You're going to give him—the kidnapper—the formula?" Laura asked, still trying to absorb the incredible idea that her aunt had invented something valuable and important enough to attract the interest of a kidnapper.

"I shall give him the six disks he asked for," Stefano said, turning on the shower. "Most certainly. Let us hope that is sufficient to secure the release of your aunt." He took Laura by the shoulders and pushed her gently in the direction of the door. "The second bathroom is down the hall," he said. "Hurry up and get dressed and we'll talk in the car."

Sick and shaking with anxiety, Laura headed toward the shower.

Chapter Five

LAURA, WHO HAD ALWAYS taken pride in her common sense and cool efficiency in the face of a crisis, found her competence crumbling. The thought of Aunt Bette in captivity left her paralyzed with worry. However sprightly Bette appeared, she was seventy-two years old, and her reserves of strength weren't great enough to cope with the horrors of being kidnapped. Laura fought back tears as she showered at record-breaking speed. Pulling on jeans and a T-shirt, she shoved her feet into a pair of sneakers at the same time as she swished mouthwash around her teeth. Her fingers were shaking so badly she gave up on her hair and simply shoved it into a haphazard ponytail.

Stefano heard her leave the bathroom and called to her. "I am in the kitchen," he said, poking his head around the door and thrusting a mug of coffee into her hands. "This will help the morning blues."

She swallowed a couple of scalding sips, then set the mug on the counter, glancing nervously at her watch. "We don't have time for this, Stefano. It's past seven..."

He picked up the mug and wrapped her hands around it. "You need something to drink," he said softly. "Finish this, *cara*. You have time, I promise."

"But Aunt Bette—"

"Laura, we are ten minutes away from the campus, fifteen at the absolute most. We will achieve nothing by sitting in a empty parking lot waiting for the kidnappers to arrive. Let's take five minutes to drink coffee and make our plans."

"Okay," she agreed reluctantly. She took another sip of coffee and the roiling sickness in her stomach calmed a little. Pacing, unable to stand still, her eye caught sight of a flat plastic box lying on the counter with Stefano's car keys sitting on top.

"Are those the disks the kidnapper wants?" she asked.

"Yes, all six of them."

Laura shook her head. "I don't understand. Bette's the one who set up the experiments, so why doesn't she have a record of her own experimental data? Why doesn't she have a set of disks?"

"She does."

"Then why in blazes didn't she just give the damn disks to the kidnappers?" Laura's voice snapped with tension. "My God, she's risking her life for the sake of a stupid formula! What good will that do her if she's dead?"

"The formula is very important to your aunt," Stefano said.

"More important than staying alive?" Laura slammed her coffee mug down on the counter. "I don't understand what's gotten into her. Bette's never cared about money, and anyway, her income is enough to live on comfortably for the next forty years."

"You misread your aunt's character," Stefano said quietly. "She cares nothing for the money. She wishes only to show you—to show all those who have doubted her—that she has both the determination and the genius to make a great contribution to society."

Laura closed her eyes. "She doesn't have to kill

herself in the effort to prove she's important. The whole family adores her. She's like a second mother to me. Good grief, *everyone* loves her."

"And admires her?" Stefano asked.

"Of course," Laura said, but her split second of hesitation betrayed her.

Stefano made no comment. He didn't need to. "You must not imagine the worst," he said, putting his arm around her shoulders. "You are picturing your aunt being tortured or threatened, but that probably has not happened. She also has an excellent reason to conceal the existence of her copies of these disks—"

The sharp ring of the doorbell interrupted Stefano's attempt at reassurance. "It's too early for regular visitors," Laura whispered. "Who can it be?"

"Whoever it is, we must get rid of them quickly."

The ring of the doorbell changed to a thunderous knocking. "Immigration and Naturalization. Open up. This is Agent Dennis speaking."

Agent *Dennis?* Laura smothered a gurgle of nervous laughter. She turned to Stefano. "Oh, my God! Dennis the Menace. What are we going to do now?"

Stefano glanced toward the window. "It is too high to jump," he said regretfully. "And Dennis is blocking the stairs, so I'm afraid we shall have to open the door and let him in."

"My God, Stefano, it's seven-fifteen. We don't have time for chitchat with some overzealous despot from the INS!"

"Then we will get rid of him as soon as possible," Stefano said, walking to the front door. He pulled it open. "Good morning, sir. How may I help you?"

Without waiting for an invitation, the INS agent stepped into the tiny entrance hall.

"Please do come in," Stefano said affably.

The agent glared at him. Then his gaze swiveled around, lighting on Laura with blatant disapproval. He didn't speak to her, however. He directed his attention to Stefano, waving a sheaf of multicolored forms and puffing up his chest. "Mr. Corelli, it's come to our attention that you are illegally employed in the United States. Under the terms of your student visa, you have no right to take paid employment. Furthermore, your visa has expired, and you no longer have right of residence in this country. You may, if you wish, return to Italy on the next available flight and avoid all penalties. Otherwise, under the terms of the Immigration and Naturalization Act of 1990, I am authorized to detain you until a hearing can be arranged in an appropriate federal court." Agent Dennis recited his piece in a singsong monotone. Drawing breath, he continued almost without pause, "You may, of course, request release from custody while awaiting your hearing, and your application will be processed through the appropriate channels." With clear and ominous intent, Dennis put his hand over a pair of handcuffs hanging from his belt. "Now, Mr. Corelli, you're a sensible man, and I'm sure you understand all the reasons why you need to come with me. Your efforts to avoid us have gone on quite long enough."

"But, Officer, I cannot come with you now! Trust me, you're making a terrible mistake."

"That's what they all say." Agent Dennis sounded weary.

"Look, be reasonable." Stefano kept his voice carefully controlled, but Laura could see the involuntary flick of a muscle in his jaw. "Let me call the university lawyers," he said. "We'll arrange a meeting in your office first thing on Monday morning. It's simply a case of clerical error, I promise you."

"You can call for your lawyer after we get downtown, Mr. Corelli."

"But you can't put Stefano in jail!" Laura exclaimed. "For heaven's sake, he's done nothing wrong."

Agent Dennis frowned at her. "I'm not taking him to jail," he said. "Contrary to popular opinion, the INS isn't staffed by sadists. We're simply overworked, understaffed and trying our best to do our duty. I'm taking Mr. Corelli downtown to our offices in response to a complaint filed by a U.S. citizen. Once he's downtown, Mr. Corelli can call his lawyer and make a legal deposition concerning—"

"Wait!" Laura had a great deal of experience dealing with government officials, and Dennis was obviously one of those people who followed department rules to the letter. Stefano was seconds away from being marched downtown, and once he was locked up in an INS office, Laura hated to think what would happen to Aunt Bette.

She suddenly remembered that she and Stefano had gone through a wedding ceremony yesterday precisely to take care of his problems with the INS. She took Stefano's hand, holding it up to display their wedding rings.

"Look, Officer, you can see there's been a mistake," she said, flashing him one of her best and friendliest smiles. Agent Dennis looked thoroughly unimpressed. Laura let go of the smile, drew herself up to her full five foot six and switched to cool and dignified. "I'm a U.S. citizen," she said. "Born and bred, third generation. How come my husband has no right to live with me?"

"Your husband?" Agent Dennis blinked, then jerked his thumb toward their clasped hands. "You tellin' me this man's married to you? Since when, I'd like to know."

"Since yesterday," Laura said. She found her purse and scrabbled with feverish haste through its once-orderly contents. "Here!" she exclaimed triumphantly. "Here's our wedding certificate, signed and sealed by Judge Sol Waterman. You know the immigration judge will give Stefano permission to stay in this country now that he's married, so couldn't you wait until Monday to have him fill out the paperwork?"

Agent Dennis looked momentarily taken aback, but he soon recovered. He directed a withering glare at Laura. "I hope you know, Miss...er, ma'am, that it's a federal offense to aid and abet a foreigner to obtain legal residence status in the United States by entering into a false contract of marriage—"

"Officer, how could you even suspect us of such a thing?" Stefano asked, hugging Laura and smiling at her with sickly sweetness. "This is not a false contract of marriage. Can you not see that we are in love? Passionately in love."

"Surely it's not part of your duty to break up a happily married couple," Laura said, resisting the strong urge to tell Agent Dennis to go to hell and let them get out of here while her aunt was still alive.

"How long have you known each other?" the agent asked.

"A very long time," Stefano said.

"Not too long," Laura said simultaneously.

Stefano managed a chuckle. "Well, I guess the wait seemed longer to me than it did to Laura. I have been wishing to call her my wife from the first moment we met."

"And when was that?" Agent Dennis asked. He held up the handcuffs. They rocked gently back and forth, the stainless steel glinting in the morning sunlight. Laura gulped and wiped her sweating palms against the sides of her jeans.

"At a party," Stefano said.

"At my aunt's house," Laura said simultaneously.

They exchanged wan smiles. "At a party at my aunt's house," Laura amended, sick to her stomach as she heard a clock chime in the distance. Seven-thirty. The minutes were ticking away inexorably toward eight o'clock. She pleaded with Agent Dennis. "Officer, now that you know we're married, couldn't you let us go? We have to leave right now—it's really very important. Someone's life might be at stake."

Dennis snorted. "Right," he said dourly. "Like I said before, it always is. But I'm a nice guy. Since you're claiming to be married and your papers look to be in order, I'm willing to promise that Mr. Corelli will get a prompt hearing. You can come downtown with me to the office and we'll take depositions from both of you—"

"*Now!*" For once, Stefano and Laura said the same thing at the same time. "Both of us?"

"Of course *now*. Of course both of you. You're married, aren't you? You should do this together."

Good Lord, mentioning the wedding had only made things worse, Laura thought. Now neither of them would be able to meet up with the kidnapper. Despairingly she turned to Stefano. "What are we going to do?" she murmured, not caring if Dennis overheard. "Can we tell him the truth?"

"I think he would not believe us," Stefano said quietly. "We have waited too long to mention Bette and now he would think we are making one more excuse." He appealed again to Dennis. "Officer, we do not have time to confer with you right at this moment. As my wife promised, we will come to the INS office first thing on Monday morning, I swear to you. But we have an appointment that cannot be broken."

He might as well have spoken to a block of concrete. Agent Dennis didn't yawn in their faces, but his bored expression suggested that he had heard every impassioned plea imaginable, several times over, and no longer allowed himself to be swayed by the trivia of everyday life. He opened the handcuffs and dangled them from his fingers. "Mr. Corelli, we can make this easy or we can make it nasty. You can come willingly, which I'd sure like, or I can take you out of here cuffed. The choice is yours."

"Yes," Stefano muttered, "I can see that it is." He smiled brightly. "Then I make my choice and face the consequences, no? I hope you approve." His hand shot out, landing a solid punch square on Dennis's jaw, followed by a blow that smashed into the agent's stomach. Dennis's eyes crossed, rolled upward and swiftly closed. He collapsed neatly into Stefano's waiting arms.

"Oh, my God!" Laura stared at the agent's limp body.

"Get the disks!" Stefano said, arranging Dennis on the hall carpet and stuffing a cushion under his head. "We must get out of here."

Too shocked to do anything other than obey, Laura

jumped over Dennis and grabbed the disks and car keys from the counter. Her heart pounded and her mouth felt dryer than cotton fluff, but she was aware of a surge of relief, along with the shock and the anxiety. At least they could now keep their appointment with the kidnapper.

"Where in the world did you learn to hit like that?" she asked, handing the keys to Stefano.

"On the street corners of Milan during a notably misspent youth." Stefano took her hand and ran toward the stairs. "Come on. Let's get out of here before he wakes up. We have only a few minutes."

"Maybe you should hit him again."

"How unexpectedly bloodthirsty you are, *cara*. But there is no need to compound the crime. We will be on our way before he recovers, and he will have no idea where we have gone."

"True." Laura ran down the stairs behind Stefano, adrenaline pumping into her system. She was in the car when the enormity of what she had just done suddenly occurred to her. "My God! I've aided and abetted a brutal physical assault on a representative of the U.S. government. I've committed a major crime! I could go to jail!"

Stefano didn't seem to take her worries with the seriousness they deserved. In fact, he laughed. He raised her hand to his lips and kissed the tips of her fingers. "If you go to jail, then I will certainly be condemned, also. I will write you love letters from my cell, *cara*."

The man should have that damn smile of his registered as a lethal weapon, Laura thought. "Great," she muttered, ignoring an illogical flutter in the region of her heart. "That certainly makes it all worthwhile."

To Laura's relief, the traffic was light, and Stefano obviously knew where he was going. He drove aggressively but within the speed limit, so that they ran no risk of attracting attention from a skulking traffic cop. Laura spent the journey on pins and needles, but they arrived at the café parking lot with a couple of minutes to spare.

The café was undergoing renovations, its windows and entrance sealed by heavy-duty sheets of plastic tacked onto wooden frames, and the parking lot itself was cluttered with construction debris. There were no other cars in the lot, although the parking area across the street contained a small Chevy pickup, three bikes locked to a rack and a couple of cars. Of Aunt Bette and her kidnapper there seemed no sign.

Stefano stopped the Buick in the middle of the lot, where it was instantly visible from all sides. He left the engine running and the windows rolled up. Ready for a quick getaway, Laura realized, not sure whether to be impressed by his forethought or worried by his expertise in dealing with criminals.

The car's air-conditioning was on full blast, but the sun was already hot, and Laura's T-shirt was beginning to stick to her back. She felt hot, disheveled and scared. She drew a deep breath. "What do we do now?"

"We wait."

His cool self-control irritated her raw nerves. "How can you be do damned relaxed?"

"Because it is necessary. For Bette's sake."

"Maybe the phone call was a hoax. Maybe Bette's at home, tucked up in bed."

"Could be. Thanks to our friend Dennis, we did not have time to drive by her house and check. But if the call was a hoax, we have lost nothing save nervous energy by coming here as he instructed."

Laura was about to mention that they were looking at life in jail for punching an INS agent in the nose when she heard the faint ring of a phone. Stefano had the car in gear before she could say anything. He drove quickly to the side of the parking lot where a public phone box stood in the shade of a scraggy hedge. Lowering the car window, he picked up the phone without getting out of the car.

"Hello."

Laura leaned across the seat, straining to hear the kidnapper's reply.

"You haven't come alone, Doctor. That wasn't smart of you."

If the kidnapper knew Stefano wasn't alone, then he had to be calling from somewhere nearby, where he had a clear view of the car. Laura glanced around, squinting against the bright sun, but she couldn't detect any sign of the caller or of Bette. That didn't mean much. The parking lot was ringed on two sides by office buildings, and the kidnapper would be able to see their car from any number of windows.

"Laura is Bette's niece and my wife," Stefano said. "She was with me when you phoned this morning. Would you have preferred her to stay at home and report your call to the police?"

"Don't try to get smart, Corelli. You're not in any position to get smart. Do you have the disks?"

"All six of them. I trust that you have Bette."

"If you have the disks, we're ready to do a deal. Here are your instructions, Corelli. Get out of the car *real* slow. Keep your hands away from your body and hold the disks in your left hand. Go into the café and turn to your right. You'll find an open door. We'll be waiting inside. Understood?"

"Understood."

"And, Dr. Corelli?"

"Yes?"

"Make sure the broad stays in the car." The kidnapper disconnected the phone with a gentle click.

Laura thrust the box of disks into Stefano's hands, allowing herself to feel hope for the first time. Impulsively she reached up, pulled his face down and kissed him hard on the mouth. "Take care," she said. "Don't get yourself hurt."

He paused in the act of exiting the car. "You sound as if you really care." His voice held none of its usual teasing undertone.

"Well, of course I care." Under his steady gaze, she blushed, then tried to make light of her feelings. "I don't want to be left alone to face charges of assaulting Dennis the Menace."

Stefano touched his fingers to her lips. "I will not fail you," he said. "That is my promise."

He got out of the car before she could reply. Laura watched him cross the parking lot to the café. She saw a man with an athletic build, his thick hair gleaming blue-black in the sun, walking with his hands held carefully away from his body. *Her husband.* She let the words rattle around inside her head, but they no longer sounded quite as incredible as they had yesterday. Which, Laura decided, probably had something to do with the fact that she'd spent most of the previous night making love with *her husband* to mutually mind-blowing effect.

Stefano disappeared into the café and Laura unclenched her hands, willing herself to wait patiently as instructed. The hum of distant traffic drifted in through the open car window, punctuated by the barking of a dog and the thunk of tennis balls landing on a nearby court. The parking lot itself remained quiet, the uneven surface baking in the morning sun. However hard Laura strained her ears, she could hear nothing from inside the café.

Half a minute ticked by. Two minutes. What the heck was going on in there? How long could it take to swap a set of computer disks for Aunt Bette?

A sputter of sound drew her attention to the parking lot across the street. A gray Ford Taurus drew out from its half-concealed parking spot behind a dumpster. JMT 261. Laura strained to see the driver, but the sun was shining on his windshield, and she had no more than a blurred impression of a gray-haired man wearing dark glasses, before the car turned into the alley behind the café. She heard the engine cut, then nothing.

Laura considered her options for about a second and a half. Then she grabbed the keys, jumped out of the car and crept toward the café, keeping close to the perimeter of the parking lot, where the leafy branches of the hedge gave her at least the illusion of being protected from immediate discovery. She sneaked up to a window on the far side of the café and carefully lifted a loose corner of plastic so that she could see inside.

What she saw was Stefano, struggling in the midst of wood shavings and discarded paint cans to fight off the attacks of two masked men. He was a much stronger and more coordinated fighter then either of his attackers, but it was two against one, and they were smart enough to keep coming at him from opposing angles.

With a swift whirling turn, Stefano delivered a kick that knocked one of the men clear to the ground, but even as he swung back around to defend himself from behind, the second attacker, a giant wearing an oil-stained athletic shirt, grabbed a plywood board and brought it crashing down on Stefano's head. Stefano swayed for an instant, then fell to the floor, landing in a pile of wood shavings. Laura barely managed to smother a cry of outraged sympathy.

"Was that really necessary, Joe? You know how much I loathe violence." A stout gray-haired man stepped out from behind the ladder that had obscured him from Laura's sight. The man who'd been driving the Ford Taurus, she realized. He took off his sunglasses and she recognized him at once. She'd seen him just yesterday, lurking in the bushes outside the restaurant where they'd gone for their celebratory lunch.

Aunt Bette's kidnapper, Laura thought grimly, loathing the man's self-satisfied smirk. He might claim to hate violence, but apparently not enough to leave poor Bette safe in her own home.

Joe looked sulky at the reproach from his boss. He poked Stefano with his foot. "Damn dago wouldn't hand over the disks until he saw the old woman. He said if she ain't here, he ain't dealin'."

The man Stefano had knocked over got to his feet, brushing sawdust from his hands and wincing with pain. "The son of a bitch kicked me right in the crotch. Damn near castrated me."

The kidnapper-in-chief had no interest in the state of his underling's health. "I hope you didn't crush the disks when you fell," he said. "Give them to me and let's get out of here."

"We ain't got the disks yet."

"What?"

"I'm getting 'em now." The oil-stained giant rolled Stefano onto his back and gave a grunt of satisfaction. "Here they are." He aimed another kick at Stefano's rib cage. "Damn foreigners. I hate 'em all. Takin' jobs from honest Americans."

"And even from dishonest ones," the elderly man murmured. Smiling at the sight of the computer disks, he moved across the littered floor with a speed and agility that belied his girth. "I'll take care of those," he said, seizing the box of disks. He paused and stared at Stefano. "Dr. Corelli, are you awake?"

Silence.

"I hope you can hear me, Dr. Corelli, because I'm not planning to repeat myself. If these disks contain the promised information, Bette will be released later today. I will call your apartment at two o'clock and tell you where you may go to pick her up."

Either Stefano was unconscious or he chose not to reply. The kidnapper prodded him a couple of times, then shrugged. He waddled back to the rear door, the disks cradled protectively against his chest. "Let's move it, my friends. We need to print out the information on these to make sure he's not selling us a bill of goods."

Ducking below the level of the windows, Laura sped to the corner of the building. She waited just long enough to see the three men jump into the Taurus and take off in a northerly direction before dashing back into the café, no longer bothering to hide. Stefano was already hauling himself to his feet, using a carpenter's trestle to help lever himself upright.

"Can you walk?" she asked. "Did you hear what the fat guy said?"

"Yes to both questions." He spoke through gritted teeth. "Lend me your shoulders, will you?"

Laura grabbed his arm and draped it around her neck, torn between the need to get back to the car and give chase to the kidnappers and the equally urgent need to get Stefano some medical help. "How badly are you hurt?" she asked.

"I'll live." His mouth twisted in a parody of his familiar teasing grin. "Maybe."

His attempt at a smile produced in her the craziest impulse to burst into tears. She took his hand and held it briefly against her cheek. "Ready to go?" she asked.

"Yes." Stefano's face was white beneath the streaks of dirt and sawdust, but he was already moving at a fast clip, his spare arm wrapped around his waist, nursing his bruised ribs.

"I recognized one of the kidnappers," she panted. "He was the same man who was lurking in the flower bed outside the restaurant."

"Which means he is also the man who tried to break into Bette's house last month," Stefano said, reaching into his pocket for the car keys. "You drive."

She took the keys and turned on the ignition while Stefano eased into the front passenger seat in dogged silence. Neither of them made any comment about the sweat beading his forehead as she reversed out of the lot, or about the rigid line of his mouth as they bounced over the speed bump at the exit onto the street. "Do you think the kidnappers really will release Bette later?" she asked.

He hesitated. "I do not believe they will harm her. She is their only bargaining chip."

Laura drew what comfort she could from his reply. She calculated that the kidnappers had less than a two-minute head start. She knew in her heart of hearts that they might as well have had two hours. How in the world could they hope to pick up the trail of a gray Ford Taurus, the most popular car in America, even if she did know the license-plate number? Nevertheless, she headed north at high speed, praying for a glimpse of the kidnappers' car. Praying for a miracle.

Stefano leaned forward and opened the glove compartment, taking out a small device that looked like a cross between a fuzzbuster and an electronic game board. Frowning, he fiddled with the dials until the machine began to emit a thrumming intermittent beep. His face broke into a beatific smile. "We have them!" he said. "Turn right here. They are obviously heading for the interstate."

"How do we have them?" Laura asked, turning right as directed. "How can that...thing possibly tell you where the kidnappers are going?"

"I bugged the plastic container that holds the disks," Stefano said, looking extremely pleased with himself. "Provided the kidnappers do not get outside a ten-mile radius of our car, we can follow them on screen. With luck, they will lead us straight to Bette."

"You managed to make coffee, get dressed *and* bug a package of computer disks all while I was taking a thirty-second shower this morning?" Laura asked.

"Of course not. I had the package of disks already bugged. Just as a precaution."

Laura should have been delighted at Stefano's news, but she wasn't. What sort of man built an electronic homing device into a package of computer data just in case it got stolen? Her doubts must have shown on her face, because Stefano laid his hand on her knee. "Remind me never to gamble with you as my partner, *cara*. You have the most expressive pair of eyes I have ever seen."

"Do I? Then you must know that I'm wondering why you seem to have expected Aunt Bette to be kidnapped."

"If I had expected Bette to be kidnapped, I would never have left her alone," Stefano said coolly. "However, I did expect someone to make another attempt to steal the computer disks. Naturally I took precautions."

"*Another* attempt?"

"I told you about the burglar I surprised outside Bette's house a couple of weeks ago. Besides, to take precautions was entirely logical. Somehow, word has gotten out that your aunt has developed a process that will revolutionize cloth production. Naturally the sharks are circling. If those disks had truly contained details of Bette's new process, they would be worth at least a million dollars, even on the black market."

Laura's ears pricked up. "What do you mean, *if* those disks had truly contained details of the process?"

Stefano grinned. "I prepared them with a built-in self-destruct program. The moment anyone tries to print out the information on any of those disks or send it over a modem, the entire contents of the disk will automatically erase." He broke off. "Take the next exit. Quick, move into the right-hand lane! They're leaving the highway."

Laura looked into her rearview mirror as she prepared to shift lanes, and her stomach clenched with fright. "Oh, my God! Police! Lights flashing, sirens blaring, the whole works."

Stefano glanced over his shoulder. "Damn! They look as if they are coming after us."

"Dennis the Menace must have called in the license number of your car."

"Lose them," he said. "We don't have time for explanations."

Laura shot across two lanes of traffic, leaving a trail of blaring horns and infuriated drivers. What's happening to me? she wondered, not slowing the car. She'd left New York a law-abiding accountant, who had dated the same man for ten months without ever exchanging more than a chaste good-night kiss. Since arriving in Columbus, she'd married a man she barely knew; she'd spent the entire night making passionate love to him; and now she was being chased down the interstate highway by a cop who wanted to arrest her for assault and battery. Obviously she'd lost her mind in midair, somewhere between Manhattan and Columbus, Ohio. Obviously she had no choice but to pull over to the side of the road and apologize profusely. Perhaps the cops would accept a plea of temporary insanity. Perhaps they'd recommend a good psychiatrist.

"Double back once we've lost the cops!" Stefano yelled. "Get back on the highway if the lights aren't against you."

The lights were against her. Laura sped out of the exit lane, veering right so that she didn't have to brake for more than a second or two. She doubled the car back on itself, and when another set of traffic lights impeded her progress, she spun right again and sped down a deserted side street.

"Great driving. I am impressed." Stefano gave her knee an admiring pat.

"Have we lost them?" she demanded, staring anxiously into her mirror and executing another swift turn just to be on the safe side.

"We have lost the policemen, for sure," Stefano said.

"But?" she queried. "I hear a 'but' in your voice."

"Unfortunately, *cara*, I'm afraid we have also lost the kidnappers."

Chapter Six

THEY PARKED the Buick at the rear of a busy McDonald's, deciding they were as safe from discovery there as they would be anywhere. Once inside the restaurant, Stefano disappeared into the men's room and emerged wet-haired but free of dirt streaks and sawdust. They ordered french fries and orange juice so that they'd have an excuse to sit down and discuss what to do next.

"We should probably consider going to the police," Stefano said, not quite hiding a wince as he slid along the bench and his sore ribs hit the table.

"Good grief, we just spent ten minutes escaping from them!" Laura protested.

"And that's what changed the situation. Until the police chased us off the highway, we had a good chance of following the kidnappers and finding Bette quickly. Now that hope is gone, and so our options have narrowed."

"Going to the police might put Aunt Bette at greater risk," Laura said. "Remember, the kidnappers warned us not to tell the authorities anything."

"What else would you expect them to say?" Stefano slammed his fist into the palm of his other hand. "Damn, this is my fault! We need to be in my apartment to take the next phone call from the kidnappers, but we cannot return to my neighborhood without running the risk of being arrested for assaulting Dennis the Menace. *Dio mio,* I thought I was so smart, with my fancy electronic gadgets. I was sure I would be able to find Bette before the kidnappers realized the disks I had given them were programmed for self-destruct."

He didn't need to point out that the kidnappers would be furious when they saw their stolen data unraveling into gobbledygook right in front of their eyes. Nor did he need to point out that angry kidnappers were almost guaranteed to take out their frustration in physical violence. Laura's imagination was working overtime, and she was sure his was, too.

Stefano pushed his french fries away untouched. "We really have no choice," he said. "We'd better find the nearest police station. I hope to God they believe our story and take quick action."

Laura wasn't optimistic. She could visualize all too clearly the painful delays as the lumbering wheels of a police investigation rolled into operation. Her chest tightened with panic. She had a mental flash of Aunt Bette's cherubic face as she'd last seen it, eyes twinkling, laughter lines crinkling her cheeks, when she raised her champagne glass to toast the newlyweds. A picture of the kidnapper's smirking features superimposed itself on the happy memory, and Laura's entire body turned cold with dislike. Even when he'd been hiding in the bushes outside the restaurant, the kidnapper had worn an infuriating expression of smug self-satisfaction.

A nagging sense of familiarity tickled at the edges of Laura's anger. She'd seen those sneering features somewhere before, and recently, too. But where? She lived in Manhattan, and the kidnapper presumably lived in Columbus. So where in blazes could she have met him? Or even glimpsed him?

The answer came in a flash of subliminal memory. "In the photo on Aunt Bette's dressing table!" she exclaimed, grabbing Stefano's hands in her excitement. "Good grief, that's it! He's in Aunt Bette's wedding picture!"

Stefano looked understandably blank. "Who is in Bette's wedding picture? What are you talking about?"

"Aunt Bette's ex-husband." Laura jumped to her feet, unable to sit still any longer. "Except he wasn't her ex-husband then, of course. He was the bridegroom."

"Well, I daresay the bridegroom has every right to appear in his own wedding picture—"

"I'm talking about the kidnapper! *Bette's husband*—that's who kidnapped her. Or I should say her ex-husband, Walter what's-his-name! Come on, let's go find him!"

"You believe Walter Willis is behind this kidnapping?" Stefano rose to his feet, but he could hardly have looked more skeptical if she'd accused Mother Teresa. "But he is a most respectable man! He is a college professor."

"So are you," Laura pointed out. "That's no guarantee of virtue. You're being chased by half the Columbus police force."

"But that is a misunderstanding—"

"It all fits." Laura insisted, already halfway to the exit. "Walter is a chemical engineer. He and Bette met in college, and she dropped out in her junior year to marry him. Bette mentioned that they'd run into each other at a college reunion a few months ago, and I'll bet she couldn't resist telling him what she was working on. And who better than Walter to know that Bette is brilliant enough to have discovered something valuable?"

Panting but triumphant, Laura arrived back at the car. "Get in," she said, annoyed with Stefano's lack of excitement. "Let's go!"

"Go where?"

"To Walter's house!" Stefano was really being infuriatingly dense. Laura almost stamped her foot with impatience.

"Even if Walter Willis has taken Bette back to his house—and that's a big if—do you know where he lives? I don't."

Laura's mouth opened, then closed again. She collapsed against the side of the car, as deflated as yesterday's balloon. "Damn!" she exclaimed softly. "I haven't the faintest idea where Walter lives, except that it's probably somewhere in Columbus. My God, isn't there any way to track him down?"

"He might be listed in the phone book," Stefano suggested.

She brightened. "It's sure worth a try. Where can we find a directory?"

"There's a phone booth over there." Stefano pointed to the corner of the parking lot.

Unlike any public phone Laura had ever seen in New York City, this one actually had two current directories suspended from metal binders just as they were supposed to be. Midwestern living, she decided, had its advantages. They searched swiftly through the directories, but without success. No Walter Willis, no W. Willis, not even somebody Willis with W. as a middle initial, appeared anywhere in the area listings.

"I guess that's that," Laura said gloomily. "At least we know what we have to do next. We have no choice but to go to the police. Thank goodness we have a name to give them." She bit her lip, scowling anxiously. "I'm scared they'll throw us in jail for assaulting Dennis the Menace and ignore our story about Aunt Bette. Of course they won't keep us in jail for very long, but Bette's nowhere near as strong as she looks, and time isn't on our side...."

Stefano was looking progressively more miserable as she spoke. "Unfortunately I'm afraid we may have a worse problem than you know."

"What's that?"

"Even if the police believe Bette is being held hostage, I'm sure they won't believe our claim that Walter Willis is responsible for the kidnapping."

"Why not? Ex-husbands are mean and vicious to ex-wives all the time. They're usually the prime suspects."

"True, but in this case, I'm afraid the police will think we are accusing Walter out of a desire for vengeance."

"Why would they think something so silly? We'd never even met Walter Willis until he pulled this dumb stunt."

Stefano grimaced. "I have been wondering for the past couple of weeks why the INS pursued me with such determination. After all, this country is swamped by illegal immigrants, and a college professor with a clerical error in his paperwork doesn't merit a full-time agent working on his case."

"It is strange," Laura agreed. "But you told me the INS must have decided to make an example of you."

"That's what I believed until this morning. But do

you remember what Agent Dennis said when he waved that bundle of official papers at me? He said a complaint had been filed with his department 'by a U.S. citizen.' According to him, a U.S. citizen had sworn that I was involved in illegal activities, and because of that, the INS checked into my visa status and discovered it had expired."

"Yes, you're right, Dennis did say that, and it explains why the immigration people are pursuing you so actively." Laura frowned. "But I don't see..." She paused. "Good grief, are you suggesting that Walter reported you to the INS?"

"Do you not find it a most strange coincidence that very soon after I foiled Walter's attempt to break into Bette's basement, my problems with immigration began?"

Laura breathed in sharply. "Bette always said her ex-husband was a snake, but it never occurred to me that he was reptilian enough to swear a false complaint about you so that Aunt Bette would be left to market her new miracle fiber without your help and advice."

"But that is what happened, I am almost sure of it. Walter had very good reasons to want me out of the picture, and so he set the INS on my tail."

"It sounds horribly logical," she admitted.

Stefano's eyes darkened with foreboding. "Can you imagine how the police will react if we march into the local station and tell them that Walter Willis has kidnapped Bette?"

"They'll think you're trying to get back at Walter...."

"Or even that I have kidnapped Bette myself," Stefano said glumly. "If we mention her great discovery, they will think I wish to steal it. After all, what do they know about me except that a U.S. citizen has accused me of being a criminal—probably a member of the Mafia—and that I am in the country without the correct visa? Not to mention the fact that I brutally assaulted Agent Dennis."

"What can we do?" Laura asked, her voice cold and flat with fear. "If your theory's correct, we daren't risk going to the police, but we sure can't leave Bette in Walter's hands. The man's a monster."

"Or a jealous scientist, which sometimes is close to the same thing."

At that moment, a squad car cruised by on the opposite side of the road. Laura's stomach plummeted to her sneakers. Quick as a flash, she jumped into the Buick, and Stefano followed almost as fast. His attention caught by the blur of movement, the cop glanced across to the parking lot, but he didn't stop or turn around. Laura's stomach gradually eased back to its normal resting place, but her heart continued to pound at twice its normal rate.

"This is ridiculous," Stefano said. "We cannot carry on like this, ducking and hiding every time we catch a glimpse of a police car."

"If only we could get into Aunt Bette's house," Laura said. "We could check her address book and see if she has a listing for Walter Willis. They might have exchanged addresses when they met at their college reunion. When people have been divorced for as long as Bette and Walter, they forget all the reasons they split up and start to think they can be friends again."

"For what it's worth, we *can* get into Bette's house," Stefano said. "I have her house key."

Laura smiled delightedly. "You do?"

He nodded. "Right there on the same ring as the car keys."

Laura was so relieved she flung her arms around his neck and kissed him exuberantly. "Stefano Corelli, you are a wonderful magnificent man."

He slanted her a sideways look that was hard to interpret. "You almost sound as if you mean that, *cara*."

"Why shouldn't I mean it?"

His eyes gleamed. "When you arrived in Columbus, I am not sure you would have called me wonderful. Arrogant, perhaps, or more likely...a scoundrel."

"I didn't know you then," she said.

"We both had misconceptions." He looked at her, his dark melting gaze suddenly intense. "Getting to know you has been a great pleasure for me, *cara*. I hope for you, too."

"It's been...interesting," she said.

His gaze became quizzical, and she felt herself grow hot and flustered. "What are we going to do if we can't find Walter's address at Bette's house?"

Stefano accepted her change of subject without comment. "Call a priest or a psychic," he said. "Or maybe both. If we don't soon find out where Walter lives, we are going to be in serious need of divine intervention."

THE MORNING'S EVENTS had not left Laura in an optimistic mood, so she was overjoyed when they discovered Walter Willis's address and phone number listed in Bette's Rolodex, not under *W*, but under *E*.

"How in the world did you know to start looking

at the beginning of the alphabet?'' Stefano asked, tugging the card free and shoving it into his pocket.

"She files my address under *N* for niece, so I didn't expect to find his under *W*." Laura hurried toward the back door, where they'd parked their car out of sight, they hoped, of passing policemen.

"But why under *E*?" Stefano asked.

She grinned. "I'm guessing *E* stands for ex-husband."

"You're right, of course." Stefano chuckled. "Just when I think I have finally fathomed the way Bette's mind works, she surprises me again."

Memories of Bette crowded in thick and fast, all of them warm and happy. Fighting back unexpected tears, Laura reached for the door handle. "God, I hope we find her soon."

"We will. Worthington isn't all that far from here and it's still barely lunchtime— Don't touch the door!" Stefano lunged for her hand, but he was a split second too late. A cacophony of howling sound broke out, blasting the quiet neighborhood.

Belatedly Laura remembered the fancy burglar-alarm system Stefano had installed. "I thought you disarmed the darn thing when we came in," she yelled over the blare.

"It has an automatic re-arming system, and it's keyed straight into the local police station," he yelled back. "Come on! Let's get out of here before we have the entire Columbus police force on our heels."

Given that they already had half the police force out looking for them, adding the other half seemed almost a minor problem to Laura. The noise of the alarm, however, was earsplitting, disrupting the entire neighborhood. "Can't you turn it off?" she asked.

Stefano was sprinting to the car, dragging her with him. He ignored the neighbors who were beginning to poke their heads out of various doors and windows. "Only from the master panel in the basement. No time. We must get out of here and rescue Bette."

Laura scooted behind the wheel of the Buick and slammed the door with one hand, simultaneously turning on the ignition with the other. She reversed out of the driveway at a speed that would have terrified her under normal conditions. One of Aunt Bette's rosebushes encountered a spinning car wheel and bit the dust. The tires burned rubber as she swung out onto the road and depressed the accelerator so hard the car fishtailed. She hung on to the steering wheel and fought to bring the car back under control without losing speed.

"See any cops?" she asked tersely as soon as the car was secure on the road.

"None. At least a dozen astonished neighbors, however."

"They'll get over it." The blare of the alarm finally faded into the distance. "Give me directions," she said. "Where am I going?"

"Right at the second light, then left lane onto the highway." He leaned across and locked her seat belt.

"Thank you." Laura drew a calming gulp of air and forced her fingers to relax their death grip on the steering wheel. "Maybe it's a good thing the burglar alarm went off," she said. "The cops are bound to investigate a signal, aren't they?"

"Sure to. Is that good news?"

"The cops will at least know Aunt Bette isn't at home and that someone tried to break into her house. Maybe they'll chase us right to Walter's lair."

"I'm beginning to suspect you like being chased by police cars."

"Of course I don't!" Her denial was instant and indignant. "Except...except today it might be convenient as long as they don't actually catch us."

Stefano laughed, the sound oddly tender. "Do you know something, Laura? You are a complete and utter fraud. A total impostor."

His words stung. She stared ahead, mouth held firm against an ominous tendency to quiver. "I'm sorry you feel that way. This is a difficult situation, and I've tried to—"

He put his hand over her knee and squeezed gently. "I did not make my meaning clear. I intended to pay you a compliment."

"I don't see how it's a compliment to call me a fraud."

"Then let me explain. You have spent so many years trying to make yourself look and sound like the woman you think you ought to be that you have forgotten the woman you really are."

She shook her head. "I'm very much aware of my own basic character."

He grinned. "On the contrary, my love, you are delightfully deluded. You would like to believe that you are dedicated to your career. You struggle to create the impression that you have all your feelings boxed into neat rational compartments. The truth is something quite otherwise."

Laura could feel herself blushing. "You're wrong," she said, her voice low and oddly husky. "I'm exactly the person I appear on the surface. I believe it's essential for people to conduct their lives in a logical manner, to base their decisions on reason, not on impulse and half-baked emotions—"

"Liar," he said softly. "You know very well that the most important decisions we make have little to do with reason. Quite often we must grope and feel our way to the truth. Sometimes we must risk a leap into the unknown, trusting only our gut instincts."

"Not me," Laura said firmly. She cleared her throat, trying to get rid of the thickness that refused to go away. "I *never* take chances. I base all the important decisions in my life on a careful analysis of the facts—"

Stefano burst out laughing. "Right," he said, still chuckling. "I have seen that prudent behavior pattern a lot over the past two days."

"What does that sarcastic remark mean?"

"Well, let me see." He ticked off on his fingers. "First, you came running from New York to Columbus just because Bette said she needed you. You didn't even bother to call first. Then you married me, a virtual stranger. You made love to me within twelve hours of our marriage—a wonderful glorious experience that I am burning to repeat. So far this morning, you have helped to vanquish Dennis the Menace, unmasked the identity of Bette's kidnapper, led the police on a high-speed chase, and now you are about to confront Walter Willis in his lair, all without batting the eyelash, I think you Americans say. And you wish to claim, *carissima,* that you are a woman who doesn't take chances?"

Laura gulped. "But I'm not really the way you make me sound," she protested. "I'm not irrational and...and undisciplined. Everything that's happened in the past two days is completely out of character for me."

"On the contrary," Stefano said. "I believe that in the past two days you have behaved as the woman you truly are. Impulsive, emotional, brave." She heard the smile enter his voice. "Passionate. Loyal. Sexy. Not to mention very beautiful. Shall I go on?"

He thought she was brave? And passionate? Not to mention beautiful. Laura blinked, telling herself to concentrate on the traffic and not allow herself to melt into a puddle of warm chocolate. Why did his assessment of her character leave her feeling so admired, so...cherished? In truth, she disapproved of people who acted impulsively. She was the member of the family who could be relied on to behave sensibly no matter what the provocation. Good grief, the last thing she wanted was for Stefano to start believing she was passionate and impulsive—the sort of woman who met the man of her dreams and fell instantly in love with him.

She drew her mouth into a tight line, trying to look stern. Making love to Stefano last night had obviously been a major mistake. In view of the wanton feverish way she'd behaved, he had every right to wonder if she was falling in love with him. And of course she wasn't even a tiny bit in love with Stefano. She couldn't be. Falling in love was a slow process that took months and months of careful consideration. She still hadn't managed to fall in love with Brett Hotchkiss after dating him for almost a year. How could she have fallen in love with Stefano after only two days? She knew nothing about him. Well, only a few unimportant things. Like the fact that he made her laugh, and that he was the most exciting lover she'd ever dreamed of, and that he was a unique source of strength in a crisis...

"You must be thinking very interesting thoughts, *cara*." Stefano's voice was husky. "Your eyes are full of dreams, and your cheeks have turned the most delightful shade of pink."

"I'm hot!" she snapped. "That's all." Good Lord, if she carried on like this, blushing and simpering every time he looked at her, he'd start to wonder if she wanted to turn their fake marriage into a real one. Which would be embarrassing, to say the least, because obviously a man like Stefano would never tie himself for life to a plain boring woman like her. Except he didn't consider her boring, she reminded herself, or even plain. He'd said she was passionate and beautiful. And sexy.

Laura's thoughts skittered to a confused halt, and she gave her throat another clearing rasp. "How much farther to Walter's house?" she asked. This time her voice emerged as a high-pitched squeak, instead of a throaty growl.

"The next exit." Thankfully, Stefano accepted the change of subject without comment. He glanced through the rear window. "This is the most subdued ride I have taken with you, *cara*. Not a police car in sight. Not even an eager INS agent pursuing us."

"That figures," Laura muttered, still trying to get a grip on her wayward feelings. "There's never a squad car around when you need one."

"I see your point," Stefano said. "If Bette really is being held captive at Walter's house, it would be quite helpful for us to turn up with a police escort." He read from the card they had taken from Bette's address file. "1762 Hillview Road. Make a left turn here, *cara*. It should be about halfway down the block."

Number 1762 turned out to be a slightly shabby bungalow in a row of well-maintained houses dating from the sixties. Its quiet exterior and lace-curtained windows gave no hint that it might contain a trio of kidnappers and their seventy-two-year-old victim. Laura drove past the house once, turned at the end of the road, then drove back and parked the Buick a couple of doors down on the same side. They both sat in silence for a second or two, considering their next move.

"As far as I can see, our only choice is to march up to the front door and ring the bell," Laura said.

Stefano gave her a faint smile. "I share your impatience, *cara*, but they are more likely to cut and run than to answer the door. It would seem wise if we could first check out the lay of the land a little."

"But we can't see anything from outside. There are blinds or curtains at every window."

"At the front that is true. But perhaps if we check in the back of the house, we shall find an uncurtained window and some sign of your aunt's presence."

Laura frowned, squinting against the midday sun. "Can we get to the back of the house without being seen by any people who are inside?"

"If we walk around by the garage, I believe we can reach the backyard without being observed."

"Then let's go." Laura was out of the car in an instant, compelled by a nagging sense of danger. "I have this horrible feeling that we don't have time to hang around out here twiddling our thumbs and hoping Aunt Bette's okay."

"You are right." He followed her out of the car

and took the keys, unlocking the trunk. "If we have to do any breaking and entering, this tire iron might be useful," he said.

Laura swallowed hard, but she didn't protest when he tucked the lethal-looking weapon under his arm. Stefano brushed his knuckles lightly across her cheek. "Don't look so worried, my heart. We shall rescue your aunt, never fear."

My heart. Why did the wretched man choose the most ridiculous moments to say something that sent her pulses careering into overdrive and her lungs into a state of instant oxygen deprivation? Spine ramrod straight, Laura walked down the path at the side of Walter's house and rounded the corner into the backyard.

A screened porch, jutting out some eight feet or so, ran across most of the rear of the house, and a chestnut tree, thickly festooned with the bright green leaves of early summer, shielded the far corner. Fortuitously, they had ended up by the kitchen, the only part of the rear not blocked by the porch. From inside the house, wafting out through the porch, they heard the murmur of masculine voices, several of them seeming to talk at once.

The sounds were clear enough that it seemed likely that the doors leading from the house to the porch were open, but not quite clear enough to identify individual voices. Unfortunately, however hard she strained, Laura couldn't detect any trace of a female voice that might be Aunt Bette's.

Stefano cupped his hands together, then mimed to indicate that he would give Laura a leg up so that she could see in through the kitchen window.

She shook her head. "I'll hurt your ribs," she mouthed into his ear.

"No choice," he mouthed back. "You are light. I will survive."

Reluctantly Laura stepped into the cup of his hands, clutching the window ledge with her fingers and using as much of her own strength as she could to pull herself up high enough to peek inside. The kitchen window was uncurtained and the blind was rolled up. Despite his battered ribs, Stefano was very strong, and within seconds her nose was resting on the sill, and she had a clear view of the interior.

There was nobody in the kitchen, although a couple of glasses in the sink still had ice in them and an open box on the counter contained a slice of fresh-looking pizza. Someone had obviously eaten lunch, but there was nothing in the kitchen to indicate if that someone was Bette or her captors or some totally innocent householder. Laura wriggled her foot free of Stefano's supporting hands and jumped quietly to the ground.

"I saw pizza and ice water," she said softly. "No people. The house looks as if it has a standard suburban-home layout. The family room leads off to the side of the kitchen, and I think that's where everyone is, but I couldn't see in."

Stefano's gaze became speculative. "I could get a clear view of the family room through the roof," he said. "Look, there is a skylight right in the center."

"But how would you get up there?"

"That chestnut tree is better than a ladder."

Just as he spoke, a howl of mingled dismay and fury exploded through the porch screens. "What the hell is happening to this program?" yelled a voice.

This time the question was so loud Stefano and

Laura had no difficulty in hearing it. They exchanged glances. "Walter Willis?" she murmured.

"Sounds like him, no?"

"God awmighty!" A stream of profanity wafted out into the backyard. "What the bloody hell is going on?"

"Exit the freakin' program!" Another voice, shrill with panic, shouted the instruction.

"I can't! It's not responding to any cues."

"My God, we're losing the whole data base!"

"Shut the friggin' system down! The main drive is going to crash!"

Stefano grinned. "I do believe our friends have discovered the special feature of my disks," he whispered.

Laura swallowed the urge to laugh. Stefano spoke into her ear. "Don't move. Stay out of sight. I'll signal if I see Bette."

Before she could respond, he had swung himself up into the chestnut tree and was lost in its leafy branches. A couple of seconds later she saw the top of the tree sway and heard a soft thud. Stefano had landed on the roof of the porch and was scrambling toward the skylight, tire iron grasped firmly in his right hand.

He moved with amazing speed and agility. Even so, Laura was sure his presence would have been detected if the kidnappers hadn't been too busy yelling, cursing and hurling accusations at each other to hear anything beyond the sound of their own voices. Stefano reached his goal and crouched down, staring into the room beneath the skylight. Then he turned, standing up just far enough to give Laura a thumbs-up. She felt a flash of jubilation. Bette was here! And presumably Stefano wouldn't look so cheerful unless she seemed in reasonably good condition.

Laura returned his signal, following it up with an enthusiastic wave. Stefano didn't get off the roof. Instead, he hunched once again over the skylight, slipping the tire iron under the frame and levering with all his strength. Laura's momentary good cheer vanished. Surely this crazy man wasn't planning to drop down from the roof into the family room below! Who did he think he was? Superman? Batman? The Italian Terminator?

Above the noisy thumping of her heart and the sporadic shouts of the kidnappers, Laura became aware of another sound—the unmistakable wail of a police siren. Within a few seconds, the kidnappers would hear it, too. Laura didn't know whether to cheer for the arrival of the cavalry or panic at the thought of how the kidnappers might react. Joe, the oil-stained giant, had not seemed the sort of man likely to hold out his hands and wait politely for a policeman to snap on a pair of cuffs.

Stefano obviously heard the same mournful wail and must have decided Bette was at risk. He abandoned any attempt to work silently and brought the tire iron crashing down on the skylight, smashing a hole in the glass and then levering the broken twisted remains to the side of the roof. They fell onto the path with a resounding crash, spraying splinters of wood and glass in all directions. Simultaneously Stefano swung himself into the hole left by the empty skylight and disappeared from view.

Laura had absolutely no intention of cowering in the safety of the backyard while Stefano and Bette faced the brunt of the kidnappers' anger. She ran across the yard and grabbed a hunk of wooden frame from the wrecked skylight. The wailing of the police siren reached a crescendo, cutting off all sounds from inside the house. Spinning around, poised on the brink of making a dash for the porch door, she automatically jumped back behind the chestnut tree as Aunt Bette stumbled into sight.

Her hands were bound, her mouth was taped, and ropes dangled from her ankles where she had presumably been tied to a chair. But her blue eyes flashed fire, and her hair stood up in a frizz of outraged gray curls that seemed to epitomize Bette's indomitable spirit. Laura's split second of joy quickly turned to horror when she saw that Aunt Bette hadn't escaped, but was being forced out into the backyard at the point of Walter Willis's gun.

Laura's hands tensed around the hunk of wood that was her only weapon. What in blazes was she supposed to do now? Even if she managed to get behind Walter and bring the piece of skylight frame crashing down on his skull, she might do more harm than good. What if she caused Walter to give a reflexive jerk on the trigger and fire the gun?

The police were already here, Laura reasoned. Stefano was inside, presumably playing superhero and taking care of Joe and the other thug. Walter was a scientist, a man dedicated to rational assessment of the facts. He would have to accept that the game was over and that he'd lost. Right now, all that mattered was saving Aunt Bette before Walter stumbled over a tree root or a rabbit hole and caused a terrible fatal accident.

Drawing a deep breath, Laura stepped out from behind the chestnut tree. "Aunt Bette!" she called. "Professor Willis! I'm over here!"

As she had hoped, Walter and Bette spun around. Quick as a flash, Bette assessed the situation, realized that Walter's gun was no longer pointed at her and dodged back into the house. Hallelujah! Laura's plan had worked. She would have raised a hearty cheer—except for the unfortunate fact that Walter's gun was now aimed at a point somewhere between her second and third ribs.

"Well, well, well," Walter said, looking at her with acute loathing. "If it isn't the interfering niece from New York. You're a chip off the old block if ever I saw one."

Laura tried to keep her voice calm. "Listen," she said. "The police are at the front door. Put the gun away, Walter. You're not going anywhere and neither am I."

"Want to bet?" Walter's breath was coming in puffs and pants. Sweat poured from his forehead, dripping down his cheeks and along his nose. Worst of all, his eyes were wild and his movements uncoordinated. Rationally, he must know he had nothing to gain and much to lose by continuing to threaten Laura. With a surge of fear strong enough to set her entire body shaking, Laura realized that Walter was long past the point of being rational.

Walter started to walk across the grass toward her. Laura tried to move behind the chestnut tree when, horrifyingly, she heard the thunderous sound of a gun being fired. She froze in place, clutching the tree trunk and half expecting to feel the searing pain of a bullet exploding in her gut.

Instead, she saw blood spurt from Walter's arm in

a gush of bright scarlet. He stared down at his hand, and the gun he was holding dropped to the ground. "I've been shot!" he moaned. "My God, I'm dying!" He swayed, eyes rolling upward, and fell in a crumpled heap on the grass.

Laura had no time to think or even to react. Within the space of a heartbeat, Stefano was at her side. He pulled her into his arms, smothering her with kisses. "Are you all right?" he demanded, his voice rough with fear. "He did not hurt you?"

"You shot Walter," she said, her voice blank with shock.

Stefano held her tight. "Only in the arm," he said. "Trust me, *cara,* he will recover in plenty of time to stand trial."

Aunt Bette trotted into the backyard, still trailing rope from her ankles and wrists, but with no trace of a gag. She was followed by a young policeman, who was trying hard to look as if he knew what he was doing and not succeeding very well.

"Darlings!" Aunt Bette rushed over to Stefano and Laura and wrapped them in an all-purpose hug. "You rescued me! I knew you would." She beamed at them both, then gestured to the policeman who was kneeling beside Walter Willis and looking more bewildered by the second. "This is Officer Paderewski. He came to arrest Stefano, but I explained to him that he should arrest my kidnappers, instead."

"Right now, I'm calling for the paramedics and reporting the situation to my superiors," the policeman said.

"Wonderful." Bette smiled at him as if he'd made an astonishingly wise suggestion. She placed an arm around Stefano and Laura. "My niece and her husband are on their honeymoon."

"Congratulations," Officer Paderewski said sourly. He eased the collar of his shirt and swallowed hard, clearly aware that the situation was slipping out of his control.

"Where are the other two kidnappers?" Laura asked.

"They're handcuffed to the dining room table," Bette said with obvious relish. "You should have seen Stefano when he jumped down from the ceiling! My dear, your husband was simply magnificent! He had the two of them stretched out unconscious within seconds of touching the ground."

Laura avoided Stefano's eyes. "Just what I've always wanted in a husband," she muttered. "A man who can swing from the ceiling and knock kidnappers unconscious."

Stefano took her hands and pulled her gently into his arms. "I have other qualifications," he said, "although none quite as splendid as that one, of course." His voice was warm with laughter, but his gaze was entirely serious.

Laura felt the inevitable breathlessness that always seemed to afflict her whenever Stefano took her into his arms. "What other qualifications do you have?" she asked.

"Well, let me see. I can drive almost as fast as you," he said. "I am sure not many men could make such a claim." He kissed her lightly on the nose. "I make better spaghetti sauce than you—"

"You do not!"

He silenced her protests by the simple method of

kissing her senseless. "I am a most expert deliverer of kisses," he said softly.

"Why you arrogant, macho—"

He kissed her again. "And then, of course, there is the minor fact that I have fallen hopelessly, totally and crazily in love with you."

Laura was afraid to let herself feel the joy that was waiting to burst inside her. "You can't be in love with me," she said. "We haven't known each other nearly long enough."

He took her hands and carried them to his lips. "My heart, falling in love has nothing to do with how long we have known each other. I love you, and I believe you love me. Now all we need to do is make the commitment to share our lives, so that our love can become deeper. Will you do that, Laura? Will you share my life? Grow old with me? Have my babies?"

She let down the barriers and happiness flooded her. "Yes," she said softly. "Yes, yes, yes. I love you so much, Stefano."

Bette watched her niece and her nephew-in-law melt into each other's arms. She turned to Officer Paderewski, her face alight with smiles. "Look what I did!" she said. "And I didn't even need to blow up my garage."

The Little Matchmaker
Muriel Jensen

CHAPTER ONE

SHERIFF ETHAN DRUM swept his flashlight in a wide arc in front of him, willing the missing little boy to appear out of the rainy darkness. The three-hour search had become desperate and very personal. As a parent himself, he didn't have to guess at the anguish of the mother who waited at home; he knew it all too well.

His daughter had once disappeared at a family picnic, and he could still remember how the unthinkable possibilities had driven him and Diana to the brink of madness. Then a Search and Rescue volunteer had walked out of the woods with her, and Ethan's heart had almost stalled with relief.

He wanted to bring that same relief to this boy's mother. It wasn't that he wanted to be a hero. He'd been the sheriff of Butler County long enough to know that the job wasn't about heroics, but about maintaining peace and order in a little corner of Oregon, where the Columbia River met the ocean.

Generally people weren't the problem here; nature was. The pine, fir and cedar woods that ran along the beach could hide a boy in their dense undergrowth so that a man could walk right by him in daylight and not see him.

Tonight there was no moonlight, and a steady soaking rain served to blot out any remaining visibility. At least the temperature was on his side—a reasonably moderate midforties rather than the just-above-freezing levels usual for early February.

And nothing was impossible. Ethan's ancestry was Portuguese, French-Canadian and, somewhere way back, Mohawk, which was as hardheaded an ethnicity as could be created in any gene pool. It meant he liked to have his way and was willing to go to any lengths to see that he did. He was damned if he was going to be deprived of delivering this boy alive and well, home to his mother.

He flipped the switch on the shoulder mike connected to the radio at his belt and called the office. "500," he said, indicating his call number.

"500," a woman's voice answered. "Go ahead."

"Ebbie, it's Ethan."

"You found him?" she asked hopefully.

"No," he replied. "I was just checking to see if he'd turned up at home."

Evelyn Browning, secretary and reliable source of gossip both in and out of the office, sighed audibly. "No. His mother left a friend waiting at home and came into the office. She, ah…she'd like to borrow a car."

Ebbie's tone suggested that the mother was standing within earshot. He frowned at the darkness as rain dripped off the brim of his hat and into his jacket. "What?" he asked.

"Well…you know…she wants to help. But she doesn't have a car."

Ethan could imagine Ebbie smiling reassuringly at the woman as she spoke to him.

"She was thinking," Ebbie went on, "that she could go up the dump road while you're—"

"No."

"She says she's an excellent driver."

"No! I don't care if she's Michael Andretti. Do *not* give her a car. I know she's upset, but it's an abso—"

"Sheriff Drum." This was a different voice—younger, deeper. "This is Bethany Richards. I know the idea might sound foolish to you, but your assistant here tells me that Search and Rescue is all tied up looking for a group of missing campers and you're searching for Jason alone. We could cover twice as much ground if I was searching, too. And please don't tell me the county's insurance wouldn't cover me. I don't care. I'll sign a waiver."

He'd been about to bring up the safety rules governing county vehicles until he'd heard the fear and the end-of-her-rope torment in her voice. To mention such practical matters in the face of that seemed insulting.

"Mrs. Richards," he said patiently, "I'm going to find your son. You've got to have faith."

"I've *got* faith!" she said, her voice rising as she lost the calm with which she'd come on the line. "What I want are wheels!"

"You don't need wheels, Mrs. Richards," he said firmly. "You need to stay right where you are so that when I bring Jason back, I can put him right into your arms. I don't want to have to tell him when he's cold and scared that you're driving around somewhere and we don't know where *you* are."

He heard an inrush of air—a swallowed sob, he guessed. "But you *aren't* finding him, Sheriff," she disputed hoarsely. "And he's only seven—he'll be eight tomorrow—"

"But I *will* find him," he insisted. "You told us that Forest Beach is one of his favorite places. I've walked the beach and checked the woods. He must be on the hill." The road at the top of the gradual thickly wooded slope behind the woods was a favorite parking spot of teenagers because of the seclusion it provided. He prayed that was where Jason Richards had gone to hide.

There was a moment of silence. "What if he isn't?" she asked finally. The question had an edge of despair. The mile of darkness and woods that separated him from the voice on the radio disappeared, and Ethan knew exactly what she was feeling.

"I thought you had faith," he chided gently, rubbing the chest of his bulky jacket with a gloved hand. Inside him, frustration was burning a hole.

He heard that sound again, the little inrush of air.

"What time is it?" he asked her.

She hesitated. He imagined her looking up at the ancient round clock on the wall over Ebbie's desk. "Ah...five minutes after ten."

"All right," he said, knowing this was risky but unable to stop himself. "You watch that clock, and by five minutes after eleven, I'll have Jason back to you."

He heard her sigh of acceptance. He knew it didn't mean she believed him; it just meant she'd give him the hour because she had nothing *else* to believe in.

He switched off the radio and headed for the hill, sweeping the beam of his flashlight methodically from side to side.

"YOU JUST SIT right there." The plump middle-aged woman in the beige-and-brown county uniform, whose gold badge was inscribed with "E. Browning," pointed Beth to a chair. Beth had avoided it since she'd walked into the office an hour earlier, because she'd been afraid that if she sat down it would be an indication she was prepared to wait—and she wasn't. She wanted Jason back now!

The woman pressed a steaming mug of coffee into her hands. "Drink this and watch that clock just like Ethan told you. If he said he'd be back with your boy in an hour, he will be. Ethan Drum is a man of his word."

Beth wanted to believe that, but it was a night out of a horror movie. Jason, just a day short of turning eight, had been frightened and angry when he'd left; if he wasn't already unconscious from hypothermia, he might hide from the sheriff rather than be brought back home to face the risk of being taken away by his grandparents.

Beth took a long sip of the coffee. Her eyes widened when the generous dose of brandy in it hit her tastebuds.

The sheriff's staff assistant had gone back to her desk and now turned to wink at her. "Nothing like a good medicinal cup of coffee."

Medicinal, indeed. There was enough alcohol in the cup to pickle her for posterity! Still, the warmth of the brandy brought a measure of relaxation to muscles that had been clenched in terror ever since darkness had fallen. Ever since she'd realized that Jason had followed through on his threat to run away.

Beth had explained to him over and over that her mother-in-law's threats to take her to court for custody of Jason were a bluff, and that nothing and no one would ever separate them.

She and Jason had moved here to Cobbler's Crossing three months ago. Some bully at the school, who'd overheard Jason expressing his fears to a friend, had been teasing and tormenting him. And all her assurances that his grandparents had no legal cause to take him from her hadn't comforted him. She imagined that when a boy's father died, his sense of security died, also, leaving him to feel that everything else he held dear could be taken, too.

Beth looked at the clock. Ten-fifteen. She took another sip of the coffee-cum-brandy, or rather, the brandy-cum-coffee, leaned her head back against the wall and closed her eyes, remembering the man she'd been married to for thirteen years.

They'd met in high school. Steve Richards had been of average height, with a handsome face and muscular build. She'd admired his drive to achieve and accomplish, especially when other boys seemed to spend much of their time avoiding homework and skipping classes. It was in wood shop that they'd become fast friends; they were the class misfits—she, because she was the only girl, and he, because he had no skill for carpentry.

Her parents had died in an automobile accident when she was six, and she was raised in a Seattle suburb by a grandmother who was loving and supportive, but possessed slender financial means. Steve's parents were indulgent but overbearing, and he'd been anxious to strike out on his own.

And so Steve and Bethany had married right out of high school. He'd gone to work at a furniture store, part of a retail chain, while she'd worked in the office at the community college—which enabled her to take art classes without charge.

For two years they were very happy. She'd produced painted wooden art and worked every craft show in the area, and he'd worked long hours at the store, eager to get ahead.

Beth became pregnant with Jason at the same time Steve was put in charge of the chain's newest and largest store, in downtown Seattle. And then everything changed.

By working night and day, catering to all his customers' needs and demands, and keeping costs down by serving as both clerk and manager, Steve put the store in the black the first year.

Over the next two years he made enough in bonuses and stock options to strike out on his own. Though Beth knew he loved her and Jason, she also accepted that he put them second to his career. What had once seemed such an admirable trait had become, in her eyes, an insatiable and obsessive drive to succeed at any cost.

In search of some adult contact, she'd joined a coop of artists that required each member tend the small neighborhood shop several mornings or afternoons every week. But many of Steve's contacts called him at home, and he resented their having to deal with an answering machine rather than a person. He wanted Beth there.

"Steve, the co-op is important to me," she'd tried to explain.

He'd made a sweeping gesture with one hand that encompassed the vaulted ceiling and floor-to-ceiling windows of their new house on Puget Sound and said, "The store means this house and the way we live. If I land the deal to furnish the redecorating of the convalescent home on Markham Road, it's going to mean two weeks in the Caymans for us."

She'd sighed, tired of the argument. "If you don't

slow down, Steve," she'd warned, "you're going to land *in* the convalescent home on Markham Road."

"That's what it takes to build a business, Beth," he'd said. "You have to work at it all the time."

It had been on the tip of her tongue to tell him that what built a business could also destroy a marriage, but Jason adored his father and she'd made a vow. She'd looked around—at the oversize sofa with its distressed-velvet slipcovers, the Scandinavian pine dining table under the iron rope chandelier—and decided that she was caught in a very elegant trap.

So she'd left the co-op and worked on her art at home, unwilling to discard the time and emotion she'd invested in her marriage or to dismiss the love Jason felt for his father.

Then one day a little more than a year ago she'd received a telephone call from a client with whom Steve had a lunch meeting. He told her Steve had collapsed as they were leaving the restaurant and had been taken by ambulance to the hospital.

She'd left Jason with a neighbor, and by the time she'd arrived at the emergency room, her thirty-two-year-old husband was dead of a heart attack.

She'd grieved for months over the loss of the man that driving ambition had robbed of his potential as a husband and father. The bank holding Steve's loans took everything, including most of the money Beth made by selling the house, which, thank God, had been paid off by mortgage insurance.

When she'd signed the check over to the bank and was given only a small fraction of it back, she'd stood on the sidewalk in front of the bank with Jason beside her. A curiously quiet happiness stole over her.

She was free.

For the first time in years she was free of Steve's crippling need to do more, to have more. Free of the terrifying debt that resulted. Free of all the pressures that suppressed who she really was and who she really wanted to be.

She'd called Kelly Braxton, one of her co-op friends who'd moved to the Oregon coast and with whom she'd kept in contact. Kelly had sent her the newspaper from Cobbler's Crossing, population two thousand, and Beth had seen the picture of the old cannery that was for sale at the end of a pier on the waterfront.

Kelly had checked it out with the Realtor for Beth. She reported that a previous owner had tried to put shops into the old building, and that some of the interior had been painted; plumbing and wiring had been installed, along with a furnace. Then the small-town entrepreneur had run out of money.

"But the rest of it's pretty primitive," Kelly had warned over the phone. "The walls to break it into shops are up, but they're not painted. There's flooring, but the roof leaks on the river side. The dock would probably also have to be checked for safety before you could allow any commercial traffic."

Beth had looked at the photo of the cannery and seen everything she'd always wanted—space for a studio combined with living space so that she had only one set of expenses. And if she was willing to work hard, the place had income potential as a location for rental studios. Artists were always looking for big inexpensive spaces.

She put a down payment on it sight unseen and moved with Jason to Oregon, sure it would be a fresh start for both of them. But Steve's parents, who adored their grandson but only tolerated Beth, had come to visit two weeks after she and Jason moved into the cannery. They'd been appalled by the general condition of the building, by its location at the end of a pier and by the tiny living area, which was the size of a very small apartment.

Beth took them through the rest of the building in an attempt to show them its possibilities. But all they'd seen were the ceiling and walls stained with water from the leaky roof, and the stark bareness of the building, not the happy little art community she envisioned.

Joanne, her imposing, haughty mother-in-law, had met Beth's eyes and said ominously, "We can't let Jason live like this. Steven would be appalled. We'll see you again when we've looked into our options."

Beth had swung her gaze from Joanne to Zachary, her father-in-law. "You have no options, Jo," she said. "Steve let you intrude on our lives, but I won't. I want Jason to be able to see you, but don't think for one moment I will let you take him from me. Jason is *my* son, and he's not going to replace Steve in your lives."

Her in-laws had left in a huff, Zachary making threats of suing her for custody.

Beth hadn't know Jason had been listening until they'd slammed the door behind them and she'd turned to find him in the doorway to his tiny bedroom, his eyes wide with fear.

She'd done her best to reassure him, but he'd been convinced that, since his grandfather was a judge, he'd be able to carry out his threat. When Zachary had called yesterday to tell Beth that he and Joanne were coming to Cobbler's Crossing for Jason's birthday tomorrow, Jason had been sure they were coming to take him away.

Now Beth was wondering if indulging her dream had been selfish and irresponsible. It was one thing for an adult to leave family and friends and flirt with poverty to fulfill an ambition, but had it been right to uproot her son? At this moment she wasn't sure. She'd gladly go back to life in Seattle if it meant the sheriff would walk through the office door right now with Jason by the hand.

THE GRASSY HILL was slick with rain and difficult to negotiate, but the muddy trail was worse. So Ethan tacked across the face of the hill, swinging his light in wide arcs, careful not to miss anything.

"Jason!" he shouted. "Jason, are you here?"

For the first time in hours of searching, he thought he heard a faint response. His heart lurched and he swung the beam of his flashlight up the hill in the direction of the sound.

But the wind was howling and the rain was noisy; he couldn't be absolutely sure. The light revealed nothing.

He waited for a lull in the wind, then shouted again. "Jason! Where are you?"

So weak he wondered if he'd imagined it came, "Over here!"

"Where?"

The answer was a little louder. "In the tree at the top of the hill!"

Relief surged through Ethan as he pressed on up the slope. He knew precisely what tree Jason meant. The lone mangled fir that leaned east from a lifetime of being buffeted by the wind.

He stopped under the tree and shone his flashlight beam upward. About fifteen feet above his head he saw a small sturdy figure in jeans and a red waterproof parka. The boy was straddling a branch and holding on to the trunk with both hands. He was crying.

"Hi," Ethan said, propping the flashlight in the fork of a branch so that its beam remained on the boy. "I'm Sheriff Drum."

"Yeah," the boy replied, his voice shaking. "I know."

Ethan reached for a branch above the one in which he'd propped the light. He pulled himself up, then bracing himself against the trunk with his feet, reached for the next branch.

"You mean we've met," Ethan said when he was only a few feet below the boy, "and you'd make me come out on a night like this to find you?"

"You...you came to school to talk to us," Jason said haltingly. "And the other kids told me all about you...."

"Ah." Ethan's head was now level with Jason's feet. He could see that the tree had kept the boy reasonably dry. "Okay, just hold the branch above your head and swing your leg over the branch you're sitting on."

Instructing the boy step by step, cautioning him to always keep a hold on the branch above, Ethan soon had him down to his level and clinging to his neck.

"Well done," Ethan said, pleased. "You okay?"

Jason, teeth chattering, wailed, "I want my mom."

"Right. I know." Ethan was afraid to risk freeing a hand to comfort him, so he had to use his voice, instead. He spoke quietly and with confidence. "She's waiting for you in my office. All we have to do is get down this tree."

"I'm okay," Jason said after a moment, tightening his grip on Ethan's neck and wrapping his legs around his waist. "I'm ready."

Ethan smiled into the darkness. At fourteen his daughter was fiercely independent and resisted all his efforts to help or counsel her. And though she never said so directly, he suspected she considered him generally useless and unable to function competently in her world. So having a child willingly depend upon him was a treat he hadn't experienced for a while.

"Here we go. Hold on tight." Ethan moved slowly, the boy's sixty or so pounds a challenge to his balance. Still, he reached the bottom branches without incident.

"Okay," he said into Jason's ear. The boy's cheek was pressed so tightly against his that conversation was easy. "Now I need you to let go of me and hold on to this branch so I can jump down and catch you."

"No," the boy said adamantly, fearfully.

"Jason," Ethan explained, "if I jump holding on to you, we'll get hurt."

"I don't want to let go!"

"It'll only be for a minute. If I bring you back to your mom with a broken bone, she'll be really mad at me."

The boy apparently considered that something to think about. "She's gonna be really mad at *me*."

"I talked to her on the radio," Ethan said. "She sounded much more worried than angry."

"Yeah, but after she doesn't have to be worried anymore, she'll be mad."

Probably true, Ethan thought. "Well, running away isn't the best way to handle whatever the problem is."

"But *he's* coming for me."

"Who's 'he'?"

"Grandpa Richards. And Grandma. He's a judge and he's gonna take me away." Jason began to cry again.

Ethan decided it was time to be firm. "Look. I want to hear about this, but you're going to tell me about it in the car after we get out of this tree and down the hill. So listen to me."

Jason sniffed. "Okay."

"Take your right arm from around my neck and hold the branch that's over our heads."

"I don't want to!"

"I know, but you have to. Just do as I say, and this'll be over in a minute."

Still whimpering, Jason freed one hand, reached up and grasped the branch just above his head. The pudgy face now visible in the light from below was pinched and pale, and the blue eyes were wide with fear.

"Good," Ethan said. "Now reach up with the other hand and catch the other branch." Jason complied.

Ethan's neck was free, but the sturdy legs around his waist felt riveted to him. "Great." Ethan uncoiled one of Jason's legs and placed that foot on a branch.

"Feel that?" he said.

"Yeah," Jason replied thinly. "It's wobbly."

"It only has to hold you for a minute."

He did the same with the other leg, and before the boy could realize what he was doing and complain about it, he jumped backward to the ground.

"Hey!" Jason shouted.

Ethan clapped his hands and reached up for him, bracing himself to take his weight. "Come on. Just—" Before he could complete the command, the boy fell into his arms. Ethan, his hat dislodged and rolling away, landed on his back on the wet grass with the boy on top of him.

"We did it!" Jason said exultantly, sitting up on Ethan's stomach. "And I didn't even get a broken bone! Did you?"

"No," Ethan replied with a half laugh. "I'm squished. You want to get off me so we can radio your mom that you're all right?"

"Oh. Yeah." Jason scrambled to his feet, found Ethan's hat in the process and handed it to him.

Ethan drew the boy back under the shelter of the tree and called Ebbie.

"You found him?" she demanded.

It gave Ethan great pleasure to be able to say yes. "Put Mrs. Richards on," he said. "Here's Jason."

Ethan disconnected the mike from his shoulder and held it to the boy's mouth. "Mom?" Jason said, then he whispered to Ethan, "Am I s'posed to say, 'Over'?"

Ethan bit back a grin. "No. Just talk."

"Mom? Hi. It's me."

Ethan heard the voice he'd spoken to half an hour ago laughing and crying at the same time. "Jase, are you okay? Where are you?"

"I was in a tree, Mom, only I couldn't get down 'cause it was too slippy, but Sheriff Drum came up and got me. He jumped down at the bottom and then he caught me. It was really cool!"

Cool, Ethan considered, shaking his head. That's not what *he'd* have called it.

Jason's voice lowered and he asked gravely, "Mom, are you mad?"

"Jase, right now I'm just happy and grateful you're

alive and all right," she answered. "But by tomorrow I'm going to be mad. It doesn't mean I don't love you, it just means..." There was a sigh. "But we won't talk about that until tomorrow."

"Tell her we'll be there in twenty minutes," Ethan prompted.

Jason repeated the information.

"I'm waiting for you, sweetie. I love you." Her voice was a comforting sound in the roaring blackness. Then she added softly, "Tell Sheriff Drum that I love him, too."

Jason handed the mike back to Ethan. "She said—"

"Yeah." Ethan had to cope with a weird sensation in the pit of his stomach. "I heard her."

It had been five long years since a woman had said those words to him—his wife, Diana, only days before she'd died of ovarian cancer. And this time, of course, the words were simply an exaggerated expression of gratitude. All the same he found them touching.

CHAPTER TWO

ETHAN LED THE WAY down the muddy trail, one hand holding Jason's, the other holding the flashlight. They slipped and slid and finally arrived at the small parking lot, which was empty except for the brown-and-white patrol car.

Ethan put Jason in the front seat, retrieved blankets from the trunk, then took the boy's jacket off and wrapped him in one of the blankets. He pulled the seat belt over him, then covered him with another blanket, unmindful of the mud that caked him from foot to thigh. At last he climbed in behind the wheel, cranked up the heat and turned the car toward the road.

The wipers beat hard against the rain sheeting the windshield.

"Warm enough?" Ethan asked. When Jason didn't answer, Ethan glanced over to find the boy staring at him.

"Yeah," Jason said finally. Then he fell quiet, but continued to stare at him.

"How'd you get this far from home?" Ethan asked.

"On my bike," Jason answered. "But I crashed on the trail when it started to rain and bent my front wheel. Then my bike fell down the hill."

Ethan turned his full attention back to the road. They were approaching a long series of hairpin turns that led to the state highway. Ethan could still feel the boy's eyes on him.

"What?" he asked. "You worried about your mom coming down on you when you get home?"

Jason sighed. "No. Well, yeah, but that's not what I'm thinking about."

"What are you thinking about?"

"I was thinking," Jason said hopefully, "that you could maybe...arrest me."

Ethan glanced at him again. The blue eyes looked serious. "If it was up to me," he replied, "I *would* put you in jail for scaring your mom like that. Unfortunately the law doesn't consider running away criminal."

"But you're the sheriff." The boy shifted in his seat, turning toward him, his voice going to a higher pitch as he warmed to the idea. "You can do whatever you want."

"No, I can't," Ethan corrected. "I can only do what the law tells me."

"Well...you could say I resisted arrest. I'd tell everybody that I really did."

"But you're not *under* arrest. You haven't committed a crime."

"You could say I stole something."

Ethan shook his head. "Now, how do you think your mom would feel if I told her that?"

"She'll feel worse if Grandma and Grandpa take me away! And if I'm in jail, they can't get me, right?"

Ethan heard the very real anguish in the boy's voice. "What makes you think your grandparents want to take you away?" he asked.

"They told Mom it's 'cause of the cannery."

"What cannery?"

"Mom's an artist," Jason said, wiping rain off his cheek with an edge of the blanket. "We bought the old cannery out on the pier."

Ethan nodded, remembering his brother mentioning that some gullible out-of-towner had bought the old Baldwin Cannery building.

"We're gonna make an art mall out of it," Jason went on excitedly. "And when it's all rented, we'll make enough money to send me to college. But right now it looks pretty awful. And just one little part of the building's fixed up, and that's where we'll live till Mom gets the rest of it done. Grandma said my dad would be *appalled*." He gave the word dramatic emphasis.

"Pretty strong word."

"Yeah, well. Grandma doesn't like a lot of stuff. She doesn't like artists, so she doesn't like Mom."

"Your mom and dad are divorced?"

"No. My dad had a heart attack and died." Jason's voice became very faint.

Ethan turned to the boy and was encouraged to see that he looked sad but not destroyed. He reached over to pat his knee. "I'm sorry. It's hard to lose a dad."

"He wasn't home that much, but when he was, I really liked him. My mom says he loved me a lot."

"That's a good memory to have."

"Yeah."

Ethan heard the lack of conviction in Jason's reply and realized that a memory, especially to a little boy, was a poor substitute for the real thing.

"I bet you miss him a lot."

"Yeah." Jason heaved a sigh. "I used to miss him a lot *before* he died, too." He shifted in his seat, then asked, "Where do *you* live?"

"In a big old house in town. In fact, you can see it from the cannery. It's gray with green shutters."

"That one?" Jason's voice was reverent. "Wow! It has that tower thing?"

"That's the one."

Jason sighed again. "I wish I lived there."

"Oh, I don't think your grandmother would like it any more than she likes the cannery. It's not very fancy, just comfortable." Jason grinned at the boy. "You warm enough?"

Jason nodded, then sat straighter. "Hey. Maybe you could arrest my *grandpa!*"

The boy definitely had a future in law enforcement, Ethan thought. He was determined to have someone arrested—anyone. "But he hasn't done anything against the law."

"If he tries to take me, wouldn't that be stealing?"

"Ah...that would be kidnapping," Ethan said. "And if your grandfather's a judge, I'm sure he wouldn't try to take you away without first getting a judgment from the court. And to do that, he'd have to prove that your mother wasn't doing a good job of being your mother."

"She does a great job," Jason said staunchly.

Ethan could believe it. From the way she'd sounded on the radio, it was clear she was very caring.

"Then you probably don't have as big a problem as you think you have."

"Yeah, I do." Jason's voice was anxious again. "Taylor Bridges's dad is a lawyer, and he says my house is awful enough to prove my mom's a bad mother."

"Taylor said, or his father said?"

"Well, Taylor."

Ethan sighed as he turned off the highway and down the road into Cobbler's Crossing. "Think about it, Jason. What does an eight-year-old kid know about it, even if his father *is* a lawyer?"

"Taylor's nine." Jason seemed to think that was significant. "He's in the fourth grade."

"Well, I don't think you learn much about the law in the fourth grade. He probably just likes to rattle you."

Jason looked at him in surprise. "That's what Mom says. How did *you* know that?"

"Evreybody's got somebody like that in his life. You just have to let them talk, but you can ignore it and hold to what you know to be true." Ethan turned into the parking lot of the small complex that held the sheriff's office and the jail. "If your mom's a good mom, you don't have to worry about what Taylor Bridges says."

"I wish Grandma and Grandpa weren't coming for my birthday," Jason said plaintively. "Then I could have a pizza party like the other kids have. With balloons and video games."

Ethan brought the car to a stop directly in front of the office's back door. "I'm sure your grandparents love you a lot and just want to help you celebrate."

"Uh-oh," Jason said. His voice had a despairing note.

Ethan turned off the engine and unbuckled his seat belt. "What?"

Jason pointed to the white Cadillac two spaces over. "That's Grandma and Grandpa's car."

Ethan removed the blanket he'd put over the boy and unfastened his seat belt; Jason was wrapped too tightly in the other blanket to do it himself. "When your mom came to the office tonight, she left a friend at your house in case you came home. Your grandparents probably got there, heard you'd run away and came down to the office because they were worried about you."

Jason shook his head adamantly. "But don't you see? Now they're really gonna think Mom's bad!"

"We'll explain everything," Ethan promised. He reached for his door handle and found his neck caught in Jason's death grip.

"Let me stay with you," the boy pleaded. "Just till Grandma and Grandpa are gone. You can tell them you had to arrest me, even though it isn't true. And I'll wash your car and sweep out the jail. I can paint, too. I helped my mom paint the bathroom. Please?"

Ethan held the boy close and let him absorb the comfort he seemed to need so desperately. But he had to be honest. "Jase, if I had a way to help you, I would. But your mom's been worried to death about you, and we can't keep you away from her any longer. Now let's go in there and explain what happened."

Jason groaned and clung to his neck.

Ethan backed out of the car, holding the boy to him, and ran the few short steps to the door. Once inside the vestibule, he grinned at the still-clinging Jason and said, "You can stand now." But the boy only wrapped his arms and legs around him even more tightly.

Loud voices from the office filtered back to them.

"Yes. Well." The two simple words were spoken perfunctorily and in a high disdainful voice. "You can make all the claims to good motherhood you want, but the fact remains your eight-year-old son has been missing for hours in a raging storm and the police had to be called out to find him."

"That's Grandma," Jason whispered.

"We're the sheriff's office, ma'am," Ebbie said in the no-nonsense tone she used on drunks and attorneys, "not the police. Search and Rescue is a county function. Though we do have a very small police force and we often back them up."

"Moving here was irresponsible, Bethany," a man's pompous voice accused. "You should never have taken Jason from Seattle."

"Grandpa," Jason whispered to Ethan.

"Steve always said you had no sense of what's important in life," the man went on. "You snatch a child away from all that's familiar less than a year after his father's death and drag him to this godforsaken place. You make him live in a hovel where he can't even play outside for fear of falling in the river!"

"The sheriff found Jason," Ethan heard the beleaguered Bethany reply mildly. "I'm sure it was frightening for you to arrive to such confusion, but he let me talk to Jason and he sounded fine. They'll be back anytime now."

Ethan waited for her to tell them that they were the reason Jason had run away. But she didn't.

He felt a sense of outrage he couldn't have explained, except that in the dark stormy night he'd made a connection with that voice on his radio and knew with a certainty born of long experience that she hadn't been careless about the boy he now held in his arms.

And he felt guilty about trying to minimize the boy's fears about his grandparents. They did indeed sound like people to be feared.

Jason clung to his neck. "Can't you tell them you lost me again?"

Ethan smiled grimly, then settled Jason on his hip and pushed his way through the door into the office.

A young woman ran at him instantly, a blur of red coat and dark hair pulled back in a disheveled ponytail. For a moment, he had a second pair of arms around him, crying and clinging.

"Jason! Oh, Jase." The woman buried her face in the boy's hair, then looked up at Ethan, her head just topping his shoulder. Her eyes were enormous in a face that was pale with worry. "Is he okay? Is he hurt?"

"Just a little scared," Ethan replied, having to think about words with those blue eyes so like her son's, on him. "He had a warm coat and the good sense to take shelter in a tree."

Jason looped an arm around her, but his other arm remained securely fastened to Ethan's neck. "Yeah, Mom," he said, "I'm okay."

"Sheriff, thank you!" A portly balding man in glasses and a raincoat came forward to clap Ethan on the shoulder. "I can't tell you how grateful we are. Jason. Come see your gramps."

The man tried to pull Jason out of Ethan's arms, but the boy held on to Ethan with one arm while retaining his hold on his mother with the other. "Hi, Grandpa," he said.

Jason turned his gaze to Ethan and looked him in the eye. Ethan recognized it as a man-to-man communication. He and the boy had shared a lot tonight, and something in Jason's eyes told him he was going to test their developing friendship.

A tall full-figured woman in a silky lavender raincoat came near, her features hard—until she put a hand on the boy's back. Then the contours of her face softened.

"Jason," she said in a gentle, yet wheedling tone, "why did you run away? You can tell Grandma. Are you tired of living in that awful cannery place?"

Jason stiffened. "No. I ran away because I thought you and Grandpa were gonna try to take me away from Mom, but Ethan says you can't."

The older woman looked momentarily horrified. Then the horror dissolved into confusion followed immediately by suspicion. "Oh, really?" she asked. "And who is Ethan?"

Jason pointed in the vicinity of Ethan's nose. "This is Ethan. The sheriff."

The woman assessed Ethan haughtily. "I have rights as a grandmother," she said, then redirected her gaze to Jason. "And it's not that I want to take you away. It's that I want to make sure you're well taken care of."

"I am," Jason insisted. He looked at Ethan, and Ethan couldn't fail to notice the strange plea in his eyes. Then the boy said, "And now that Ethan and Mom are getting married, I'll have a dad to take care of me, too. So now there's no problem, right?"

For the tick of ten seconds there was absolute silence. Through his own shock, Ethan felt the woman in his arm clutch at the back of his jacket.

So that's what Jason's man-to-man look had meant—*Watch it, buddy. I'm about to shaft you.*

"He has a neat house on the hill where you can see the cannery," Jason went on, undeterred. "We live there now."

While Ethan tried to decide how best to cope with the situation without denying Jason's claim and humiliating him in front of his pompous grandparents, Bethany Richards looked up at him, her eyes stunned.

The press of bodies around Jason had forced her right into Ethan's arms. Jason's grandfather took a step back and looked at them in shock. The grandmother made a strangled sound.

"So you don't have to worry anymore," Jason said, adding to his little fiction. "We have a dad now and a great house."

Jason's mother looked from man to boy, and Ethan saw understanding dawn in her eyes. She knew what her son was doing. The eyes she fixed on Ethan were suddenly sad and apologetic.

At last she turned to her in-laws, apparently prepared to refute Jason's claim, but Ethan interrupted her to introduce himself.

"Ethan Drum," he said, offering his hand to the older man. "How are you, Mr. Richards? I'm sorry it's been such a harrowing night for you."

He had no idea what in the hell he was doing. He was an agent of the law, for God's sake! He couldn't make up stories to deceive people. But he also couldn't shatter Jason's story or let this woman admit to her bullying in-laws that her son had lied.

Jason's mother was staring at him. He evaded her by tipping the brim of his hat at the grandmother. "Mrs. Richards. Did my assistant, Ebbie, give you some coffee?"

"I don't believe it!" the woman said, drawing herself up like some kind of dangerous blowfish. "I don't believe it for a minute!" She turned accusing eyes on her daughter-in-law. "You never said a thing about seeing anyone. You never even *hinted* you were getting married. This is just a trick to try to stop us from getting custody of Jason."

Before Bethany Richards could speak, Ebbie got to her feet from the other side of the counter. "Oh, it's true, Mrs. Richards," she said with a smiling glance at Ethan and Beth. "In fact, the wedding's taking place at my house."

Joanne Richards's expression tightened.

"Next Saturday," Ebbie added.

"I don't believe it," the woman repeated.

Beth Richards stared at Ebbie as though she'd lost her mind. Then she turned to her mother-in-law. "Jo—" she began.

"Guess you'll have to come and see for yourself, won't you?" Ebbie interrupted.

Ethan hadn't a clue what his staff assistant was doing, either. He only knew she was everyone's self-appointed mother, and she must have taken a real liking to Bethany Richards.

Jason's grandmother turned to her husband, who shrugged helplessly. Then she spun toward Ethan, who still had Jason on his hip and Bethany in his arm, and said adamantly, "No. You're all lying. And just to prove it, Zachary and I will stay and attend...the wedding." She spoke the last two words with scornful disbelief.

"Great." Ethan decided, now that he'd been drawn into Jason's scheme, the only way to play it out was with all sincerity in the hope that the Richardses finally believed them and—God willing—remembered some previous appointment that conflicted with the wedding day. "Meanwhile," he said, "you'll want to come to Jason's birthday party tomorrow. We're having it at Dinosaur Pizza."

Jason's eyes ignited with pleasure and he tightened his grip on Ethan. "All the kids have their parties there!" he said.

Bethany Richards frowned at her son. But before she could speak, Jason grinned convincingly. "At three-thirty," he said. "Right after school."

Bethany gasped.

Ebbie smiled at the grandparents. "I'll add two more to the reservations."

Joanne Richards studied the staff assistant closely, obviously suspecting collusion. But Ebbie met her eyes with that same friendly smile. The other woman finally turned away.

"We'll be there," she said. Then she turned her attention to her grandson. "Jason, are you sure you're all right? Where are your shoes?"

"They were muddy and wet and Ethan pulled 'em off me." He strangled Ethan with a hug. "'Cause he's gonna be my dad."

Ethan was treated to that disbelieving stare again, then the woman began to button her coat. "Dads don't usually lose track of their children."

"I sneaked away," Jason said quickly. "It wasn't his fault. He's prob'ly gonna spank me. Aren't ya?"

Ethan tried to back him up. "No. I don't spank. But I do yell and take away privileges."

Jason looked pleased and relieved. "That's what Mom does. Only she doesn't yell. She talks like a queen."

Ethan couldn't quite interpret that. "Like a queen?"

Jason lifted his chin and assumed an expression of royal displeasure. "'Jason Peter Richards,'" he said in a deeper adult tone, "'I've warned you about that before. This time I have to take action.'" He relaxed and assumed his own voice again. "And then I can't watch TV or go out and play."

Joanne Richards put her purse over her arm and pulled up the collar of her coat. "I'm happy you've agreed on parenting techniques," she said with a disdainful lift of an eyebrow, "but I think they'll have to improve considerably before we're convinced they're good enough for our grandson. We'll see you at your party, Jason."

"We're gonna have a cake from the bakery!" Jason called after them, thespian skills at full throttle.

Ebbie exchanged a grinning glance with Ethan.

At the door Zachary turned to add, "We're staying at the Coast Motel if you need us, Jason." Then he slammed the door behind him.

Beth took her first full breath in hours. She extracted Jason from the sheriff's arms and let him slide through her hands to his feet. The blanket puddled on the floor.

She pulled it up over the boy again and gave him a little shake. "Jason Richards, what do you think you're doing?" she demanded. "You've been lying like Pinocchio since you came through that door!"

The anguish of this interminable night was still very clear in her mind, and added to this incredible little drama her son had just performed—with the help of the sheriff and Ebbie—she felt as though she'd lost complete control of her life.

"Grandpa won't take me away," Jason replied simply, somewhat subdued in the face of her displeasure, "if he thinks I have the sheriff for a dad."

She pulled her son close for a moment, in sympathy with his fears of being taken away. Over his head, she met the eyes of the wet and muddy sheriff, who was the lead in Jason's drama. He seemed to be studying her.

He was a big man, with a good solid look about him. And he'd rescued Jason—possibly even saved his life. She understood his appeal for her son, because at the moment she'd like nothing better than to run into a pair of arms like his and let him deal with her in-laws and all her other troubles, too. But unlike her son, she was a grown-up and understood that real life had to be dealt with in a real way.

She held Jason at arm's length and looked into his eyes. "Jase, I understand why you ran away, because I would rather die than be separated from you." She swallowed hard, as emotion and the strain she'd been under threatened her composure. "But I promise you that isn't going to happen. Your grandparents are just making threats. But we can't involve the sheriff in a lie to make those threats go away."

Jason shrugged. The blanket slipped and he caught it and pulled it tightly around himself again. "Why can't we just make believe he's gonna be my dad until Grandma and Grandpa go home?" He turned to look up at the sheriff. "Why can't we?"

Beth caught the boy's chin in her hand and turned him back to face her. "Jason, because of what you told Grandma and Grandpa, they're not going home until *after* the wedding." She shook her head. "But there's not going to be a wedding. So they'll know you lied and then they'll really think I'm a terrible mother."

Jason smiled cautiously. "Then let's have a wedding."

"My house is too small," Ebbie said, "but my garden is available."

Ethan frowned at her. "It's February."

"So I'll borrow the Ladies of Law Enforcement's tent. We use it at the Winter Festival and everyone stays dry."

Beth turned condemning eyes on the sheriff's staff assistant. "And you, Ebbie, *what* were you thinking?"

The woman smiled, obviously unaware she'd probably just blown a hole right in the middle of Beth's life. "That you needed a little help against a pair of bullies, however well-meaning they are."

"But you told them I was getting married." Beth was trying to sound reasonable. Difficult when you were on the verge of panic. "What do you think they'll do when I *don't* get married? They'll tell one of Zachary's judge friends that I'm delusional and a liar, and they'll get custody of my son!"

Ebbie folded her arms, looking concerned at last. She unfolded them, frowned at the sheriff and sighed penitently at Beth. "I'm afraid I didn't think that far ahead. In the time I've spent with you, I got to sympathize with you and wanted to help."

Beth reminded herself that this woman had come back into the office after a full day's work to man the radio and keep in touch with the sheriff while he searched for her son. Anger seemed out of place.

She moved to the counter and put a hand on Ebbie's. "Thank you. I know you meant to help."

Ebbie placed her other hand atop Beth's and patted it. "Don't worry. The sheriff's always got a solution. When the county cut our budget, he found a way to keep me on. When the van died and we didn't have money to replace it, he bought one at an auction and got his brother to overhaul it. He shut down the drug house near the middle school when the police department claimed they didn't have enough manpower to do it. We only had four people in the department at the time."

Those accomplishments enumerated, she looked up at the sheriff expectantly. "So, how about it, boss? How do we get Beth and Jason out of this mess?"

Beth turned to him, too, hoping against hope that Ebbie was right and he would have a solution. He looked capable of it. He pulled off his muddy jacket to reveal a muscular chest and broad shoulders. But in his dark eyes and the thoughtful lines of his mouth were a wit and intelligence that said he wasn't just another set of pretty pecs.

He tossed the jacket at a chair, removed his hat and flung it atop the jacket. His dark hair was a little too long and curled just above his ears and at his neck. It was still wet from his hours outdoors.

Beth watched him run a hand through it and was surprised to find herself wondering if it was as coarse and thick to the touch as it looked.

She pushed the thought away, equilibrium held on to by a thread. She focused her attention on the sheriff's face as he smiled. Thank God! He had a solution.

"I guess," he said, "we have a wedding."

CHAPTER THREE

JASON THRUST a fist in the air. *"Yes!"*

Beth's heart began to thump wildly, not with joy and excitement, but thanks to a surge of adrenaline brought on by her body's "fight or flight" reaction.

An index finger raised in protest, she began, "Ah—"

"You come with me." The sheriff caught Jason by one arm, then pushed open the gate in the counter with the toe of his boot and urged him through. "You, too," he said to Beth. "We have to get this guy into some dry clothes and then we have to talk." He glanced at Ebbie. "You can go home, Eb," he said firmly.

"But I want to know what's happening," she said, then added righteously, "After all, I'm hosting the wedding."

When his response was a darkening of his expression, she reached for her purse. "Fine. I'm out of here. But don't worry about the cake for the party tomorrow. I'll pick it up."

The sheriff's inner office was a small beige room furnished with a plain oak desk littered with paperwork, four gray metal file drawers and two old ladder-back chairs. A venetian blind covered the room's only window, and there were certificates, maps and a wildlife calendar on the wall.

The sheriff pointed Beth and Jason to the chairs and opened one of two doors. A small closet was revealed.

Beth sat, but Jason stayed glued to the man's side and peered into the closet with him. She watched the sheriff pull a brown sweatshirt off a shelf and turn, prepared to walk toward the chairs with it, only to find himself nearly tripping over the boy.

With a look of amused exasperation, he pushed the blanket off Jason's shoulders and dropped to one knee to pull the sweatshirt on him. Its hem fell almost to the boy's knees. Then he cuffed the sleeves back until they were inches thick around her son's small wrists.

She felt an almost physical pain at the sight of them together. Jason glowing with the attention and a full-blown case of hero worship, and the sheriff a seemingly perfect male specimen who obviously related to children, this one particularly.

The sheriff rose to his feet, reached into the closet again, snatched another pile of fleece and turned, only to find once again the boy standing squarely in front of him.

"You know, you're like a wart on my knee," he said to Jason with a grin, handing him what turned out to be a pair of sweatpants. He pointed to the door beside the closet. "Bathroom. Put those on, tie them as tight as you can around your waist—see the string?—and roll up the cuffs."

"Cool," Jason said. "These yours?"

"Yes. I get muddy a lot in the line of duty. I usually have a change of clothes here."

Jason walked into the bathroom, carrying the brown sweatpants as if they were royal robes.

The minute the door closed behind her son, Beth got to her feet and confronted the sheriff. "I appreciate your willingness to help me and Jason," she said to his back as he reached into the closet for another sweatshirt. "But there's no way out of this mess." She moved a little closer, afraid he hadn't heard her. "The only thing I can do at this point is explain to my in-laws why Jason told such a tale and pray they'll understand."

He turned suddenly in the doorway of the closet and had to catch himself from tripping over her, just as he'd done with Jason. For one protracted moment her nose was a fraction of an inch from his second shirt button.

She could smell the outdoors on him, the rain in his hair. She could feel the warmth emanating from his big body.

She took two quick steps back and said flatly, succinctly, "It'll never work, so thank you for all you've done, but I'll just take Jason home and get on wi—"

"How?" he asked. He walked past her, the sweatshirt thrown over his shoulder as he unbuttoned his flannel shirt.

"How what?" she asked, a little impatient with him because this evening had been all too frightening and then weird, and he didn't seem to notice.

"How will you take Jason home?" The shirt unbuttoned, he pulled it off, revealing a rock-hard torso tightly clothed in simple white cotton.

Beth saw the jut of his chest and the concavity of his stomach, which disappeared under his belt. "My friend...at the cannery. She'll come and get us."

He pulled the sweatshirt over his head and yanked it into place. "You go home to the cannery," he warned, "and you'll make a liar out of Jason in front of his grandparents."

"Well, he *did* lie." She walked around the office, arms folded. "That's the problem here. And anyway, they've gone back to the motel. In the morning I'll—"

"No, they haven't," he said. He threw the flannel shirt at the bottom of the closet. "I just saw the white Caddy turn into the trees across the road. They've doused the headlights."

Beth frowned. "What do you mean?"

He caught her wrist as she started toward the window. "I saw the car through the blinds when we walked in here. I imagine they decided that a little simple spying might tell them something and get specific evidence on you, so they thought they'd hang around and watch us leave. *Don't* turn around. Relax."

It was just a touch, a hand on her wrist, but it claimed control of the situation.

It wasn't that she wanted to give over control of her life for any length of time, but it would be delicious to let someone else be in charge for a little while. After an absolutely hideous year, she'd been trying against overwhelming odds to rebuild her life in a simpler, cleaner pattern. Then her in-laws had intruded, casting a pall over her newfound happiness and, worse, stealing Jason's comfort in his new surroundings.

Now there seemed to be more wrong with her life than she could ever fix.

"If you can see them," she said, the emotional knot inside her tightening, "they can see us."

He drew her toward his desk and sat on a corner of it, retaining his grip on her wrist. "That's my point. Your taking comfort in the arms of a loving fiancé will only lend believability to Jason's story. And you look as though you're going to dissolve into a puddle any minute."

"I don't need comfort," she denied as he drew her closer. Everything in her was trembling now.

"What *do* you need?" he asked quietly. He was watching her with gentle dark eyes that moved over her face feature by feature. There was no judgment in them, no demand, no criticism. It seemed forever since she'd looked into a man's eyes and found simple interest there.

Her composure unraveled. She had no idea why this man should even ask the question, much less care about the answer. "Why does it matter to you?" she asked. Instinct told her to pull away from him, the warm serenity he represented had never been her destiny. All her life she'd moved from one demanding, unsatisfying situation to another. A tempting taste of comfort and security would only remind her of what life *could* be like, but wasn't.

As though sensing her need to pull away, he put his free hand to the middle of her back and used it to draw her between his knees. "This is my county," he replied. "Everyone in it matters. You can cry if you want to. I think that's what you need."

She sniffed resolutely. "Thank you, but I'm fine. Maybe you could just...walk over and close the blinds."

He ignored her suggestion. "My daughter was lost once for a couple of hours," he said, rubbing gently between her shoulder blades. "When she was finally found and my wife and I took her home and put her to bed, we cried for hours. The fear of what could have been just sits in your gut if you don't."

Yes, Beth thought. She could feel it there, hot and heavy, with barbed edges that continued to hurt even though the danger was over.

Ethan had never seen a woman—or a man, for that matter—under such tight control yet with an urgent need for release in her eyes. And he guessed it had to do with more than just this night.

The rigidity in her back had to be tension of very long standing. His father had been gone a lot, Jason had told him, and then he'd died.

Had she gotten what she needed from her husband? he wondered. If she had, he knew from personal experience that the death of a spouse was like a fresh wound every day for years.

If she hadn't, that was a different kind of tragedy. Either way, he couldn't imagine having to cope with grief and then having to deal with the threat of someone trying to take your child away.

"Jason's safe now," he said. Her fists were clenched between her breasts and she'd closed her eyes. There was a frown line between her eyebrows that seemed to deepen as he rubbed gently up and down her spine. "And we can deal with the issue of his grandparents."

"How?" she whispered.

"I don't know. We can talk that over, explore the options. But if you're going to stand up to it, you have to do two things."

"What?"

"You have to let this tension go and let yourself be human." She opened her eyes to look at him, the anguish there so great he swore he could see sparks. "And you have to trust someone to help you. It looks like I'm it."

He felt something snap in her. She lifted a hand to cover her eyes, and below it her mouth contorted on a sob. "All I want," she said in a high desperate voice, "is to be left alone to make a life with Jason. That's all! Is that so much to ask? Is it?"

He knew he didn't have to answer. He simply pulled her the rest of the way into his arms. She wrapped hers around his neck with a strength that might have surprised him if he hadn't seen the intensity in her eyes close up.

She clung to him and sobbed and he held on, sure the Richardses were watching. The way they operated, he'd probably be brought up on charges of sexual harassment if they weren't convinced that he and this woman had a relationship.

He couldn't believe the bizarre turn the missing-child call had taken tonight. He'd been able to relate to Jason and hadn't wanted to make a liar of him when he'd made those outrageous claims in front of his grandparents. And then he'd looked into Beth Richards's blue eyes and known he had to help. He wasn't sure why, except that he cared about everyone in his jurisdiction, and she'd touched the same chord in him Jason had. What could he say? He was the paternal type. That was what had led him to law enforcement in the first place. It hadn't been the excitement of high-speed chases or pistol-drawn stand-offs. It had been the simple desire to keep safe the people and the place where he'd grown up.

But when Beth Richards drew back from his shoulder and shifted her weight, her hip brushing the inside of his thigh, he experienced a reaction that was decidedly not paternal.

He absorbed the startling impact of it for an instant, then cleared his expression when she sniffed and looked into his eyes. Her own were like a turbulent sea, her eyelashes wet and spiky against her pale skin.

"Are they still there?" she asked.

"Who?"

She frowned at him. "My in-laws. Are they still watching?"

He pulled himself together. "Ah...yeah, I think so. The car hasn't moved."

"So what do we do now?"

"I guess," Ethan answered, thinking it was going to be interesting explaining this to Nikkie, "we go home."

The bathroom door burst open and Jason came out, his muddy jeans over his arm and more of the sweatpant legs rolled up than not. In spite of his ordeal, he looked pink-cheeked and clear-eyed.

Until he noticed that his mother had been crying. He crossed to her. "What's the matter, Mom?"

She took him in her arms and held him, resting her cheek on top of his still-damp curly hair. "Nothing," she replied, putting her concerns aside to reassure him. "I'm just very glad you're all right."

"I'm sorry I scared you." He gripped her tightly around the waist. "I was just gonna hide out till Grandma and Grandpa were gone, but then it got raining so hard." He leaned away from her to smile at Ethan. "I was really glad when you came to find me. Are you gonna take us home with you?"

Ethan suspected the little devil's penitence stretched only so far. Jason was getting what he wanted, at least temporarily, and he was unashamedly pleased about that. Well, hell. What lonely little kid didn't deserve to pretend he had a father who cared about him?

And what lonely frightened woman didn't deserve a buffer between herself and the bullies in her world?

"Yes, I am," Ethan said, getting to his feet. "Then

tomorrow, while you're in school, your mom and I are going to decide what to do about all the fibs you've told.'' Ethan gave him back the blanket he'd been wrapped in earlier. ''Put that around you. We'll get your jacket washed tomorrow.''

Jason did as he was told, then said, ''Ebbie fibbed, too.''

Ethan took a clean jacket out of his closet for himself. ''I know. And I didn't bother to correct either one of you. I'm not saying it's all your fault. I'm just saying it's going to take some doing to straighten it out.''

''Why do we have to?'' Jason asked, watching Ethan as he put on his hat.

''Because they're lies, Jason,'' Beth said.

''But the sheriff doesn't have a wife,'' the boy said reasonably. ''And you don't have a husband. Why don't we just have a wedding? He's got that house on the hill with the cup thing. Grandma would like that.''

Beth looked at Ethan in surprise. ''The cupola? That's your house?''

She smiled. He'd seen enormous relief and gratitude on her face when he'd walked into the office with Jason. But he hadn't seen pleasure there before. ''That's a wonderful house,'' she said. ''Jason and I used to imagine who lived there. We thought maybe the mayor.''

''Nope.'' Ethan caught her arm and drew her with him to the front office. Jason followed. ''Just the sheriff. You want to call your friend and tell her where you'll be? You might want to invite her to Jason's birthday party so we can get some bodies in the pizza place to make our story look good.''

She made a wry face but finally seemed resigned to

going home with him. "This is all so unreal," she said, dialing the number while Ethan put a clean pair of big tube socks on Jason's feet.

Her friend Kelly did not understand the simple explanation Beth gave.

"What do you mean, you're going home with the sheriff?" she asked. "You mean he's...holding you or something? Your in-laws have filed charges?"

"No," Beth said. "Jason sort of told them that... that we're..."

"Yeah?"

"Getting married," she said in a rush, watching the sheriff cuff the long socks on her son's ankles.

"Who?" Kelly demanded.

Beth turned away and lowered her voice. "Me," she replied, "and the sheriff. Jase told my in-laws we were getting married, and they didn't believe him. They think he did it just to make them leave me alone—which he did—so they're hanging around outside waiting for me to go home."

There was silence on the other end of the line. "So you're really going home...with the sheriff?"

"Yes."

"I see." There was a note of interested speculation in Kelly's voice.

"No, you don't," Beth said. "It's just a stopgap measure until we can talk it over and figure out what to do."

Kelly cleared her throat. "It's odd that telling the truth hasn't occurred to anybody."

That was true. And it was something Beth didn't care to give much thought to because, in retrospect, she realized she should have firmly denied her son's claims at the time.

But Jason had seemed so thrilled with his solution to the problem of his grandparents, and frankly, she'd rather enjoyed their shocked surprise. Throughout her married life they'd cajoled and coerced Steve into doing what they wanted rather than what *she* wanted, and since she'd moved here they'd bedeviled her with their threats of taking Jason away.

It had been thrilling to see them outsmarted, if only for the moment.

She sighed. "I'm sure it'll have to come to that, probably tomorrow at Jason's birthday party. Oh. You have to come. Okay? Dinosaur Pizza at three-thirty."

"Ah...sure. But I didn't know you were planning a party."

"I wasn't. It was all rather impromptu. Kelly, listen." Beth wished she had her friend in front of her to give her a hug. In the blackness of her despair when she'd realized Jason was gone, she'd had no one to turn to but Kelly, who'd hurried to help. "Thank you so much for coming over and for staying so late. I owe you big. Go into the gallery on your way out and take that welcome sign you've been admiring."

"No, I—"

"Kelly, please. Take it." Beth glanced over her shoulder and saw the sheriff sitting in a chair by the back-vestibule door, her son in his lap. "I've got to go. See you tomorrow for pizza?"

"I'll be there. Beth?"

"Yeah?"

"You know...be careful. The sheriff's a hunk and all, but this is all kind of...sticky."

"I know. Don't worry."

The ride to the sheriff's house took less than ten minutes. Ethan checked the rearview mirror and grinned without looking away from the road. "Guess what?"

Beth played the game. "We're being followed by a white Cadillac?"

"Yep. And they're coming with us up the hill."

The neighborhood was old and comprised of beautiful turn-of-the-century homes. The old sidewalks were broken by the roots of oaks and cedar trees that had probably been there when the town was settled 150 years before.

It was now almost midnight, most porch lights were off, and only the occasional light glowed in an upstairs window. Ethan's house was dark as he pulled up in front of it. He checked the rearview mirror again.

"Are they still with us?" Beth asked.

"They're maybe two hundred feet back. Just turned off their lights."

Beth held the car door open while Ethan pulled Jason out of the vehicle and into his arms. "I hope we don't wake your daughter," she said. "You must worry about her when you have to leave her alone at night."

When he looked surprised that she knew about his daughter and that the girl was alone, she explained. "Ebbie told me that your wife died and you live alone with your fourteen-year-old daughter."

He shook his head. "It's a good thing Ebbie works for me and not the CIA," he said. "National security would be a thing of the past."

"It was a long wait," she said in Ebbie's defense. "We exchanged confidences."

"To her that's like oxygen. No wonder she offered her garden for our wedding. Follow me."

Beth trailed Ethan up the porch steps and waited

while he held Jason with one arm and fitted his key in the lock with his free hand. "My brother lives next door," he said, indicating a large Craftsman-style house on the neighboring lot. "He watches out for her."

The door open, Ethan set the boy on his feet just inside and flipped on a light.

Beth saw a short-haired calico cat race down the stairway to the right, then stop abruptly at the sight of strangers, big green eyes peering at them through the balusters.

Ethan went to the stairway and reached a long arm up to scratch the cat between the ears. "This is Cindy Crawford," he said with a light laugh.

Beth noticed the small black spot above the cat's mouth. It did indeed look like a glamorous mole.

Jason went forward to get acquainted, but Cindy meowed once and darted upstairs.

"My daughter's a cat lover." Ethan led the way up and beckoned them to follow. "She also has a big gray Persian named Simba, but he's usually too lazy to investigate visitors after he's gone to bed. Cindy, on the other hand, has to know everything."

Beth noticed the subtle green-and-yellow-flowered wallpaper and dark woodwork as she and Jason followed Ethan. They proceeded down a corridor softly lit by a night-light in a bathroom, and Ethan paused to look behind a partially open door. His daughter's room, Beth guessed.

Apparently satisfied that all was well, he continued to the end of the hallway where he pushed open a door and reached inside to flip on a light. He ushered Beth and Jason inside.

The room was fairly large, despite a sloping wall

under the eaves. The walls were white, the curtains blue-and-white gingham, and a pair of maple bunk beds had red-white-and-blue bandana-print coverlets.

Jason launched himself gleefully at the ladder. "I get the top one!" he declared.

Beth shushed him, aware of the sleeping girl down the hall and the major inconvenience their presence in the house had to be to the sheriff.

"It's not ideal," Ethan said, indicating the bunks, "but it should do for tonight. I'll get you some pajamas. You saw the bathroom?"

"Yes, thanks."

Ethan disappeared and Beth looked around, experiencing a strange sense of distance from the situation. She felt as though she was watching her son move around on a stage as he shed his blanket and crawled, still wearing the oversize brown sweats, under the blankets of the top bunk.

"Isn't this cool?" he demanded in an exaggerated whisper. "Bunk beds!"

Beth looked at the narrow bottom bunk and decided that even a king-size water bed could not have been more inviting at the moment. She was exhausted.

"Every woman's dream," she said, pulling off her jacket. She opened a door under the eave and found a garment rod, several empty hangers dangling from it. She hung up her jacket, feeling as though she was establishing at least a modicum of order to the chaotic jumble her life had become.

She picked up the blanket Jason had draped over the ladder and folded it at the foot of the top bunk. She turned to find Ethan standing behind her, a pair of gray pajamas in his hand.

"Nikkie could probably lend you something more suitable," he said, "but I hate to wake her."

"Of course." Beth took them from him. "These'll be fine."

"There's a fourth bedroom, but at the moment there's no bedding in it and not much furniture."

"The bunk will be fine. Thank you, Sheriff. I—"

"If you call me Sheriff in front of your in-laws," he interrupted, "it's not going to help sell our story."

"Right." She held the pajamas to her, feeling suddenly as though she needed a shield. Ethan looked comfortable and relaxed in his home environment, and she felt as though she'd landed on an alien planet. Not an unfriendly one certainly, but far removed from where she'd thought she'd be spending the night when she'd awakened that morning.

She felt compelled to chatter. "Of course. Ethan, thank you for spending hours in the cold and rain looking for Jason. And thank you for trying to help him with his grandparents. I know you've put yourself out on a limb and probably turned your household upside down. I'm very sorry we got you into all this."

"I'm not," Jason said, chin resting on his folded arms on his pillow. "This is gonna be fun!"

Beth turned to her son in complete exasperation. "Jason—"

Ethan chuckled. "He's not going to see it your way, so don't even try. Just sleep well and we'll sort it all out in the morning."

She couldn't imagine how they could sort it all out without either admitting the truth to Zachary and Joanne or staging a wedding. But she was too tired to think about that now.

"All right. In the morning."

Ethan turned to Jason. "You have everything you need?"

"Yeah." Jason reached out and caught Ethan around the neck. "Thanks. Are Grandma and Grandpa still watching from outside?"

Ethan shook his head. "I checked out my bedroom window when I got the pajamas. They're gone."

Jason freed Ethan and grinned broadly. "So they're probably thinkin' right now that everything's going to be okay with Mom and me."

Ethan imagined they were thinking they were going to hang around and see how this all played out on the supposed wedding day. But Beth didn't look as though she could deal with that right now, so he said nothing.

"Do you think I could have Buzz Lightyear on my birthday cake?" Jason asked. He fell back against his pillow. Ethan stepped forward to pull up his blankets and tuck him in.

"Sure. Who's he?"

"A space hero in *Toy Story*," Beth explained. When Ethan still looked puzzled, she added, "The Disney movie."

Ethan nodded. "We'll see what we can do. I'll call Ebbie in the morning."

Jason kicked his feet under the covers as though his delight with the prospect of his birthday party couldn't be contained. "Thanks. This is gonna be so cool!"

Ethan turned away from the bunk to find Beth standing behind him, the pajamas still clutched to her chest. She looked uncomfortable.

"I'll pay for the party," she said.

He took her by the arm and pulled her with him to the doorway. "Good night, Jase," he called, flipping off the light.

"Night, Ethan," Jason called back.

Ethan drew Beth into the hallway and said quietly, "We'll work that all out later, all right? Why don't you just change into the pajamas and try to get some sleep."

"But I don't want you to—"

"I do pretty much as I please," he said mildly, pointing to the bathroom. "You're welcome to shower if you want to, take a bath, whatever. Just try to relax and don't sweat the details."

"Life, Ethan," she said, a little prudishly, he thought, "is all about details."

He folded his arms and shook his head. "No, I don't buy that. Life is about the big picture and not getting all hung up on the details. And right now the big picture is seeing that Jason has a great birthday."

She folded her arms, too, over the pajamas. "I agree, but I just want to make it clear that I'm the only family Jason has. Therefore I will pay for the party."

"I'm afraid I don't buy that, either." He watched her sigh and firm her jaw, as though intending to resist whatever he was about to say. He found something challenging, even stimulating, about that. "Jason and I developed a friendship tonight. I know from what he told me about you that you've done your best this past year to be everything to him. But he's coming to a point in his life where he needs more than you can give him. Maybe you're going to have to share him a little. So let's not worry about who pays for the party."

Her eyes widened in the shadowy hallway. "Did he say he's unhappy? I mean, besides the worry about his grandfather?"

"No," Ethan assured her quickly. "He seems to

understand and accept his situation. And he was proud to tell me about the cannery and all you intend to do with it. But he said he missed his father. In fact, he said he used to miss him even *before* he died."

Beth heard those words and felt the impact of them right in the middle of her chest. So much of her grief over Steve's death was because they'd had so little of him the last few years he was alive.

"His father loved Jason very much," Beth said gravely. "But he failed him."

Ethan spread both hands in an expansive gesture. "So let's indulge the kid a little. Let him have his fantasy for a while. We'll do his party up big and between us, try to convince the grandparents we're making a cozy home for him."

"That sounds reasonable," she said on a sigh, "but if you carry that plan to the conclusion my in-laws will demand, you may very well find yourself married to me."

He leaned a shoulder against the wall and grinned. "Are you suggesting I might find that unpleasant?"

Beth did her level best to quell the spark of excitement those words generated in her. For the last five or six years of her marriage, she'd wondered what it would be like to live intimately with someone who was aware she was there.

And she had the feeling the sheriff was always sharply conscious of who was around him and what went on.

"I'm an artist," she said, thinking she could erase that grin from his face, "and not very domestic. I'm a marginal cook and I often forget things like laundry and shopping." She let her eyes run lazily over the attractive length of his body. "I imagine a man like you pictures the perfect wife as a cross between Martha Stewart and a Playboy bunny.''

He laughed softly. ''I had a perfect wife,'' he said, ''and she was nothing like that. She often forgot to do laundry, too, though she was a lawyer and not an artist. She was loving and funny and forgiving.'' He sighed, his voice taking on a moody quality. ''And I had her for only twelve years—she died five years ago. I miss her often, but it's never her domestic skills I think of, only the warmth and laughter she brought to my life.''

Beth felt small for having tried to force him to a distance by suggesting he was in any way typical.

''I'm sorry,'' she said. ''I guess it's because I haven't been appreciated as anything but a business prop for a very long time. It sounds as though you had a wonderful marriage.''

''I did. I'm sorry you didn't.''

She shrugged, having long ago accepted that domestic bliss would never be hers. ''It was good in the beginning, I learned to live with what it became, and now it's over. Art and marriage aren't compatible, anyway.''

Now he shrugged. ''A lot of people think law enforcement and marriage are incompatible because the job comes first.'' He grinned again. ''So that makes cops and artists compatible, doesn't it?''

She blinked. ''I believe that's a flawed equation,'' she said. ''I think it means neither of us should get into a relationship. Anyway—'' she squared her shoulders and cleared her throat ''—thank you again for finding my son. And for being his friend. I...I do appreciate your concern for him. I just don't think it has to extend to me and my problems with my in-laws.'' She smiled at him hesitantly. ''So, good night. We'll organize the party and the...the problem in the morning. Okay?"

It was a moment before he nodded. She got the distinct impression he was simply humoring her. "Okay," he said. "Sleep well."

"Thank you. You, too."

She stepped into the bathroom. She'd change into the pajamas and shower in the morning. As she closed the door and stood in the dark, her heartbeat skipped erratically. She attempted to analyze her feelings and finally concluded that they didn't appear to be caused by worry or fear.

Her racing pulse was caused by excitement. She groaned, knowing that suggested big trouble.

CHAPTER FOUR

BETH TURNED OFF the shower and stood for a moment in the warm steamy space, pulling her arguments together. After a good night's sleep and in the sunny sanity-restoring light of day, she felt in control again.

Her in-laws were forceful and demanding and single-minded, but she was sure she could make them see reason if she was calm and logical. That was certainly a more acceptable solution to her problems than marrying the sheriff.

She reached beyond the shower curtain surrounding the old tub, caught a towel off the rack and wrapped it around herself, wondering what had happened to her that she'd even considered such an outrageous scheme.

Actually the answer was simple. Her son had been missing for hours in rain-filled darkness, and when he'd finally been restored to her, she'd have done anything to ensure she'd never be parted from him again.

But such dramatics weren't necessary. Last night the storm had heightened the dangers of her situation. But this morning she was thinking more clearly. She would thank the sheriff for his help and be on her way.

Wrapped in a fluffy green towel, she pushed the shower curtain aside—and found herself face-to-face with a girl in a red chenille bathrobe with tabby-cat faces embroidered on its big patch pockets.

The girl was probably as tall as she was. Her long

curly mass of dark hair was disheveled, and the expression in her dark eyes as she stared at Beth was one of complete disbelief.

Beth stared back, searching her mind for some brief and reasonable explanation to give the girl for her presence there.

The girl smiled suddenly. "Hi," she said in a voice still groggy with sleep. "I'm Tanika. But nobody calls me that. It's Nikkie." She laughed a little nervously, then indicated Beth's towel. "So. You stayed the night?"

"Ah...yes," Beth replied. Then realizing what the girl was suggesting, corrected her quickly. "Oh. No, no. Not like that. I mean...my son was missing and your father searched for him for hours. Then...well, he brought us home because—"

"Hi!" Jason burst into the little room, still wearing the brown sweats. His thick dark hair stood up in spikes, and his blue eyes were as filled with excitement as they'd been the night before when he'd discovered the bunk beds.

Nikkie's friendly smile turned to confusion.

"Nikkie," Beth said, stepping out of the tub, "this is my son, Jason. Jase, this is Ethan's daughter, Tanika."

Jason looked at her as though assessing her worthiness to associate with his hero. "Weird name," he said.

"It's American Indian," the girl replied somewhat stiffly. "My mother liked it." She looked from Jason to Beth and asked, "What are you doing here?"

Beth opened her mouth to explain, but before she could form the words, Jason said with considerable pride, "The sheriff's going to be my dad!"

Nikkie stared at him for a full ten seconds, then demanded in an over-my-dead-body tone of voice, "What? *What?*"

"Hey." A quiet male voice spoke from the doorway of the crowded little room. "I see you've all met. Who needs a family room when you've got a bathroom? Good morning, Nik."

He was already showered, Beth noticed, and dressed in a beige shirt with all the brass buttons and pins of his office, a brown tie and brown slacks.

"Daddy." Nikkie turned to her father, a formidable picture of indignation not at all diminished by the kitty faces on her bathrobe. "I want to know what's going on. *Now.*"

Beth clutched the towel closely, feeling her cheeks redden as Ethan's eyes ran over her. "Good morning," he said, his attention diverted from his daughter. "Sleep well?"

"Yes, thank you," Beth replied awkwardly, feeling apologetic that his daughter was upset, wishing desperately that she was anywhere but this tiny packed room. "I, ah, was hoping to be out before Nikkie got up, but—"

"The kid says you're going to be his father!" Nikkie indicated Jason with a disparaging wave of her hand. "Is he delusional or was I left out of the loop on something important?"

Jason threw his arms possessively around Ethan's waist. "Tell her," he said, wrinkling his nose at Nikkie. "Tell her about you and Mom getting married."

"What?" Nikkie shrieked.

"We are *not* getting married!" Beth told Nikkie, hoping to defuse what was rapidly becoming a little war. The source of the dispute, she accepted wryly, was the sheriff. Nikkie felt he belonged to her, and while she might have been willing to share him with a woman who'd spent the night in his bed, that generosity didn't extend to another child.

And Jason, who didn't want anyone or anything to endanger the flimsy hold he had on security, was also staking his claim on Ethan.

Beth couldn't help but feel left out. She was the only one in the room with no claim on the sheriff, and her own son didn't even seem to notice her presence in his determination to make sure that Ethan noticed *him*.

Ethan put a hand to Jason's back, then extended his free arm to Nikkie. "Jason, why don't you get ready for school while I catch Nikkie up on what's going on," he said. "Beth?"

"Yes?" She looked up, a little surprised to be noticed after all, even if it wasn't by her son.

"Brodie'll make you breakfast."

"Brodie?"

"My brother comes over every morning to eat. Don't let him scare you. He's all talk."

And with that he patted Jason's shoulder and left the room with Nikkie.

Jason stared after them longingly. "You don't think he'll change his mind, do you?" he asked, his voice small and pitiful.

Beth, her early-morning confidence shaken by the volatile confrontation, found that she could neither reassure him that Ethan wouldn't change his mind, nor explain to him that it would probably be better all around if he did. At the moment she wasn't sure of anything.

And there'd been something friendly, even...needy,

in Nikkie's eyes when she'd introduced herself to Beth. As though a woman in her life might be welcome.

But that tentative extension of friendship had been shattered when she'd thought Beth—and particularly Jason—might be intruding on her life with her father.

Beth closed her eyes for a moment, wondering how things could possibly get more complicated. She quickly dismissed the thought, afraid maybe they would.

"Take your shower," she said briskly to Jason, "and remember, when you're a guest in someone's home, it isn't polite to tell them you think their name is weird."

Jason sank onto the closed lid of the toilet. "She doesn't like me. Do you think Ethan'll change his mind because she doesn't like me?"

"I don't know what will happen, Jase," she said frankly. "Take your shower and get ready for school, and I'll try to figure everything out today."

He looked at her doubtfully. "You'll tell Grandma and Grandpa the truth because you won't want to lie. Then...then it'll all be over."

She took his face in her hands and leaned over to kiss the tip of his nose. "Sweetie, it never began. The sheriff is *not* your father, even though you'd like that very much. And you can't make it happen, just because you want it. He belongs to Nikkie, not to us."

Jason's eyes brimmed with tears. "Well...how come we don't get a dad?"

"We had one," she reminded gently. "Remember?"

A tear spilled over onto Jason's cheek. "Not very

much. Mostly it's just been you and me. I love you and all, Mom. But he's...he's got muscles."

Beth wrapped her arms around her son and hugged him. "The heart's a muscle, too, Jason. And mine works just for you."

He returned her hug and giggled. "It's funny to think of a heart being bulgy."

Now she laughed, relieved to hear the humor in his voice. "At my age, Jason, everything gets bulgy, only not in a good way. Now hurry up and get showered and dressed so you can have breakfast before you go."

"Okay." Momentarily distracted from his problems, Jason pulled off the brown sweatshirt as Beth hurried to the bedroom to put on the undies, old jeans and sweater she'd been wearing last night before this whole drama had begun.

ETHAN SAT on the blue-and-yellow coverlet on the edge of his daughter's bed and watched her pace in front of him, much as he'd seen her mother do during opening or closing arguments in court. He felt a bittersweet pang in his chest.

"I thought we were in this together," she said with an air of injured pride as she marched past him. Her cats watched her movements with interest, one on each of her two pillows. "That's what you're always saying when you want to learn something from me. 'Nikkie,'" she quoted him, "'we're in this together. There isn't anything you can't tell me or ask me.'" She gave him an angry glance as she went past him again, headed in the other direction. "I thought that applied to you, too."

He caught her arm and pulled her down beside him onto the bed. "It does apply to me, too." He put an arm around her shoulders. "But I just explained what happened. Jase was a little kid in trouble, and Beth looked like she was at the end of her rope last night. And while I imagine the grandparents have the boy's best interests at heart, they were terrifying. I had to do something."

"So you brought them home." Nikkie sighed with exaggerated patience. "Fine. But what's this stuff about you becoming the little twerp's father? You're not going to do that, are you? Marry her just so the grandparents won't go to court to get the kid?"

Ethan rubbed his forehead. He hated starting the day with a headache. "I don't know what I'm going to do. I thought I'd wait till the birthday party this afternoon and see how the grandparents react."

Nikkie played with the belt of her robe, knotting and unknotting the ends. "You always wanted to have a boy, didn't you?" she asked moodily. "Only, Mom died before you could do it."

"No," he replied honestly, pulling her closer. "We never talked about having another baby. You were great and your mom had a busy career. You were enough for us."

"But you always took me fishing with you and out to cut wood and to football games at the park."

"I thought you liked coming with me."

"I did. I do. But it'd be more fun for you with a son. All your friends bring their boys and you just have me."

He wasn't sure where this was coming from and he tried to tread carefully. "You're a good sport. They all like you. It's never been a problem, has it?"

"No," she replied with a certain lack of conviction. "But I'm getting older now. Worms are losing their thrill for me, and I hate having to go to the bathroom in the woods."

He laughed. "Your mom did, too. But the point is, you never gripe and that makes you one of the guys."

She leaned into him and put her arms around him. He knew he had her sympathy if not her understanding. "I think it'd be a little scary around here if you got married—even if it wasn't for real. I mean, they'd have to *live* here, right?"

"Beth and I are going to talk about that later." He squeezed her to him and kissed the top of her head. "But you must know you're the most important person in my life and I'd never do anything to hurt you."

"I know. But you have to fall in love again *sometime*. I mean, you're still a young man." She said the words seriously and with some surprise.

He bit back a laugh. "Thank you."

"But it'll be hard for me to share you. What if she doesn't want to go to Bailey's for breakfast on Sunday mornings and read the paper while we eat? What if she doesn't like 'NYPD Blue' and wants to rent some mushy movie?" She sat up, her eyes wide and horror-filled. "What if she doesn't like cats?"

"Then," he said with a theatrical sigh, "I guess you'll have to make pancakes on Sunday mornings, sit through *Love Story* on Tuesday nights and...I don't know, give the cats to some lab-animal bounty hunter who—"

That earned him a doubled fist to the chest and an indignant "Da-ad!"

He laughed and dodged a second punch, catching her wrist. "Come on. You know I'd never let anyone deprive you of your cats. And the rest of the stuff is something all families have to deal with. Sometimes you give up something to get something else. It's life."

"I like *this* life," she said petulantly.

"I know." He grew serious. "I do, too. And I promise not to do anything that'll change it too radically. Trust me, okay?"

She appeared to consider that. "I always trust you. But I never got up to take a shower and found a woman wrapped in a towel in the bathroom before."

Yes, he thought with a slight quickening of his pulse. That had been quite a sight. Soft breasts pressed under the enveloping edge of the towel and two long shapely legs visible below. He'd had to force himself to focus on Nikkie and Jason.

"Right. But everything happened too suddenly last night, and too late for me to explain it to you. I thought I might get to you before you got up this morning, but apparently Beth's an early riser."

"So." Nikkie went to a dresser drawer and pulled out a pink sweater. "Her name's Elizabeth."

"No." He stood. "Bethany. Bethany Richards. She's an artist. She bought that old cannery on the waterfront."

Nikkie pulled a pair of jeans out of the closet and turned to frown at him. "An artist? You mean, paintings and stuff?"

"Yeah, I guess. I'm not sure." He went toward the door, then turned as he opened it and asked, "What are you doing after school?"

"The drama club's meeting to decide what play to do for the Winter Festival weekend." She retrieved a pair of fat-heeled boots from the bottom of her closet. They were the ugliest things he'd ever seen, and he remembered paying a fortune for them. "Why?"

"We're having a birthday party for Jason at three-thirty at Dinosaur Pizza. If you have time to come, it'd help his story in front of his grandparents."

She rolled her eyes. "You want me to come to an eight-year-old's birthday party?" Then she huffed impatiently. "And how come *you're* giving him a party? You just met him last night."

Ethan nodded. His daughter definitely had some of her mother's gift for argument. "He happened to mention when I was returning him to his mother that he wished he could have a birthday party like all the other kids have, rather than one where his grandparents come to bully his mother. So when he started telling his story about me becoming his father, I backed him up by inviting them to the party—which hadn't really been planned but which Ebbie's supposed to put together this morning."

Nikkie tossed her boots at the bed, then yanked open a drawer and pulled out a pair of thick flowered socks. "And it'd help your story if I show up and act like a big sister."

"You don't have to act like anything. But it'd be great if you could come. And pizza will likely be dinner tonight."

She tossed the socks after the boots and moved toward him. "The meeting'll probably break up too late for me to make the party," she said with little visible sign of regret. "But maybe you could bring me home a couple of pieces of pizza. Sausage, pepperoni and onion—no olives."

"Right." He leaned down to kiss her cheek. "Have a good day."

She hugged him briefly. "You, too. And, Daddy?"

He stopped in the hallway and leaned back into the room. "Yeah?"

She hesitated, as though considering what she was about to say, then blurted, "Did you and...Beth have sex last night?"

It always startled him when his daughter brought up the subject of sex. He understood that she was no longer his *little* girl and that it was far healthier for her to bring him her questions than talk about them to someone else, but the subject was so important it unnerved him.

He was always tempted to tell her horror stories about how sex at too young an age ruined lives and futures, but that wasn't smart. He didn't want to frighten her into never discussing sex with him again. Still she was pretty and shapely already, and he knew that several of her classmates were experimenting. The prospect that she might terrified him.

"I prefer the term 'making love,'" he said, trying not to betray his fears. "But no, we didn't."

"You'd only known her a few hours." Nikkie studied him gravely. "You couldn't possibly have learned to love her in that amount of time. So you couldn't have made love to her. But you could have had sex. People have recreational sex all the time."

Dear God! He leaned a shoulder against the wall as much for support as to appear casual. "*I* don't. Sex is for love...and for communication and procreation, but not recreation."

"She's very pretty," Nikkie persisted. "And you've been celibate a long time."

He closed his eyes briefly. He certainly could never be considered guilty of having stifled his child's curiosity. "Like I said, love's important. I had it with your mom, and that's made it impossible for me to ever use sex just for fun. Though it certainly can be."

She sighed, apparently satisfied. "I sure would like to know what it's all about," she admitted wistfully.

He found relief in her admission that she didn't know. "It's all about things that are just too big to deal with at fourteen," he said, leaning down to kiss her again. "Even for a fourteen-year-old as smart as you are."

She gave him a rueful and knowing look. "But someday I'll be ready. Right now, though, there's enough going on in my life."

"Amen to that," he said. "See you tonight."

He went into his room to retrieve his utility belt and jacket, praying he would be much older and wiser by the time she *was* ready.

BREAKFAST BRODIE-STYLE was bacon, eggs and hash browns with onions and garlic. Beth considered herself lucky that she had a preference for onions and garlic, because Ethan's brother had been generous with them. She poured coffee while he brought their plates to the table.

Brodie Drum was a little taller and leaner than his brother, but had the same rich dark hair and eyes. He wore a blue-and-white-striped shirt with a large sewn-on patch on the back embroidered with "Drum's Garage." His name was on the front pocket.

He exuded energy and a confident sexuality that Beth concluded was the reason for Ethan's warning, but he was friendly and welcoming. She guessed he was four or five years younger than Ethan.

They sat across from each other at the small table in the middle of the sunny yellow kitchen. Ethan had explained her presence to his brother earlier, and Brodie had commiserated with her while he cooked.

"So what we have to do now," he said, sounding eager, "is convince your in-laws you're marrying into a solid loving family. I'll come to the birthday party."

"Thank you," she said, shaking salt and pepper on her egg and potatoes. "I'd like that, but we're not sure what we're going to do about the...the wedding thing."

Brodie seemed surprised. "But what other solution is there? And you can't do better than Ethan, even if it's just a temporary thing. He's a solid citizen, good provider, and he knows all that—" he waved his fork over his plate "—all that sensitive stuff. He shouts only when he's exhausted every other option, and he's willing to lend a hand to people everybody else has given up on."

Brodie's eyes softened. "His wife, Diana, I know, was very happy with him. And he's great with Nikkie. She's a good kid and he's raised her by himself the last five years."

"Hi!" Jason burst into the kitchen, jacket held by its collar and dragging on the floor. Someone had laundered it already. It was easy to guess who.

He came to Beth's side and smiled at Ethan's brother.

Brodie pushed his chair back and reached across the table to shake Jason's hand. "Hi, Jase," he said, pulling a chair out for him. "I'm going to be your uncle. Sit down. I'll get your breakfast."

Beth opened her mouth, prepared to remind him that the wedding issue was undecided. But Jason followed him to the stove and said excitedly, "Wow! I never had an uncle before."

"Well, you're going to like it," Brodie replied, carrying the warm plate to the table with a hot pad. Then he went to the refrigerator and poured a glass of milk. "Uncles spoil you. They let you do things your father won't. Want some chocolate in that milk?"

"Yeah!"

Jason sat in the chair at a right angle to Beth and dug into his breakfast while Brodie poured a generous amount of syrup into a dessert spoon, then stirred it into the milk.

"I'm coming to your party this afternoon." Brodie resumed his chair. "What'll I bring?"

"What do you mean?"

"For a present."

"Oh! You know those *Toy Story*..." Jason began a complicated description of the movie's action figures, then caught Beth's reprimanding eye and stopped. "You don't have to bring me anything." The denial was offered with a smile but lacked conviction. "I'd just like you to come so I can introduce you to Grandma and Grandpa."

"I'll be there," Brodie promised.

Beth had difficulty taking issue with her son's ear-to-ear grin of delight. Brodie was as comfortable to be with as Ethan was and just as indulgent with Jason. But he also seemed as bent as his brother on believing that marriage to Ethan was the solution to her in-law problems. She'd tried to stop him from letting Jason think that was going to happen, but he hadn't seemed to notice her protests.

"Hi!" Jason said when Ethan entered the room.

The concern that Ethan would no longer like him because Nikkie didn't showed clearly in his expression. But Ethan touched Jason's shoulder as he passed him, and the expression evaporated.

Ethan went to a far corner of the kitchen where a large bag of cat food was tucked away. He lifted it easily and shook food into two bowls.

Cindy and a gray ball of fur Beth presumed to be Simba ran into the room and began to eat. Ethan stroked each down-bent head, then crossed to the oven to retrieve his plate.

He poured a cup of coffee and brought it and his plate to the table. He grinned at Jason as he sat opposite him. "Mm," he said. "Smell those onions and garlic."

He picked up his cup without using the handle and took a sip, smiling at Beth over the rim. "Did Brodie ask you to run away with him to the Seychelles yet?"

"I was saving that for after she gets to know me." Brodie winked at Beth. "Think you could take to island living?"

"Easily," she replied. "I like the thought of warm beaches and blue water."

"But Gauguin already did the island thing in his paintings," Ethan said. "Don't you want to do something else?"

Beth laughed. "I wouldn't complain about where I was if I had the time to paint." She chewed and swallowed a bit of crisp bacon. "But I don't, at least not right now. All my dreams of being a real artist—you know, doing oils on canvas—have to take second place to paying the rent, so to speak. I make signs, plaques, decorative boxes, children's chairs, stuff like that."

"In the Seychelles, you could make those little figures you see made out of shells in tourist shops." Brodie drew a picture in the air with his fork.

Beth made a face. "I don't think so. But we could make our living pearl-diving or something. Maybe you could open a garage there."

Now Brodie made a face. "No. When I make it to the Seychelles, the only thing I'm doing is beachcombing. No more squeaks you can't find, brakes that don't act up when I'm test-driving them, no customers unwilling to pay for the time it takes to repair a transmission..."

"You mean you'd be expecting monthly checks from me," Ethan said, clarifying his brother's daydreams. "Or Beth would have to support you."

Brodie chewed thoughtfully on a mouthful of potatoes, then shook his head. "No, I don't want Beth to have to lift a finger. And you owe me for all the times you beat me up when we were kids."

Ethan made a scornful sound. "You deserved it. You were such a whiner, always running to Mom over every little thing. Like the time I gave you a little tap on the nose in the grocery store."

Brodie sat up indignantly. "That wasn't a tap. It was a punch! My nose was bleeding all over the candy aisle!"

"You tried to steal a package of bubble gum."

"It might have had a trading card in it that would have made me a rich man today!"

Ethan shook his head at Beth. "I wouldn't go anywhere with him if I were you. No matter how inviting he makes island living sound."

"Me, either." Jason grinned from brother to brother, happy to be part of their banter. Then he said staunchly to Ethan, "I'm staying with you."

"Well," Brodie said, pretending to be affronted, "Forget getting any *Toy Story* character for your birthday."

The three of them laughed and Beth forced a smile, but she felt a mild resentment over how quickly her son's allegiance was switching from her to Ethan.

Nikkie flew through the kitchen calling goodbye to her father and her uncle as she reached into a cupboard, snatched a granola bar and headed for the door. To Beth and Jason she threw a polite smile and a casual "See ya."

The door closed behind her just as a school bus pulled up in front of the house.

Brodie pushed his empty plate away and made a conciliatory face at Jason as the boy downed his last swallow of milk. "My shop's a couple of blocks from your school. Do you want to come with me or do you want to wait for Ethan to drive you?" He turned to Beth. "Is it all right?"

"Of course." She smiled gratefully. "I'd appreciate that."

"Good." Brodie stood and carried his plate to the counter. "Then I'll pick him up after school and bring him to the party."

Jason followed his example with his own plate. "Even though I won't go to the seashells with you?"

"The *Sey*chelles," Brodie corrected. "And I'm sure you'll eventually come to your senses. I'm a much nicer guy than Ethan."

Jason cast an adoring look at Ethan. "Nobody's nicer than Ethan."

Ethan gave him a thumbs-up. "You're okay, Jase," he said.

CHAPTER FIVE

"YOU LOOK RESTED," Ethan said as he got up to get the coffeepot off the warmer and bring it to the table. His gaze skimmed Beth's face and lingered on her hair before he topped up her coffee mug and then his own. "If you can sleep in a bottom bunk with a squirmy kid over your head, you can sleep anywhere."

She added cream to her coffee, then pushed the small jug toward him, resisting the impulse to touch her hair. She'd combed it and left it swinging free this morning because she had no idea what happened to the pins and fastener she'd had in it the day before. "You've had the experience?"

"Brodie and I had bunks," he said over his shoulder as he returned the coffeepot to the counter. "He sleeps with the same energy he displays when he's awake. And he makes great hash browns."

"That he does." She kept her eyes on her plate, wondering how best to explain to Ethan what was on her mind.

"So, do you want to talk about the birthday party and the problem with your in-laws?" he asked between forkfuls of food.

She put her own fork down and squared her shoulders, his direct question reminding her that the only way to deal with this man was with the same directness.

"Yes," she said, "but *I'm* going to talk and you're going to listen." She waited for him to object. When he didn't, she was surprised into silence for another moment.

He pretended to cock his ear. "I don't hear anything."

"I expected an argument," she admitted.

He raised an eyebrow. "Arguments are generally two-sided. 'I'm going to talk and you're going to listen' doesn't really encourage that."

She felt her shoulders sag a little. "True. But you saved my son's life and I'm a guest in your home and at your table. I...I guess I'm having second thoughts about the way I phrased that."

He grinned at her. "I'm not that delicate, Beth. If I want to argue, I'll argue, whether or not you try to stop me. Speak. I'm listening."

She collected her thoughts, the corner of her mind not occupied with her son and his grandparents thinking that this man would be interesting company if her circumstances were different. And if she didn't mind always being in a dither. But they weren't. And she did.

"All right." She pushed her plate away and leaned toward him on folded arms. "I could never repay you for all you've done. I can't tell you what my son means to me, but I don't suppose I have to because I can see how much you and Nikkie care for each other." She smiled, despite her determination to make her point. "She's lovely, by the way. Before Jason managed to annoy her, she was very warm and polite to me."

He smiled, too, the gesture filled with pride and amusement. "Thank you. That was because she thought you'd spent the night." He gave the phrase significant emphasis.

Her smile widened. "I know. And then Jason flew into your arms and she became Warrior Woman, protecting her home."

"I'm sorry."

"Don't apologize. It's a quality that admits her to our sisterhood—even at fourteen." Beth's expression sobered. "But that's not what I wanted to talk about."

"I'm still listening," he said, then took another sip of coffee and leaned back in his chair.

"I wish it was possible for me to let Jason go on thinking he can have you for a father," she said quickly before she could lose track of her arguments. Ethan's quiet dark eyes were focused on her, and she found their intensity unsettling. "But let's face it. Getting married to keep my in-laws out of my hair would be ridiculous."

"Why?" he asked. "Or is it my turn to talk yet?"

She sputtered, wondering how he could possibly ask such a question. "What do you mean, why? Because you don't love me and I don't love you. We don't even know each other. And even if we did it just to appease them for now, Joanne and Zachary will be a threat to me until Jason's an adult. You'd have to be married to me for at least ten years!"

Ethan watched the fire in her eyes, saw the color tinge her creamy cheeks, saw her eyebrows disappear under rich brown bangs as she strained to make him understand her position. He remembered how her voice had sounded over the radio when her son was lost and she wanted to take one of the county's cars and go look for him herself.

He was beginning to think she was wrong in believing he didn't love her.

Well, maybe *love* was too strong a word. Maybe it wasn't love at all. But he had feelings for her. A very powerful...*like*. And that seemed a pretty good basis for a relationship.

"Fifty percent of the marriages supposedly based on love," he said calmly, "end in divorce. And many of the couples who stay married do so out of laziness. Even *you* said you'd simply gotten used to what yours had become."

"That's right!" she said fervently. "And that's precisely why I've sworn I'll never get married again."

"Maybe something more reliable than love should be the reason for marriage. Like a mutual need."

"I'm thirty-two years old, I'm finally free to do what I want to do with my life, and I'm determined that no one is going to get in the way of that."

"What makes you think I would?"

She looked heavenward in supplication. "You would. I'm sure it would upset you if I didn't cook and forgot to do laundry and stayed up all night finishing a project for a craft show."

"I can cook," he replied reasonably. "Nikkie does our laundry, my uniforms go to the cleaners, and I wouldn't care how late you stayed up if you finally came home to me."

She stared at him in disbelief, opening and then closing her mouth several times as she apparently considered, then discarded one argument after another.

"Are you forgetting the kids?" she asked finally, her voice high and a little desperate. "Do you think it'd be good for them to know we married to perpetrate a hoax?"

"I think," he said, "that Jason really likes the idea of having me for a father."

"But Nikkie," she argued, "*doesn't* like the idea of sharing you, which is perfectly understandable. And I seriously doubt it would be good for a fourteen-year-old girl to have her life upended like that."

"Nikkie's been without a mother for five years." He leaned his elbows on the table, cupped one hand over the other and looked at her, his eyes reflecting that he, too, had been without someone he loved. "That was an important time for her. I did my best to be there for her and I think we've held our own, but I know she's lost out on some things because I can't be what Diana could have been to her. And now I'm looking at an even more critical time in her life. A time when she should have a woman to turn to."

Beth felt her arguments growing fuzzy in the face of his emotional honesty, but she struggled to clear them. "Ethan, I can't be what Diana could have been to her, either. I'm me, and unfortunately I'm not at all a typical mother. And, anyway, if you married me, I think she'd see me as a threat, rather than someone to turn to and confide in."

"Maybe in the beginning," he agreed, "but she's a smart kid. She'd see how much you have to give to our lives."

Beth shook her head in disbelief. "Why do you *say* that? I just told you—"

"I know. You don't cook, you forget to do laundry, and you hang out in your studio all night." He sighed, lowered his arms and leaned toward her. "I guess because your husband resented the artist in you, you have trouble understanding that when a man really loves a woman, he wants her to be who she really is.

Whatever inconvenience that brings him is tolerable—particularly if she loves him back."

"But you don't *love* me!" she said emphatically, slapping both hands on the table so hard the crockery shook.

He didn't even blink. He smiled, instead, and that completely unsettled her. "I like you a hell of a lot, though. And you like me."

She closed her eyes and put a hand over them. "What I really like," she said with quiet exasperation, "is a man who listens to me when I'm talking."

He laughed softly. "I've heard every word. I think what you mean is that you like a man who listens, then does what you want him to do. Which seems to be in direct contrast to how *you'd* like to be treated by *him*."

Beth dropped both hands to her lap, fell against the back of her chair and eyed him with weary frustration. "If we were married," she said, "I'd probably kill you the first time we had a fight."

He grinned wickedly. "I don't think so. I'm BPST-trained."

"Who trained?"

"Board of Police Standards and Training. But I might let you wrestle me down just to see what happens."

"You're impossible."

"You're not the first to tell me that."

"I can't marry you."

"Okay."

For all his wily arguments, he made that concession easily and with seemingly little regret. Beth felt a strange pinch of disappointment in the suddenly quiet aftermath of their head-to-head confrontation.

"No hard feelings?" she asked.

"Of course not." He pushed away from the table and picked up his plate and mug. "Come on. I'll give you a ride to the cannery."

She followed him with her dishes. "And I'm paying for the party," she insisted, hoping to take advantage of his amenable mood.

He nodded, putting his things in the sink. "Whatever you want."

"Why?" She put her dishes in after his, then turned to face him suspiciously.

He appeared confused. "Why what?"

She put a hand on her hip. "Why are you suddenly saying yes to everything? To show me what an easygoing husband you'd be?"

"No," he replied, reaching up to button the collar he'd left undone under the loose knot of his tie. "To show you how dull and unfulfilling it would be to have such a husband."

So, he was using reverse psychology on her. She felt warmed and amused. "Ah." She smiled. "The toothless-tiger theory."

"Pardon me?"

"Challenge. Where's the glory in taming a toothless tiger? Is that what you're trying to tell me?"

He considered that a moment, then shook his head. "I don't think so. Generally men don't like to hear the word 'tamed' used in a sentence about them. Some of us can be domesticated but never *tamed*."

"Then what was your point?"

"That you'd be bored in a week by a man who did exactly what you wanted him to do."

She laughed. "That's a myth put forth by men who want everything their *own* way."

"Really?" He shifted his weight and she had the skin-prickling awareness of being hunted. "Do you want me to kiss you?"

She parted her lips to answer, but couldn't decide on yes or no. In her current state of confusion, either answer seemed a lie.

Then with a swiftness that validated her notion of being hunted, his hand went under her hair and caught her nape, gently but firmly. He tilted her head slightly as his came down to block out the sun streaming in through the kitchen window.

And he kissed her. He wasn't forceful, but he wasn't tentative. His lips had the same gentle but confident strength as the hand at her neck, as well as an artful mobility that made her put both hands on his waist to steady herself.

She felt the tip of his tongue against her lips and opened to admit it. But all he did was explore the rim of the inside of her lips. Then he withdrew, ending the kiss with the lightest nip of her bottom lip, effectively erasing any comparison of him to a toothless tiger.

When he raised his head, she felt as though someone had worked her over with a foam bat.

He frowned down at her, looking a little unsettled himself. "I expected you to say no." His voice was quiet, thoughtful. "And because I was sure kissing you would be wonderful, I was going to make the point afterward that you'd have missed the pleasure if I'd done as you asked." His frown deepened. "But you *didn't* say no."

Still shaken, she pulled his hand from her neck. "I didn't say yes, either." Then because she knew he'd won that one, she admitted with a thin smile, "But your point was made, anyway."

He cleared his throat. "Good. Get your jacket. I'm leaving in five minutes."

ETHAN FOUND a sales receipt on his desk for a sheet cake. There was a note scrawled on it that said, "Pick up at three." Beside it was a bag that contained paper plates and napkins with *Toy Story* figures on them, as well as a giant package of colorful balloons.

"Your share is seventeen dollars," Ebbie called from the outer office, her telephone receiver cradled on her shoulder. "I'm holding for Chuck. He's rousting a pair of homeless men out of that empty house down the street from your place. I wish that somebody would buy it and restore it, or that the city would condemn it. Between the drifters who break in for a refuge from the rain and the kids who dare each other to go in, the damn thing's on the log every other day. Yeah, Chuck?" She responded to a question on the other end of the line, logged the call on the computer, then called the shelter to tell them Chuck was bringing them a couple of clients.

At last she hung up the phone and grinned at Ethan, who stood in his doorway. "I bought Jason a basketball. You think he'll like that?"

"Sure." He pulled the right number of bills out of his wallet and put them on Ebbie's desk. "You made the reservations at Dinosaur?"

"Yes. But I couldn't tell them how many. I guessed twenty, with kids from school. What do you think?"

"Sounds good to me." He patted her graying curls. "Thanks. Even if his grandparents foul up his life, he'll have a party to remember."

Ebbie looked concerned. "I thought you and the

mother were getting along when I left. The wedding's off?"

He shrugged, trying to ignore the feeling of something important missed, of two lives destined to entwine, yet somehow evading each other and moving in opposite directions.

But that was ridiculous. This time yesterday he hadn't even known Beth or Jason Richards existed. He'd known Diana a lifetime. He and she had planned on Nikkie for years.

Last night had just been a strangely emotional accident. Jason's fantasies about a father couldn't be safely indulged without completely upsetting four lives.

The hell it couldn't.

"Her last marriage wasn't great," he told Ebbie, then went into his office and stood beside his desk, pretending to study the calendar. "She's determined not to do it again. It was an outrageous idea, anyway."

Ebbie got up from her desk and crossed to his doorway. "Well, *un*determine her. She's afraid of you, that's all."

Ethan looked up from his calendar, eyes narrowed. "What?"

"Afraid of you," she repeated, folding her arms over her matronly bosom. "Because you…light her fire, so to speak. I don't understand it, but I suppose a competent in-charge sort of man could appeal to a woman who was ignored by her first husband."

He shook his head over her homegrown psychology. "Apparently not. She was very emphatic about it. No wedding."

Ebbie studied him for a moment, then asked, "Disappointed?"

He turned a few pages on his calendar. "No. Nikkie doesn't like Jason and was annoyed that he and Beth spent the night. It was just that..." Ethan abandoned the calendar and sat down in his chair, trying to look busy. "The notion put a little excitement in my life for a few hours, that's all. When you've lived in the same place for thirty-seven years and have nothing in your life but work and a daughter who's trying hard to keep you out of *her* life, there's a certain seduction in a change of pace. Now beat it, all right? I'm busy."

"No, you're not," she said. "I keep your calendar, remember? What does she intend to do about her in-laws?"

He pulled a file toward him. "I'm not sure. I think she intends to tell them the truth at the party this afternoon."

Ebbie looked horrified. "You saw them. You know what they'll do with that bit of information."

Ethan shuffled papers. "It's her decision, Eb. Our job was to find her missing child and we did. The rest of her life is up to her."

"Your job's not over yet," she said.

He looked up at her with strained patience. "Why not?"

She angled her chin with that superior maternal air she assumed when she thought he was being dense. "Because now *she's* the one who's lost."

Her telephone rang and Ethan shooed her away. "And close the door!" he called.

She did.

Ethan forced his mind from thoughts of Bethany Richards, from the woman who looked at him with eyes that seemed to devour him, then told him she'd vowed never to marry again and was sure they'd only make each other miserable.

He'd see what the musts were on today's schedule, give serious thought to Jason's birthday present—Then it hit him like a bolt out of the blue. A bike! Jason had said he'd bent the wheel on his bike and that it had fallen down the hill. He could use a new one, Ethan was sure.

The bike would need a light, a bell, a water bottle. Jason would need a helmet. He resolved to check out Bike-King on his lunch break.

KELLY SAT ON a stool beside Beth and hung over her as she painted a whimsical angel with patchwork wings on a yellow-painted pine board. It was for the door of a little girl's room.

She watched as Beth rimmed the patches with a fine black line and added broken lines to look like stitches.

"You are so clever," Kelly said, propping her elbow on Beth's worktable and resting her cheek in the palm of her hand. "I should order a couple of those for my nieces. The name goes there, right?" She pointed at the expanse of bright empty yellow to the right of the angel.

"Yes. Julia Marie. But I won't let you order any more stuff from me." Beth dropped the brush in the water, then selected a wider one for the lettering. "You do it just to make work for me so you can pay me. I appreciate it, but *you're* an artist. You can make signs for your nieces yourself."

"I'm a potter." Kelly delved a hand into a bag of microwave popcorn at her elbow. "And don't tell me what I can and can't buy. I hate painting. It's so tedious."

"Then I'll paint you a couple gratis." Beth dipped an inch-wide brush into bright pink acrylic paint.

Kelly groaned in disgust. "You know, that's what's wrong with you," she said, continuing on a theme she'd begun earlier, before she'd paused to admire the angel. "You're too generous. You're also too honest."

Beth concentrated on forming a simple block-letter capital *J*. "And that's a bad thing?" she said absently.

"It is when you turn down business, refuse to let a friend rent space in your art mall and decide to come clean about the sheriff to your in-laws when you know they'll probably end up taking you to court over it! That's...*stupid* honesty."

Beth made a face at her as she dipped the brush in paint again, a perfect *J* executed. "There's no such thing as stupid honesty. Honesty is always smart."

"Then why," Kelly asked smugly, "when I asked you if these narrow-legged jeans made my backside look fat, did you say no?"

Beth bit back a smile and concentrated on the lower-case *u*. "Because they don't."

"Liar."

"Diplomat," Beth corrected with a grin as she dipped for more paint. "And anyway, they don't make you look fat. They make you look...lush."

Kelly waited while Beth formed the *l*, *i* and *a*, then expelled a breath. "Well, I'm not being diplomatic with you. You're insane."

"You don't need to rent space in my mall," Beth said, dipping the brush again. "You have that enormous garage, which you don't have to share with anyone."

"It doesn't have north light."

"You don't need it. You're a potter."

"I want to have a studio in your building!"

"You're just trying to give me money."

"You *need* money."

"Not yours."

Kelly groaned and watched her dot the *i* in Marie with a tiny heart with a patch on it.

"You know," she said, pointing to the heart, "that's your problem right there."

Beth leaned back to get a better perspective. It looked fine to her. "What's wrong with it?"

"Not that one—*your* heart. I swear to God, Beth, sometimes you're such a blonde! Your heart has a patch on it—that's why you won't let me help you and why you've decided against marrying the sheriff."

Beth dropped her brush in a jar of water and snatched the bag of popcorn from Kelly. "My heart does not have a patch on it. I'm heart-whole, and you've helped me too much already. You have to support yourself and your house and studio. My cannery is *my* responsibility. And I'm not marrying the sheriff because…"

Because for a few hours it had been a delicious notion to share her problems with someone else, to see Jason blossom under the man's attention and to speculate what it would be like to be noticed. Not loved necessarily, just noticed. But thinking she could have that under these circumstances was absurd.

"Because it was a dumb idea. In fact, if you recall, last night when I phoned you to tell you Jason and I were going home with him, *you* told me to be careful. That he was a hunk and all, but the situation was sticky."

Kelly looked her in the eye. "I think you know you need a man, and you're afraid of that."

Beth slid off her stool and reached into the bag of popcorn. "No, I don't. I can live without it."

"It?" Kelly looked smug again. "I wasn't talking about sex. I was talking about the need for companionship, emotional support."

"I have you for that," Beth said with a smile as she crossed to the small refrigerator against the wall. She opened it and took out two bottles of juice.

"Yeah, well, I'm about to withdraw my companionship and emotional support if you don't wise up," Kelly threatened. "Come on. Don't tell your in-laws anything, team up with the sheriff and see what happens. I've asked around. Everyone has nothing but the highest praise for him. Maybe you shouldn't be careful at all. Maybe you should go for it."

"We're talking *marriage,* Kelly. That's a little different from a simple 'teaming up.' And what happens to my son and his daughter when it doesn't work out?"

"Maybe it would."

Beth handed Kelly a bottle of juice and hitched herself back up on the stool. "Yeah, right. You're an artist and you know what happened with *your* marriage. Your husband left you because he was sure you were having an affair with some guy named Art. He couldn't believe you could find a clay pot more interesting than he was."

"That was my mistake," Kelly said after a moment's moody reflection. "If I'd truly loved him, I *would* have found him more fun than a clay pot. I'd have done my pottery, but I'd have wanted to go home to him."

Beth shrugged and took a long swig of her cranberry-apple juice. "Look, the way things are for us now, neither of us is forced to make the choice. That's the safest thing."

"Is life supposed to be about being safe?"

Beth put her juice down and picked up another brush. "It's about being able to do what you want to do. And we are."

"But we're doing it alone."

"I'm happy about that," Beth said, touching up a patch on the angel's wing. "But if you insist on complicating your life, I've got just the man for you. He's going to be at Jason's party."

Kelly put her juice down. "Really? Who?"

"Ethan's brother, Brodie. He owns a garage and he's a great cook. Seems very nice, too."

"Well." Kelly looked interested, then cast a disparaging eye at her jeans. "Well, you can just bet I'm not wearing these. Lush and fat *are* the same thing." She was silent a moment, then said, "You know, if you married the sheriff, we could double-date."

Beth pushed the plaque out of her way and put her head in a hand stained with pink acrylic. "Kelly," she pleaded, "if I let you rent a studio, will you leave me alone about the sheriff?"

Kelly's cell phone rang before she could reply. She dug in her big suede backpack for it, pulled up the antenna and pressed the talk button.

Beth glowered at her friend as she addressed her caller. "Gone to Pot. This is Kelly."

Beth left the plaque to dry, then pulled another similarly designed board toward her, the angel already painted, the empty expanse for the name in blue. She dipped a brush in white paint while forming the name Jessica by eye. Now she was preparing stock for the Winter Festival Art Fair.

"Ah...yes," Kelly said hesitantly.

Beth looked up at the odd note in her friend's voice. Kelly pointed to her phone and made a face. Beth raised an eyebrow in question.

"Yes," Kelly said. "Yes, I knew her in Seattle. Why?" She listened, then blinked and shook her head at Beth. "Yes, I know you're asking the questions, but if you expect me to answer them, you'd damn well better tell me what this is about."

Beth dropped the brush back into the water and felt her shoulder muscles tense. Someone was talking to Kelly about *her*.

"Yes. She bought an old cannery to turn it into an art mall." Kelly's voice grew increasingly antagonistic. "Yes, that's a formidable venture, but the woman is very smart, hardworking and a fine artist herself." She paused to listen. "Yes. He's healthy and bright and a real credit to his mother."

Now they were discussing Jason. A little frisson of fear inched up Beth's spine. "Who is it?" she mouthed.

But Kelly was concentrating on another question from whomever was on the other end of the line.

"Rush Weston!" she said in surprise, her eyes widening at Beth. "Yes, I imagine she knows him. He teaches at the college and we've both taken classes there. I believe he'll be renting studio space in her mall when it's ready. No! No, there is nothing romantic between them."

Kelly's mouth worked uncertainly, her eyes rested on Beth in grave concern, then she swallowed and said with singular firmness in her voice and apology to Beth in her eyes. "I don't care who told you that, it isn't true. She's about to be married to Ethan Drum, our sheriff."

Oh, God. Beth put both hands to her face. "And if you want to know any more about them," Kelly continued, "I suggest you call *him* and see how he reacts to your snooping!"

Beth guessed by the sudden silence that the conversation had been terminated. She lowered her hands and asked with a sense of dread, "Who was it?"

"He said he was a reporter for an art magazine, but I'm sure the name he gave me was phony. I subscribe to everything, and I've never heard of it. And why wouldn't he have called you? My guess is he's a private detective hired by Joanne." Kelly looked reluctant to impart that information and she put an arm around Beth's shoulders as they slumped.

"I'm sorry about telling him you were getting married," Kelly continued, "but he seemed to be trying to make something out of your relationship with Rush Weston."

Beth spread her hands helplessly. "But I don't have a relationship with Rush, except as a fellow artist and possibly as his landlord when the building's ready."

"I know that, but you know what a flamboyant gasbag Rush is. This guy had already spoken to him because he knew about his participation in the art fair. Apparently Rush was indulging his fantasies again and told him that he'd be renting space from you and the two of you would be sharing more than that very soon."

"Oh, God, oh, *God!*" Beth paced across her studio, a knot of panic forming in her stomach.

As though reading Beth's mind and her fears, Kelly said, "Imagine what Joanne could do with that. Jason tells her you're marrying Ethan, Rush tells her detective you're marrying him. She could use you for a hockey puck in court with that!''

Beth put a hand to her chest where terror was building up a full head of steam.

"Do you hate me?" Kelly asked warily.

They'd done it, Beth thought. They'd actually put a private detective on her with the intention of discrediting her. Or they'd hired an attorney and he'd hired the detective. Either way, the result would be the same.

She couldn't believe it. She'd worried about her in-laws' interference, but she'd never thought they'd go this far.

She was confident they'd find nothing on her that would prove her an unfit mother, but if she fought them, she was looking at probably months of litigation, months that would be even harder on Jason than on her and her efforts to get her art mall going. And that would incur more expense than she could possibly pay for even if she sold the cannery.

"You *do* hate me," Kelly said, her miserable expression reflecting what Beth felt.

Beth went to her friend and put her arms around her. "Of course I don't. You were trying to help."

Kelly hugged her tightly. "You've got to do something about this, Beth."

"Yes," Beth said, dread and fear like a lead ball in her stomach. "I intend to."

CHAPTER SIX

ETHAN PULLED the red-and-silver Blazer into the parking lot of Dinosaur Pizza and drove around the back. He parked beside Ebbie, who was lifting a wide pink bakery box out of the trunk of her old Toyota.

She came around to greet him as he climbed out, then lifted the lid of the box to show him the contents. Buzz Lightyear had been formed in the middle of a cake with green-and-white icing, his features perfectly drawn with piping gel and a little dome of plastic serving as his helmet.

Jason's name was written on the cake with Buzz's highly quoted "To infinity and beyond!" under it.

"Think he'll like it?" she asked.

Ethan nodded. "If he doesn't, it's mine. Good work, Eb. Thanks for doing all the running around this morning and for making the arrangements."

"No problem," she said. "My grandkids are so far away I don't get to do this stuff. See you inside. I've already brought the cups and plates in, and we're going to need your help with the balloons."

He grinned. "I'm ahead of you. I borrowed the helium tank the Red Cross used for the blood drive."

"Clever devil." Ebbie backed away toward the restaurant's rear entrance. "See you inside."

"Right." Ethan opened the Blazer's tailgate and pulled out a blue bike with all the pertinent accessories and a giant silver bow attached to the handlebars. The bike shop had put the helmet in a box, wrapped it in colorful paper and attached another silver bow. With the box on the flat of one hand, Ethan lifted the bike by its frame with the other and was halfway toward the restaurant with it when a little yellow MG convertible came whipping around the corner at a speed that suggested the driver hadn't slowed for the turn. It screeched to a halt inches from him.

He was about to threaten the pretty redhead behind the wheel with arrest for reckless driving when her passenger leaped out of the car and ran into his arms.

Well, not precisely into his arms; both were occupied with Jason's gifts. But Beth caught the front of his tweed jacket in both fists, her blue eyes wide and troubled. He was about to tell her to give him a minute to put the bike down when she said anxiously, "Ethan, I *have* to talk to you."

He sighed. "Is this one of those all-I-get-to-do-is-listen things?"

She didn't seem to mind his sarcasm. "No. Actually your input will be very important. Please. Can we talk before we go in? Brodie just pulled up in front with Jason."

"Want me to take that?" The pretty redhead had backed up and pulled into a parking spot with the same speed and screech of brakes and now stood beside Beth.

She smiled and offered her hand. "Hi. I'm Kelly Braxton, a friend of Beth's. I'm invited to the party. Want me to walk the bike in so you can talk?" Then realizing he didn't have a free hand to shake hers, she said, "Oh, sorry," and took the wrapped box from him.

Ethan shook her hand. "Hi. Ethan Drum."

Her smile was wry. "Yes, I know. Center of the vortex." She handed him back the box.

"Vortex?"

"Beth will explain." She took the bike from him with both hands and set it on the pavement. Then she grasped the handlebars and pushed it toward the restaurant's rear entrance.

Ethan stood face-to-face with Beth, her hands still clutching the lapels of his jacket. She looked a little like she had the night before when Jason told his grandparents she was getting married.

"You want to sit in the Blazer?" he asked, gesturing toward it with the gift-wrapped helmet.

"No," she said. "I need fresh air. Can we just walk up the block?"

"Sure. Let me get rid of this." He sat the gift on the back of his vehicle and closed the tailgate. When he turned to her, she slipped her arm into the crook of his and led him out of the parking lot and up the street. Lined with a print shop, a dog groomer's, a furniture store and a supermarket on one side, and an old brick turn-of-the-century post office on the other, it was surrounded by ancient maple trees, their bare branches like lace against the blue sky.

She leaned into him slightly, her tone quiet but urgent. "I don't have time for small talk, all right?"

He put both hands in the pockets of his gray cords, her arm still looped in his left. Things were looking as though she might have changed her mind about marrying him, after all, but he'd been a cop long enough to guard against too optimistic a view.

He kept walking at a leisurely pace, careful to keep

what he thought to himself. "As I seem to say often when I'm around you—I'm listening."

She sighed. The wind blowing from the direction of the river had a sharp bite. She didn't seem to notice. "While Kelly was visiting my studio today," she said, her breath puffing out ahead of her, "she got a call on her cell phone. Someone was full of questions about me."

"Who?"

She shook her head, her hair moving in loose waves with a gloss and grace that caught his eye. He looked his fill for a moment while she stared ahead, a pleat between her eyebrows, then concentrated on her eyes when she looked up at him. They were filled with fear.

"He said he was an art-magazine reporter, but she thinks he was a private detective. He knew that Kelly and I had known each other in Seattle, and that Jason had run away." She shook her head and added with a mocking twist of her lips, "And he tried to make something out of my relationship with Rush Weston."

He felt instant and profound annoyance, but he kept that, too, to himself. He'd picked up Rush Weston while breaking up a brawl in a waterfront tavern on a Friday night a couple of weeks ago. The man had behaved with scornful superiority, and Ethan had enjoyed pinning him to the bar and cuffing him when he'd resisted arrest.

"What about Rush Weston?" he asked calmly.

"Nothing. Well, you could say we're friends. He's an artist, too, a sculptor, and when he's not being obnoxious, he can be very nice. He's renting a spot in my art mall when I open."

Although Ethan knew his attitude was unwarranted, he resented that she even knew Weston. "That doesn't sound like anything a detective could use against you," he said, sounding mature and magnanimous. What he really wanted to do was warn her to stay away from the guy, but he could imagine how that would go over. And anyway, depending on the point she intended to make with this conversation, he might have very little to do with her life from now on.

They stopped at the corner where the pedestrian light read Don't Walk, and she took the moment to lean her forehead against his upper arm. The wind stirred her hair and strands of it drifted across his chin and throat. He felt a stalling of his brain function. When she lifted her head again, her cheeks were pale and pinched with the cold.

Without giving thought to the action, he reached down to pull the zipper of her red jacket up from between her breasts to her chin.

The light changed. They crossed the street and started back in the direction of Dinosaur Pizza. "You might have guessed by the fact that I'm walking you around like some fraternal organization sergeant-at-arms that there *is* something the detective can use against me."

"And what's that?"

Her grip on his arm tightened. "When the detective spoke to Rush, he implied that there was something between us. He said we'd be sharing studio space and that soon we'd be sharing…more."

That fanned Ethan's annoyance. "How did Rush get that impression?"

Beth stopped walking and looked into his face. She dropped her arm from his and jammed her hands in the pockets of her jacket. Her eyes were speculative, surprised. She'd detected his irritation and it seemed to have sparked her own.

"I don't know," she said finally, her tone a bit stiff. "He did ask me out a couple of times and I refused. Some men have difficulty taking no for an answer. Certainly a man like you who generally does as he pleases can understand that?"

He narrowed his eyes at her for using his words against him. She looked at him in all innocence.

"I'm acquainted with Rush Weston," he said, then added with relish, "professionally."

Her look of innocence vanished. "What do you mean?"

"It made the paper."

"I don't subscribe," she said impatiently. "It's a way to pinch pennies. I count on gossip. How do you know him professionally?"

"I picked him up in a brawl at a tavern on the waterfront." He provided that information with satisfaction. "If you're trying to present a squeaky-clean image to your in-laws, Weston is not the way to go."

"He and I are not..." she began angrily, a little loudly, then remembering where they were, lowered her voice. "I said he's a fellow artist, that's all. His suggestion that there's something more between us is just a lot of bull. Everybody who knows him understands his tendency to fantasize."

"Your in-laws," he reminded her quietly, "don't know him."

Her lips firmed and she shifted her weight. "You're absolutely right," she said. "That's why I need you to marry me."

Beth spoke the words quickly before she could lose courage, then resisted the impulse to cover her eyes and watch for his reaction between her fingers. Instead, she squared her shoulders, held his seemingly unsurprised gaze and waited for his reaction.

If she'd expected something dramatic, she was disappointed. He simply started walking slowly back toward the restaurant. She had no choice but to follow.

"What exactly did you have in mind?" he asked when she caught up with him.

"I'm desperate," she admitted candidly. "So, I guess, pretty much whatever you want. If you really hate the idea, if you'd just do it for me for now to get us through this week, we can annul it the moment they leave town and I'll find a way to disappear with Jason. Or…something." That wasn't fair to anyone, she knew, but right now her need for a solution was too immediate to allow contemplation of future consequences.

"Or," she continued, trying hard to sell him on the idea, "if you want someone to cook for you and keep house, I'll do it for as long as you want me to. And I'll do my best to help with Nikkie, if she'll let me, provided you do the same for Jason."

He stopped to look down at her with open skepticism. "What about all your denials of domestic competence?"

She nodded, willing to grant him the right to wonder. "I have no domestic competence, but I can do anything I set my mind to. And I'm a damned good mother. I'll do my best for Nikkie."

He moved on again. She kept pace with him.

"Well, so far," he said, "we've talked about your abilities as a housekeeper and a mother, but not as a wife."

"In my experience," she said, doing her best to

keep up with his long strides, "that's all a wife is. Maybe an answering service, too."

They'd reached the corner opposite the restaurant and another Don't Walk light. He frowned down at her. "What kind of a marriage did you have, anyway?"

She'd been trying to avoid thinking about those days. Cobbler's Crossing was supposed to be a fresh start for her and Jason. But now that opportunity sat squarely in the hands of Ethan Drum. So she answered his question with one of her own—the only one that mattered now.

"What kind of a marriage do you want?"

His dark eyes told her in detail. To her horror she blushed. He noted that and groaned.

The light changed. He caught her arm and pulled her with him across the street and toward the Blazer. They could hear the excited sounds of children's voices and the lower notes of adult laughter coming from the restaurant.

Ethan stood her squarely in front of him against the back of the Blazer, then put a hand to the roof on either side of her. Her heartbeat accelerated and all the air seemed to leave her lungs.

"What I *don't* want in a wife," he said quietly, "is a woman who blushes at the mention of sex."

She tried to fold her arms to put some distance between them, but he was too close. She dropped both arms and flattened her hands against the cold metal of the car behind her. That was steadying somehow.

"You *didn't* mention it," she said, "but I saw it in your eyes. That made it more intimate. I'm sorry."

He seemed annoyed with her apology. "So you hadn't considered intimacy as part of our marriage?"

It was hard, she decided, to allow a fear to surface that she'd suppressed for years. Particularly since it was a fear she'd never shared with anyone except Kelly. She'd borne it for a long time, then when Steve made it clear there was little need to deal with it, she'd simply put it away. And her choice never to marry again allowed her to let it remain hidden.

But her present situation changed all that.

"Frankly..." Her voice came out thin and reedy, and she cleared her throat. "Frankly, I hadn't thought that far. When Kelly repeated what that caller said about Rush Weston, I knew there was only one way out of this, so I came to you. But—" she cleared her throat again, blushed again and closed her eyes when he watched her in obvious confusion "—there's something you should know."

She was hyperventilating and she felt as though she was about to faint. She opened her eyes and found that he still appeared confused, but not angry. He simply waited.

"Do I have to tell you again that I'm listening?" he asked quietly.

He didn't. But a man who listened to her was something new; she suspected that that was why it unsettled her so much. That, and the nature of what he was waiting for her to explain.

"I'm not very good sexually," she said at last.

There was a long moment of silence in the parking lot. Children laughed and shrieked in the restaurant, cars drove by on the street, a siren whined somewhere in the distance. But Beth felt as though she'd been covered with a glass dome, as though she could see out but was isolated.

Ethan studied her for an endless moment, as though

that remark might make sense to him if he stared long enough at the woman who'd made it. At last he stepped back, folded his arms and asked, "What do you mean?"

That was the very question she dreaded. She looked at him imploringly. "I mean," she said, her blush draining, pallor replacing it. "I'm not...very skilled at...making love." Her lips twisted in self-deprecation. "I think I'm even worse sexually than I am domestically."

Now that he'd moved away, she could fold her arms, too, but it didn't seem to work as a defense mechanism. She still felt exposed. She dropped her arms and put her hands in her pockets. "It doesn't mean I won't do it," she said, her eyes miserable with humiliation. "It's just a warning that you shouldn't expect...great things."

He studied her another moment, then turned and leaned against the Blazer, too. "What makes you say that?" he asked, his voice filled with disbelief.

When she tipped her head back and looked up at the sky, agonized by the thought of going into detail, he said gently, "I'm sorry. I can see that this is difficult for you, but I want to understand. So tell me. When did you arrive at this conclusion?"

She was asking this man to let her into his life for her own purposes, she reminded herself. She had an obligation to let him into hers. Even into the places she didn't like to go.

"About five years ago," she said, staring at the toes of her shoes. "I...never found it wonderful, although it was all right the first couple of years of my marriage. But then Steve became very busy and, when he did think about me, sex was always after he'd made some lucrative deal—and then it was sort of quick and triumphant. I sort of...lost interest."

"And it never occurred to you that it was his fault and not yours?"

"I'm not sure it was entirely," she said, remembering the humiliation she'd felt at the time. "I...I'd suggested we try something new. He was disgusted by it and I was embarrassed. Then I realized somewhere along the way I'd lost all appeal for him." She sighed. "And then, I guess, I gave up."

Ethan turned to face her, but she couldn't meet his eyes. "He was disgusted?" he asked incredulously.

She shook her head. "Please don't ask me to tell you what it was."

"I won't." He reached up to catch her chin with his index finger and turn her face toward him. She found his expression gentle and surprisingly easy to look into. "But I want you to know that if you ever want to tell me, I like to consider myself... adventurous."

He pushed away from the Blazer, drew her a short distance from it, then opened the tailgate again. Handing her the gift-wrapped bicycle helmet, he closed and locked the door, put an arm around her shoulders and led her toward the restaurant.

"We'll get married on Saturday," he said. "You can do your art, not worry about the housekeeping, we'll do our best with the kids, and we'll let sex take care of itself."

She stopped him a few feet from the door, her expression serious. "Ethan, I appreciate how well you're taking my news, but...I can't let you get into this if you don't understand that there's a real problem here."

He shook his head, apparently failing to grasp the severity of her warning. He tapped her temple with his index finger. "I think the problem's here, not anywhere else."

She blinked at him, torn between exasperation and admiration. "How could you possibly know that?"

"Because I kissed you this morning," he replied with a grin, "and you kissed me back. The interest is there. Maybe you just need more inspiration than you've had in the past." He pulled the door open. "But some things are better done than analyzed. Come on. Jason's waiting for us."

CHAPTER SEVEN

BETH WATCHED her son surrounded by school friends cheering him on as he maneuvered around monsters in a video game. She guessed there was not a happier child anywhere that sunny afternoon.

A couple of teenage boys in white aprons with triceratops printed on them cleared two long tables of the debris generated by eight large pizzas and four pitchers of soft drinks.

In one corner of the room was a veritable treasure trove of presents. Because of the party's short notice, Jason's friends had not had a chance to buy gifts, but Brodie had arrived with the entire set of *Toy Story* figures down to the barrel of monkeys and the green rubber soldiers. Ebbie had bought a basketball, and Kelly had wrapped several videos in a backpack. Several sheriff's deputies in uniform, whom Ebbie or Ethan had probably commandeered to fill out the party for the sake of the grandparents, appeared with a fleet of toy trucks and a set of Goosebumps books.

The deputies had left early, explaining that they were on a dinner break, and Beth and Ethan had walked with them out to the parking lot.

"Thank you for coming," Beth said sincerely, shaking their hands. "I know you were bullied into this. You really shouldn't have brought gifts."

The taller of the two, whose badge read "Curtis"

shrugged off her thanks. "What's a birthday party without presents?"

The other deputy, shorter, stockier and a few years older, was Billings. "And when Ethan speaks, we obey," he said in a heroic tone. "Right, Chief?"

"Yeah, right." Ethan's tone suggested that wasn't true at all. "Has it been a quiet afternoon?"

Billings nodded. "Yeah. We feel neglected, but we'll adjust."

Ethan put a hand on each man's shoulder. "That's the spirit of the department, gentlemen. Now get out there and make me proud."

"But, Chief," Curtis said gravely, "pride's been your problem all along."

Ethan gave him a shove toward their county car. "Goodbye, Curtis."

As they moved off, Curtis could be heard asking loudly, "Did that shove qualify as boss brutality?"

"No," Billings replied as they separated to walk around opposite sides of the car. "But I'm getting out of here before he does something that does."

Ethan and Beth went back into the restaurant. "Incidentally," Beth said quietly as the boys continued to carry on loudly at the video game, "why did you buy Jason a bike? An expensive bike, at that."

There was scolding in her tone, and he turned just before they reached the tables to fix her with a silencing frown. "His was totaled," he said, "and I wanted to buy him a bike. All right?"

She glanced in the direction of the table and saw that Zachary and Joanne were watching them. Kelly and Brodie seemed completely absorbed in each other, and Ebbie was busy slicing and packaging leftover cake.

"I just don't want you spending a lot of money," she said.

"What *is* it with you and money?" Ethan demanded, keeping his voice low. "Were you frightened by a savings-and-loan bailout or something?"

She gave him a speaking look. "My in-laws are watching," she warned, "and don't get smart with me. I used to have a lot of money and nothing else. Now I have only a little and...and many concerns. But Jason and I do not require much, so there's no point in your indulging every extravagance he—"

She stopped because he'd run a hand over his face as though he'd had about all of her he could take.

"If you play your cards right," he said, smiling—which she was sure he did for Joanne and Zachary's benefit, "you can have everything I have. It's not a lot of money, but usually enough. And you can have everything else—all that was missing in your life before. But not if you keep ragging on me."

"I wasn't ragging, I was—"

"You were ragging."

A glance toward the table told her that her in-laws were still watching. "Now you've probably made them think we're not getting along," she accused him.

"Then maybe," he suggested under his voice, "you should do something to make them think otherwise."

She studied him with suspicion. "Like what?"

"Your call," he said mercilessly. "What comes to mind?"

In view of what she'd explained to him just before they joined the party, her mind was blank. Then she realized that all her in-laws needed to see was a loving touch.

She drew a breath and looped her arms around his

neck. His came to her waist. She felt the press of his leg between her thighs, the hardness of his chest against the softness of hers, the hair at the back of his neck against the inside of her wrist.

She smiled in the interest of her performance and asked sotto voce, "How's that?"

Apparently also performing, he returned her smile. "A little lukewarm."

"We're in a pizza parlor."

"I don't think passion has a sense of place. It's as combustible in a downpour on a street corner as it is in the bedroom."

And with that he pulled her against him. She was sure her body's instant clamoring response was only one of surprise.

Then he nuzzled under her hair and kissed the side of her neck, and she knew she was wrong. Her heart jolted and sent what felt like a little stream of lava right down the middle of her being. The pulse of excitement she felt had nothing to do with surprise.

But before she could analyze it further, Ethan said in amused warning, "Uh-oh. Incoming."

She began to step back out of his arms, but Jason collided with them, wrapping an arm around each of them. His face was almost too bright to look at.

He took a fistful of the sleeve of Beth's sweater and pulled her down to his level. "Is Ethan gonna be my dad?" he whispered. "Be real quiet, Mom. Grandma and Grandpa are looking this way, and I think they're trying to listen."

She kissed his cheek. His happiness was infectious, and it would be easy for the sake of today's performance for her in-laws, to let herself believe as her son did—that her marriage to Ethan was the best thing that could possibly happen.

"Yes," she said, smiling into his hopeful expression. And with that admission, she let go of all the potentially grievous problems the situation presented. If she was going to do this, she would have to do it with certitude and enthusiasm, to be both convincing to her in-laws and fair to the man who was giving her this chance to avoid messy and expensive litigation. "Yes," she said again, "he is."

With a whoop of delight, Jason leaped at Ethan, who bent slightly and caught him in one arm. The boy reached up and gave him a strangling hug.

"I'm gonna really like being your kid," he said in a loud whisper. "And thanks for the bike and the helmet! And the cool party! I've never had so much fun. Never, never, never!"

"Well, good." Ethan straightened and exchanged a wry glance with Beth. "'Cause I think the fun's just starting."

Half a dozen of Jason's friends who were crowded around the video game shouted that it was his turn. Jason raced back to join them.

Ethan wrapped an arm around Beth's shoulders and led her to the table where Brodie, Kelly and the Richardses sat. Ebbie stood at the end of the table, still wrapping up leftovers.

Brodie and Zachary were enthusiastically discussing basketball scores. Ethan joined the men on one side of the table, and Beth sat between Kelly and Joanne on the other.

A young man in a Dinosaur Pizza apron arrived with a tray filled with cups and a pot of coffee.

"We're soft drinked out," Kelly explained, helping

the boy distribute cups. "But it doesn't look as though the kids are ready to go yet." She pointed to the knot of little boys cheering excitedly in the corner as Jason turned a wheel with one hand and operated a joystick with the other. His laughter was loud and gleeful.

Kelly laughed just watching them. "Have you ever seen such unbridled delight? Ah, to be eight again!"

"When I was eight," Brodie said, holding his cup out as the waiter poured, "Ethan made me slide down the banister into the basement of our parents' house."

Ethan passed him the cream, his expression unrepentant. "You could have refused."

"You had my Tonka dumptruck and wouldn't give it back."

"Because you had a fear of the basement stairs and wouldn't go down. I was trying to help you deal with your problem. Get past it."

"Sure."

"It worked, didn't it? You no longer have a fear of basements."

"That's true. Now I have a fear of sliding down a banister, falling off and losing my front tooth."

"Lighten up. The implant looks great. Women love your smile." Ethan turned to Kelly. "Don't they?"

"Ah...um..." Kelly stammered. Beth watched with interest as her usually quick-witted friend seemed to lose the power of speech. Beth looked at Brodie, who was giving Kelly the reputed smile, then at Ethan, who also appeared to be studying the action with interest.

"Yes," Kelly said, finally pulling herself together. "It's a charming smile."

"See?" Ethan said to Brodie. "Quit whining." Then he turned to Zachary and asked politely, "Did I overhear you say you're having trouble with your car?"

Zachary stirred sugar into his coffee and eagerly launched into a detailed explanation of the Cadillac's behavior.

"When did you meet Ethan?" Joanne asked, her arms folded on the table.

"It's a small town," Beth replied carefully, certain the question was a trap, "everyone gets to know newcomers pretty fast, and Ethan's job requires him to be very involved in the community."

Joanne nodded, her smile suggesting acquiescence, but her eyes suggesting suspicion. "But when exactly? How?"

Aware that a lie of any kind could mean trouble, Beth took a sip of coffee to give herself a moment to think. Had Joanne already asked Ebbie how they'd met? Or Jason? Or Kelly? Was she just waiting for Beth to contradict that information?

Beth suddenly remembered something Jason had told her and decided that a grain of truth in her reply was better than none at all.

"Ethan went to Jason's school to talk to the kids about the sheriff's office. I volunteer there a few hours a week."

She hadn't been there the day Ethan visited the school, but that wasn't what she'd claimed, anyway. She'd simply stated two separate truths.

Joanne glanced across the table at Ethan, who was deep in conversation with Brodie and her husband, then turned back to Beth. "You've only been here three months. That isn't very long to know someone."

"Well," Beth said, thinking fast, "when it's right, it's right."

That, too, was true. Saving herself from litigation over her son was very right.

Joanne's dark eyes focused on her with disapproval. "Can it *be* right when you've just lost Steve?"

"That was a year ago, Jo," Beth replied, thinking that she'd really lost him years before his death. But his mother didn't know that.

"One can't help but wonder," Joanne said, raising her coffee cup, "how deeply you felt about him if you can get over him in a year."

Mercifully Beth was saved from having to respond by Ebbie, who leaned between them and placed a foil-wrapped package in front of Joanne. "There you go," she said. "A little cake to enjoy tonight in your motel room."

Ebbie offered another foil package to Brodie.

He accepted it with a smile, then pursed his lips in imitation of a kiss. "When are you moving in with me, Eb?"

"When Mel gets tired of me," she replied offhandedly.

"Mel?" Brodie asked.

"Gibson," she said, as though it should be obvious. "You didn't know he's been flying in on weekends to see me?"

Brodie made a face. "Ebbie, do you really think a pretty face can make you happy?"

"No, but he's a pretty face with millions."

Brodie looked chagrined. "But...women love my smile."

Ebbie gave a derisive snort. "You can't buy diddly with that, sweetie," she countered. She closed the box, which still contained a third of the cake.

Brodie leaned toward Kelly. "Would you prefer a man with millions, or me and my smile?"

Kelly leaned toward him. "I'm looking for a smile like yours *on* a man with millions. I need someone to support my art habit, but I need him to do it cheerfully so he doesn't inhibit my creativity."

"I thought artists needed to be in pain to work," he said.

She shook her head. "Not me. Pain just makes me miserable. And I can't throw pots when I'm miserable."

"Well—" he seemed to be thinking seriously "—is there anything that'd keep you happy, besides millions?"

"Ah…" She pretended to consider the question seriously, then said firmly, "Nope," and pushed away from the table. She bent down to hug Beth, then went around the table and hugged Ethan, too.

Beth exchanged a surprised look with Ethan, then realized Kelly was pretending she'd known Ethan for some time—something the Richardses would expect of Beth's best friend.

"Great party, guys," she said. "Thanks for inviting me." She pushed Brodie's shoulder as he tried to stand. "Don't get up. Nice to meet you, Brodie. Mr. and Mrs. Richards. See you at the wedding?"

Joanne's manner was cool. "Of course. We'll be there."

"Wonderful. Ebbie, I'll call you about the hors d'oeuvres."

Ebbie looked up from pouring a pitcher of leftover soda into a large carryout cup and covered her momentary surprise with a quick smile. "Thanks. I planned the menu, but left it at the office."

As Kelly waded through the crowd of little boys to find Jason and give him a hug, Joanne said with feigned amiability. "This is a little last minute to be planning a menu, isn't it, four days before the wedding? Or is the entire wedding spur-of-the-moment?"

"The wedding," Ethan said easily, reaching across the table for Beth's hand, "is a tribute to my success in finally convincing Beth I can't live without her." The look in his eyes was intimate and ardent. Beth was ensnared by it and couldn't free herself until he turned to Joanne. "I understand your concern for your grandson and your daughter-in-law, but I promise you I'll take good care of them."

Joanne's mouth worked uncertainly as she obviously struggled with disbelief and the convincing quality of his declaration. Zachary studied Ethan uncertainly, too. Then he exchanged a glance with his wife.

Kelly blew kisses as she passed the table on her way out to the parking lot. Brodie watched her walk away with an interest Beth was thrilled to see. Kelly had sworn off men after her divorce three years before. She'd loved her husband, a football coach at the high school where she taught art. But he'd resented the time she spent on her pottery outside of school and her dedication to the Seattle co-op where Beth had met her.

He'd finally given her an ultimatum—him or her pottery. It had amazed Beth that he hadn't known better.

Kelly and Beth had commiserated over seafood salads at Pike Place Market the day before Kelly was to leave for Cobbler's Crossing. Most men, they'd concluded, despite their claims of appreciating a woman's skills and talents, still wanted a woman who was traditional, who conformed to their conservative notions of what a wife should be.

Yet those conclusions notwithstanding, here was Kelly now, walking out of the restaurant with her charming derriere being considered with more than casual interest by Brodie Drum, and she, Beth, was about to marry his brother.

What, she wondered, was the world coming to?

The world seemed even a little farther off its axis when the restaurant's front door swung open and five teenagers poured into the shadowy barnlike interior of Dinosaur Pizza.

Nikkie, in a black wool jacket that ended in a band at her tiny waist, an impossibly tight pair of black jeans and boots that looked as though they belonged on a logger, led the way to their table.

Ethan stood up to welcome them, and Nikkie walked into his arms.

"Hi," she said with a shy glance around the table. "Did we miss the party? Hi, Unc. Hi, Beth."

"No," he said, giving her shoulders a squeeze. "We've got cake left, and we'll get you guys some pizza. I thought you had a meeting."

He looked over Nikkie's head to the two girls and two boys who stood behind her. One of the girls was small like Nikkie and had short purple hair with a side part and black lipstick. The other was a tall and glamorous blonde in a long leather coat. Both boys were tall, one gangly with thin-rimmed round glasses and the other thickly built with a blond buzz cut and an earring.

A collective groan rose from the group and Nikkie said morosely, "Mr. Fogarty decided on *Henry V* for our Winter Festival play. We're really bummed out."

Ethan looked surprised. "Why? You love Shakespeare."

"We all love Shakespeare," the buzz cut said, "and it's a play we can get everybody in, but we're looking at Medieval clothes, armor, shields and weapons for twenty."

"On a fifty-dollar budget," the girl with the purple hair said.

"Yeah," the spindly boy concurred. "And he says it's our problem. That learning to mount a production with no money is as important for a drama student to learn as acting."

The blonde sighed. "I wanted to do *Streetcar*. I can do Blanche's lines in my sleep."

The spindly boy turned to her. "Well, you'll have to wake up to do Katharine."

Purple Hair frowned. "*I* want to do Katharine."

The blonde looked down her nose at her. "I have the tiara." Then she spread both arms in a ta-da sort of pose. "And the height to be royalty. You'll have to be happy as my lady-in-waiting."

Nikkie rolled her eyes at her friends, then turned to her father. "And the worst part—besides my cast mates—is that I'm in charge of props *and* I'm playing Isabel, Queen of France."

Ethan smiled sympathetically. "Then you're going to need a really big pizza. First let me introduce you to Jason's grandparents, Mr. and Mrs. Richards. Joanne, Zachary, I'd like you to meet my daughter, Tanika."

The girl smiled and waved. "Nikkie," she said, then introduced her friends. Bradley was the spindly boy, the blonde was Vanessa, Rosalie the one with the purple hair, and the buzz cut was Cameron.

"Guys, you know Brodie," she went on. They all nodded and murmured greetings.

"And you know Beth," she finished casually.

Beth expected instant denial or at least looks of confusion, but Nikkie must have apprised them of the plan—that she and Ethan would appear to be engaged during the birthday party.

It was easy to see why these kids were in the drama club. Their acting skills were excellent. Beth was treated to friendly smiles, a "How's it going?" and a "Love your sweater!"

Nikkie pulled a small gift-wrapped box out of her pocket and looked around. "Where's Jason?"

As though his personal radar had sensed more loot, Jason appeared at Nikkie's side. He looked up at her in astonishment. "You came!"

Beth read annoyance in her eyes, then Nikkie tossed her hair and thrust the gift at him. "I felt like pizza. Here."

He had the wrap off in a matter of seconds and held up a watch with Buzz Lightyear on it. Buzz's arms served as the hands.

"Wow!" Jason's eyes were huge. He turned to Beth. "Mom, look!"

"How did you know?" Beth asked Nikkie. Too late she realized that maybe this was not a question she should ask when trying to convince her in-laws that she, Jason, Ethan and Nikkie spent a lot of time together.

"Because Buzz Lightyear is all he ever talks about," Nikkie said with a laugh. She reached down to push a button on the side of the watch, and a tinny voice said, "Buzz Lightyear to the rescue!"

Jason gasped, beside himself with delight. He raced back to his friends to show off his newest gift.

Ethan patted Nikkie's shoulder. "Come on. We'll get you guys some pizza."

Ethan led Nikkie and her friends to the counter. Jason returned to the table with the announcement that he was out of quarters. Brodie, delving into the pocket of his coveralls for change, went with Jason back to the game.

And Beth found herself alone with her in-laws.

Joanne sighed, gathered up her purse, her coat, the foil-wrapped leftover cake and mumbled crossly, "I feel as though we've been set down in the middle of Paramount Studios!" Then she turned to Beth with a coldly polite, "Thank you. We've enjoyed the party. And thank you for the cake."

"Would you and Zachary like to come back to the house for a while?" Courtesy had forced her to ask. She prayed they'd refuse.

Her prayer was answered. "It's been a long day and Zach's arthritis is acting up." Beth saw Joanne shoot her husband a glance that warned him not to contradict her. Apparently she wanted to get away as much as Beth wanted her to. "We might spend the next few days sightseeing if there's nothing seriously wrong with the car, but we'll be in touch before the... wedding." As usual she applied cool disbelief to the word.

"Good." Beth walked the couple to the door of the restaurant. "I have to get you Ebbie's address."

Ethan appeared suddenly behind Beth. He placed both hands on her shoulders as Joanne climbed into the passenger seat of the Cadillac and Zachary went around to the driver's side.

"You'll have to come over," he said, "and help Jason with the Legos you bought. We have a worktable in the basement where we can really spread out."

Zachary looked interested, but Joanne said only, "We'll be in touch."

Beth and Ethan waved till the white Cadillac was out of sight.

Beth stood on the windy street corner with Ethan behind her and knew her life would never be the same. The first time she'd married she'd been hopeful and in love, yet her life had fallen apart, anyway. This time, she was getting married to a man she hardly knew to avoid a legal battle for custody of her son.

Perhaps, she thought, it was the influence of Nikkie and her drama-club friends, but this moment was like being center stage and having the houselights go out as the curtain came down. Stagehands were about to change the set and move all the pieces of her life around.

It would be interesting to know if she was starring in a comedy or a tragedy.

CHAPTER EIGHT

FOR THE NEXT THREE DAYS, Beth went to her cannery studio in the morning and left for Ethan's house in the evening with a grocery bag or a box in which she'd packed some of her and Jason's clothes and personal items. She did this on the chance that her in-laws' detective was watching her.

She had, in fact, noticed a man sitting in a car not far from the cannery the past two mornings, then noticed the same car parked about a block from Ethan's last evening. Was he taking photos of her comings and goings? It would be difficult to convince her in-laws she'd been living with Ethan for a while if she was photographed with a U-Haul and a group of friends to help her move.

Beth had left the room with the bunk beds to Jason and now occupied the fourth bedroom upstairs. She'd brought her bedspread and curtains from the cannery in a laundry bag. The closet had a small built-in dresser, and Ethan brought up an old wooden desk from the basement to put in an empty corner.

"Diana bought it at a church rummage sale, thinking she'd clean it up and paint it one day, but she was always too busy."

Beth thought she heard a wistful note in his voice and went to sit on the edge of her bed. Ethan knelt on one knee by the desk and dusted off the legs. It was a simple maple desk with a spindly-legged chair.

"Are you *sure* you're willing to do this?" Beth asked. "I mean, if you had a great marriage once, this might be harder for you than you anticipate."

He turned from the desk, his forearm resting on his bent knee, the soft chamois in his fingers. His eyes were quiet, relaxed. "Life is full of surprises. It's entirely possible that *our* marriage could be great."

She nodded, then looked away, occupying herself with finding pairs in a pile of loose socks in the middle of the bed.

"Are you sure *you* want to do this?" he asked, pushing to his feet and sitting beside her, leaving only a small space between them. "Considering how you feel about marriage? I know how important Jason is to you, but I really don't think your in-laws could win a case against you in court."

"I don't think so, either," she admitted, concentrating on folding a pair of woolly blue kneesocks, "but it would be expensive and nerve-racking to have to defend myself against them. I also wouldn't want to put Jason through that. Their threats have frightened him enough already."

Ethan nodded, taking the socks from her and putting them aside. He turned to face her and looked into her eyes.

"I know. I'm just trying to make it clear that a halfhearted effort in this marriage won't be good for any of us. If you're having second thoughts, I'd rather help you find a good lawyer and lend you the money to fight Joanne and Zachary. And I'll do my best to be a friend to Jason, instead of a father."

She sat up stiffly, concern budding in her chest, then

doubling and tripling quickly into a big ugly worry. Did he want out of this? Did *she?*

She tried to examine what she felt, a difficult task under his watchful dark gaze. What she found was an understandable fear of something new, the possibly irrational but very real fear of disappointing Ethan in bed and, under all that, an urgent willingness to try, anyway.

"The wedding's tomorrow afternoon," she reminded him.

"Yes, but you haven't signed a contract. If you want to cancel, just say the word."

"Jason," she said softly, "wants a father more than he wants a friend."

He shook his head at her. "That's familiar ground. I'm asking what *you* want."

She shrugged, reluctant to tell him that she found him attractive and appealing and that just being within sight of him calmed her and made her feel secure. And that the thought of being married to him, of sharing his life and his bed, lit a spark in her she'd been sure had died long ago. She'd bared her soul to Steve so many times and been ignored that she'd put a tight cap on what she felt.

And though she knew Ethan Drum could never be confused with Steve Richards, her defense mechanism remained in place.

"I want what's best for my son," she replied.

Ethan would have taken great satisfaction in shaking her. He saw many emotions cross her face and wished she'd explain them in words. But she was like a mystery without a clue, a case without a lead.

"Fine," he said. "I'm in, as long as you understand that I intend to be a husband, as well as a father."

She bobbed her head. "I'm in, too, as long as you remember...what I told you."

"Right. Your claim to be sexually inadequate." He got to his feet and offered her a hand to help her to hers. "I don't believe it for a minute."

She held on to his hand when he tried to withdraw it and give the chair one more swipe with the chamois.

She swallowed, put a hand to her hair, then dropped it, high color filling her cheeks. Her control seemed to wobble and she looked up at him, her eyes filled with a curious combination of determination and reluctance.

He tossed the chamois at the desk and gave her his full attention.

"You've been honest with me," she said, nervously tucking her hair behind her ear. "I appreciate that, so I want to be as honest with you. You're a confident virile man and it sounds as though Diana was a devoted and wonderful woman. So you had what it takes for...love to be wonderful."

By love, he knew she meant lovemaking. He listened quietly, wondering what her point was.

She heaved a sigh, as though continuing required great courage. "My experience has been significantly different, and I'm not entirely sure that...you'll be able to change the way I am."

He had every confidence that the problem was not with her but with the man who'd made his business more important than his wife. He opened his mouth to tell her that, but she had more to say.

"So I was thinking—" she looked into his eyes, then down at her hands, then up into his eyes again "—it would be one thing if we were getting married with the intention of getting an annulment the moment we thought it was safe. But if you want a *real* marriage out of this, you...you might want to make sure, first, that you're not going to regret it later...."

Ethan was blown away by her offer. And guessing by the widening of her eyes, the strong emotion he felt went from him to her through the hand he still held.

He was both touched and angry, and couldn't determine which feeling dominated. He was furious that her self-esteem had been pounded so low she felt obliged to make that suggestion. But it also turned his spine to spaghetti to know that she'd made it because she was trying to be fair to him.

As tempting as her offer was to his longtime celibate body, he knew that accepting it would only strike another blow to the pride her husband had driven into the ground.

He took her face in his hands and kissed her gently and slowly. Her lips were soft, pliable. A bit surprised.

"Thank you," he said when he raised his head, "but that won't be necessary. I'm sure I won't regret anything." He smiled. "Excuse me. I'm going to shower before dinner."

"SHE'S MAKING *frozen* lasagna for dinner," Nikkie said, her voice laced with disdain. She stood in the doorway of Ethan's bathroom, arms folded, shoulder leaning against the doorjamb.

Showered and dressed in jeans and a chambray shirt, he stood before the mirror over the sink and combed his hair.

"You do that all the time," he said, leaning forward to frown over a spray of three or four gray hairs in his sideburns. Damn. He'd have sworn they weren't there yesterday.

"But she's a mother."

Ethan gave the back of his hair one more swipe with the comb, then tossed it onto the blue-tiled counter and turned to face his daughter.

"Your mother brought home take-out from the deli a couple of nights a week, and we ate fish sticks and tater tots a lot." He leaned a hip against the counter and smiled. "But we didn't love her because she was a great cook. We loved her because she was warm and funny and she loved us."

Nikkie's expression firmed. "You're not expecting me to love *her,* are you?"

"No, I'm not. I'm expecting you to be polite and helpful and understand that she's doing her best in a strange and difficult situation."

"Do you?"

"Do I what?"

"Love her."

"I like her a lot," he answered, the words coming easily. "Liking often turns to love."

Nikkie absorbed that, then straightened away from the doorjamb with an expression of disapproval. "Well, I think it's barbaric." Then she marched off through his room and across the hall to hers.

He followed, stopping in her doorway and watching her yank a silky white blouse off her bed and move to the closet to hang it up.

"Would you find it less barbaric," he asked, "if she was fixing roast chicken and twice-baked potatoes for dinner?"

She glanced at him over her shoulder with a look he could only describe as parental. "Please, Daddy.

You don't like it when *I'm* snide," she said, hooking the hanger on the rod in an angry motion, then closing the closet door.

"Why did you come to Jason's party?" he asked as she smoothed a bedspread that didn't need smoothing.

"Because our meeting broke up early and I wanted pizza."

"I think," he said carefully, preparing for an explosion, "that you secretly like the idea of having Beth and Jason around."

When his daughter gasped and gave him a look that said he was crazy, he raised a silencing hand. "I know. You're concerned about what it'll do to the life you and I have grown used to. In a way so am I. But deep down, I think you sometimes get a little lonely. I think you're afraid you might like having a stepmother and a brother."

She glared at him, fists clenched, and he congratulated himself. He knew that look; he saw it regularly. He didn't know if it was the teenager in her or the woman, but she hated it when he read her mind.

"I think you should know," she said, her chin angling stubbornly, "that if she tries to push me around, I'm not going to stand for it."

"I don't think she's the pushy type."

"You've only known her five days."

"It only took me two days with you," he said, wandering a few steps into her room, "to know that *you* were pushy. Had us up all night. Allergic to this, allergic to that. But we kept you, anyway."

Her shoulders sagged and she appeared on the verge of a smile. "Daddy, I'm half you. You're, like, the motherlode of pushy! Hey!"

Suddenly her expression changed to anger and she rushed past Ethan into the hallway. He followed, wondering what had upset her, and caught up with her halfway to the stairs. She stood glowering at Jason.

The boy had Simba in his arms, the cat's furry legs and tail hanging heavily.

"That's *my* cat," she said, taking the gray bundle from Jason's arms.

"He was on my bed," Jason said, sounding more hurt than defensive. "I was gonna give him some milk."

Nikkie cuddled Simba like a baby. "Milk's bad for cats!" she snapped.

"But everybody gives cats milk."

"It makes old cats sick. Just leave my cats alone and go play with all your new toys."

Jason's voice rose. "Well, excuse me all to hell!"

Nikkie turned to Ethan, the picture of mortification. "Daddy. He said *hell*." She stalked back to her room and closed the door.

Jason looked up at Ethan beseechingly. "He was on my bed. And I thought cats liked milk!"

Ethan put a hand on Jason's head and led him toward the stairs. "They do, but that cat's pretty old and it does make him sick."

"Nikkie hates me."

"No, she doesn't. She's just grumpy because things are changing a little around here."

"She's jealous 'cause I had a birthday and got lots of stuff."

While that observation did have some truth, Ethan said, "I don't think so. But she hasn't had to share my attention with anyone else for a long time. Just like you haven't had to share your mom. But Nikkie'll be okay, don't worry."

They'd reached the stairs and Ethan caught Jason by the shoulder before he could start down. "No hells and damns around here, okay? No four-letter words."

Jason appeared confused about that. "H-e-l?" he spelled. "D-a-m?"

"Hell has two *l*s. And damn has an *n*."

Jason's eyebrows went up. "It does? Where?"

"On the end. I know it's weird and you don't hear it, but it's there."

"Oh. Taylor Bridges says that all the time. And I don't usually say hell, but Nikkie was yelling and she's bigger. I wanted her to hear me."

"Yeah, well, you can say regular words just as loudly as swear words. So don't pollute the conversation with bad language."

"Okay." Jason looked abashed. "Sorry."

Halfway down the stairs Ethan caught the acrid smell of something burning. With Jason right behind him, he raced to the kitchen and found it filled with smoke.

Beth had opened the window over the sink, as well as the back door and was waving at the smoke with a dish towel. On the counter was the foil pan of lasagna. It was incinerated.

"God, I can't believe it!" she said when she saw Ethan. "I usually prepare frozen meals just fine, but I'd gone down to the basement to put a load of laundry in and got distracted by all the paintable things you have down there—clay flowerpots and wooden boxes and that galvanized tub. I didn't hear the timer."

She tossed the towel at the counter, opened the refrigerator and pulled out a large white bowl. "How do you feel about salad *without* lasagna?"

Ethan was not one to be dismayed by small domestic crises when his work showed him repeatedly that the world was filled with such big ones. He could see that Beth was very upset, however, so he dismissed the ruined lasagna with a shake of his head. "Don't worry about it. Salad's great. Jase and I'll pick up some ribs and chicken to go with it."

He took his jacket from a hook near the back door and tossed Jason's at him. The boy pulled it on, eager to accompany him.

"Oh, boy!" Jason's blue eyes shone as he zipped up his jacket. "I like chicken and ribs better, anyway! I'm *glad* you're a rotten cook, Mom!"

Beth met the amused look in Ethan's eyes and had to smile. "Thank you, Jason," she said, leaning down to kiss her son's cheek. "It's nice to be appreciated."

Jason raced through the open door toward the Blazer. Ethan adjusted the collar of his tweed jacket and challenged her with a raised eyebrow. "Want to practice kissing me goodbye?"

She went toward him, her pace lazy, her heartbeat picking up. Steve had hated it when dinner wasn't ready or not as painstakingly prepared as he preferred. And though he seldom shouted, he'd always shown his disapproval with icy politeness or stiff silences.

And here Ethan was going out with a smile to bring dinner home. Unbelievable.

She stopped within inches of him and asked in surprise. "You're not annoyed?"

"Over food?" he asked. "No. I save annoyance for bad calls by referees or deputies who call in sick on

Mondays—stuff like that. Anyway, I seem to remember we'd agreed you don't have to fix meals."

She laughed mirthlessly. "I was trying to make a good impression."

"You could still save it with a kiss."

An unfamiliar sense of well-being made her close the small space between them and tip her face up toward his.

He lowered his head without touching her until their lips met, and the kiss he gave her was sweet but lingering.

Beth unconsciously rose on tiptoe to maintain contact. He responded by parting his lips. She dipped the tip of her tongue into his mouth—and the contact changed suddenly from casual to intense. He wrapped an arm around her waist, pulling her against him. She put both arms around his neck, and the kiss deepened.

She experienced the sensation again of having ingested lava. It shocked her to realize that what she felt was sexual excitement. She pulled her lips from Ethan's and looked into his face, wondering if he could be right about her. Was it possible she *did* possess a strong sexuality?

His eyes were stormy with a decidedly desirous gleam. He drew an uneven breath and grinned. "That kind of a kiss will never send a man on his way," he said, running a hand gently up and down her spine. "It only makes him want to stay."

That sense of sexual well-being seemed to double. "The kids'll be hungry," she said. "You should go."

"I can't."

"Why not?"

"You're standing on my feet." He pointed to his

Nikes on which her black flats stood. She must have used them for leverage during the kiss.

She stepped off him, shooed him backward and closed the door behind him, her heart beating like the wings of a hummingbird. She turned toward the counter to find Nikkie, Simba hanging from one hand and Cindy Crawford riding her other shoulder, standing in the middle of the kitchen and glaring at her.

"That was quite a kiss for two people who've just met," the girl said.

Beth knew she wasn't going to get anywhere with Nikkie if she wasn't just as forthright.

"Yes, it was," she admitted. She went to the counter to toss the burned lasagna into the trash. Then she took the plastic container of cat food from the corner and placed it near the empty bowls on the floor. "But sometimes, when two people find themselves in a situation that forces them to make big decisions together...something happens."

"Love?" Nikkie asked sarcastically.

"Closeness," Beth corrected, pulling the lid off the cat-food container as Nikkie put her furry friends down in front of their bowls. "A kind of mutual dependence that means they have to trust each other. And discovering that your trust is well placed inspires a certain...affection that—" Beth stopped abruptly, remembering her promise to herself to be honest.

"It's pretty complex, Nikkie," she said. "I don't entirely understand it myself. I just know that I like your dad a lot—probably for many of the same reasons you do. He's kind, understanding and supportive. My first husband wasn't like that, so I probably appreciate those qualities more than another woman would."

Nikkie scooped cat food into the bowls. Simba,

nudging Nikkie's hand in his eagerness to eat, got sprinkled with the multicolored pellets. Cindy Crawford, far more dignified, sat a small distance from her bowl and when it was full approached with a graceful twitch of her all-black tail. Simba sniffed at Cindy's bowl as though to be certain they shared the same menu. The calico growled, and the gray Persian, satisfied, went back to his meal.

Nikkie leaned against the corner of the counter, watching her cats eat, then swung her gaze to Beth. It was clear she had more on her mind.

"I'm not going to give you a lot of trouble," Nikkie said, "Because Dad seems to want you here. But don't expect me to drool all over you like Jason does with my father. I loved my mother, and Dad and I were doing fine by ourselves."

Beth nodded over the merciless statement of fact. Maybe there was something steadying about knowing exactly where you stood. "I've always thought drool was pretty unattractive," she said quietly. "Perhaps you can just treat me as you would any other friend of your father's."

"His friends don't *live* here."

"Life's full of exceptions. But I'll do my best not to get in your way."

"I'd appreciate that." Nikkie gestured to the back door. "Where was Dad going?"

Beth smiled in self-deprecation, suspecting she was in for more flack. "To get chicken and ribs to go with our salad. I burned the lasagna."

Nikkie made a face. "It was frozen."

"I know," Beth said. "I was doing laundry in the basement and noticed all the neat old pots and things down there. The sort I paint for craft shows. I didn't hear the timer."

Nikkie rolled her eyes. "I can see you're not going to be much help around here."

Beth shook her head. "Probably not. But you and your dad were doing fine. It doesn't sound like you need me for that kind of thing." She turned to open a utensil drawer. "I can set the table, though. So if you'll excuse me, I'll do that."

Nikkie walked away.

Beth put napkins and silverware around the table and replayed their exchange in her mind. It wasn't precisely negative and it certainly wasn't positive. It had simply been a sort of honest declaration of territory—like Simba sniffing Cindy's bowl.

BETH'S FIRST WEDDING had taken place before a justice of the peace in a small town in eastern Washington. She'd worn a simple blue dress and carried a bouquet of carnations and baby's breath bought at a nearby supermarket.

But she'd been excited and in love.

Her second wedding took place in Ebbie Browning's backyard in an elegant canvas tent against which a torrential rain beat unmercifully. She wore a long-sleeved ivory wool dress with a roll-necked collar and a tea-length flared skirt. Kelly and Nikkie stood beside her. Nikkie had not been pleased about being a bridesmaid, but she hadn't refused.

Ethan wore a gray suit, the jacket of which he'd draped over her shoulders in the middle of the brief ceremony when she'd shivered against the rawness of the day. All the guests were prepared for the cold rainy weather, but Beth had had nothing to go over her dress but her bright red parka.

Brodie served as Ethan's best man, and Jason as usher.

The two deputies Beth had met at Jason's party and several other people Ethan had introduced to her from his office stood behind them as they recited their vows.

Joanne and Zachary were there fully expecting, Beth imagined, she would turn to them at any moment and admit it was all a farce. But the ceremony continued and finally concluded with the traditional directive to the groom.

"You may kiss the bride."

Ethan complied gently and briefly with a promise in his eyes for later.

Beth huddled a little deeper into his jacket as they turned to face her in-laws and Ethan's friends.

There were cheers and applause followed by a buffet of hors d'ouevres Kelly had put together.

"Coconut prawns?" Beth said in amazement. "Bacon-wrapped scallops? Crab-stuffed mushrooms and heart-shaped watercress sandwiches?" Beth said to Kelly as she stood between her and Ethan in the small buffet line. "I didn't know you could do this kind of thing. All you ever eat is chicken strips and egg rolls."

Kelly grinned at her astonishment. "My mom was a caterer. I learned to prepare a lot of fancy things. I just don't like to bother—unless, of course, my best friend is getting married."

Behind her Brodie bit a huge coconut-dipped prawn in half and closed his eyes in ecstasy. "That does it!" he said, piling several more onto his plate. "I have to win the lottery."

"Why?" Kelly asked.

"You're looking for a man with millions, remember?" He reached around her while she remained still and helped himself to two stuffed mushrooms. "And I'm looking for a woman who can cook."

"You missed something, Brodie," she told him, slapping his hand when he reached for another mushroom. "Other people might like them, too. I said I *can* cook, but I don't like to."

"You might want to if you adored the man you were married to."

"I'm not married."

"Only because you don't know me well enough yet."

Kelly sighed dramatically and turned to Ethan, who'd reached the end of the buffet and was pouring coffee for himself and Beth. "What is it with him? He seems bright enough, but he doesn't listen."

"It's a problem he's always had," Ethan explained with a straight face. "Our mother always excused him by saying he was a forceps delivery. I think he's just nuts."

"Go ahead," Brodie said. "Have your fun. But when I win the lottery or become an auto-mechanic mogul—" he pinned Kelly with a glance "—and *you're* begging me to marry you—" his glance went to Ethan "—and you need help IDing tire tracks or repairing the county's dilapidated fleet, I'll tell *you* to take a flying leap. And I'll tell you…" He looked back into Kelly's eyes and something there seemed to stop him and snare his attention. "I'll tell you…" he said absently as Kelly gazed into his eyes. "I'll tell you that I'll take you under any terms. Any."

Ethan turned to Beth with a whispered, "What's going on there?"

She smiled and whispered back, "Can't you guess?"

He looked at his brother and Kelly again and found they were still gazing at each other. People in the buffet line were beginning to move around them.

"You're kidding!" Ethan said as he held both their coffees carefully in one hand and followed her to the head table, one of four set up to accommodate the guests.

"No, I'm not," she said, putting down her plate. She took the cups of coffee from Ethan's hand and put them down, too. "Don't be shocked. Kelly's wonderful. But she has the same problem I have."

Ethan pushed in Beth's folding chair and sat down beside her. "I think she's great. What problem?"

"She has to do her art. Her first husband wanted her attention exclusively and finally left. At least she wouldn't burn the frozen lasagna."

"In the space of a marriage, how important is that?"

"I suppose it depends on how much you like lasagna."

"Oh, just be quiet and eat," he said, grinning. Then he waved at the Richardses as they left the buffet line. "Joanne! Zach! Come join us."

When everyone had gone back for seconds, Brodie rose to make a toast. "To Bethany and Ethan, who have what it takes to make the perfect life—a man dedicated to protect and a woman who beautifies the world with her art. May your lives be joyful and secure, and may there be just enough smudges and just enough risk to make you appreciate what you've found in each other. Happiness and long life."

Beth noticed that as her in-laws raised their glasses,

they both appeared to be struggling with emotion. She wondered if they were remembering how they'd been forced to miss their son's marriage because of the elopement.

Afterward Ethan and Beth cut the cake and Kelly and Ebbie distributed it. By the time guests began to leave, dusk had fallen.

Ethan and Beth were talking to Curtis and Billings and their wives when there was a scream and a commotion from the driveway of Ebbie's house. The six hurried to investigate and found a group gathered around Zachary, who was on his back near the hydrangea that bordered the side of the house.

"Zach!" Joanne was on her knees beside him.

He was conscious but groaning. "My leg," he told Ethan as he squatted down next to him. "Broken, I think. I slipped on the wet grass."

Curtis pulled out a cell phone and dialed 911. Ebbie brought out a pillow and blankets and an umbrella which Beth held over him. Everyone stood around Zach as protection from the weather until the ambulance arrived.

Joanne rode in the ambulance with Zachary, and Ethan and Beth followed in the Blazer. Brodie took Nikkie and Jason home.

The leg was broken, a simple fracture of the tibia.

"We'll keep him overnight," the doctor told Joanne, Beth and Ethan in the waiting room. "It was a clean break, and I don't foresee any problems, but the pain can be a little hard to deal with and we can take care of that here. If he's doing as well tomorrow, I can send him home with a prescription for a painkiller, but he'll need crutches for at least three weeks."

Joanne's brow furrowed in concern. "We were

heading home tomorrow. If I lay him down in the back seat of the car, do you think…''

The doctor shook his head before she'd finished. ''I wouldn't recommend that. He should stay put a couple of days. He'll be too uncomfortable to move.''

Joanne nodded. ''Whatever you say. May I see him now?''

''Of course. Come with me.''

Joanne turned to Beth. ''You two can go home.'' For the first time since Beth had known her, the woman looked vulnerable. ''I can get a cab back to the motel.''

Beth turned to Ethan, but didn't have to say a word.

''We'll wait for you and take you home with us,'' he said. ''You and Zach can stay at our place until he's feeling well enough to go home.''

Joanne looked stunned—also a first in Beth's experience of her. ''Thank you,'' she said after a moment. ''I'm sure that would be more comfortable for Zach than the motel. I'll try not to be too long, but I won't sleep tonight if I don't see for myself that he's all right.''

''Take your time,'' Beth said. ''And give Zach our best.''

Joanne hurried off after the doctor, and Beth and Ethan settled back into the upholstered chairs in the waiting room.

''How did you know,'' Beth asked Ethan, ''that was exactly what was on my mind?''

He leaned back in his chair in an attitude of false modesty. ''I'm your husband,'' he said, smoothing his tie. ''It's my job to know what you're thinking.''

''You've only been my husband—'' she glanced at her watch ''—three hours and forty minutes.''

"I'm a fast learner."

She sat sideways in her chair, resting her elbow on the back and studying him. His long legs were stretched out and crossed at the ankles. He looked pretty wonderful in a suit, she thought.

"Joanne's worried about Zach and so she's subdued right now," Beth warned, reaching over to brush a speck of something off his shoulder. "But it might be difficult to have her around the next few days. She always puts herself in charge of the situation, whatever it is. It was generous of you to offer to let them stay with you...us."

He shrugged, then sent her a questioning glance. "Have you thought about what it'll mean to *you* to have them in the house?"

"Yes," she said dryly. "Constant tension."

"I mean physically."

"Why physically?"

"Because," he explained, "we'll have to give them your room. We can tell them your things are in there because my closet's too small, but you'll have to sleep with me. It won't do for them to see you and me sleeping in separate bedrooms."

Her heart gave a surprised thud. Why hadn't she considered that? There wasn't an extra room for the Richardses.

She did her best to appear at ease as she said, "Well, I thought that was what you'd intended all along."

"I did," he admitted, "but I was willing to give you time to adjust. To come across the hall when you were ready."

"I'll just have to be flexible."

Amusement shone in Ethan's eyes. "Not *that* flexible," he said. "I'm not into anything gymnastic."

She punched his shoulder. "Ethan, I meant—"

"I know what you meant." He laughed, reaching over the arms of the chairs that separated them and cupping her head in his hand to pull her toward him. He kissed her cheek, then settled her against his shoulder. "I was just trying to lighten the mood. You get so serious when we discuss lovemaking."

"I was trying to be casual."

"I know. But your eyes become the color of a bruise and...I get the feeling there are some things I'll have to help you unlearn."

"I'll do my best," she promised.

He squeezed her shoulder. "One of them," he said, "is the notion that the outcome is entirely dependent upon you. It isn't. And anyway, the fact that we're sharing the same bed doesn't mean we have to share anything else until it seems like a good idea to you. But eventually I'm going to show you how mistaken you are about yourself."

Beth's hand rested on his pectoral muscle and she rubbed it gently in silent gratitude for his consideration.

But again she had that feeling of hot lava pouring through her, and she knew they would one day very soon make love. Though her mind and her emotions were confused about her abilities in the bedroom, her body seemed anxious to be proved wrong.

CHAPTER NINE

ETHAN STARED at the glowing numbers on his digital clock: 2:21 a.m. God. He felt as though he was in a sort of time warp where the last three hours had been a week long.

He and Beth had driven Joanne to the Coast Motel, picked up her and Zachary's things and brought her home. Beth had helped her settle into the room, while Ethan had explained to Nikkie and Jason that the Richardses would be staying for a while.

"How long?" Nikkie had asked sullenly.

"I'm not sure," he'd explained. "Maybe a week, maybe two. Depends on how quickly Zachary heals." He'd given Nikkie a significant look. "And that will probably be affected by how comfortable he is in his surroundings."

Nikkie sat in a corner of the sofa, her legs curled under her, a pillow wrapped in her arms, the picture of defensive resistance. "And I suppose we'll be inviting *them* into the family, too?"

"They *are* in the family," Jason said, his tone as aggressive as hers. "They're Grandma and Grandpa." He sat in the middle of the sofa, arms folded, feet not touching the floor. He frowned at Ethan, who was perched on the edge of a hatch-cover on legs that served as a coffee table. "But I don't want them to stay, either. They're gonna start picking on Mom and trying to get me to go home with them."

"I won't let them pick on your mom," Ethan said firmly, "and your home is right here. Nobody's taking you away."

Jason's frown turned to a fragile smile. "You promise?"

"I promise."

Nikkie got to her feet and threw the pillow onto the sofa. "Well, maybe somebody could take *me* away! If one more person moves in with us, there won't be room for me, anyway!" And she'd stormed off to her room.

Brodie had wandered out of the kitchen, a dish towel over the shoulder of the white shirt he'd worn to the wedding. He'd removed the tie. "I guess I'll have breakfast at the Crossing Café for a while," he said, handing Ethan a mug of coffee. "Looks like you're going to have a full house."

Ethan had hooked an arm around his neck and walked him back into the kitchen. "Bro, if you don't come, there will be no one to cook breakfast. We'll find room for you around the table."

"You mean in front of the stove."

"Yeah."

"Nikkie tells me Beth burned a frozen lasagna."

Ethan smiled. "She was doing laundry and got distracted by all the artistic potential of the junk in my basement. Come on. Weekends are still yours, but save us from toast and peanut butter during the week."

"Okay, okay. I'm such a pushover."

Ethan had put his cup down on the counter and hugged his brother. "Thanks for bringing the kids home and staying with them. And thanks for standing up for me. It wasn't a bad wedding, was it?''

Brodie grabbed his suit coat off the back of a kitchen chair. "We got rained on, I was pursued by a wacky redhead, and one of your guests broke his leg and is moving in with you. No, not bad."

Ethan was thinking that, when all was said and done, he had Bethany. And that made the wedding pretty remarkable.

Ethan opened the door for Brodie. "Ah, about the redhead... Just who was pursuing whom? It looked to me as though *you* were the one hot on Kelly's trail."

Brodie stepped onto the back porch. The night was dark, and rain continued to hammer the sloping porch roof. He pulled on his coat.

"Okay, I was," he said. "Then...in the buffet line, she gave me that look."

"What look?"

Staring out at the rain, Brodie shrugged in frustration. "It's hard to put into words. But I think it means...you're it."

"It?"

"Him."

"Who?"

Brodie turned to him, mouth curled in exasperation. "Think, man. You're not usually this obtuse. I think she might think I could be...you know..."

Ethan shifted his weight and leaned a shoulder against the four-by-four that held up the right side of the porch. He thought he knew what Brodie meant, but he wanted to hear him say it.

"Could you spell it out for me?"

"A lasting love!" Brodie shouted. "Husband material!"

"And that's bad?"

"Very. I'm not interested."

"That's fascinating, because I recall you asking her if she could be interested in you if you had millions."

Brodie continued to stare moodily at the rain. "Yeah, 'cause I don't have millions and have no prospect of getting millions, so I thought I was safe."

"Uh-huh. That's why you were coming on to her all day?"

Brodie sighed and shrugged again. "You know me. That's what I do. Most women understand the game."

"You play this game because of Paulette."

Brodie stiffened. "I don't talk about Paulette."

Ethan shook his head. "Bro, you're getting too old for that game," he said, figuring his love for Brodie gave him permission to dispense with tact. "It's a seventeen-year-old, busting-beer-cans-on-your-head kind of game. And you don't talk about Paulette because if you did, you'd have to admit that you fell in love with her and then got dumped."

Brodie went rigid with anger. "Don't preach to me!"

"Somebody should!" Ethan retorted. "You chase down every woman for miles as some kind of proof of your virility, and then when she stops to let you catch her, you pull back. What is it, exactly? Are you hurting them as some kind of revenge on Paulette, or did Paulette destroy your self-esteem so much that when a woman finally does show some interest, you're afraid she won't find anything in you and she'll leave?"

Brodie swiveled his body toward Ethan and drew back his fist. As though reliving an old scene from their teenage years, Ethan squared his stance and prepared to block the blow.

But Brodie didn't throw it. After one tense moment he dropped his fist and drew a breath, his eyes still dark with fury. "My life is none of your business," he said flatly. "You'd better go inside and take care of your own. I have a feeling this marriage isn't going to be the walk in the park you had with Diana." Then Brodie's eyes shifted somewhere to the left of Ethan, and his tight angry features seemed to collapse in distress.

Ethan turned to find Beth standing beside him. She'd heard Brodie's remark, he was sure, about his seemingly perfect first marriage.

Ethan put an arm around her and drew her close. The night air was cold. "Hi," he said. "What're you doing out here?"

"I heard the two of you shouting at each other," she said, her eyes going worriedly from him to his brother. "Is something wrong?"

Brodie smiled and shook his head. "You haven't been around long enough to know that we usually end up shouting at each other. It's nothing serious."

Beth studied him skeptically, then changed the subject. "Brodie, thank you for staying with Jason and Nikkie."

"My pleasure." He turned to Ethan, his expression neutral. "You'll have to move the Blazer so I can back out."

Ethan followed him at a run through the rain, but stopped at his truck. "What are you doing?" Brodie demanded as he yanked open his door. "You'll get drenched."

Ethan felt rain soak the shoulders of his shirt, but

ignored it. "I want to make sure you understand that Paulette was an idiot, not you. When you're not being psychotic, you're really all right. And I hate to think of you spending a lifetime alone because you can't see that."

Brodie looked back at him, his jaw rigidly set. "Will you get the Blazer out of my way before I back over it?" he asked.

Deciding that any further conversation would be profane and irretrievable, Ethan ran to the Blazer and backed onto the street.

In a move that Ethan thought looked like something out of a slapstick comedy, Brodie backed out with a squeal of tires, raced the twenty feet to his own driveway and turned into it with another squeal of tires and a spray of rainwater, then rocked to a stop. He went into his house without a glance in Ethan's direction.

Ethan pulled into the driveway and ran back into the house. The place was silent as a tomb.

The kitchen clock said it was just after eleven. He shot the bolt on the front door and turned off all the downstairs lights. Upstairs he looked into Nikkie's room and found her asleep, a cat curled up on each side of her. Simba looked up and gave him a faint meow. Ethan pulled the door silently closed.

The door of the room Joanne was using was also closed, and there was silence behind it. He could only conclude that meant everything was fine.

Jason's door was open and Ethan looked in to find that he, too, was fast asleep, one arm hanging over the side of the upper bunk. Ethan tucked it back up and resettled the blankets. The boy expelled a comfortable little sigh and settled more deeply into his pillow.

Ethan walked into his own room to find Beth turning down the bed. She wore a simple blue cotton nightie that skimmed her knees. She looked up at him with a smile he imagined was supposed to assure him that she was quite comfortable with the situation, and if he wanted to make love to her tonight, she was willing.

In her eyes, though, was concern, trepidation. When eventually they did make love, he wanted her to be more than willing. He wanted her eager, confident that she was doing what she wanted to do.

"How was Joanne when she went to bed?" he asked, unbuttoning his shirt.

Beth fluffed a pillow. "Exhausted but fine. Now that she knows Zachary's going to be all right, she'll probably be her old self in the morning. So be prepared to listen to suggested changes for your uniform and possibly even the county code." She smiled as she walked around the bed to the other side and fluffed the other pillow. "Do you sleep by the door or by the window?" she asked, still sounding quite composed.

He knew it was perverse, but he took a certain satisfaction in making her control slip. "I usually sleep in the middle," he said, pulling his shirt off and giving it a hook shot into the hamper by the bathroom. "You can have the two sides."

She tossed the pillow on the bed and looked at him, obviously trying to decide if he was being difficult or funny. Then she smiled. "It's nice to know that even so close to midnight you retain a sense of humor."

It was on the tip of his tongue to tell her there were moments in a man's life when that was all he had left, but he thought it sounded self-pitying, so he kept the thought to himself.

He pointed to the side of the bed nearest the door.

"That side," he said. "You go on to bed. I have to take a shower." He opened the closet door to find that a few of her things had been hung beside his. Seeing her colorful fabrics lined up beside his darker things gave him a weird sense of déjà vu. He remembered when Diana was still alive and his uniforms and sports coats had shared space with silky blouses and pastel linen suits. But the sight also projected him into the future, because he couldn't help but wonder how well this would work, how long those things would be there.

Beth gestured at the closet. "I brought some of my stuff here so I wouldn't have to disturb Joanne in the morning. I hope that's all right."

"Of course." He pulled off his shoes and tossed them into the bottom of the closet.

"She believed me when I said my clothes were in there because your closet was too crowded."

"The best lies are those that have a grain of truth," he said, pushing the closet door closed and heading for the bathroom. But Beth stood squarely in his path, a line of concern between her eyebrows.

"What's wrong?" she asked.

Again he got an unexpected glimpse of Diana, this time in the direct way Beth approached a problem. But at the moment he was tired and would have preferred to forget the whole thing. After all, in just a few short days he'd fallen for and married a woman who was afraid to go to bed with him. And he'd been looking forward to ending what had seemed like an interminable period of celibacy. But he couldn't take what she offered when he knew she'd rather be having an IRS audit or something equally unpleasant. So what could possibly be wrong?

"Nothing," he said, then he leaned down to kiss her cheek and got a disorienting whiff of a spicy rose fragrance. "Go to sleep. Good night." He walked around her and went into the bathroom.

But she followed him and stood in the doorway, preventing him from closing himself in. He saw the rosy tips of small firm breasts under her thin gown and had to tear his eyes away and concentrate on her face. It was pale and anxious.

"You're annoyed with me," she said, "because I'm nervous about...tonight. Is that it?"

"No. I—"

"Well, I'm nervous, but...I want you to make love to me." She looked directly into his eyes, though he could see that took courage.

"Beth," he said patiently, leaning a forearm on the doorway molding, "you say you want to make love with me, but your eyes tell a different story. You don't really want it. And I won't make love with you until you do."

"But I explained." She spoke quietly but urgently. "My feelings are very complex. Part Steve's fault, probably part my fault. But I don't want...the experience diminished for you because of that. I don't want to hurt you—yet there seems no way to avoid it. If you make love to me and I have trouble responding, you'll be hurt. But if we don't make love..." She spread her arms helplessly. "I mean, who *doesn't* make love on their wedding night? I understand that you're annoyed, I just want to make it clear that I—"

He put a hand gently over her mouth to silence her, although he was fascinated by her stream of chatter. The control she always tried so hard to maintain was puddled at her feet. He liked that. And he thought it boded well for their *eventual* liaison.

"Rule number one in this house," he said, lowering his hand when it appeared she'd remain silent, "is that we don't hold ourselves to other people's standards. Each of us does what he or she decides. And if I'm annoyed with anyone, I'm annoyed with myself."

He paused to draw a breath, because being completely honest with a woman, he was just beginning to remember, was harder than it seemed. "I'm used to being in charge of myself and the situation. I thought it would be easy to wait for you to be ready to make love. But I'm discovering that I'm not as strong as I thought. That I'm more vulnerable than I thought. And that's difficult for a man to admit to himself."

A subtle change took place in her eyes. The suggestion that he found her desirable seemed to surprise her. God. He wished he could have had five minutes alone in an interview room with Steve Richards.

She put a hand to his face with a reverence he found humbling. "I hope I can be what you want," she whispered.

He put his hand over hers, turned his lips into her palm and kissed it. "You *are* what I want. That's the problem."

"I meant in bed," she said.

"When two people care about each other," he said, kissing her knuckles now, "they usually have no problem making the other happy—in bed or out. When that time comes for you, we'll be ready. In the meantime, I really need a shower and you need some sleep."

"Okay." She wrapped her arms around his waist and held him fiercely for so long he was ready to chuck his noble attitude and carry her to the bed. Then she took a step back from him and said with a mystifying disappointment in her eyes that completely confused him, "I usually drop off to sleep the minute my head hits the pillow, so I'll see you at breakfast."

"Right," he replied, and watched her stiff-backed form in the thin cotton walk away before closing the bathroom door.

AND THAT WAS WHY he lay staring at the clock in the wee hours of the morning. He'd taken his time in the shower, grateful to find Beth asleep when he joined her in the bed. She was lying on her back, the fingers of one hand folded against her cheek.

He flipped onto his other side and closed his eyes, thinking how different it was to realize he was married again. Diana's absence had made such a change in his life, and the love they'd had for each other would be with him always. But the image that formed behind his closed eyelids now was Beth's.

As if she'd detected his thoughts, she turned toward him and curled up against his back, her knees tucked up right under his buttocks. His confused libido was confused no longer, and he cursed himself for taking a sympathetic stand with her. They could be making love right now, and he'd have bet everything he owned that he'd have already cured her of her feelings of inadequacy.

But he could tell by the gentle pulse of breath against his spine that she was still asleep. She hadn't chosen to snuggle against him; she'd done it in an instinctive but unconscious search for warmth and security after a long taxing day.

He tried to clear his mind of thought so that he could get some sleep. That was surprisingly easy.

What he couldn't turn off was the reaction of every nerve ending in his body. The part of him in contact with her silky flesh was screaming for him to do something about it. But he'd promised, and she trusted him.

So he lay still even as she snuggled closer. It was character building, he told himself. And he realized he was going to have to be quite some paragon to hold his own in this relationship.

ETHAN AWOKE to the pleasant smell of coffee and…pancakes? French toast? He wasn't sure which, but the aromas wafting upstairs were enough to set his stomach rumbling.

The other side of the bed was empty, but *could* Beth cook anything without burning it? Nikkie was good with eggs, but couldn't seem to get the hang of flipping pancakes, so she never made them. Brodie slept in on Sundays.

Jason appeared in the doorway of Ethan's room, still wearing *Toy Story* pajamas. "Do you smell that?" he asked.

"Yeah." Ethan tossed the blanket back and swung his legs over the side of the bed. "Who's cooking?"

Jason shook his head. "It can't be Mom, and Nikkie's door is closed. It's either Grandma or Uncle Brodie. Come on!" Jason called, then disappeared from view. Ethan could hear his footsteps heading for the stairs.

"Right behind you," he said, going to the closet and pulling on jeans and a sweater. He hadn't fallen asleep until sometime after four, but still he was more ravenous than tired.

And, masochist that he seemed to be, he couldn't wait to see Beth. She should be bright and fresh this morning, all the sleep she'd gotten in direct proportion to all the sleep he'd missed!

Joanne was holding forth at the stove, a pristine counter suggesting that whatever she was preparing had required little effort—or at least none that showed.

It was pancakes. Jason was hard at work on a tall stack drenched in syrup, and Beth sat across from him with two pancakes half-eaten. She wore a red turtleneck and had bundled her hair up in a loose knot. Bangs skimmed her eyebrows when she looked up at him, and silky tendrils of hair had escaped to caress her neck.

The look she gave him was cautious and watchful. He wondered if she'd awakened curled up tightly against him and was embarrassed by it.

Joanne turned away from the stove to see who'd walked into the kitchen. She wished him a pleasant if somewhat haughty good-morning.

He returned the greeting, then went to lean over Beth's chair and give her a kiss. He did it partly for Joanne's benefit, but partly for his own.

"I thought I'd make myself useful," Joanne said, her gaze lingering on him as a new dollop of batter sizzled on the griddle. "I know that cooking isn't one of Beth's strengths."

It annoyed him that she would feel called upon to say so, particularly when she was a guest in what was supposed to be Beth's home.

He gave Beth a calculatedly lascivious look and kissed her again. "She has other qualities that far outweigh cooking in importance."

Beth eyes widened, first in surprise, then in amused appreciation. "Thank you, darling," she said, falling in with his loverlike performance.

"But it's wonderful to have someone around who *can* cook," Ethan said, going to the stove to peer over Joanne's shoulder. He wanted her to know he appreciated her efforts, but he didn't want her picking on Beth. "Anything I can do?"

She stepped aside and pointed to the oven with her spatula. "Your plate's in there."

"Why don't *you* take it?" he suggested. "Since the batter's made, I can probably prepare my own."

"Nonsense." She pulled open the oven door and handed him an oven mitt. "Careful with it. Is your daughter coming down?"

"I don't think so. Sunday's her chance to sleep in."

Joanne nodded. "Well, I'll put a plate in the oven just in case."

Ethan carried his plate to the table. "How's Zachary this morning?" he asked. "Have you called the hospital?"

"Yes, and he had a fairly good night," Joanne replied, expertly flipping a pancake. "The doctor says he can go home this morning if we can pick him up."

"Sure." Ethan reached for the syrup. "We can go as soon as we're finished breakfast."

Joanne turned away from the stove to face him. "We could compensate you for the room and the—"

"No," Ethan said simply. "We're happy to have you here."

"I appreciate that," she said with an upward tilt of her chin that seemed more aggressive than grateful, "but it'll cost you in a dozen little ways. More groceries, more hot water, more laundry, more—"

"No," Ethan said again. And when she opened her mouth to offer further argument, he added quietly, "and that's final."

Her chin went up an extra notch, and she appeared confused, as though receiving generosity and being overruled were foreign experiences for her.

"Zachary might have something to say about that," she persisted.

Ethan cut into his pancakes without looking up. "No, he won't," he returned. "It's my house."

She might have continued to argue, but the smell of something burning turned her back to the stove with a cry of distress. She jabbed the spatula under a smoking pancake and lifted it out, obviously looking for the trash.

"Around the corner of the fridge," Beth told her. "Near the cat food."

The spatula held out in front of her, Joanne followed Beth's directions, then walked back to the stove frowning fiercely.

So Beth wasn't the only one capable of burning food, he thought. He looked up from his plate and caught Beth's eye, then winked and went back to his breakfast.

CHAPTER TEN

ETHAN DROPPED Beth at the cannery on his way to work Monday morning. Their efforts to convince Joanne and Zachary that they were a real family were aided considerably by the built-in stress of getting two adults and two children showered, dressed and fed in order to leave the house at the same time.

Nikkie was carrying a mock-up of a medieval shield she'd made out of cardboard and foil, and therefore she couldn't take the school bus. But she apparently considered arriving at school in a car filled with her new stepmother and stepbrother a severe breach of cool and ignored Beth and Jason completely.

Jason was out of sorts because Ethan had thwarted his plan to ride his bike after school to the old deserted Appleby house in the next block. Ethan had explained that transients often took shelter there, and that though children and teenagers found it fun to dare one another to go in and explore the place, it wasn't safe. Jason had tried wheedling but to no avail.

Beth thought Ethan seemed a little edgy when she suggested he looked as though he hadn't slept well. And by the time the foursome headed for the car, they were all snapping at each other. Beth had a parting glimpse of Joanne and Zachary sitting across from each other in the kitchen. Zachary's leg in its cast was propped on an extra chair, and Beth wondered what they thought of her "happy family."

Nikkie left the Blazer without speaking, and Jason climbed out with only a terse goodbye.

Ethan pulled up to the pier on which the cannery stood and caught Beth's arm when she would have pushed her door open.

"I apologize for my mood this morning," he said with a sincerity that surprised her—apologies had not even been in Steve's makeup. "I haven't been getting much sleep lately."

She turned back, giving him her full attention, wanting to know what was troubling him and to help if she could. "Why not? What's wrong?"

"It's not 'wrong,' precisely," he said with a half smile. "It just keeps me awake."

"What?"

"You," he replied. "You're a cuddler."

Color rose to her cheeks, but she smiled. "That's strange," she said, "because Steve always said that my body up against his made him claustrophobic. So I always stayed on my side of the bed. But—" her color deepened "—when I woke up Sunday morning, I was all wrapped around you. I'm sorry."

"Don't apologize," he said. "It doesn't make me claustrophobic at all. It makes me..." He considered a moment, then apparently changed his mind about telling her. "Never mind. It was no reason to grouse at you. *I'm* sorry. I'll pick you up about six. You said Jason will just walk here from school?"

"Yes. It's not far, so he doesn't have to be picked up. And Nikkie'll get the bus home?"

"She has a drama-club meeting after school, so

she'll get the city bus. That usually gets her home by five.''

"Okay. Do you want me to call and check on her, make sure everything's all right?''

"She'll tell you she's too old to be checked on," he warned, "but I always do, anyway."

"All right. I'll handle it. Besides, I'll have to check on Joanne and Zachary."

She pushed open her door again.

"Hey!" he called.

"Yes?"

"No kiss goodbye? You're forgetting the private detective.''

She leaned toward him. "Do you really think he's watching?" she asked, glancing surreptitiously beyond Ethan, then to his left and right.

"I do," he replied gravely. "I imagine he's using binoculars, so you'd better make it good."

Her smile held amused suspicion. "You aren't by any chance taking advantage of this situation, are you?"

He tipped his head and closed the few inches that separated his mouth from hers. "Of course I am," he admitted shamelessly, and kissed her until she couldn't breathe or think.

At last he raised his head, and she tried to reestablish a sense of emotional balance, thinking that if he made love with the same artful skill with which he kissed, he might very well be right about teaching her to enjoy it.

She stepped out of the car and blew him one final kiss. He drove away with a tap of the Blazer's horn.

Kelly was perched on a piling by the door to Beth's studio. She was dressed in her studio garb—a ratty denim jacket, old beige cords and a blue sweatshirt stained with clay and glaze. Her short red hair was tumbled, and her eyes were bright with mischief.

"Well, that was quite a kiss," she said, leaping down from the piling as Beth unlocked the studio door.

"We thought the detective might be watching," Beth replied, making her way into the studio, careful not to meet Kelly's eyes.

"Come on," Kelly cajoled. "That was no performance. That was the real thing."

"Well..." Beth flipped light switches, and fluorescent tubes fluttered, then came to life, filling the middle of the cavernous room with a bright glare. Tables around the room were covered with signs and all kinds of hanging wood art that was drying for the Winter Festival Art Fair.

In the middle of the room under another bank of lower hanging lights a large worktable stood, and Beth crossed to it. She dropped her purse under it and pulled off her jacket, hanging it on a nearby coat tree.

"Well, what?" Kelly encouraged, doing the same with her jacket and pulling up a stool without waiting for an invitation.

Beth wondered how to explain to Kelly what she felt for Ethan and decided that she couldn't. It would sound absurd, even to her best friend. "Well, I don't know," she said finally. "He's like a composite of the perfect man. Tough, gentle, firm, kind, funny, warm..." She stopped to grin. "Shall I go on?"

Kelly shook her head and made a gesture Beth interpreted as "Please don't." Then she pulled a circle of pine toward her, one that Beth had yet to decide what to do with, and traced the rings in the grain with the blunt tip of one finger.

"Actually I understand," she said, glancing up at Beth under her lashes. The look in her eyes, Beth noted in surprise, suggested embarrassment. "I've spent quite some time talking to his brother."

Beth wasn't sure what that meant. "You mean he praises Ethan, or you know about Ethan's qualities because you saw them in Brodie?"

Kelly sighed and concentrated on the rings. "If you'd asked me before your wedding, I'd have said it was because Brodie was all those things, too. But on the day of your wedding…" A pleat appeared between her eyebrows. "I don't know. Something changed."

Beth climbed onto her stool and leaned an elbow on the table. She studied Kelly's uncharacteristic frown and put a hand to her friend's knee. "What changed?" she asked. "It looked like the two of you were getting on so well. In fact, in the buffet line, I'd have sworn you made some kind of emotional contact."

Kelly's eyes became unfocused and Beth guessed she was remembering that moment. "Yes. We did. I looked into his laughing face and realized how nice it must be to be fussed over. How much I missed someone laughing about things, rather than finding problems with everything. It came over me as though he'd dropped a net. I was interested. *Very* interested." She sighed and made a face Beth couldn't quite decipher. "But you know what?"

Beth was almost afraid to ask. "What?"

"I think he's one of those men for whom the chase is everything."

"Why?"

"Because the minute I stopped evading him and let him know I could be interested in a relationship, it was as though someone blew up the power station and the lights went out."

"Sometimes," Beth suggested tactfully, "when your emotions are engaged and because you care so much, something that's insignificant can seem bigger than it really is."

Kelly sighed and pushed the pine disk away from her. "I don't think that's the case here," she said, knotting her fingers together and drawing a knee up until her foot was hooked in a rung of the stool. "His ardor cooled considerably the last hour of the reception. When your father-in-law was hurt, I asked Brodie if it would help if I went back to Ethan's with him and the kids, and he told me rather firmly that he'd be fine and that I probably had a lot of cleaning up of food and stuff to do."

That didn't sound good to Beth at all. And suddenly she remembered Ethan and Brodie shouting at each other on the back porch Saturday night.

"Maybe he was just being considerate," she said thinly.

Kelly gave her a look that told her she knew that excuse to be as false as it sounded. "Penny Curtis and Jan Billings were going to help Ebbie clean up so that I could help Brodie. I told him that. But he brushed me off."

Beth tried again. "He might just be a little frightened. You know, the old commitment bugaboo and all that." She smiled. "And you're pretty heady stuff, you know. If he's attracted to you and he thinks you're beginning to notice him, he might just be overwhelmed."

Kelly considered that grimly for a moment, then tipped her head from side to side as though it could be a possibility about which she remained undecided. "Well, I'm not going to give him another thought. I was well rid of my ex because he could never understand me. I'm not going to get involved with someone else who's going to make me feel unsure of myself. So let's talk about you." She caught both feet on the rung of the stool and leaned toward Beth, her eyes gleaming with curiosity. "How was...the weekend?"

Beth pulled a stack of boards nearer, setting them out in neat rows to prepare them for painting. "Nikkie's nose is a little out of joint because not only is she dealing with a stepmother and brother, now there's Joanne and Zachary. Of course, Zachary's stuck in bed for a few days, but Joanne takes a little getting used to. She did make breakfast yester—"

Beth abruptly stopped when she looked up and found Kelly staring at her and shaking her head.

"What?" Beth asked.

"You know what I want to know," Kelly said. "Did a couple of nights with him spark your interest in sex again?"

Beth sighed and met Kelly's gaze. "We haven't had sex."

Kelly blinked. "You're kidding!"

"I know. I know. I would have, but the day of Jason's party when I asked him to marry me and he agreed, we talked about what each of us wanted out of it, and we agreed that it wouldn't simply be a convenience thing—"

"So far," Kelly said, "I don't understand."

"Well, let me finish," Beth returned with mild impatience. Not that even the complete story would clarify anything for Kelly. Beth herself still felt confused. "I told him how it was with Steve and me and how I've...been ever since. He seems to think I'm wrong and that making love with him will be entirely different."

"Well, why didn't you?"

Beth leaned both elbows on the table and rested her chin in her hands. The weekend seemed like something that had happened to someone else—a wedding, a trip to the hospital, a beautiful but suspicious stepdaughter, a man who kissed her with dark-eyed ardor, then gently pushed her away when she said she was willing to make love with him.

"I told him I was willing," she said, running her fingertips over one of her boards. "But he said my eyes told a different story. That he wanted to wait until I was sure it was what I wanted."

"Willing," Kelly said with a wince, "is a pretty insipid word."

Beth straightened and jumped off the stool. "I know it is," she said loudly. The words echoed in the nearly empty room. "But what if I'd behaved otherwise, then he put a hand on me and I froze, sure he'd start telling me at any moment I was cold and unresponsive and completely unappealing? That would have been harder on him than waiting...wouldn't it?"

Kelly slid off her own stool to put an arm around Beth's shoulders. "Steve was a jerk, Beth. And before you get all defensive, I know you had a good thing going in the beginning, but he didn't uphold his end of the relationship. He ignored you when he was busy. He was too ambitious to spend any time with you, to remind you that he cared. Then when he made some big deal, he came home and treated you like...like the spoils of victory. What woman wouldn't conclude that this was no fun and she wanted no more of it?"

Kelly turned Beth to face her and grasped both her shoulders. Her gaze was fierce. "The thing you have to remember here, Beth, is that you're no longer dealing with Steve. This is Sheriff Ethan Drum—the man who scoured the countryside at night in the rain to find Jason. The man who supported Jason's story so he wouldn't humiliate him in front of your in-laws, who agreed to marry you to help you through this. It's not going to be like it was with Steve. *You're* not going to be like you were with Steve."

Beth knew that. She just wasn't sure her brain could translate that information to a body that had turned itself off long ago.

"All right, enough about men," Kelly declared, hooking an arm in Beth's and leading her toward the door that led into the rest of the cannery. "Let's talk about something we understand—art. Show me where my studio will be."

Beth spent the next hour and a half walking Kelly through a series of large separated spaces that would ultimately become the long-dreamed-of art mall. She showed her how each room could be partitioned to make a small showroom in the front and still leave a big working area in the back. There'd be north light from the long series of small-paned windows facing the river and the state of Washington on the other shore.

Kelly chose the space closest to Beth's and insisted on writing her a check. Beth tried to refuse, protesting that it would be another week at least before she had the place painted.

"For a slight reduction in price," Kelly bargained,

"I can paint it myself. You've had the building inspector in, so we know the pier and the structure are safe. All I have to do is paint the walls something soft and light, spruce up the showroom area, and pretty soon I can be here working beside you every day and checking on the progress of your love life."

Beth snorted. "Oh, good."

They laughed, then Beth walked Kelly out to her car.

JASON CAME to the cannery from school looking no more cheerful than he had when she and Ethan had dropped him off.

"Taylor Bridges," he said, munching on an apple Beth had brought for him, "doesn't believe Ethan's my dad. He says I'm making it up."

"Maybe you should invite him over sometime," Beth suggested. She knew it wasn't fair to hold a grudge against a child, but the Bridges boy had been a thorn in Jason's side since her son's first day at Cobbler's Crossing Elementary. "Maybe for dinner. Then he can see Ethan for himself."

Jason chewed, swallowed and perked up. "Yeah!" he said. "That'd be cool! Can I do it tomorrow?"

"Let me check to make sure Ethan doesn't have anything scheduled." With a fine-tipped brush dipped in silver paint, she put whiskers on a cat on one of her door plaques. "He has meetings at night sometimes."

"Okay." Jason came up beside her and leaned into her free left arm as she worked. "You know, coming here's turning out to be a good thing, isn't it?"

Beth wrapped her arm around him and pulled him

closer. She dabbed silver dots in the cat's wide green eyes. "You mean because of Ethan?"

"Mostly." As she turned to look at him, he added, "You like him, too, dontcha?"

"Yes, I do," she replied, kissing his forehead.

Jason grinned, his eyes alight with secret information. "You kiss him a lot. I seen you."

There was no denying that. "Uh-huh."

"You're not gonna be having babies, are you?"

"No. No babies."

"Nikkie said you were." He threw the apple core into the wastebasket under her table. It landed with a thunk. "She says if you and Ethan had babies, you wouldn't need us anymore."

Beth stopped in the act of tipping the cat's ears with silver and set down her brush on her palette. She wiped her hands on a rag and gave her son her full attention. "Jason, you know that isn't true. You have always been and will always be the most important thing in my life."

He leaned against the edge of the table. "Yeah, but if you had a baby that was part you and part Ethan, then it really belongs to you. I'm part somebody else and so's Nikkie."

Horrified that he might have been worried about that all day long, she waved him onto the other stool.

"First of all," she said, choosing her words carefully, "all children belong one hundred percent to both their parents."

He frowned, unable to grasp that. "But my dad's dead and so's Nikkie's mom."

"Yes," she said, "but though people die, love doesn't. Your dad and Nikkie's mom still love you from heaven, just like you both love them from down here. Only now you have even more love because you have Ethan."

He considered that and added cautiously. "And Nikkie has you?"

"Yes." She wasn't certain Nikkie would hold the same enthusiasm for the concept that Jason did. "And it doesn't matter to Ethan that he wasn't there when you were born, and it doesn't matter to me that Nikkie was born to another woman. I love her because now we're all a family. And it wouldn't matter if Ethan and I did have a baby, because we wouldn't love it more than we love you and Nikkie."

"So she was wrong." Jason seemed pleased by that possibility.

"She was mistaken," Beth corrected diplomatically. "It's a new situation for all of us, so it's easy to be confused about the way things will work. But I promise you that Ethan and I will always love you and Nikkie, even if we did have a baby."

He smiled, that problem solved. "Can I have a board to work on till Ethan picks us up?"

"Sure." Beth found him a board with a slight irregularity on one edge, and the box of odds and ends paint tubes she'd given him to use when she'd first set up her studio.

On a sudden impulse she drew two cats on a board with a pale yellow background, a fluffy gray Persian and a sleek calico with a black spot above the muzzle. She had the cats painted in an hour or so, then added pink collars on which she carefully printed their names with her fine-tipped brush—Simba and Cindy. Then she added Nikkie's name in mossy green block letters at the bottom of the board.

She made a few fine-lined flourishes for a border, then pushed the board aside to dry.

"That's cool, Mom!" Jason was her biggest fan. He jumped off his stool. "I'm gonna get my sign. We can put it up at Ethan's, can't we?" He ran across the studio to the small apartment they'd lived in before to retrieve his name plaque from his bedroom door. She saw the yellow kitchen wall through the door Jason had left open; it seemed like an eternity, she thought, since they'd lived there. Their lives had changed so completely.

Remembering her promise to Ethan, Beth called home. Nikkie answered.

"Hi," Beth said cheerfully. "It's Beth. I'm just checking to make sure everything's okay."

"Why wouldn't it be?" Nikkie said rudely.

"Because there's a man there with a broken leg," Beth replied patiently, "a woman who isn't really familiar with the house and a young woman who's helping to plan a play that's in a crisis over props. So my checking to make sure no one needs anything doesn't really seem out of line, does it?"

There was a moment's silence, and Beth could imagine Nikkie sticking her tongue out at the receiver but keeping any further rude remarks to herself because her father had insisted she be polite to her wicked stepmother.

"Zachary is fine," she said with rigid courtesy. "I know because he shouted at me to turn my music down. Joanne is fine. I know that because she told me that chocolate has empty calories and will give me zits."

Beth couldn't help but feel sympathy for the girl at home alone with the Richardses. "And how are you?"

she asked, her concern genuine. "Is there anything you need?"

"If you want to help me," Nikkie said with a despondent sigh, "you can find me medieval shields and weapons for twenty. Mr. Fogarty thought my foil-and-cardboard stuff wouldn't be convincing. I'm supposed to try to come up with something else."

"I'll look around the studio," Beth volunteered, "and see if I can find anything that'd help."

There was another silence, then Nikkie said politely but despairingly, "Thanks."

"No problem. See you in an hour or so. We'll bring home something for dinner."

"Don't bother," Nikkie said. "Joanne took a cab to the market and came back with all sorts of stuff. She's making pot roast for dinner."

"See? Everything has an upside."

"If you say so. Bye."

Beth rummaged through a stack of wooden shapes she'd cut out and hadn't had a chance to use. At last she found what she was looking for. It was shield-shaped and full-size. Pleased with herself, she took it to her table and began to trace a shape with pencil.

It was an hour later and she and Jason were admiring each other's work when a cheerful voice shouted from the doorway of her studio. "Bethie! How the hell are you?"

She turned to the studio's entrance to see a tall lanky figure standing there dressed in a white jumpsuit stained with paint. He had graying dark hair pulled back into a long curly ponytail. His eyes were pale blue, his cheekbones angular and his square chin had a cleft in it.

Rush Weston was too attractive for his own good,

and he bore the burden with a self-awareness Beth had never seen before in an adult. He was funny, charming, sometimes thoughtful, and always a brilliant sculptor, but he had the ego of a spoiled two-year-old.

"Hello, Rush," she said, meeting in the middle of the room to shake his hand.

He wrapped her into a crushing bear hug, instead. "Bethie, how are ya? Feels like it's been an age! I met Kelly at the coffee bar and she said she'd just rented a studio from you. So I thought I'd better get my deposit in before all the studios are taken."

Beth patted his shoulder, then pushed him firmly away. "No danger of that," she said. "Kelly insisted on giving me money because she thinks I need it. And she's painting her own space so she can get in earlier. Oh, and I've had the building inspector in since you looked around, and everythng's secure."

He nodded. "Good. Good. So if I paint my own space, I can get in early, too?"

"Sure. If you want to. We'll have to see how efficient the furnace is. I might have to get something bigger, which could take a little time. Can you put up with that?"

Rush snaked an arm around her shoulders and squeezed. "I'm unveiling my piece for the county's art association at the festival, and I'd like my studio set up here by then so everyone can come in and look around. And, baby, I can put up with an ice floe in my studio if it means I get to be near you."

Beth looked up at him and said with a certain relish, "Rush, I'm married."

He stared at her a moment, clearly stunned, then dropped his arm.

"I'm married," she repeated. "To Ethan Drum, sheriff of—"

"I know who he is," Rush said with a sharp downturn of his features. "Are you crazy? I thought you didn't want any part of marriage again."

"I didn't. He...changed my mind." That was true. She needed a husband and he was available and willing.

"He's going to let you keep this place?"

"Why wouldn't he?"

Rush wandered around the room, pausing to look at the boards spread out on her table. "I told you I've met the sheriff. Struck me as a hard nose. Doesn't believe in gray areas. Things are black or white. Not the kind of man an artist should tie up with."

"He isn't at all like that," Beth insisted.

"Maybe not now." Rush glanced up, warning in his eyes. "Now that he's landed you, I'll wager he becomes more demanding and possessive."

Beth made a sound of exasperation. "I'm not a fish, Rush. He didn't land me. He decided to spend his life with me—the way I am. He knows how I am about my work and he's willing to live with that."

"So he says."

"So he *is*."

"We'll see." He waved an index finger above the cat plaque she'd painted for Nikkie, then shook his head over the shield. "When are you going to stop doing this cutesy stuff and concentrate on *real* art?"

Beth bristled. She'd be the first to admit that the plaques weren't art, but she didn't have the luxury of being an art snob at this point. "They pay the bills, Weston," she said. "And if I'm going to be your landlord, don't pick on my stuff. I might raise your rent."

He turned back to her, his eyes brimming with the passion that always lay just under the surface. It was what made him a brilliant sculptor—and something of a Casanova. "Maybe we could make a deal where you take it out in trade." The lewd suggestion was made quietly and he tried to put his arms around her again.

Beth raised both her arms to block the attempt, so he simply caught her wrists, instead. "There's something between us, Bethie. You know it and I know it."

"You're right, Weston," Ethan's voice said lazily from the doorway. "The something between you is me."

CHAPTER ELEVEN

"I'M SURE that little scene played really well for your in-laws' detective," Ethan said as he pulled the Blazer up to a stoplight. His profile had all the animation of a figure on Mount Rushmore.

Beth was growing tired of explaining. She'd done it once when Ethan walked into her studio to find Rush with his hands on her. She'd done it a second time after Rush had left. And she'd done it a third time while Ethan had helped Jason on with his jacket and walked him out to the Blazer.

"If I explain it all a fourth time," she asked, a weary, slightly antagonistic note in her voice, "do you think you might actually listen?"

He turned to look at her, anger bright in his eyes. Before he swung his gaze back to the road, she saw something else there she found a little thrilling. Jealousy.

The light changed and he accelerated with more speed than necessary. "I heard you all three times," he said as the tires screeched. "It still doesn't make sense."

Swallowing an angry retort, Beth glanced over her shoulder at her son, who was sitting quietly, his eyes uncertain. She gave him a reassuring smile, then turned back to Ethan.

"Can we save this for a more private moment?" she asked stiffly.

"Yes," he said without looking away from the road. "But we *will* get to it."

"Oh, yes," she said, perversely unwilling to let him have the last word. "We will."

He gave her a dark glance, which was soundless but served as the last word, anyway.

As they marched from the driveway to the house, Beth caught Ethan's arm and pulled him to a stop. He turned to her, his eyes glowering with temper and impatience.

"I was just going to suggest," she said calmly, dropping her hand, "that you try not to look quite so much as though you intend to eat us all for dinner. Joanne and Zachary saw the four of us leave the house this morning snarling at each other. If we come home the same way, it might not matter what their detective reports. They'll be sure our marriage is doomed, anyway."

She was right. Which only served to irritate Ethan further.

He'd lain stoically awake beside her for two nights while she'd wrapped herself around him in her sleep and drove him to the brink of insanity. But except for a few moments of general irritability, he hadn't complained.

Then he'd walked into her studio and found her in the arms of a former client of the Butler County Jail. She hadn't appeared to be offering much resistance.

Well. Maybe it was time to stop being patient.

But not in front of her in-laws. Jason was standing between him and Beth now, looking anxiously from one to the other, wondering, Ethan was sure, if his life was going to fall apart. If his mother's three-day marriage was about to end and launch him into the custody of his grandparents, after all.

"You're absolutely right," Ethan said with a forced amiability. Then he pulled the back door open and gestured Jason inside. "Come on, buddy." He continued to hold the door for Beth.

Her expression remained icy for a moment, then with a toss of her head, she swept past him with a smile and a "Thank you, darling."

"There you are," Joanne said, meeting them at the door. She wore a flowered apron over her slacks and shirt and wielded a meat fork. "Potatoes are almost done. You just have time to wash your hands."

The aroma filling the kitchen would have soothed Ethan's mood if he hadn't had to follow Beth's shapely derriere up the stairs and into his bedroom.

While she tossed her jacket onto the bed and went into the bathroom to wash her hands, he hung up his uniform jacket and threw his shirt at the hamper. He pulled on a dark blue sweatshirt and was changing his uniform pants for a pair of jeans when Beth walked out of the bathroom.

"All yours," she said, her tone brittle. She carried her jacket to the closet, and he noted her quick glance at him as he drew up the jeans and zipped them. Her cheeks pinkened, and she looked away.

"You're embarrassed at seeing me dress," he challenged, heading for the bathroom, "yet you can let another man hold you in front of your son and be comfortable with that?"

He concentrated on washing his hands, hearing her firm footsteps come around the bed to the bathroom door. "First of all," she said, her voice breathy with anger, "for explanation number *four*—" this last word was spoken very loudly "—I did not let him hold me. He'd tried to, so I raised both arms to prevent him and he caught my wrists. That was when you walked in."

He glanced at her as he reached for a towel, his eyes rejecting the explanation—for the fourth time.

"And Jason knows Rush. He knows we're... friends, that Rush tends to be physically demonstrative and that it means nothing. I'm sure he didn't give it a thought."

Ethan tossed the towel over the rod without comment and stalked past her into the bedroom and out to the hallway, Beth following. He noticed Zachary's partially open door and went to it, intending to say hello. But Zachary was sound asleep, his leg in the colorful blue cast propped on a pair of pillows, the pajama leg trimmed to midthigh. A sock had been fitted over his partially bare foot.

Ethan pulled the door closed without latching it so that if Zach called out, he would still be heard.

But Ethan didn't want to risk Beth's father-in-law overhearing their argument.

Cooperating, Beth lowered her voice as she trailed Ethan to the stairs. "And I looked away when you were pulling on your jeans," she said as though they hadn't been interrupted, "because it occurred to me that you have nice muscular legs, and I was too angry with you to entertain a complimentary thought."

He stopped in his tracks at that admission and she almost collided with him. He turned to look at her, hands on his hips, torn between anger and pleasure that she found *something* about him appealing.

She stood quietly in front of him, apparently as ensnared by the moment as he was. Then she angled her chin and added haughtily, "Unfortunately your brain seems to be all muscle, too. Let's move it. Joanne doesn't like to have to wait dinner for anyone."

Ethan could have eaten a mastodon raw—and not because he was hungry. He couldn't remember ever feeling so elementally angry. Even when a perp was resisting arrest and started swinging, he was able to keep his cool and react only in department-approved ways.

But seeing Beth being handled by Rush Weston, then listening to her defensive responses to his questions about the incident, had done something to his equanimity. He didn't have the control over his emotions he usually had—and he didn't like that at all.

During dinner he asked Joanne about Zachary, complimented her on the excellent dinner, asked Nikkie about her day and learned that the drama teacher had been less than enthusiastic about her shield and weapon cardboard prototypes for the Winter Festival play.

"But Beth was going to look for something in her studio," she said with a grudgingly hopeful glance across the table.

"Oh," Beth said, pushing back from the table. "I did bring something home for you to look at. I was so ang—" She stopped, obviously not intending to let her ex-mother-in-law know about her anger at Ethan. She continued with a smile, "I was so anxious for dinner that I forgot it in the car. We could smell the pot roast even in the driveway," she said to Joanne. Then to Nikkie, "I'll go get it. Excuse me a minute."

Jason, seated beside Ethan, paused in his hearty attack on his plate and asked eagerly, "Can we have Taylor Bridges for dinner tomorrow?"

Ethan grinned at him, grateful for the boy's cheerful presence. "You think he'd be good to eat?"

Jason frowned while Nikkie groaned at Ethan's joke. Suddenly the boy caught on and laughed.

"No. I mean can he come over here for dinner. Mom said it was okay, but I should check with you 'cause you might have a meeting."

Tomorrow was Tuesday. That meant a county commissioners' meeting. "I do have to go to the courthouse for a couple of hours, but you can have him over even if I'm not here." He turned to Joanne. "That is, if your grandmother doesn't mind cooking for one more."

Joanne actually smiled. "Of course not."

"No." Jason was adamant. "You *have* to be here. That's why he's coming."

"What do you mean?"

"'Cause he doesn't believe you're my dad now. He thinks I'm lying. So Mom says the best thing to do is show him."

Beth returned with something large wrapped in white paper. Ethan had been so furious when they'd left her studio he hadn't noticed she'd been carrying it.

She'd caught the end of Jason's report and now met Ethan's gaze with an apologetic look. It wasn't quite convincing, because her eyes still snapped with annoyance.

"Taylor's been giving him a hard time for months," she said. "So let's have him come for dinner and see that Jason isn't lying."

"Okay, then let's make it Wednesday," Ethan said. "Is that all right with you, Joanne?"

"Perfectly," she replied, passing platters around the table for seconds.

Ethan half expected Nikkie to react negatively to an attempt to prove he was now Jason's father, too, but she was concentrating on the package Beth was unwrapping.

Shaped like a medieval shield, it had been fashioned out of half-inch-thick board and divided into quarters, the upper left and lower right painted blue with three gold fleurs-de-lis, and the upper right and lower left painted red with three gold lions guardant.

Nikkie's mouth fell open in awe. Ethan's annoyance with Beth was overridden with pleasure and satisfaction at what she'd done. It was a hard-won first step in building a relationship with his daughter.

"Wow," Nikkie breathed, getting up to inspect it.

"I'll have to look up the coat of arms of Henry V to be accurate," Beth said, "but I think it's something like this. And we can check out the coats of arms for Henry's nobles. These are easy enough to make if you think they'll work. I can cut them out, draw the patterns, and you and the drama club can paint them."

Nikkie took the mock-up of a shield in her hands and inspected it in detail, then looked at Beth in astonishment.

"Mr. Fogarty will think this is brilliant!" she said, her usually careful pose of disinterest dissolving in the face of such an impressive solution to her problem of props.

"How would we hold them?"

"Two leather straps on the back, I think," Beth said. "One off to the side to slip an arm through, and another toward the other side for your hand to grip." She looked at Ethan. "That's right, isn't it?"

He nodded, guessing she'd consulted him not because she needed to, but because she was feeling generous in her success. "Yes, Madam Armorer. I believe that's right. Of course you could use something less expensive than leather. Vinyl or some kind of plastic. No one'll notice from the audience."

"And I have a heavy-duty stapler for putting them on." Beth touched Nikkie's arm in a manner not intended to be maternal but simply friendly. "You take it to school and see what the consensus is. If your drama teacher and the club like it, we'll go into production."

Nikkie was still staring at the shield, touching a fingertip to the beautifully executed lion guardant. "I will," she said. "Thanks."

"Sure." Beth pulled out the sign she'd made with Nikkie's cats on it. "I was making these for the fair and thought you might like one."

Nikkie studied it wordlessly and Beth asked with a wince, "Too childish?"

Nikkie shook her head. "No. Not at all. Thanks. I really like it."

Beth went back to her chair. "I'm sorry," she said to everyone else around the table. "I didn't mean to interrupt dinner."

"Can you make me a shield?" Jason asked eagerly. "With Buzz Lightyear on it?"

"A wooden shield," Ethan said, holding the platter of meat and vegetables for the boy while he forked more food onto his plate, "is a little primitive for Buzz. Shouldn't he have a cloaking device or something?"

Before Jason could reply, a deep voice bellowed from upstairs. "Jo! I'm starving!"

Joanne smiled wryly at Beth as she pushed herself away from the table to make a plate for Zachary. "Maybe you could make me one with a wooden spoon on it," she said. "Or a knife and fork. There's a brown Betty in the refrigerator if someone wants to dish it up."

Ethan cleared the table and Beth loaded the dishwasher while Joanne took a plate upstairs to Zachary and remained there. Nikkie and Jason had gone to their own rooms to do homework.

Ethan put the small amount of leftovers into a plastic container and handed Beth the platter. The kitchen had taken on a kind of peaceful ambiance he wouldn't have thought possible, considering his and Beth's anger at each other, his daughter's usual moody defensiveness and Joanne's aggressive personality.

But something had happened at dinner. There'd been an unexpected and surprisingly successful give-and-take that came close to creating a familylike atmosphere.

Joanne had been happy to have people to cook for while she was stranded in Cobbler's Crossing with a temporarily invalid husband, and everyone else had been most appreciative of her meals. Nikkie had been astounded and grateful for the shield Beth had produced to help her with props for the play, not to mention her delight at the sign for her door. Jason had been happy when Ethan agreed to let him invite Taylor Bridges to dinner, and Ethan had been gratified by the boy's obvious pride in having him for a stepfather.

Peace reigned everywhere, but he wasn't going to be happy until he was sure Beth had no feelings for Rush Weston. And he was going to see that she wasn't happy, either.

"So you're telling me that Weston's in the habit of putting his hands on you," he asked, resuming the argument with a vengeance, "with your consent?"

As he gathered up place mats and tossed them into a hamper in the hallway, he heard the slam of the dishwater door, then the rush of water as Beth started the wash cycle.

When he came back into the kitchen, she was standing in the middle of the floor with an expression that could have ignited fuel. She pointed to the back door. "I'd like to speak to you outside," she said, her voice barely steady.

Even though the subject had really been settled hours ago, he still wasn't ready to give in. He hated Weston and felt outrageously possessive about Beth, and he was spoiling for a fight.

"Certainly." He pulled the back door open for her and followed her onto the back porch.

"I would have thought," she said, turning to face him the moment the door closed behind them, "that a man who'd had such a happy marriage for all those years would understand a little something about trust."

That punched a hole right in the middle of his anger, but it was easy to fill it up again.

"I never found Diana being groped by another man," he said. He knew he was being unfair, but he wanted convincing, damn it.

She put a hand to her forehead and he saw her lips move unsteadily. Regret brimmed in him, fighting the anger for space.

"I know Diana was a paragon," Beth said, lowering her hand to her throat and tugging at the high collar of her red sweater, "and I'm just a woman you think is using you just to hold on to her son. You probably imagine that this isn't really a marriage, and therefore I don't feel called upon to be faithful.''

That was precisely the fear he'd experienced when he'd walked into her studio and found Weston there, touching her.

"And I'm sexually repressed," she admitted, looking him in the eye, "which means that after two nights of sleeping alone...well, not alone but apart, you're thinking you can be patient until doomsday and you'll get nothing out of this marriage."

That rankled. He sat on the railing near the porch support and leaned back against it. "I might think that," he said, "if all I wanted out of this marriage was sex. But it isn't. That's why I hated seeing you with Weston."

"I wasn't *with* Weston," she said, a desperate note in her voice. "I mean, I was physically beside him, but there was no 'groping' and no emotional tie that makes me *with* him, except a sort of casual friendship. He came to ask about renting his space early because he'd run into Kelly, and she'd given me a deposit this morning. They both want to be in and set up for visitors by the Winter Festival, so they're doing their own painting."

"Beth," he said, knowing he was the one who had to be conciliatory here, though not about his opinions on Weston. "I told you I picked him up at a brawl on the waterfront. He was drunk and abusive. I don't like the idea of your life entangled with his."

She moved closer and leaned a shoulder against the post. "I met him when I first arrived here, and you'll notice that I bear no evidence of bodily harm." She looked tired and strained. He thought he could have refuted her claim, but didn't. "I'm sorry you don't like him, but he's an eccentric. I know he drinks sometimes, but that doesn't matter to me because—" the next four words were delivered with slow emphasis "—*we are not involved*. When I first moved here, he gave me a job assisting in his sculpture class and introduced me to other artists, who are now my friends. I promise you that's all he is to me."

"Did you tell him you were married?"

"Yes." She smiled thinly. "You'll be pleased to know he's no fonder of you than you are of him."

"I don't give a rip about him," Ethan said, hooking an arm around her waist and pulling her to him. "You're the one I care about."

She rested a forearm on his shoulder and asked quietly, "If that is true, why won't you trust me?"

"It *is* true," he said, pulling her closer. "And I trust you, but I don't trust him."

"If you trust *me*," she said quietly, clasping her fingers behind his neck, "you don't have to worry about him. He's going to rent a space from me and that's it. So you can stop yelling at me."

He nuzzled under her hair and kissed the sensitive skin behind her ear. "I'm sorry," he said, planting another kiss, his brain a little muddled by her rose scent. "I'm not usually a man who yells. I'm just... grumpy."

"Hm." She rubbed her cheek against his, then kissed his eyelids, first one, then the other. "Is there a cure for that?"

He groaned with the effort to stop from telling her. "Just...thinking positive, I guess," he said.

Beth knew the answer he withheld and decided it

was time she took action. She squeezed him to her and kissed his forehead. "I have a positive thought."

He looked into her eyes with suspicion. "You do?"

"Yes." She leaned her cheek against his forehead and prayed she wouldn't disappoint him. "I want to make love to you tonight."

He didn't move a muscle and she couldn't see his face, but she felt the reaction in him, the punch of one erratic heartbeat, the sudden tension of every muscle.

He drew his head back so he could look into her eyes. "Why?" he asked. She smiled in response, knowing he wasn't interested in lovemaking as a way of making up after a quarrel.

She gave him a quick kiss, thinking what a turn-on kindness was. A curious loosening was taking place within her—strange, she thought, after they'd just had a fairly serious disagreement.

Then she realized it was because he hadn't stalked away from her and left her to absorb the blame. He'd stated his position, fought it out, and when she'd convinced him he was mistaken, he'd apologized.

This was entirely new in her man-woman experience. She felt as though all doors and windows had been thrown open, and she couldn't help the soft laugh that escaped.

"You told me when I was eager to make love with you that I should let you know," she said. "That when it seemed like a really good idea to me that it was time. Well—" she kissed him again "—it's time. Except that we have to wait until everyone's asleep."

He winced and let his head fall back against the post with a thunk. "What time is it?" he asked.

She glanced at her watch. "Seven-thirty-seven."

"Oh, God," he groaned. "Three hours. Maybe more."

"Anticipation should heighten the experience," she said philosophically, giddy with the rush of freedom she felt.

"I vote we sedate everyone, cats included."

This time she kissed him slowly, seductively, letting him know with the deep sensuous exploration of her tongue that she'd never been more serious about anything. "We'll just wait. And think about how it'll be."

The door from the kitchen opened suddenly, and Joanne stood in the doorway. "There you are," she said, then noting their tangled pose, said apologetically, "Never mind. It isn't anything that can't wait."

"What do you need?" Beth asked, thinking talk was cheap. She might try to convince Ethan of her confidence in her ability to be an enthusiastic love partner, and that the three hours or so that would have to pass until then would only heighten the experience, but she knew she would have to have something practical to do in the interim to keep herself from panicking. She did feel a new freedom and knew he'd given it to her. She was just a little concerned about her ability to give back.

Both she and Ethan straightened and headed for the door.

"Zachary's feeling a little better," Joanne said as they walked into the kitchen. "He isn't needing as much pain medication, so he's getting bored. I was wondering if you had books or magazines he could read."

"How about if I bring the TV and VCR from my room into yours?" Ethan asked.

"But what'll you do?" Joanne asked.

Beth caught the quick amusement in Ethan's eyes and bit her lip. "We're going to bed early," he said. "It's been a rough day."

"But what about tomorrow?" she persisted. "I hate to deprive you of—"

Ethan shook his head. "We hardly ever watch it, anyway. And if there's anything we really want to see, we'll go downstairs."

"Well, if you're sure..."

"I'm sure."

While Ethan moved the TV and VCR and reconnected them in Zachary's room, Beth made a cup of tea to calm her nerves.

Jason appeared with the sign for his bedroom door. "Mom, can you help me hang this?" he asked.

At any other time she might have begged off until she'd finished her tea, but tonight she looked forward to gainful employment. "We need a hammer and a nail," she said, wondering if Ethan kept them in the basement.

"Ethan's got his tools upstairs," Jason informed her. "He brought 'em up to move the television. They're watching a cowboy movie."

Beth walked with him upstairs. "You haven't been bothering Grandpa, have you?"

"They told me to go in," he said, looking offended, "'cause it's a guy movie."

"I see. I'm sorry." She ruffled his hair, enjoying his pleasure in being considered one of the guys.

Beth was pleased and flattered to see that Nikkie had hung up her sign.

The sounds of guns and galloping horses came loudly from the television in Zachary's room. A large metal toolbox stood against the wall just outside the door.

Beth peered around the door and saw Zachary propped up against the pillows, and Ethan sitting in the chair by the bed, his legs stretched out before him.

"There's nobody like the Duke," Zachary said, his eyes riveted to the screen. "Jo always insisted he was going to be her second husband." He grinned, still staring at the screen. "Smart man checked out before it could happen."

Beth waved her hand to claim Ethan's attention.

He walked around the bed and came into the hall, his eyes alight with humor and passion. "Tell me we've moved up the time," he said, catching her hands. Then he noticed Jason standing beside her.

A rueful acceptance replaced the desire in his eyes. The frustration was something they shared, though hers was mixed with more than a little trepidation.

He put a hand to Jason's shoulder. "What's up, Jase?"

"We need a hammer and a nail," the boy said. "I want to put this on my door." He held up his Buzz Lightyear sign. "Mom made it for me before we moved here."

"Ethan," Beth said, "if you can just point me to a hammer and a nail, I can put it up."

Ethan squatted by the toolbox, lifted the top tray, reached into the bottom and handed up a hammer. "You won't hit your thumb or anything?" he teased.

She pretended to swing the hammer at his head. "I probably use woodworking tools more than you do. At the studio I have saws, sanders, dremels, lathes, you name it, and I have yet to lose a thumbnail or a pinkie finger."

He straightened and waggled an eyebrow. "Ooh. I love it when you talk tough."

"Ethan, come and see this!" Zachary shouted.

Beth pushed him toward the room. "Go. We'll rendezvous later."

He sighed and kissed her again, his eyes lazy with desire. "Words I've longed to hear," he whispered.

Beth hung the plaque with several experienced strokes of the hammer. Jason's pleasure in it made her feel as though it should have required much more effort.

She went into his room to encourage him to get ready for bed and was a little horrified to discover that in less than a week he'd managed to make it look like a warehouse for boy's clothing—one without hangers.

"Jason," she scolded gently, picking up jeans, shirts and underwear off the floor, "you know better than this. Underwear and shirts and dirty jeans go in the hamper. Stuff that's still clean should be hung in the closet."

He followed her as she gathered his things. "But I can't reach the hanger thing."

"The rod," she said, folding clean jeans at the zipper and draping them over a hanger. She was about to suggest he stand on a chair, but a maternal second sense told her that wasn't a good idea. "Then you can put things on your chair and I'll hang them up for you until we can put in a lower rod."

She collected underwear and carried it to the bathroom hamper. He waited for her in the doorway of his room, a pair of battered tennis shoes in his arms. "Are you happy here, too?" he asked, appearing anxious for the right response. "I mean, you weren't really at first, but you are now, aren't you?"

"I'm happy wherever you are," she said, taking a jacket off the bedpost and hanging it up in the closet.

"I mean you're happy you got married to Ethan," Jason said in exasperation.

A man in the making, she thought wryly, direct and insistent.

But at least she could give him the answer he wanted. "Yes, I'm happy I married Ethan."

"And Nikkie's starting to like you, too."

Beth plucked a pair of pajamas off another bedpost and handed them to him. "We might have to wait a little while for that to really happen. She liked the shield I made, but I'm not sure she likes me yet."

Jason took the pajamas, then wrapped his arms around her waist. "She will 'cause you're a great mom," he said, his eyes alight with a contentment she hadn't seen there in some time. "Aren't we lucky I ran away and all those campers were lost so that the only one who could come and look for me was Ethan?"

He lowered his voice and glanced toward his open bedroom door. "And aren't we lucky I lied to Grandma and Grandpa, and then Ethan helped me?"

Beth almost hated to be reminded of how their situation had come about. It made it seem so fragile, and the possibility that it could all dissolve one day was something she didn't like to contemplate. Particularly tonight.

"We're lucky nobody's caught us," she whispered back conspiratorially.

Jason seemed to like that and ran off giggling to take a shower and get ready for bed.

CHAPTER TWELVE

BY TEN O'CLOCK Jason and Nikkie were asleep, and Zachary had turned down the sounds of battle in deference to the late hour.

Beth piled her hair in a loose knot on top of her head and took a shower, wondering where Ethan was. He'd left Zachary's room a short while ago and she'd heard him go down the stairs, but he had yet to return to their bedroom.

Heart thudding nervously, she spritzed cologne and slipped on a berry-colored silk nightie Kelly had given her years ago but she'd never worn. The color made her flushed cheeks appear to be on fire, and she put her hands over them to cool them.

"You look like you're about to ignite," she told herself with a moan.

"You are," a quiet male voice said from the doorway.

She spun around. Ethan stood there in jeans, barechested and barefoot, a tulip glass of something bubbly in each hand. His hair was damp, suggesting he'd showered in the other bathroom. A mild frown creased his brow. "Second thoughts?" he asked.

"No," she denied, moving toward him. "A little nervous, though."

He smiled and handed her a glass. "Me, too," he

said with a sincerity that turned her spine to oatmeal and made her heart swell with love.

He beckoned her out of the bathroom and toward the bed, where he'd turned back the blankets and banked the pillows against the headboard. He held her glass while she climbed into the bed and sat against the comfortable backrest he'd made.

He followed, drawing her into his arm and tipping the rim of his wineglass against hers in a toast. "To learning to communicate."

She drank to that, then leaned against him. His warm shoulder was muscled and smooth under her cheek. She tipped her head back to kiss the underside of his jaw. "That means 'I love you' in…in Romanesque," she said fancifully. His arm around her and his easy manner were beginning to banish her nervousness. She watched his eyes darken at her admission and it was a moment before he whispered, "God, I love you, too." Then he cleared his throat and smiled.

"Romanesque? Really?" He kissed the top of her head. "I thought Romanesque was a style of architecture."

She made an airy gesture with her glass. "It's a mistake everyone makes. It's actually a language."

"Ah. A romance language?"

"No." She turned her face into his chest and kissed his pectoral muscle. She felt his heartbeat accelerate and her own race to match it. "The language of romance. There's a difference."

"I see." He sipped his wine. "And you're fluent in this?"

"Not really," she admitted, leaning her cheek

against him again. "It wasn't spoken where I lived before, so I've had little chance to practice."

"Well." He ran a hand tenderly up and down her bare arm. "I don't want to one-up you, but I happen to be a Romanesque scholar."

She smiled. "I guessed that."

"Yes." She heard the light clink of his glass against the top of the bedside table. "I have a Ph.D. in it. Unfortunately I've also had little chance to practice. But I'd be happy to share what I know." He took her glass from her and placed it beside his. When he turned to her, his eyes were dark with intent. "Together I'll bet we could write the definitive text on it."

She slid down into the bed, her heart thudding, and he leaned sideways over her to rearrange the pillows under her head. Then his eyes met hers and she saw everything he was in them—tough, strong, gentle, funny. And at the moment she held his complete attention, and the realization gave her both profound comfort and unbearable excitement.

She put her hands to his face and rubbed a thumb gently over his upper lip. "I know how to say, 'I'm glad I found you.' Want to hear?"

"Please," he replied softly.

She pulled his head down to her and kissed him with all the tender passion he inspired in her. She parted her lips, he opened his mouth, their tongues met and stroked...and she finally had to draw back to catch her breath.

"Excellent pronunciation," he said, his voice low and a little rough. "What else can you say?"

She traced the line of his jaw with her fingertips, then trailed her index finger down the middle of his throat to his collarbone.

"I can say, 'You've changed my life,'" she suggested.

"Mm." He ran a hand down her side, over her hip to the top of her thigh. "I'd like to know how to say that, too."

She felt the warmth of his hand through the thin layer of fabric, and a frisson of anticipation arced through her.

She leaned up to kiss the base of his throat, then dropped a series of soft kisses down the middle of his chest. She pushed away from the mattress, forcing him backward until he lay on his back on the bedspread and she kneeled over him.

Ethan felt her lips and her breath at the waistband of his jeans and prayed that his cardiovascular system was up to this. Letting her remain in control so that he didn't frighten her was almost more than he could do.

With the denim blocking her path, she strung kisses across his waist from his left side to his right. He couldn't withhold a groan.

"Do you want," she asked on a whispered breath, "to try to...repeat that after me?"

Everything inside him roared, but his reply was a throaty, "Yes, I would."

He reached under the hem of her gown and moved his hands slowly up the backs of her smooth legs, then down and up again, inching his way to the warm flesh of her bottom.

She eased her weight on top of him, buried her face against the side of his and lay still as he explored her.

Her long sigh fractured as she finally sat up on him to pull off her gown. The action took the loose clip in her hair with it, and the dark mass tumbled to her shoulders, curly and fragrant.

He reached up to touch it, but she caught his hand and brought it to her breast. The small mound filled his palm, and he felt its tip pearl.

"This means," she said, her voice a little unsteady, "'You've changed *me*.'"

He slipped his hands around her and, sitting up, eased her onto her back among the pillows.

He kissed the slight convexity of her stomach, her hipbones, the juncture of torso and thigh.

Her hands at the waistband of his jeans unzipped them. He sat up to push his jeans down and off, and the instant he was free of them, she reached for his arm to draw him back to her.

He lay beside her and pulled the blankets over them. She pushed herself against him and bent her knee, rubbing it along his thigh as her hands moved down his back and over his hip.

"This means 'I need you,'" she said, her whisper a little feverish. She nipped at his shoulder.

He caught her in the crook of his arm and held her to the mattress when she tried to wriggle against him. She stroked a hand over his belly and downward, but he caught her fingers and stopped her, enfolding her hand in his and carrying it back to her waist.

"Now I have a few things to say," he murmured softly. She settled back with a languorous smile. He stroked a hand down her abdomen and placed it possessively right where she longed for his touch.

Beth was certain she would explode. Her heart couldn't beat this fast, her breath couldn't come in such shallow gasps, her nerves couldn't be stretched this tight without snapping.

He dipped a finger inside her, then found the spot Steve had never believed was there, and said, his lips just above hers, his other arm holding her to him, "This means 'I love you and you're everything to me. Everything.'"

His clever hand began to move, and as she absorbed the wonder of those words, pleasure rushed at her headlong so that the declaration still echoed when fulfillment overtook her.. The sensory impact of the miracle created by love and understanding given and taken pinned her to the mattress with its force. It filled her, bathed her, and just when she thought it might drown her, she rose with a gasp of astonishment, and let it wash over her in breathtaking waves.

She opened her eyes to see Ethan's pleased and slightly self-satisfied expression. Then she closed both hands over him and felt her own satisfaction when his expression turned from smug to seduced, and he grew ready under her touch.

"This means," she said as he moved quickly over her, "'Let me be as generous as you are.'"

Even as he lifted her hips and entered her, she saw his eyes react to her eagerness to please him. She closed her eyes and ran her hands up his arms, hoping that it would be as good for him as it had been for her.

He drove into her and she lost all ability to concentrate. Pleasure rose again all around her, and just as she'd begun to suspect that she'd somehow gotten this wrong, that her intention had been to give Ethan the same delicious pleasure he'd given her, he burst inside her with a cry that he silenced in her hair.

She'd done it. She'd given him pleasure. The past wasn't her fault.

As his body pulsed over her, she came alive again like the molten middle of the earth. In astonishment, she clung to him as they shuddered together for long, long moments.

As the ripples of pleasure cleared, Beth burst into tears.

Ethan cradled her to him, his voice filled with concern. "What?" he demanded. "What?"

How did a woman tell a man, she wondered, that he'd just restored her faith in herself as a sexual being? How did she explain that though she was logical and clear-thinking in every other way, she'd allowed a selfish lover to convince her that the unsatisfying results of his lovemaking had been her fault?

Ethan tried to ease her away to look at her, but she put a hand over her eyes. "Nothing," she said, sniffing. "Nothing. I'm fine."

There was a sharp pain on her left buttock. She yelped and dropped her hand, staring at him in stunned surprise. He'd pinched her!

"In Romanesque," he said gravely, "that's 'Don't lie to me.' What is it? Did I hurt you? Upset you?"

And suddenly the momentous revelation she'd just had about herself seemed to lose all importance in this very sane and comfortable world Ethan had provided. Her tears turned to laughter and she wrapped her arms around his neck.

"Oh, good," he said, turning them so that she lay in the hollow of his shoulder, "I've married a split personality."

She hitched a leg up over his and kissed his throat. "But I'm multilingual. You liked my Romanesque."

"I did indeed. I, however, am single-minded, and I want to know what you were crying about."

"They were good tears," she said, snuggling closer. "Not bad ones."

He drew her arm across his waist. "Great. Then it should be easy to explain to me."

She did. It didn't take very long, and it was like being purged of the past. He listened, understood, commiserated.

"But as of tonight," he said, "it no longer matters. That's over, and I think we proved—" she heard the smile in his voice "—rather forcefully, I might add, that he was wrong and I was right."

"I love you," she said, suddenly exhausted.

"Brilliantly." He stroked her hair, then kissed it. "I love you, too."

"Also brilliantly. Jason said we were lucky."

LIFE WAS IDEAL. For the next week Beth worked like a fiend in her studio and made love with Ethan like a wild woman every night.

The night Taylor Bridges came to dinner, Ethan took the boys to the gym with him afterward, then dropped Taylor at home.

Jason was the picture of self-satisfaction when he and Ethan returned. As Beth tucked Jason in that night, he said that Ethan called him "son" when they were shooting baskets, and that later, when Ethan took them for ice cream and Jason and Taylor went to the bathroom, Taylor told him he was the luckiest kid in the whole world.

Beth thought he probably was.

She wished she was doing as well with Nikkie as Ethan was doing with Jason. Yes, Nikkie was visibly pleased with the shields, but her friends from the drama club, who came nightly to work on them, were warmer to Beth than she was.

Nikkie was polite and no longer overtly hostile, but except when her friends were over, she kept to herself and showed Beth no sign of friendship.

Zachary was comfortable with his crutches by the end of the week, and Joanne declared it was time to return to Seattle.

"You're welcome to stay a few more days," Beth said, "if you think it would—"

"No," Joanne insisted. She looked from Beth to Ethan with a new ease in her manner. "We appreciate your hospitality and your generosity, but you have to get back to your routines and we have to get home. We've enjoyed watching your progress with the props for Nikkie's play, though, Beth. And of course, we'd like to be here for the opening of the cannery over the Winter Festival weekend."

"Please come back for it," Ethan said. "We'll try to get along without your cooking until then."

Joanne tried not to look too pleased, but Beth could see it was an effort.

They left on Sunday morning, and Beth and Ethan made love all afternoon by the fire in the family room. Nikkie and her friends were rehearsing the play at school, and Jason was spending the afternoon at Taylor Bridges's.

On Monday evening the blissful peace was shattered.

Beth had put in a good day at the studio. Ethan had helped her pack up the clay pots in the basement and transport them to the cannery. She'd spent the day washing them and giving them all coats of brightly colored background paint.

She and Ethan and Jason had gone for burgers after work because Nikkie had stayed late at school to rehearse, and Ethan had a Search and Rescue meeting after dinner. Ethan had dropped Beth and Jason at home and given her a lingering kiss goodbye and a whispered promise to be home early.

Jason turned on the television and Beth puttered about the kitchen, making herself a cup of tea and running the dishwasher. The house was quiet without Ethan and Nikkie, she noticed, thinking how quickly and closely their lives had become entwined. Even though Nikkie seemed to do her best to keep her distance, Beth found herself caring and worrying about the girl and wishing she could discover some magic way to bridge the gap between them.

There was a knock at the back door. Beth opened it to find Brodie standing there in a brown tweed sports jacket over a tab-collared denim shirt and casual brown slacks. In one hand he held a rather tousled mixed bouquet of flowers. He looked handsome but angry and stormed past her into the kitchen.

Apparently remembering his manners, he stopped in the middle of the room and said with an apologetic twist of his lips and a thrust of the flowers toward her, "Hi. Are you busy?"

"Not at all," she replied, closing the door. "But Ethan's at a meeting tonight."

He jammed his hands into his pants pockets. "Good. I wanted to talk to you."

"Ah...sure." She looked doubtfully at the flowers. "These are...for me?"

"Why not?" he asked defensively.

Okay. She decided to simply coast until she could

figure out what was happening here. She pointed him to the table. "Sit down. Can I make you a cup of tea?"

He looked uncertain for a moment, then nodded. "Okay," he said finally, then held up large-fingered hands permanently stained in the lines and hollows with grease and oil and whatever else mechanics dealt with. "Just don't give it to me in anything delicate."

Beth laughed as she rummaged through the cupboard for something to put the flowers in. She finally decided on a teapot with a chipped spout. She filled it with water and set the flowers in it, wondering what had happened to them. They were beautiful, but crinkled and bruised.

"Not to worry," she said. "We seem to be big on sheriff's-office mugs. Sit down, Brodie. Milk and sugar?"

He pulled out a chair and sat. "I don't know," he admitted. "I've never had tea before."

She stopped in the process of opening a teabag's protective paper envelope. "You're kidding. Well, I can make a pot of coffee if you prefer."

"No." He waved a hand dismissively. "This is my day for doing things I'm not used to."

Beth filled the mug with water and brought it to him.

"That sounds a little ominous," she said, sitting opposite him with her cup. "Do I want to know what you've done today?"

He leaned away from the table, crossed one ankle over the other leg and studied the ceiling tiles overhead. "I called in sick," he said, then quickly added when Beth began to express concern, "I wasn't, I just told my guys I was sick so they wouldn't guess I was being an idiot."

It was on the tip of her tongue to ask why, but she held off. He seemed to be collecting his thoughts, and judging by the storm in his eyes and the complete absence of his usual good humor, she guessed they weren't pleasant.

"Then I got a haircut," he continued, "went to Buckley's and bought this jacket,"

"Which looks very dapper," she interrupted.

He gave her a glance she found difficult to interpret, then leaned forward over the table and drew the steaming mug toward him. "Thanks. I'm giving it to Ethan. And this shirt with the dumb collar. I feel like I should have a handlebar mustache."

Beth was beginning to suspect where this was going. She propped her elbow on the table and leaned her chin in the palm of her hand. "I think that's the appeal of those shirts for women. Victorian men wore something like it under those old, stiff celluloid collars. But...I'm guessing Kelly didn't like it."

He looked momentarily surprised, then took a sip of his tea and shook his head. "Kelly never saw it," he said. "I went by her place tonight to see if she'd like to go to dinner. She was packing up stuff from her studio to move into your cannery. She hardly even looked at me."

"Well..." Beth struggled between an inherent preference for diplomacy in such matters and the undeniable effectiveness of the plain and simple truth. She did her best to combine both. "I think the night of the wedding, you left her with the impression that... you're not really interested in a relationship."

He drank more tea, then put the cup down, his expression moody. "I thought I wasn't," he said, leaning back in his chair. He folded his arms over his chest and let his head fall back. "I once had a relationship with this woman I met when she and her father were driving from Portland to their vacation home across the river. He owns Techno-Ware in Portland. Their Rolls-Royce broke down just this side of the bridge. It was only a hose, and I went to them to fix it because, I'm not sure, but I think you'd probably go to mechanics' hell for towing a Rolls."

Beth smiled, but Brodie didn't. He straightened restlessly in his chair, blew out a breath and took another sip of tea.

"Anyway, Paulette—that was her name—looked at me. I looked at her and it was fate. You know, *fate*, in capital letters. Her father was so pleased with me he invited me to their place, she came over a few evenings to see me. I spent a couple of weekends with them. We got along famously, and when it was time for them to go back to Portland, I asked her to marry me."

His eyes seemed to lose focus for a moment, then he rubbed a hand over them, and when he looked at Beth again, his gaze was self-deprecating and sad. He went on as though he could suddenly see it all from a comfortable distance.

"She looked so surprised," he said, shaking his head. "And now I think that's what hurt the most. That I was *so* in love, and all along she hadn't a clue. Then she blinked these velvety brown eyes and said in this husky rich-girl voice, 'But Brodie, you're just a mechanic.'"

Beth reached a hand across the table and covered his, her heart filled with sympathy and anger. "Obviously a zero, Brodie. If she was here, I'd deck her for you."

His thin smile told her he appreciated the offer. "Anyway, it was hard for me to admit I'd been that blind. In fact, I think I've resisted admitting it by deciding that love was never meant to be taken seriously and treating every woman I met that way."

"But you feel something for Kelly?"

"I don't seem to be able to put her out of my mind. Is that the same thing?"

"I'd say so."

"So how do I get her to realize I regret acting like an adolescent and I want to spend time with her?"

"Tell her that."

He blew out another breath. "I did, and I handed her those flowers." He pointed to the ragged bunch in the chipped teapot. "All she did was hit me with them and lock the studio door on me."

Beth went for the teapot to refill her cup. "Want more?" she asked, holding the pot over his.

He shook his head and made a face. "I don't think tea's my thing. But thanks."

Beth laughed and put the kettle back on the burner. "You know," she said, sobering, "I think Kelly feels about marriage the way you feel about tea. She had it once, didn't like the taste, and even though there are other kinds available, she doesn't want another cup."

Brodie frowned at her metaphor. "You mean, she doesn't want *me*."

"No," Beth corrected, leaning toward him. "She doesn't want to risk getting what she had before—which was someone who didn't appreciate her and wouldn't let her be who she is. I think she would want you if she really knew the man under the Don Juan facade."

He brooded over her words for a moment, then

pushed his cup away and stood. He didn't seem any happier than he had when he arrived, but he did seem a little more hopeful. He hugged Beth. "Thanks for listening. I'm glad I've got you for a sister-in-law."

"Well, you're all right for a brother-in-law, too." She smiled, then walked him to the door and opened it for him. "And keep the jacket and shirt. You look great in them, and if you handle this right, you might get to wear them again."

"Let's hope so," he said.

Just as Brodie went out the door, Nikkie came in, looking flushed. She called a greeting to her uncle, gave Beth a polite hello, then hurried through the kitchen toward the hallway and the stairs, all the while careful to avoid Beth's eyes.

Beth noted that, then dismissed it; her husband's daughter was simply continuing to keep her, Beth, out of her space.

"Have you eaten?" Beth called after Nikkie.

"We had pizza delivered!" Nikkie shouted back.

Ethan phoned at nine o'clock. "This is going on longer than I'd hoped," he said. Then his voice dropped a tone and took on a quality she could almost feel through the electronic connection. "But if you wait up for me, I promise to make it worth your while."

"I'll be waiting."

"More than an hour," he said with sudden briskness, "and I'm out of here. I love you."

"I love you, too," she answered, sharply aware of how sincere she was.

She hung up the phone, then turned and almost collided with Nikkie. The girl's eyes were wide and stricken, and Beth presumed she was upset because she'd heard Beth tell Ethan she loved him.

Beth summoned patience and prepared to defend her position. But before she could say a word, Nikkie asked anxiously, "Have you seen Simba?"

Surprised by the question, Beth had to take a moment to think. When Ethan had dropped her and Jason home after dinner, Cindy had been eating, but she couldn't recall seeing Simba.

"No," she said finally. "Why? Is he missing?"

Nikkie made a nervous gesture with one hand. "I think so. Cindy's on my bed, but I've called Simba and looked in all his favorite places and he isn't there."

"Did you check Jason's bunk?"

"Yes."

"Did you ask Jason? He's watching TV."

"Yes. He hasn't seen him, either."

Relieved to find herself in one of the areas of motherhood she understood and in which she felt qualified, Beth was prepared to help Nikkie find her cat. She reached into a utility drawer for the large flashlight Ethan kept there.

"Come on, we'll look around outside," Beth said, going to the hooks by the door for her jacket. "You check the yard and I'll—"

Nikkie stopped Beth with a hand on her arm before she could open the door. Beth looked at her in puzzlement, and saw more than worry in the girl's eyes. Guilt was there, as well.

Jason walked into the kitchen, his expression concerned. "So, we gonna go look for Simba?" he asked.

Instead of snapping an answer at him, Nikkie

averted her eyes from Beth and studied her fingernails. "I...I think I know where he might be."

She glanced back at Beth, clearly expecting reproof of some kind.

Beth called on her reserves of calm and good sense. "Where's that?"

Nikkie pointed vaguely west. "In the Appleby house," she said.

"But he never wanders that far. And the house is boarded up."

"You can get in through the basement window," Jason said, apparently pleased to be able to share that information. "The board's loose at the bottom."

"Ethan told you to stay away from there," Beth scolded, missing the connection.

"I have," he said in the voice of the unjustly accused, "but all the kids know you can get in that way."

The light began to dawn for Beth. She turned to Nikkie. "But how would a cat get in there?"

Nikkie met her suspicious gaze and admitted reluctantly but frankly, "He probably followed me. The drama club did have a rehearsal after school like I told you, but Cameron and Bradley thought it would be fun to have it somewhere else, since it was just us. So the club voted and decided on the Appleby house. I ran home to get some Cokes and cookies, and Simba followed me."

At Beth's surprised look she explained, "I know he's a really lazy cat, but when he's been alone all day, he sometimes just wants to be with me, no matter what." Nikkie returned to her story. "Anyway, when we left, it was dark and later than I thought, and I forgot all about him. He probably went to sleep somewhere and…" A big tear slid down her cheek. "All we did was rehearse the play, but Dad'll be really mad."

Beth glanced at the clock over the stove. Nine-ten. "All right." Beth pointed at Jason. "You stay here. Nikkie and I will be right back."

But Jason reached for his coat as Nikkie pulled hers on. "I wanna come," he said.

Beth took the coat from him and returned it to the hook. "No. I want you to stay here. Watch TV until we come back. And Uncle Brodie's right next door." She blew her son a kiss and dashed outside, Nikkie right behind her.

They hurried to the end of the block, looked both ways at the corner, then ran across the street and down another half block until they reached the deserted Appleby house.

Beth headed for the main entrance, but Nikkie caught her arm and pulled her around the house and behind a dormant rhododendron.

The house was a dark rectangle against a moonless sky. The many trees and bushes that surrounded it formed irregular shadows. The wind blew, leaves and branches rustled—and Beth did her best to ignore the gooseflesh on her arms.

"Shine the flashlight down here, Beth!" Nikkie whispered, taking Beth's wrist and pointing it downward.

The beam revealed a piece of plywood that had been nailed over the window. There was graffiti on it and obvious gouges on the bottom edge where a tool had loosened the nails that held it in place.

Nikkie removed the plywood with very little effort. Then Beth hunkered down beside her and peered through the window into the darkness. Even from outside, the place smelled dank and musty and faintly alcoholic.

"Simba!" Nikkie called in a loud whisper. "Simba! Come on, baby!"

No response.

"Simba!" Nikkie tried again.

Still no response. Beth lay on her stomach on the grass and cast the beam of light over what she could see of the basement. There were stacks of dusty boxes, some of them rotting from the dampness. Rusty old gardening tools were propped against an ancient furnace. The concrete floor was littered with the debris left by the occasional transient—paper cups, empty bottles, fast-food wrappers, a filthy jacket.

Nikkie continued to call, and at last they heard a thump. She called again excitedly, but all they heard was silence.

Beth handed her the flashlight. "Hold this for me," she said, taking all her instinctive fears of dark and unknown places and thrusting them away. "If, God forbid, there's a *person* down there, just run to the nearest house and call 911."

"Beth, I should go in," Nikkie argued, trying to push the flashlight back at her.

"No, I will," Beth said firmly. "Just do as I say and stay here."

Nikkie gave in and directed the flashlight beam to the floor just under the window. Beth sat on the window frame, cleared long ago of broken glass by transients, and swung her legs into the basement. Her feet encountered a rusty laundry sink. She stepped into it and squatted down to hold the sides and lower one leg to the floor, then the other. She reached up for the flashlight.

"Be careful, Beth!" Nikkie cautioned with a sincerity Beth would have found touching under other circumstances. Right now all she could think of was finding the cat in good health, getting out of this place and getting home before Ethan did.

She swept the light before her and picked her way across the cluttered floor calling the cat. Things scurried in corners, and it occurred to her that if the cat was alive and well, being in this basement was probably the feline equivalent of a two-for-one day at the Burger Bistro.

She swept the light under and around boxes, tools and broken parts of things she couldn't identify, then went around to the other side of the furnace. She swept all corners with the light first and was relieved to find nothing human crouched in a corner.

"Simba!" she called. "Come on, kitty! Here, kitty!"

A sudden thump behind her caused her to turn with a little scream. The thumper responded with her own scream. It was Nikkie.

"I told you to wait!" Beth whispered.

"Well, I couldn't see you," Nikkie answered defensively. "And I'd feel awful if something happened to you because you were looking for my cat."

"Then next time," Beth said, "don't leave your cat in a haunted basement!"

Nikkie took a step back. "You're yelling," she accused.

"Do you know what your father would be doing if he was here?" Beth asked, turning around again and inching her way forward in the beam of light.

Nikkie grabbed hold of the back of Beth's shirt. "I'm trying not to think about that. Do you see any— There!"

"Where?" Beth asked, and Nikkie caught her wrist and directed the beam to a set of shelves built against the wall. Simba sat between an auto-parts box and a broken light fixture, looking like just another dusty remnant of the past.

"Simba!" Nikkie cried with delight and reached up for him. Her reach was one shelf short.

The cat yawned and watched her straining fingertips with interest, carefully keeping all parts of his body beyond her reach.

"Simba," she said, impatience mingling with her delight at finding him safe. "Come on. I'll give you a can of tuna! *People* tuna!"

A sudden clatter of metal caused Beth and Nikkie to spin around, the beam of light in front of them.

"Jeez!" Jason complained, putting both hands up protectively. "It's just me."

"Jason Richards!" Beth grabbed his arm and pulled him toward her.

"I know, I know," he protested, "but Ethan says a man's got to take care of his family, and he says when he isn't here, it's my job."

"Your *job*," Beth said, leaning over him, "is to listen to your mother!"

Jason looked beyond her shoulder and smiled. "There's Simba!" he said, pointing. "I can see his eyes!"

"Yes," Beth said wearily. "Nikkie found him. But we're having trouble getting him down."

"Oh." Jason moved around in front of them and studied the predicament. Simba could be heard purring, but he wasn't moving. Jason thumped his chest like Tarzan, and Simba leaped off the shelf and into his arms.

He turned to a surprised Nikkie with a wide smile and handed her the cat. "That's how I get him off my bunk," he said. "I was just playing around one day, and he jumped on me when I did that."

Nikkie held the cat to her cheek and buried her nose in his fur, dust and all. She looked up and said gravely, "Thank you, Jason."

His eyes widened. He glanced at his mother, then back at Nikkie, and replied with another big smile, "Yeah, sure."

"All right, we're out of here," Beth said, urging Jason and Nikkie, with Simba now clinging to her shoulder, before her.

She boosted Jason up onto the laundry sink and pushed on the seat of his jeans until he could wriggle out the window. Nikkie handed up the cat, then followed Jason through.

Beth stepped into the tub, then reached a hand out into the darkness for help as she clambered up. "If we're all very quiet, we might get home without anyone—"

She knew the moment the helping hand clamped her wrist that it didn't belong to Jason or to Nikkie. It pulled her with startling ease and speed through the window to the grass and onto her feet.

On her way up she noticed a familiar pair of boots, uniform pants and jacket. Over the shoulder of the jacket she saw several cars in the middle of the street, their red-and-blue lights illuminating the sheriff's department's logo.

She groaned defeatedly and looked into an angry

pair of brown eyes under the low brim of a Stetson hat.

"Hi, Ethan," she said in a very small voice. "You're home early."

CHAPTER THIRTEEN

"ETHAN!" BETH CLUTCHED the bars of the prison cell and shouted at the top of her lungs. "Ethan Drum, you come here this instant!"

Beth heard footsteps hurrying down the hallway from the outer office and into the small bank of holding cells. She could tell by their urgent pace that they didn't belong to her husband.

Deputy Curtis's harassed face appeared on the other side of the bars. "Yes, ma'am?" he asked.

"Where *is* he?" she demanded.

"Um...he's on the phone with the governor's office, Mrs. Drum." Curtis pointed awkwardly behind him. "I'm supposed to ask you to be quiet. You're disturbing the drunk tank."

Beth could not remember ever being so enraged. If she could have gotten her hands on Ethan at that moment, she was certain the seventy-pound difference in their weights would have made no difference.

"The governor?" Beth repeated. "What—is prowling a capital offense? And don't I get a trial first?"

Curtis smiled nervously. "I don't think your case will go to trial, Mrs. Drum. The governor's visiting Butler County in a couple of months. That's what they're talking about."

"You're damned right it isn't going to trial! I haven't done anything!"

"Pardon me, ma'am, but the sheriff's got quite a list of charges," Curtis disputed courteously. "There's breaking and entering, two counts of endangering the safety of a minor, resisting arrest—"

"I did *not* resist arrest!"

"He carried you in, ma'am," Curtis reminded her. "And you were beating on his back."

"Because I hadn't *done* anything!" she shouted.

"You resisted arrest, ma'am," he repeated.

"You tell the sheriff," she said, forcing herself to speak more quietly, "that if I'm not out of this cell and on my way home in five minutes, he's going to be single again. Do you understand me, Curtis?"

"Yes, ma'am." Curtis hurried off to relay her message.

Beth checked her watch. Midnight.

It was twelve-thirty-five when Beth heard another, lazier set of footsteps and identified the tread. Ethan came around the corner, shrugging into his jacket. He gave her one dark look, pressed a button, and her cell door opened electronically.

She snatched up her jacket and stalked past him into the hallway.

"Am I free?" she asked, "or are you taking me down some dark country road where I mysteriously disappear? This is very interesting, you know. I've never seen small-town justice in action before. I always thought *Cool Hand Luke* was an exaggeration."

He pushed the cell door closed and crossed to her, every muscle in his face tight and hard. "I would be happy," he said with a calm that belied the anger in his eyes, "to exaggerate a little justice for you right now, so don't push me."

She would have, but after the past hour and the

raging surge of adrenaline brought about by her arrest, resistance and subsequent trip to the car, then from the car to the jail over his shoulder, she was exhausted. She wasn't sure that even her fury could keep her on her feet much longer.

"Where are the children?" she asked coolly.

"At Brodie's," he replied.

"Good." She punched her way into her jacket, adjusted the hem with a yank that should have made her an inch shorter, then zipped it, seriously endangering her trachea. "Then when we get home, we can talk about the divorce!"

ETHAN WASN'T generally a drinking man. He had a beer occasionally, a mixed drink at a party once in a while, but the alcohol he kept around the house was mostly medicinal. When he got home with Beth, he poured himself a third of a barrel glass of Irish whiskey, certain his blood pressure would burst his heart within the hour if he didn't relax.

He was doing his best to *appear* relaxed because Beth was raging like a woman possessed, and he knew his control was making her crazy. It was small satisfaction in light of what she'd put him through tonight, but he was enjoying it.

Still, it would be a long time before he forgot what it had felt like to get a call from Ebbie, who picked up messages whenever he was in a meeting.

She reported that one of his neighbors had called to say she'd been watching the pilot boat through her binoculars and happened to notice several figures by the Appleby house. When he'd asked why she hadn't called the police, Ebbie replied that the woman said she thought one of the figures looked like his daughter.

What particularly troubled the woman was that she'd seen a couple of young men go into the basement that afternoon.

"Well, hell, why didn't she report it then?" he asked.

"Her son had just pulled up to take her to her doctor's appointment, and afterward she forgot. Curtis and Billings are doing back-to-backs tonight. I'll dispatch them for you."

He'd raced to the site, mindless with worry. If there was a transient in the basement, there could be trouble. He knew better than anyone that the homeless weren't necessarily criminal. A certain element was, however, and even for those who weren't, the sudden intrusion of someone else into their sanctum could surprise them into reacting with fear, instead of common sense.

Then he'd arrived. Curtis and Billings behind him, to find Nikkie and Jason on the grass. He'd been giving serious thought to paddling both of them where they stood when he'd heard a voice coming from the basement. Then he'd stared in disbelief when a hand reached out, groping for help. It was wearing the simple gold band he'd put on it a little more than a week ago.

At that moment he'd had no idea what their adventure had been about, but it had sounded as though she'd been suggesting that they conceal it. In view of the fact that he'd forbidden both children to go into the Appleby house, he'd lost all willingness to listen to explanations before he acted.

He'd asked Billings to take the children to Brodie's, then told Beth he was taking her in for questioning.

She'd argued, which he'd expected, but when he'd tried to lead her to the car, she'd kicked him, which he hadn't expected. That was when he hoisted her over his shoulder, carried her past an openmouthed Curtis and put her in the cage in the back of his patrol unit.

Things had gone from bad to worse. Her fury had set off his, and now here they were, two volcanoes about to erupt.

"Would you like a drink?" he asked with strained civility before replacing the bottle in the open kitchen cupboard.

"No," she said, pacing the kitchen like some out-of-control bumper toy. "I want a divorce."

Just as they had when she'd spoken them earlier, the words struck terror into his heart. But he kept his calm facade in place and headed for the hallway to the living room, barely avoiding a collision with her as he interrupted her pacing pattern.

"Okay," he said, and continued into the living room.

He'd called a lot of bluffs in his time, and some of them had even involved weapons aimed at his heart or his temple, but he'd never awaited a reaction with the trepidation with which he awaited this one.

"Okay?" she repeated, right at his heels as he made for the telephone. "Okay? That's all Jason means to you? *Okay?*"

That was a promising response, but he ignored it and stabbed out Brodie's speed-dial number on the cordless phone.

Brodie answered instantly.

"Hi," Ethan said. "It's me. Everything all right?"

"With me and the kids or with you and Beth?" Brodie asked.

"Not now." Ethan took a pull of whiskey. "The kids all right?"

"They're fine. They're asleep. But they were pretty worried when they got here. They said you went a little Dirty Harry on Beth."

"With good cause," Ethan replied. "So are they okay there for the night?"

"Of course. They wanted to go home, but I figured you had a reason for having them brought here, instead of asking me to go to your place." He paused. "Ethan?"

"Yeah."

"Calm down, okay? If you guys are about to have it out, count to ten or something first. Have a drink. Remember that she and the kids went to the Appleby house to get the cat. They didn't have criminal intentions. And even though you think you know what's best for everybody, that doesn't require them to do it. Kids, sure, but not a woman. Even if you love her."

"I thought you weren't into taking women seriously."

"I've changed my mind."

Ethan laughed mirthlessly. "Do yourself a favor. Change it back. See you in the morning."

He pushed the Off button on the phone and put it back on its base. He took another sip of whiskey and turned to Beth. He felt fractionally calmer.

"Jason means a lot to me," he said in answer to the question she'd flung at him before he'd called Brodie. "That's why I got just a little upset knowing he'd been in the Appleby place."

"A *little* upset?" she said, her voice reaching a high register. "You didn't even let us explain! You have the kids thinking you're going to kill them in the morning and you *arrested* me."

He pulled the drapes closed and took another sip of

whiskey. "I didn't arrest you," he amended. "I only brought you in."

"Just to punish me!" she said angrily. "You had no right to subject me—"

He turned on her, temper boiling despite the whiskey and his best efforts to remain calm. "I had every right!" She stood in the middle of the room and he strode toward her. "I went to a meeting leaving my kids in your care, and what do you do? You take them with you as accomplices to help you break into a private residence. Do you have any idea what it feels like to be the sheriff and arrive at a call only to find that the perpetrators of the crime are your family?"

"The house was empty!"

"It doesn't matter!" he roared. "It's someone else's property! They just don't live here. But that's not the point, anyway. You heard me tell the kids that transients go in and out of there all the time. If some wacko had been in there, you and the kids could be hurt or dead right now!"

She was quiet a moment, assimilating that information. "I had a flashlight," she said defensively.

"Oh, good," he said flatly. "How many rounds does it hold? Or does it just allow you to see the gun before it fires at you?"

She put a hand to her forehead, and he realized suddenly that she was very pale and that her hand shook a little. Concern for her diminished his anger slightly.

"All right," she admitted in a quieter tone. "I exercised poor judgment. I knew it at the time. But Nikkie was very upset about the cat and she came to me for help."

He guessed she was being carefully nonspecific. He knew how it had all come about, but she didn't know he knew. Nikkie had told him all about it when he'd put her and Jason in Billings's car. She'd assumed all blame and made it clear that Beth had told Jason to stay home and her to stay outside on the grass.

"And you thought to look in the Applebys' basement?" he asked.

She went to the window, drew the curtain back and looked out. "Cats love dark hiding places."

"But the place is boarded up. How did you think he'd gotten in there?"

She turned away from the window and met his gaze, her own direct and suspicious. "If you wanted to interrogate me," she said, "you should have done it when you had me in a jail cell."

"If you'd just told me what happened without a lot of attitude," he countered, "you wouldn't have ended up in a jail cell."

"Oh, I understand." She let the curtain fall back into place and came around the chair to lean against its well-upholstered side. "Your deputies were there and you had to flex your muscles."

"No," he said after counting to ten as Brodie had recommended. "Our children were there, and it was important for them to see that ignoring the rules has consequences. I didn't have all the details, but I figured out what had happened, though I didn't know if it was Nikkie or Jason at fault. I'd have let them believe I was taking you to jail, let them see us drive away, then I'd have taken you for coffee somewhere and chewed you out quietly for not waiting to check on the cat until I got home."

She arched an eyebrow. "So, it's all right for *you* to disregard the rules and break in?"

"I'm an officer of the law," he replied. "I can go

anywhere. And I'm armed." He paused. "Anyway, you wouldn't *let* me handle the situation easily. You turned on all this attitude. What was that about?"

"You were just beginning to convince me that you were different from Steve," she said, "and suddenly you were acting just like him. Full of criticism and accusation, without even bothering to ask for the details."

Ethan downed the rest of his whiskey and put his glass on the coffee table. "Beth, I'm not Steve. I don't know how many times I have to remind you of that. If I acted at all like him, it's unfortunate, I guess, but I won't apologize. I answered a call in which my entire family was involved, and the knowledge of what could have happened scared the hell out of me. I'm not going to spend a lifetime tiptoeing around you so that nothing reminds you of Steve. I get upset with you, you're going to know it."

Her jaw remained taut, her chin angled. "I should have stayed with my promise to myself not to get married again. I should have taken Jason and hidden somewhere."

So. She wasn't tiptoeing around, either. Good. He had a few other things to get off his chest. "You didn't marry me to keep Jason," he said quietly, resting his hands on his hips. "You married me for me. And now that you have me, I don't behave quite the way you expected, so you don't know what to do. Your life was dictated by what Steve wanted for so long that when you were finally free, all you could think about was never having to answer to anybody again. Well, that won't be life with me."

He closed the space between them and took her chin between his thumb and forefinger. "You know me,

Beth. You know I'd never hurt you and I'd never stop you from being what you want to be or doing what you want to do, as long as it doesn't endanger you or the kids. But you do something that scares me or worries me, I'll stop you."

She caught his wrist in her hand and pulled it down. "That kind of...paternalism in a husband," she said stiffly, "is so Victorian."

He refused to budge. "So are frivolous women. I don't want to run your life. I just want to keep you safe. If you can't see the difference, maybe you're not mature enough to be married at all. Good night." He left her standing near the chair and went upstairs.

She went to bed in the room she'd used before the wedding. He'd felt sure she would, but he was too angry and too determined to make concessions.

And apparently so was she.

HE SETTLED THINGS with Nikkie and Jason in the morning. Brodie brought them home just after seven and disappeared into the kitchen. They looked terrified, more affected by the events of the previous night than he'd expected.

He took them both in his arms, then sat them on the sofa and listened again to each one's interpretation of what had happened.

Nikkie finished with, "I told you, Daddy. It was all my fault. I went with the kids to rehearse there, and I'm the one who forgot Simba. Beth just went to help me. She told me to wait on the grass."

"Yeah," Jason added. "And she told me to stay home. But you said a man takes care of his family, and you were gone, so I was the man."

In the light of day and after a long and lonely night,

Ethan was wondering if he'd made more of the incident than he should have. But then he looked into his daughter's and stepson's trusting faces and remembered how very real his anxiety had been, how important it was that they understood danger and, in that regard at least, obeyed him unconditionally.

He put an arm around Nikkie's shoulders and one around Jason's. "Nikkie," he began, "I appreciate your honesty, and I'm proud of you for not letting Beth take the rap, because she tried to."

Her lip quivered. "She did?"

"Yes, she did. She tried to make me believe you had just decided to look outside for the cat and it was her idea to check the Applebys' basement."

He let that sink in for a moment, then gave her the bad news. "But while I'm proud of you for telling the truth, I'm grounding you for ignoring the rule about the Appleby house in the first place and rehearsing there."

She nodded as though she'd expected as much.

He turned to Jason. "You're grounded, too," he said, "for not listening to your mom."

Jason looked surprised. "I was listening to *you!* You said—"

Ethan cut him off. "—that it's your job to look out for your mom and Nikkie when I'm not here. I know. And I can see where you might have gotten confused, but your mom gave you specific instructions to stay home. Disobeying her isn't the best way to look out for her."

Jason puzzled over that. Ethan knew that deep down his argument wasn't sound, but he felt obliged to back up Beth's authority. This had all come about because everyone was trying to help everyone else, but he had to hold to the Appleby-house rule.

He looked from one child to the other. "Two weeks. Nothing but drama-club stuff for you, Nik, because I know they're counting on you, but don't try to stretch it. Nothing after dinner."

"Okay."

"And, Jase, the bike stays in the garage and you stay in."

"Okay."

"Good." Ethan stood, pulling the children to their feet. "Let's get some breakfast."

Beth came down the stairs just as Ethan was urging Nikkie and Jason toward the kitchen.

"Good morning." Beth smiled at the children and opened her arms as Jason launched himself at her. She didn't bother to raise her glance to Ethan's.

"Mom!" Jason held her tightly, then looked up at her, his eyes wide with respect and admiration. "You were in the slammer! What was it like?"

Ethan kept going toward the kitchen, thinking grimly that his point about obeying rules and laws may have fallen short of its mark.

He stopped in the kitchen doorway, turning at the sudden sound of sobs. They were coming from Nikkie, who'd thrown her arms around Beth's neck and was apologizing brokenly for being the reason she'd been taken to jail.

Beth held her and spoke quietly. Ethan couldn't hear the words but guessed they were something like, *It's all right, Nikkie. It wasn't your fault. Your father's a prehistoric muscle flexer with delusions of power and we're his unfortunate victims.*

In truth, he was happy to see his daughter and his

wife finally making an emotional connection. It was just unfortunate that it had to be over what he feared was the death knell of his marriage.

He went to pour a cup of coffee and sat at the table.

"Morning, Cruella," Brodie said. "One egg or two?"

"Two. And lay off me," Ethan advised. "Cruella's a woman, so your sorry little joke doesn't work."

Brodie broke two eggs into a pan and while they cooked placed half a grapefruit in front of Ethan. "I think it does—she's the ultimate villain, man or woman, and only someone who'd collect puppies to make a coat of *their* coats would haul his own wife off to jail for helping his daughter rescue her cat."

Ethan glared at him. "I don't remember asking for your assessment of the situation."

"Too bad," Brodie replied. "It comes with breakfast."

Before Ethan could tell him what to do with breakfast, Beth and the children trooped in and the conversation was terminated.

Beth and the children chatted cheerfully as Ethan drove the Blazer on the now familiar round of elementary school, high school and cannery.

But the cheerful conversation stopped the moment Jason was dropped off and Ethan was left alone with Beth. The vehicle was filled with icy tension for the next two blocks.

Ethan pulled onto the pier and saw two cars parked at the side of the building. One he recognized as Kelly's MG. The other, a decrepit Volvo station wagon with lumber sticking out of the back, Ethan remembered being there when he'd walked into Beth's studio and found Rush Weston with his hands on her.

He said nothing, simply let the engine idle while Beth shouldered her purse and pushed open her door. She held the door an extra moment and he wondered if communication might be reestablished between them. She seemed to be struggling to put something into words.

"Nikkie asked me if the drama club could come over tonight to work on the shields," she said, her face expressionless. "I told her it was all right."

"It *is* all right." He kept his expression as blank as hers.

"Good." The wind tossed her hair, and a wicked gleam in her eyes marred her attempt to remain completely impassive when she added, "I'd hate to end up in jail for having forgotten to tell you."

She reached back inside for the lunch she'd left on the floor on her side, and he leaned over to catch her wrist. She looked at him in surprise, not frightened but clearly uncertain of what he intended. He liked that.

"Innocent forgetfulness isn't a crime," he said, injecting a warning note into his voice. "But smart sarcasm is a felony, not to mention foolish. You might keep that in mind." He freed her hand. "Have a good day."

She slammed the door.

CHAPTER FOURTEEN

BETH SLIPPED her arms into the two leather handles she'd attached to the back of her prototype shield. She flexed the muscles in her arm and was pleased that the heavy-duty staples she'd used kept the strips in place.

She'd tried vinyl and simple staples earlier, but one flex of Cameron's forearm and a staple popped. Considering Henry V's army would be composed of Cobbler's Crossing's football team, she knew she had to find an alternative. And old leather belts from the thrift shop were an economical alternative to twenty feet of two-inch wide leather from a fabric or craft shop.

Now that she knew the belt worked, she'd run back to the thrift shop in the afternoon for more.

Her studio door opened and she turned around to greet the visitor, the shield still on her arm.

It was Kelly, in black jeans with ripped knees and a man's shirt that had once been white but now looked like a Jackson Pollock canvas. Her red hair was stuffed under a paper painter's cap.

"Whoa," she said, her eyes going to the shield as she walked toward Beth's worktable. "Where's your horned helmet and pointy bra?"

"Lent them to one of the other Valkyries," Beth said, smiling as she eased her arm out of the straps. "Go away unless you have a caramel-vanilla latte."

Kelly rolled her eyes and leaned over Beth's table

to study the coats of arms she'd drawn on the shields. "I brought a bunch of stuff down this morning, but forgot the box with my coffeepot. Brodie came over yesterday while I was packing and I lost track of what I was doing."

Beth showed Kelly the finished product. "I was the recipient of the bouquet you dusted him with," she said.

Kelly admired the shield and said nonchalantly, "I can't imagine why he'd come to see you."

Beth folded her arms. "Why, hoping for a clue to your complicated psyche," she said, then added dryly, "As though I had it."

Kelly gave her a chiding glance and turned the shield over to inspect the back. "You should talk, Ma Barker. I was up late last night and listening to the scanner when I heard about the dustup at the Applebys'. So you're a big bad mama with a record now?"

Beth took the shield away from Kelly and put it aside. "No, I do not have a record. He couldn't arrest me. He just went through the motions to make me pay for having gone down there with Nikkie in the first place. And as my friend, aren't you supposed to be sympathetic to my plight and offer comfort and support?"

Kelly asked seriously, "Is it going to lower my rent?"

"It might forestall eviction."

"Can you evict me if I haven't even moved in yet?"

"We'll ask Ethan," Beth said, taking the shield from the table and adding it to one of the boxes in which she'd placed the other nineteen wooden discs. "He's good at manipulating the law in his favor."

"I imagine," Kelly ventured, "that he took you to jail to impress upon you and the kids that, as beguiling as a haunted house is, that place can be dangerous at night. And also because you kicked him. He's an officer of the law."

"He's my husband and he was being a jerk."

"At home he's your husband. At the scene of a disturbance he's the sheriff, counted upon by the citizens of Butler County to keep the peace. And you were shouting at him and fighting him, according to what I heard on the scanner."

Beth groaned and went to the open door of the studio to look out at the river beyond the pier. The water was the color of gunmetal and met a sky of the same color. The line of the horizon was almost invisible in the monochromatic world of the wintry Oregon coast.

Seagulls flew around a red-and-black tug pulling a barge mounded with wood chips from the mill on the other side of the bay. Cormorants watched its passing from their perch on old pilings, remnants of other cannery piers.

It occurred to Beth that it was a beautiful setting, but her world felt as sunless as the sky.

Kelly came up beside her. "So what happened to you last night? I saw the two of you shopping after work just a couple of nights ago, and it looked as though you'd found some common ground."

Misery welled up in Beth's chest. "He was shouting at me," she said, her voice dull, "and acccusing me of being foolish..."

"Astute of him, I would say," Kelly offered mercilessly.

Beth leaned a shoulder against her open door, feeling suddenly heavy, burdened. "He was sounding a lot like Steve,'' she explained, seeing vivid pictures behind her eyes of her and Ethan shouting at each other. ''All I could think about was how confining some of those times had been, how demoralizing, and here I'd been beginning to think that with Ethan, those days were gone forever.''

Kelly leaned against the other side of the doorway, her hands pressed behind her. ''Beth, you're not comparing Steve's selfish claims on you to Ethan's gut reaction when he arrives at a call to find his family in danger, are you?''

Beth put a hand to her head where an ache had been gaining momentum ever since she'd climbed out of the shower that morning.

''I did last night,'' she admitted.

''He's a man and you scared him,'' Kelly said simply. ''They get really ticked off when they have to admit that to themselves. And it's instinctive to take it out on whoever inspired the fear, whether or not it's entirely justified. It means he cares. I think you should forgive him.''

Beth turned to her friend with a disbelieving look. ''I have a broken bouquet in my kitchen that says you don't practice what you preach.''

''I don't have to.'' Kelly stared out at the river. ''My situation's entirely different.''

''How so?''

''Ethan yelled at you because he cares. Brodie backed away from me because I never meant anything to him at all. It was just the sort of hormone-driven game kids play.''

''Not exactly.''

Kelly met her eyes with a frown. ''What do you mean?''

Beth related the story of Paulette.

Kelly listened. There was a momentary softening of her expression, a small gasp of indignation, then she sighed and turned her gaze out to the river again. "Stupid snot. But it just proves that he's out to pay *her* back by taking it out on every other woman he comes across—get her interested, then drop her."

"He admits he was doing something like that. Until you."

Kelly laughed scornfully. "Right. 'But you're different, Kelly.' I've been around too long to fall for that one, Beth. I'm no different, I just called him on it and he caved, but he can't have any holdouts. He has to make me come around, too—and *then* he'll dump me."

"I don't think so."

"Well, I won't be finding out."

"Fraidy cat."

"Smarty-pants. I'm playing it safe."

Beth caught Kelly by the arm and pulled her back into the studio and across it to a poster hanging over her tool chest. It pictured a tiny boat on a seemingly endless ocean under a vast sky. "What does that say?" Beth demanded.

Kelly shifted her weight and read in a disgruntled monotone, "'A ship in a harbor is safe, but that is not what ships were built for.'"

Kelly turned to Beth and challenged her with a look. "Okay. If I'm going to stick my neck out, you're going to make things right with Ethan."

Beth offered her hand, secretly pleased to have an excuse to try to rectify things between her and Ethan. "Deal."

Kelly studied her skeptically for a moment, then

shook hands to seal the deal. She winced and asked in a small voice, "Doesn't this feel a lot like Butch and Sundance jumping hand in hand off that cliff?"

Beth smiled and tried to think positively. "They lived, didn't they?"

THE KITCHEN was full of laughter and loud music. Beth had spread newspaper all over the table and all over the floor. Nikkie and Vanessa knelt on the chairs and painted the shields' backgrounds while Rosalie, Cameron and Bradley sat cross-legged on the floor and painted in the details, according to the sketches Beth had made.

Jason prowled the room peering over shoulders and admiring their work. Beth was pleased to see that they were tolerant of him and that Nikkie even let him try his hand at stenciling. When his tense hand moved the stencil and created a lion with a lump protruding from its back, she patted his shoulder and told him not to worry, no one would notice.

Then she looked up at Beth when Jason was distracted by something else and made a comically distressed face.

Beth returned a wink and a nod and the unspoken assurance that she would repair the damage.

Ethan kept bowls of popcorn and corn chips filled, soda glasses topped up and the cats out of the paint.

Beth noted worriedly that he made no effort to talk to her, though she was sure their silence wasn't obvious to Nikkie and her friends. Considering her behavior the past twenty-four hours, she couldn't blame him for ignoring her. But how she was going to fulfill her part of the bargain she'd made with Kelly remained a mystery.

Brodie came over to investigate the source of the noise.

"Jeez," he grumbled theatrically, "do I have to call the sheriff and have this place raided?"

Nikkie and her friends laughed.

Ethan put a glass of soda in his hand and a corn chip in his mouth. "Eat that and be quiet," he said. "We have enough noise around here already."

Brodie took the chip out of his mouth. "I thought maybe you needed help running the roulette wheel or dealing blackjack."

Ethan shook his head and offered a supermarket tub of salsa for Brodie to dip the chip into. "The only gamble around here is whether or not these shields come out right. The guys are talking football, and the girls are talking Brad Pitt. Who knows what we could end up with?"

Rosalie held up the first finished shield. "This!" she said, her voice conveying surprise and awe.

Everyone turned to look, and silence filled the room for a moment. The shield was Henry's. The lions stood out brilliantly against the red paint, and the fleurs-de-lis were beautifully formed on a blue field.

"Beth!" Nikkie breathed, the glow on her face saying everything. "Look at what you did!"

Beth denied the credit with a shake of her head. "You guys did it. All I did was provide the wood and make the stencils. If you act as well as you paint, you're all headed for Hollywood."

"Oh, I just came from there," a female voice said from the back door. "Unless you're interested in beautiful people, big cars and lots of money, it has nothing for you. That's why I'm *here*."

The kids laughed. Beth's heartbeat shifted into second gear. Kelly was *here,* she guessed, to keep her part of the bargain.

The kids went back to work, turning their music up a notch to be heard over the adult conversation.

"Can I get you a soda, Kelly?" Ethan asked. "Coffee?"

"No, thank you," she replied with a smile, then seemed to lose control of it as she turned to Brodie. It narrowed, wavered, then disappeared altogether when Brodie didn't smile back.

Kelly glanced at Beth for support. Wanting desperately for her best friend and her brother-in-law to have at least an opportunity for another go at their relationship, Beth pushed aside her own difficulties and tried to spur Kelly on.

Ethan stood only a foot away from Beth in the corner of the kitchen into which the press of teenagers had forced them, and she reached out to hook her arm in his and lean into him. She gave a smile for Kelly that suggested she, Beth, had already taken her steps in their deal and it was time for Kelly to follow suit or be a welsher.

Ethan didn't move away from Beth, and he didn't remove his arm, but he did nothing positive, either. As she inhaled the fresh rainwater fragrance of him and felt the warm textured wool of his sweater under her cheek, she was very aware that he didn't respond.

She knew precisely how Kelly felt.

Kelly tossed her red hair and refocused her attention on Brodie. "I was hoping," she said in a voice that wasn't at all familiar to Beth, "that I could buy you a cup of coffee."

Beth watched him study her warily a moment, then lift his glass. "Got a root beer."

Kelly put her hands in the pockets of her short leather jacket, her jaw firming perceptibly. "You don't have pie. I could buy you that to go with the coffee."

He considered her another moment, bounced a glance over Beth's head to Ethan, then said to Kelly. "But it's almost ten o'clock. This is Cobbler's Crossing. Nothing's open after ten."

Kelly shrugged. "I'm a caterer, remember?"

The merest trace of a smile pulled at his lips. "I never forget anything."

"Good," she said, drawing the first even breath Beth had seen her take since she'd walked into the room. "I like that in a man. If we take my car, I can have you home in time for Leno."

Brodie put his glass on the counter, slapped Ethan on the back and leaned down to kiss Beth's cheek. "Thanks for the hospitality, guys, but I've got to run." He opened the back door for Kelly. "Can I drive your car?"

She passed through the door before him. "It's very precious to me. Are you a good driver?"

"Nothing special," he replied, "but I'm a good mechanic. I break or dent anything, I can fix it." The door closed behind them and Beth couldn't help her relieved sigh.

"God, that was an ordeal," she said, forgetting for an instant, in her delight over Kelly's preliminary success, that her own part of the bargain remained undone. She pulled her arm from Ethan's.

Jason brought her an empty plastic bowl, then returned to the table to look over Nikkie's shoulder.

Ethan moved with Beth as she went to the cupboard for the second bag of corn chips. "And what was your stake in that little scene?" he asked.

He didn't look hostile, she noted, just comfortably removed from the situation.

"Kelly's my friend." She poured chips into the bowl and carried it to the table, then went back to the counter and carefully folded the top of the bag. "And Brodie's wonderful. I think they'd be good for each other."

"And you encouraged her to try to straighten out their problems," he speculated, "by letting her think we'd dealt with ours."

She clipped the bag closed and gave him a small friendly smile. "Precisely."

"Artful trickery," he said.

"Everyone should have a skill."

There was a shout from Cameron as he looked at his watch, then a sudden flurry of activity as the young people who'd ridden in with Cameron began to pack up the project.

"Drop the brushes in the water jar," Beth instructed, "and leave all the wet shields side by side on the floor against the wall. I've got something rigged up to protect them. Don't worry about the newspaper. I'll clean that up."

Ethan volunteered to take Rosalie home because everyone else was on Cameron's way. Nikkie went with him.

Beth waved in response to the cries of "Thanks, Mrs. Drum!"

Beth hugged Jason, then shooed him off to bed while she picked up the newspapers and stuffed them into a plastic garbage bag. She covered the painted shields with overturned boxes to keep out the cats, stashed all the paints and supplies in another box and took the brushes down to the laundry sink to wash them.

At last, feeling as though she'd won Henry's Battle of Agincourt single-handedly, Beth left on the back porch light and the kitchen light, then locked up the front of the house and went upstairs to get ready for bed.

ETHAN WALKED into the kitchen with Nikkie and noticed the silence. There was something poignantly familiar about it. It reminded him of all those years when it had been just the two of them, before Jason decided to run away and changed all their lives forever.

Forever. It struck him as a strange word to use in connection with the woman he'd married on an inexplicable impulse, particularly in view of the state of that relationship at this very moment.

Still, he thought fatalistically as he reached behind him to lock the back door and turn off the porch light, the word applied. Even if she left tomorrow, he would still be changed forever. There was a lot of confusion in her, but also so much light, so much spontaneous laughter, so much grace. And so much love.

The shadowy quiet of the house reminded him of the first time he'd made love to her. It surprised him to realize that had been only last week. Every time they'd made love since had expanded and amplified his spirit so that there were moments when it felt too big for his body, as though he would have to live to be four hundred to make use of all he felt.

"Daddy?" Nikkie turned to him from the rack where she'd hung up her jacket. She helped him out of his and put it on a peg. Her eyes were bright from the hectic evening. "Thanks for letting the kids come over and work tonight. We had a great time, and we got a whole lot done."

He nodded, opening his arms in surprise when she leaned into him and stayed there. Over the past few years he'd gotten used to kisses and hugs dealt out sparingly, and usually on the run.

"I'm really sorry about going to the Applebys'," she said, her grip on him tightening "I knew better, but...you know. When you're the sheriff's daughter, everybody thinks you're a Goody Two-shoes."

He held her tightly and kissed the top of her head. "I know that's hard for you sometimes, but let me tell you that Goody Two-shoeses are underrated. They don't usually find themselves in situations where they can get hurt. Try to remember that rules aren't just to make your life uncomfortable. When you're young and enthusiastic about everything, it's hard to recognize potential danger, so I have to do it for you. You have to trust me to know what I'm doing."

"I know." She looked up at him, still holding him, her bright pretty face alight. "I'm just beginning to understand how smart you really are."

His first instinct upon hearing that was to get a tape recorder and have her repeat those words. He was certain there'd be times in the future when he'd desperately need to hear them again.

"And what brought on this revelation?" he asked.

"Beth," she said. Nikkie looked a little mystified, as though an adult truth had invaded her teenage life and confused everything. "I didn't want to like her. I didn't want things to change. But every time I turned around she was being nice to me, trying to do something for me without being pushy like Jason's grandma or sappy like some movie version of the perfect stepmother."

Her voice tightened a little. "When I couldn't find Simba, she was ready to go out in the dark and help me look. Then when I told her where I thought he was, she didn't yell or threaten or anything. I think she probably even might have told you about it when it was all over—or made *me* tell you—but we didn't take time to talk about it. We just went looking for him. And she did tell Jason to stay home, but he thought we were taking too long, so he came to help because you told him—"

"Yeah, I know. A man takes care of his family and I was gone, so he was the man."

She stood up on tiptoe to kiss his cheek. "Anyway, I love you for being so smart," she said. "And I kind of like the way things are turning out around here. Good night, Daddy."

"Good night, Nik."

Ethan turned off the kitchen light and headed for the stairs, resolved to end the standoff with Beth. He couldn't change his position on the Appleby house, but he could certainly concede that, though his entire family had ignored his instructions, they'd done it for reasons that had everything to do with responsibility and generosity, however misguided.

Nikkie's door was already closed, and the only light in the hallway came from the night-light in the bathroom. Ethan peered into the room Beth had used the night before, expecting to find her curled up under the covers, asleep.

She wasn't. The bed was undisturbed.

She'd gone to his room? He took a few steps into the room, but his bed, too, was undisturbed, the coverlet carelessly thrown across it, just as he'd left it that morning.

Where was she? Feeling that same familiar but unwelcome silence he'd recognized just a little while ago in the empty kitchen, he suppressed any notion that she might have left.

She needed him. Even if she was angry, she was too responsible to leave in a fit of pique.

Just to be certain, he went to check on the one thing she'd never leave behind. Jason was there, fast asleep in the top bunk in the room at the end of the hall, one arm hanging over the side. Simba was curled up in a ball on Jason's pillow, his head against the boy's.

Ethan felt great relief, and then a swelling of the deep affection Jason's straightforward ways inspired. He tucked the arm up onto the bunk, then stroked the cat, who'd awakened with a start.

Simba purred and went back to sleep.

Ethan walked into his bedroom and over to the window, wondering if Beth could have gone to Brodie's. But Brodie's house was dark. Of course. He'd left with Kelly.

"Ethan."

Beth's voice came from a corner of the darkened room. He turned away from the window, his heart giving an erratic lurch. "Beth." He spoke quietly, hoping to calm himself. "What are you doing in the dark?"

"I was sitting in the chair, thinking about things," she said. She was wearing his white terry-cloth robe. It fell almost to her ankles, and her face and throat gleamed above it, her dark hair disappearing in the shadows. He felt weak with the need to touch her.

She lifted her chin. "I still think your tactics last night were uncalled for," she said, her chin coming down as she spoke, the line of her shoulders softening under the big robe. "But in all fairness, so were mine. And you did have good reason, I guess, to get a little out of control. I, on the other hand, was reacting to the past, instead of the present and..."

She expelled a breath, tried to put her hands in the pockets of the robe, but they were too low for her to do more than slip her fingertips in. She folded her arms and said, "I'm sorry."

He crossed the distance between them in two strides and took her in his arms. "*I'm* sorry," he said, absorbing the rightness of holding her against him after a separation that had seemed interminable, though it had been only a day. "I was beside myself with worry when I saw all of you there, but I should have handled things differently. I should have understood. But I was feeling, rather than thinking."

She nuzzled his throat, her hands gently exploring his waist. "Me, too." She tipped her head back and asked, her voice dropping an octave, "Why don't we shower yesterday away—together? Water is a sort of dialect of Romanesque."

He didn't say anything for an instant, and Beth experienced the panicky fear that she'd overstepped. She'd often done that with Steve, offending or embarrassing him.

Then she saw Ethan's white smile in the dark and he wrapped an arm around her, and walked with her into the bathroom, stopping at the shower stall. He hooked a finger into the belt of the robe and pulled until it was undone. Then he slipped it off her shoulders.

His eyes shone with the same expression she'd seen in them the first time he'd made love to her. A very male appreciation of her body, coupled with a kind of disarming humility.

She reached her fingers under his sweater and T-shirt and pulled them up and off. Unbuckling his belt and unzipping his jeans, she slipped her hands between his briefs and his warm flesh and pushed the briefs down to his ankles. He toed them the rest of the way off.

He opened the shower, pulled her in with him and backed her into the cold tile corner to protect her from the onslaught of water until he had the temperature adjusted.

Then he brought her in front of him under the spray. It was a warm and comfortable drumming on her shoulders, and it seemed to create an answering beat within her. She put her hands to Ethan's chest. "Want me to soap you?" she asked.

He leaned down to kiss her greedily. "Later," he said, and lifted her into his arms, encouraging her to wrap her legs around him.

She complied, holding tightly to his neck, and felt a small jolt of surprise when his fingers parted her and slipped inside.

He tipped his head back to look into her face. "I won't drop you," he promised, humor in his voice.

She shook her head, his fingers distracting her. "That isn't...it."

"What, then?" he asked, kissing her lightly. "Is making love in the shower new to you?"

"Yes. Remember...I told you I wanted to...try something with...with, um..."

"Steve?"

"Yeah, Steve. And he..."

"Right. He was disgusted by it. This? Making love in the shower?"

"And standing up. He...said it...wouldn't work. That the shower was for hygiene, and the only way to have sex was...in bed. Ethan!"

"All right. I'm with you. And I'm about to prove to you that he was wrong about that, too."

Her body caught in the tight spiral that was the prelude to fulfillment, Beth held on to him in an agony of waiting. He propped a foot against the tile and entered her surely, making a seat for her with his hands as he leaned his shoulders back against the wall in the small space.

She cried out at her sudden release. It shot through her like fireworks, hot and colorful and lighting up the night.

She clung to Ethan as he erupted inside her at the same moment.

He clung to her, his hands stroking her hips and her back until the celebration finished and the sky cleared.

They soaped each other's bodies and washed each other's hair. When they got out and dried off, they sat in the middle of the bed while he rubbed her hair with a towel. Then they pulled the blankets up over them and, arms and legs entangled, drifted off to sleep.

Beth's last thought before she drifted off to sleep was that she felt sure she'd never doubt Ethan's opinion on anything again.

CHAPTER FIFTEEN

HENRY V'S ARMY lined up backstage in three tight rows, their shields held out before them, and smiled as though war was the last thing on their minds. Beth imagined that after the roaring success of their opening night and the cast party ahead of them at a waterfront restaurant, it would be the restaurant staff who would need the shields.

Ethan photographed them for posterity, and then the army tried to break ranks. But Ethan pointed them back into place and posed Nikkie and her friends in front of them, then pushed Beth into their mix. She tried to protest, but Bradley and Cameron brought her physically into the middle of the front row.

"Thanks, guys," Ethan said finally. "I'm finished." The cast exploded from their tidy rows into a moving knot of excitement. Parents and teachers milled around them, offering their congratulations and their parting instructions for the night ahead.

Nikkie rushed to where Ethan stood with Beth and Jason, and Brodie and Kelly. "The football team's going to the cast party on the rooter bus, but Mr. Fogarty's taking the drama club to the party in his van, and he says to tell you he'll have us home by eleven. My curfew's ten, so I thought I'd better make sure."

"Eleven's fine." Ethan flicked her chin and

grinned. "Just remember that you're the queen of France and act accordingly."

She struck a haughty pose. "*Mais, oui*. I have several beheadings scheduled for zee morning."

"Good. I'm glad to see you have an enlightened legal system in place."

Beth gave Nikkie a hug. "You're aware, of course, that your father's system is about as enlightened, so watch yourself. His spies are everywhere."

Nikkie looked heavenward. "Be sure to watch *your*selves, too. You're going to that dance-and-dessert thing with Uncle Brodie and Kelly. That sounds like trouble to me."

"We resent that!" Kelly said with feigned offense as she hugged Nikkie. "You were wonderful, sweetie. And all your props looked perfect from the audience."

Brodie took Nikkie from Kelly and hugged her in turn. "You were brilliant, Nik. Genius is unpredictable, isn't it? I mean, I have it, you have it, yet it managed to skip your father altogether!"

Ethan gave his brother a mock punch on the arm. "Careful," he warned. "This room is full of weapons."

"Duh! They're all phony."

Ethan gave him a cold smile. "The way you irritate me, Bro, I could run you through with a paper sword."

Brodie kept an arm around his niece. "This could prove to be a troublesome evening, Nik. We'll call you if we need bail money."

Ethan laughed. "The way she saves, we'd rot in jail. No, I think we have to count on graft and corruption if we get arrested."

"Oh, good. The job's going to be fun again." Curtis

appeared beside Ethan. "I'll look the other way for a pickup."

His wife, a plump blonde in a bright pink suit, elbowed him in the gut. "Are we talking trucks or women?"

"Trucks, Penny," Billings assured her. He and his wife, a gorgeous brunette half a head taller than he was, came up on Ethan's other side. "He's been off women ever since that gorgeous little DUI rabbited in the middle of her field sobriety test and he had to chase her down the riverbank and into the water."

"Nikkie, you did a wonderful job!" This praise came from Joanne. She and Zachary had approached the group. They'd arrived that afternoon for the Winter Festival weekend.

Zachary patted Nikkie's shoulder. "Good work, young lady." He appeared quite well, though he leaned on a brass-handled cane. "Your shields, by the way, looked very authentic."

"Beth's responsible for that," she said with a smile in Beth's direction. "We're going to sell them at the Parents' Club auction at the end of the school year to make money for the drama club *next* year."

"Wonderful idea." Joanne leaned toward Beth to be heard in the crush of people. "Would you mind if Zach and I go home rather than on to the dance? We're pretty beat."

Jason's grandparents were staying at Beth's and Ethan's for the weekend. Beth shook her head. "Of course not. I laid in some snacks, so help yourselves."

The conversation ended abruptly when the announcement was made that the rooter bus was leaving in fifteen minutes. With costumes to change and determined to be on time, the "army" cut a wide swath through parents and friends.

The friendly insanity, however, went on well into the evening. Ethan, Beth and Jason, Brodie and Kelly, and Curtis and Billings and their wives shared a table in the fairground hall for the after-theater dance and dessert.

Ethan and the deputies recounted stories of their more humorous cases, with Brodie, as the man who repaired their vehicles, making a few contributions. Jason sat beside Ethan, leaning over his arm, laughing with the men and absorbing every word. The women talked children and jobs and men, remembering wryly what it was like worrying about them when they were late.

"Who'd have guessed," Penny Curtis asked, indicating with a jut of her chin the laughing men, "that they were late because they were having such a good time?"

Jan Billings shook her head. "Bert could have fun at the dentist. What do you do with a man like that?"

"Thank God for him every day," Kelly advised.

Beth had to agree.

"All right, what'll you have for dessert?" Ebbie suddenly materialized at their table wearing an apron with the Ladies of Law Enforcement logo. The group had provided and was serving desserts as a fund-raiser for the county's new women's crisis center. "And make it snappy. Don't think that because I work with most of you that I'll take any guff. Now. We have double chocolate torte, blackberry cobbler with vanilla ice cream, or crème caramel with whipped cream. No substitutions."

She studied each face in turn. "It would help me a

lot if you'd all have the same thing and then consider seconds. It's been a long day, and this is a good cause."

Beth saw the mutiny brewing as the men from Ebbie's office exchanged glances.

"Cake," Ethan said with a straight face, "and I'd like that à la mode."

"Only the cobbler comes with—" Ebbie began.

"I'll have the crème caramel with ice cream," Curtis said.

"You can't—"

"I'll have the cobbler with whipped cream." This from Billings, who turned to his wife.

Picking up the game, Jan asked, "Is there a sampler plate with a little bit of everything?"

"Cake with whipped cream," Penny ordered briskly.

"Cake with crème caramel," Brodie said. "And the same for Kelly."

"I'll have the cobbler with ice cream." Beth gave her companions a scolding look, then when Ebbie offered her a smile for her cooperation, she added, "But I'd like my ice cream on the bottom, please. And could I have a raspberry vanilla latte to go with that, with nonfat milk but real whipped cream? Dusted with cinnamon."

Everyone laughed heartily and Ethan pulled Beth into his arms and kissed her temple in congratulations. Then they all awaited Ebbie's reaction.

She drew a breath so deep that the bib of her apron rose and fell, and she looked around the table again, desire for retribution just barely masking the laughter in her eyes. "Eight chocolate cakes," she said, scribbling on her pad, "and eight regular coffees. Jason?"

She leaned over the child whose head rested on Ethan's arm, apparently willing to give *him* a choice. But he was fast asleep.

"If he wakes up," Ethan said, "I'll share with him."

Ebbie nodded, then looked around the table one more time. "The tip," she said, her voice soft with significance, "had better be worth my while."

Curtis looked up innocently. "I didn't know you tipped at charity functions."

Ebbie patted his head. "Then you're going to be our first registration at the new home for battered *men.*"

The men groaned and booed at her threat, and she blew them a kiss as she returned to the kitchen.

Conversation and laughter began again, and Beth leaned comfortably into Ethan, his arm still around her. He eased his other arm out from under Jason's cheek and let the boy's head fall to his chest. Jason stirred restlessly, found a comfortable spot on the wool of Ethan's jacket, tucked his hand under his chin and didn't move for the next hour.

Beth couldn't remember ever being more content in her life.

SATURDAY DAWNED cold but sunny. Beth looked out the kitchen window with gratitude, knowing that even though the art-fair organizers had put up tents to protect the artwork in the event of rain, people would be far more likely to walk around—and to linger and look—if the weather was fair.

Brodie and Joanne prepared breakfast, and Beth and Kelly tried to skip it in the interest of a little extra time to set out their wares on the pier where all the tenants of the Cannery Art Mall—as Beth had named it—would be showing their work. The rest of the artists would be strung out under tents along the river.

"You have to eat something," Ethan insisted. "It's going to be a long day. You might not get any lunch." He pressed a glass of orange juice into Beth's hand as she tried to dodge him to get to her jacket.

She took several swallows and then handed it to Kelly, who finished it. "Thanks. But there'll be vendors all over the pla—"

"It's ready." Brodie carried two steaming plates of omelettes and toast to the table. "Sit down. You could have this eaten in the time you spend arguing with us."

Ethan took their jackets from them and returned them to the pegs. Brodie pulled out chairs.

Kelly sighed at Beth and, resigned, moved to the table. "I remember now why we made that pact about men and marriage."

"What pact?" Joanne asked from the stove.

Aware of the potential danger in that line of conversation, Beth tried to warn Kelly off with a severe look, but Kelly, her mind no doubt on other things, had apparently forgotten Joanne's connection to Steve on this sunny morning.

"Never to fall for another one," Kelly answered, reaching for the pepper. "My husband wanted everything his way, and Beth's usually forgot she was alive. He—"

Kelly stopped abruptly, awareness dawning on her face.

Joanne frowned and put the spatula down on the stove. Her expression changed from the almost convivial cheer they'd grown used to to that of the woman

Beth remembered all too well from the old days—defensive, judgmental, argumentative.

"What do you mean?" Joanne demanded.

Beth closed her eyes, thinking that the last thing in the world she wanted to discuss this morning was her relationship with Steve. But maybe it was time to set the issue straight. Not the ideal time, certainly, but time all the same.

"I didn't mean anything, Joanne," Kelly said, apology in her eyes when she looked at Beth. "I was talking out of turn."

Joanne moved to the table, pulled out a chair at a right angle to Beth's and sat. The smell of something burning came from the stove. Brodie picked up the spatula and turned the charring omelette. Then Ethan moved to the table, as well, and took the chair opposite Joanne. He leaned back in it as though in the role of observer, but Beth knew better now. He was making himself available if she needed him.

"Kelly was my confidant in Seattle, Joanne," Beth said with courtesy but no apology, "and she listened to my problems when Steve wouldn't. She knows what I went through the last couple of years with Steve."

Joanne went pale. "Steve gave you everything."

Beth nodded. "Everything he could buy, yes."

"He was a wonderful father."

"On the five or six times a year he actually came home before Jason went to bed, yes, he was."

"He was working for *you!*"

Beth sighed. Old pain tried to resurrect itself but failed because there was so much new love. "Joanne, he was working for himself, because some inner demon made him always want to do more, make more, get more. I don't know if he was trying to prove something to you and Zachary or just to himself, but it controlled his whole life."

"You had that wonderful house on the sound that everyone envied!"

"That's why we had it," Beth said. "Not because I wanted it, but so it could be envied. So everyone who visited would want what it contained, and Steve could make more sales, open more stores. I was the answering machine. My job was to make everyone who called Steve at home feel as though he was getting special treatment. I was a business tactic, Joanne, not a wife."

"Then why did you stay?"

Beth had thought about that often in the year since he'd been gone. Especially lately, knowing what marriage *could* be like.

"Because Jason loved him," she said, "and I'd made a vow."

Joanne's lips pinched closed and she looked away a moment, her eyes welling with tears. "So you're glad he's gone?"

"Joanne." Zachary had come into the room. His tone was reproachful.

Joanne looked up at her husband defensively. "Well, she was miserable. She hated him. She *must* be glad."

"I *was* miserable," Beth said candidly. "But it was because I'd loved him so much in the beginning and then it all disintegrated from inattention. Even in my worst moments, I never hated him, never wished him dead. I was just so…disappointed."

She reached blindly for Ethan's hand. He caught hers and squeezed it.

Joanne excused herself and left the room. With a moody glance around, Zachary shook his head and turned to follow her. Kelly put both hands over her face and burst into tears.

Beth's mouth trembled dangerously. "Kelly, stop it!" she ordered. "It wasn't your fault. That conversation was long overdue."

Ethan used Beth's hand to pull her out of her chair and into his lap as she sniffed back tears of her own.

"It isn't grief for Steve," she said. "It's…I think it's…"

"I know." He rubbed her back and pressed his cheek to her hair. "Grief for how it should have been. But I don't want you to be unhappy." He snatched a napkin from the holder on the table and gave it to her.

She dried her eyes and drew a breath. "I'm not unhappy. I just hate confrontation."

He grinned skeptically. "Really? I've never noticed that."

She laughed and kissed his temple. Then she turned to her friend, who still had tears streaming down her cheeks. "Kelly, it's okay."

Brodie dropped the spatula and crossed to the table. He leaned over Kelly and put his arms around her, then glanced at Ethan, humor glinting in his eyes. "Didn't we make a pact about staying away from women?"

Ethan held fast to Beth. "No," he replied. "As I remember, we made a pact to seek them out."

Brodie looked from the weeping woman in his arms to Beth, dabbing at her eyes with a napkin. "You mean…we're doing well?"

Ethan grinned. "Damned if I know."

People thronged the art fair. The colorful tents set up along the water made Cobbler's Crossing look like some medieval encampment. Musicians had been hired to stroll among the exhibits, and the sound of their instruments floated through the air as though sent from another time.

But it was the aroma of waffle cones that was driving Beth crazy. After her set-to with Joanne, she hadn't had time to eat her omelette, and she and Kelly had hurried to the pier on empty stomachs, after all.

Rush Weston had already arrived and, in high spirits at the prospect of the day ahead, had helped them haul out tables and set up their work. All the while he'd boasted of the special project he would unveil at one o'clock, the sculpture that would grace the lawn of the art association's newly acquired permanent home near the maritime museum.

"I beat out fourteen other artists for the commission, you know," he said several times.

Appreciating his help, Beth and Kelly agreed he was wonderful, winking at each other across the long table the three of them had carried out of Kelly's studio.

Rush was set up around the corner of the cannery building, and the tall sculpture stood under what appeared to be several bedsheets sewn together. The sheets protruded with something pointy out the top and out the back, causing Kelly to speculate.

"Knowing him," she said to Beth sotto voce as they dutifully admired his setup of sculpture and bronzes, then returned to their own areas, "it's probably a giant breast! But I'm still anxious to see it. The guy's a genius."

Beth nodded. "I'm with you. And it was nice of him to help us."

"Mm. Only, it makes me wonder what he's up to."

Ethan, with Nikkie, Jason and Taylor Bridges in tow, arrived shortly after the opening with a wonderfully aromatic bag of food from a local takeout place.

"I'll sit for you," Nikkie offered, "so you can have breakfast."

"Brodie brought breakfast for Kelly, too," Ethan said, catching Beth's hand and pulling her aside while Nikkie took her place behind the table. "So why don't the two of you take a little time to relax and look around before the midmorning crush?" He put a hand to her cheek and looked into her eyes, his own gentle but searching. "You all right?"

She nodded. Her disagreement with Joanne had put a bit of a pall over the day. But if things went well, the exposure would help her as an artist and present the Cannery Art Mall to everyone who visited as the place for unique fine art and the more commercial but one-of-a-kind handicrafts.

She turned her lips into his hand. "I'm fine," she said. "I can't believe that deep down Joanne and Zachary weren't aware of all that about Steve, but I thought it was time to say it. I'm sorry it had to be in your kitchen."

"It's *our* kitchen," he corrected with a sweet smile. It turned wicked as he added, "I just don't want you cooking in it very much. Go find Kelly and a quiet place to have your breakfasts. I promised the boys I'd take them to the carnival." He pointed to the Ferris wheel a couple of hundred yards farther down the waterfront. "Nikkie'll watch your table until you're finished."

Beth put the take-out bag down and looped her arms around Ethan's neck. His warmth and his calm seeped into her, and she kissed him lingeringly, trying to tell him how truly happy he'd made her and how much she loved him.

"Yeah," he said, his voice ragged as she finally drew her mouth away. "Me, too."

"Dad, come on!" Jason said impatiently. He caught Ethan's hand and tugged. "You guys can do that later. Me and Taylor want to ride the moon jet!"

"All right, all right." Ethan kissed Beth one more time, then strode after the boys as they ran up the pier to the waterfront path.

Only as Beth replayed the scene in her mind did she realize Jason had called Ethan "Dad." It brought a lump to her throat and seemed to seal her life in place.

"I THINK I'M DEAD," Kelly said, nibbling on a sausage roll as she and Beth wandered slowly through a Peg-Board setup of small scenic paintings done in the impressionist style.

Beth sipped at a paper cup of tea as she stepped back to study a painting of mountains and a meandering stream. "That's funny. You look very much alive to me."

"I mean dead as a single woman," Kelly said.

They were now on opposite sides of the Peg-Board setup, and Beth leaned around it to look into Kelly's face. "I know that being a potter makes your *brain* go to pot, but try to be clearer. Are you trying to tell me we're going to be sisters-in-law?" Kelly and Brodie had wandered off together the night before in the middle of a dance and hadn't been seen again until they'd appeared in Ethan's kitchen that morning.

Kelly's expression was both terrified and excited. "Will it mean a reduction in rent?"

"No," Beth said. "If I'm going to have to put up with you day in and day out, it means I'll need *more* money. Will you please speak plainly?"

Kelly came around the Peg-Board, chewing and swallowing her last bite of biscuit. Her cheeks were flushed. "Brodie asked me to marry him last night."

Beth squealed and caught her in a hug. She couldn't think of anything more wonderful than having her best friend become a part of her family.

"Brodie's wonderful," Beth said. "You're going to be so happy!"

Kelly took a step back, still holding Beth's arms. Her eyes were filled with amazement. "Who'd have thought just a year ago," she asked softly, "that we'd both end up in love with and marrying the kind of men most women only dream about?"

As they hugged each other again, Beth realized it would never have occurred to *her*.

BETH SOLD six door plaques to an older woman who was thrilled to find the names of all her grandchildren. After a trip to her car with those, the woman returned to buy four painted flowerpots for gifts, then wandered over to Kelly's table and picked up several bowls.

Beth had just secured the morning's take in a locked box in her studio and intended to take advantage of the lull to tidy up her table when Kelly strode over and took her by the arm.

"Come on," she said. "Let's go see Rush's grand unveiling."

Beth glanced at her watch. It was three minutes to one.

"You go ahead," she said. "I should haul out some more things. These people are in a buying frenzy, and I don't want to miss one patron with an impulse to overspend."

Kelly rolled her eyes. "Jeez, Louise, lighten up. All our customers are collecting at Rush's, anyway. See. Our end of the pier is empty."

Beth looked up from rearranging a pair of children's chairs she'd painted with whimsical mice to find that Kelly was right. A few people were headed for the carnival, but everyone else was formed in a large semicircle, half-a-dozen people deep, around Rush's display tables.

"All right." Beth followed Kelly to Rush's area and discovered her friend had an ulterior motive in insisting they go. Brodie and Ethan were there, too.

Kelly went right into Brodie's arms and into a kiss that made everyone nearby smile and look away. Except Beth. She watched them, feeling as though, in a life filled with miracles, she'd been given yet another.

Then Ethan wrapped his arms around her from behind and found a spot for them in the crowd where she could see. The local radio station was broadcasting remote, and the *Crossings Crusader* had sent a reporter and a photographer.

Beth leaned her head back against Ethan's shoulder. "Did you know," she asked, "that Brodie and Kelly are getting married?"

Ethan smiled. "He just told me. Well, actually he stammered around a lot and I figured it out for myself."

Beth laughed. "Ebbie'll be thrilled to do another wedding." She gasped. "Uh-oh."

"What?"

She widened her eyes in mock alarm. "Kelly catered for us. Does that mean I have to cater for her?"

"No," he replied, kissing her cheek. "I think it means Kelly'll do it and ask you to serve."

Beth pretended hurt feelings. "That's mean."

His arms around her squeezed. "I'll make it up to you later," he whispered in her ear.

Rush cleared his throat, and the broadcaster who'd attached a microphone to the pocket of the artist's chambray shirt stepped out of his way.

Beth leaned back again into Ethan. "Where's Jason?" she asked.

"I sold him to the carnival," Ethan replied.

"Did you get a good price?"

"I threw in Nikkie. She's so good at the midway games she'll bankrupt them in a month, and then they'll be home again. But we can do some high living in the meantime."

"Oh, good."

The strolling musicians had stopped behind Rush and now played a little flourish. Rush began to speak. He talked about what a beautiful spot Cobbler's Crossing was and how the area was a source of inspiration for artists, himself particularly.

"Everything's about 'himself particularly,'" Ethan grumbled softly in Beth's ear.

She jabbed him gently with an elbow, then turned her attention back to Rush, hoping the sculpture would give him the fame his ego seemed to need so desperately.

He went on to talk about himself, giving a rather lengthy history of his career, then said that everything changed for him when he moved to Cobbler's Crossing.

"I found friends here," he said dramatically, his strong profile tipped upward, "and my particular inspiration." He swept a hand toward the shrouded sculpture. "This piece, entitled *Water Woman,* is the culmination of a four-month labor of love. My heart and my soul have gone into it, and I now present it to you, the people of Cobbler's Crossing."

Rush yanked on the sheet and it fell into his arms, revealing a life-size bronze of a nude female figure. A collective cry of approval rose from the crowd.

As Beth admired the statue from the base on which it stood on tiptoe on one foot, the other leg raised and bent at the knee as though the woman had been caught midstride, she thought she noticed a slight change in sound in the common cry of approval.

But the artist in her was too busy appreciating the "movement" in the bronze. The body was poised in an upward stretch, as if toward something just beyond reach. The thighs were long and slender, the hips rounded, the waist slender, the breasts uptilted and generous, the reaching arms graceful.

And then Beth saw the face.

With a little gasp she fell back against Ethan, and that was when she noticed that the arms around her were now like rock and the tension coming from him almost palpable.

She heard someone else gasp and knew the sound had come from Kelly.

The face on the sculpture...was Beth's.

CHAPTER SIXTEEN

THERE WAS A SMATTERING of applause among the other artists assembled, enthusiastic cheers from some men in appreciation of the female form, and startled glances at Beth from acquaintances who thought she must be embarrassed. There were also the disapproving frowns of those who would never understand that nude modeling did not suggest a morally bankrupt character.

The almost painful grip of the arms around her indicated that her husband was among that group. Beth pushed her way out of his embrace and turned, thinking that if she explained calmly and carefully, he might understand.

But she knew the moment she looked into his eyes that that wasn't going to happen. He was wearing the same expression he'd worn the night he'd hauled her out of the Applebys' basement and taken her to jail.

A cold knot formed in her midsection. They weren't going to be able to come together on this. She could hear his argument now. *Do you know what it's like to be present at the unveiling of a nude sculpture and have everyone identify it as your wife?*

Beth saw her in-laws standing in the front row of spectators across the semicircle. Their expressions could only be described as horrified shock.

Embarrassment, frustration, anger and disappointment became a turbulent combination in Beth's chest. She wanted to hide, she wanted to throw things, she wanted to be sick, and then she wanted to die.

But before she did any of those things, she wanted to kill Rush Weston.

But that was self-indulgence, she told herself, and something for which she had no time at the moment. Beth Warner Richards Drum had had it with everybody.

As Rush invited people closer to study the sculpture, Beth realized she was tired of being threatened with the loss of her child, tired of having to be on the watch for her in-laws' detective, tired of having to remind Rush Weston that he didn't love her and she didn't love him, tired of having to remind her husband of the same thing.

Feeling as though she should slip an arm into one of the shields she'd made for Henry V's army, she turned to Ethan and said into his furious dark eyes, "I'll deal with you later. Excuse me."

She knew that genuine shock was the only thing that prevented him from grabbing her and telling her what he thought of her then and there.

She marched through the crowd to where Joanne and Zachary continued to stand gasping at the sculpture. She collected congratulations and pats on the back for being Rush's model and "inspiration," as well as several glares, as she crossed the pier.

She stopped in front of Joanne, arms folded with resolution. "Where is he?" she asked with the air of royal command she'd learned from Joanne.

Joanne met Beth's gaze, her own imperiousness in place. "Who?"

"The detective," Beth replied. "Where is he?"

She saw embarrassment in Joanne's eyes for an instant, then it was gone. "What detective?" she asked innocently.

"The one you hired to check me out," Beth said, shifting her weight, her voice rising a trifle. "The one who's been following me and photographing me. Tell me where he is, or I'll have you arrested for harassment."

"Really?" The imperious look now became scornful. "You're threatening me after you posed naked for that…"

Zachary suddenly pointed his cane at a youngish man in a trench coat who stood several yards away, even now taking photographs. "Right there," Zachary said. "That's Frank Bowker."

Beth pointed to the spot where she and the Richardses stood. "You stay right here or I'll come after you, I swear it."

She turned in the direction of Bowker and was on him even as he took a final photo of her. Then he was preparing to run, backing away and trying to secure his camera over his shoulder. But she had him by the lapels before he could get away.

He was several inches taller than she was, and he appeared to be fairly substantial under the coat. Nevertheless there was no Mike Hammer toughness about him. In fact, she thought she saw fear leap in his eyes when she grabbed him.

"You're coming with me," she said, giving him her best Ethan-in-a-temper look. "And I don't want to hear one complaint or feel the least resistance, do you hear me?"

He seemed to try to pull himself together. "Who do you think you are?" he asked with false bravado.

While he was posturing, she snatched his camera from him. "The woman whose privacy you've been invading," she replied.

"Following you and taking pictures is not a crime," he said, his voice faltering.

She got right into his face. "When your husband is the bad-tempered sheriff of a small town, it is," she said, disregarding the distinct possibility that Ethan wasn't going to be her husband for much longer. "And I'm also holding this...what? Six-, seven-hundred-dollar piece of equipment?"

He sighed. "Nine," he said.

She looped the camera strap over her shoulder. "Then you'd better follow me."

Beth strode back to her in-laws as the rest of the crowd dispersed to the food stands and the other tents. They stood alone, a man and a woman who suddenly looked old and rather frail. But Beth refused to let her resolution slip.

"I'd like you to come with me, please," she said. "And, Zachary, be careful with your cane—those spaces between the planks." Then she marched off toward her studio as though completely confident that her in-laws and their detective were following.

Beth saw that Nikkie was manning her table. "That's quite a bod for a stepmother," Nikkie said under her breath, then giggled. "Are you back? Where's Dad?"

"Would you mind watching the table for a little longer?" Beth asked. Sad, she thought, that it was all falling apart when she and Nikkie were finally becoming friends. "I think your father's...still looking around."

"Sure, no problem. Take your time."

"Thanks, Nikkie." Beth ushered Zachary, Joanne and Bowker into her studio and closed the door. She flipped on all the lights she had, but the cavernous space was still dimly lit everywhere but under the fluorescent bulb above the worktable. So she gathered everyone there.

She pulled a stool up for Joanne. "You might want to sit down, Jo," she said.

"I'll stand," Joanne insisted. "You don't frighten me."

"It isn't my intention to frighten you." Beth made herself speak calmly. "It's my intention to explain a few things to you, then make it clear that there is no way in hell you will ever get Jason from me."

"Beth—" Zachary began.

Beth silenced him with a raised index finger. "I know you're a judge, Zachary, and I know you have influential friends, but even you can't make a case where there is none."

"But there's a statue of your naked body!" Joanne exclaimed.

"Joanne, it's art!" Beth said slowly, carefully. "I posed for Rush's sculpture class when I first moved here to make extra money. I didn't know Rush had sculpted me, but now that he has, I'm flattered to grace the lawn of the art association's new building." That wasn't true, but it wouldn't hurt to let Joanne think it was. "And that is not against the law."

"It's—" Joanne made a face "—disgusting."

And for the very first time Beth had an insight into Steve's sexual reactions to her. Was that what Joanne had taught him? That the body was disgusting?

"It isn't disgusting at all," Zachary said quietly. He used his cane to hike himself up on the stool, then rubbed at his cast as though the leg inside it ached. He gave Beth a thin smile. "I thought it was quite beautiful."

"Zach!" Joanne's eyes widened.

He sighed. "Don't be such a priss, Jo," he said mildly. "You looked like that once, and I enjoyed looking at you. But when I was made a judge, you changed. You became full of self-importance and you assumed a dictatorial code of behavior, which you inflicted on Steve—until he became just as stiff and self-absorbed. You did it to me, too."

Beth stood paralyzed in complete surprise, afraid to breathe for fear she'd be noticed.

"Zachary!" Joanne gasped, leaning against the table for support.

"It's true, Jo," he said heavily. "We used to be fun, you and I, and now you've turned us into caricatures of stuffy old folks. And you turned a boy who was already too serious for his own good into a man consumed with status, with wanting more."

"Are you saying...?" Joanne's mouth quivered, unable to say the words.

"That the adult he became is your fault?" Zachary shook his head. "We all get to a point where we have to look the past in the eye and decide what we want for our own future. Apparently he grew blind to his wife and son, and all he saw was getting and owning. But he did that to himself."

Zachary sighed and ran a hand over his face, then he turned to Beth. "I admit I was a little worried when I first saw your apartment in this place." He looked around, nodding as he noted the fresh coat of paint and the refinements she'd made. "Steve was always telling us that your art took so much time away from him, and I believed him. I was worried for Jason. But now that we've spent time with you and I've seen you with him and with Ethan and the girl, I don't think there was every anything wrong with you. I realize now the problem was with Steve."

Beth was still afraid to breathe.

Joanne looked even more shocked than she'd been by the statue.

"I didn't want the detective, either," Zachary continued. "But Jo thought it would give us something concrete to go on, and I've found it's often easier to take the line of least resistance when her mind's made up. But no more. Give her the film, Bowker. All of it."

Bowker backed up a few steps, prepared to resist.

"Now," Zachary said more loudly. He took the wallet out of his jacket pocket. "Hand the cartridges to Beth, you'll get paid in full, and this will be over."

Beth's heart began to thump erratically. Over? The threat of losing Jason finally over? She'd talked a good line about the solidity of their case, but she didn't believe for a minute that she was invincible where the law was concerned. After all, she'd gone to jail for looking for a cat!

Bowker vacillated a moment, then apparently decided that immediate payment was more appealing than cartridges of film that would have no value to anyone else. He delved into his camera bag, produced six cartridges and placed them on the table.

Beth handed him his camera. "And I want the one that's in there now."

Bowker took it out and handed it to her. Zachary wrote him a check, which he quickly pocketed, and then he left.

Joanne put a hand to her heart. "Oh, my God," she moaned.

Beth turned to her in concern.

"Don't fall for it, Beth," Zachary said, easing himself off the stool. "She always has palpitations when she doesn't get what she wants. She'll be fine. I want to thank you and Ethan for your hospitality. We're going back to the house now to collect our things, then we'll head for home."

Beth steadied him as he braced against the cane and regained his footing. "I have to tell you something else before you go," she said.

He raised an eyebrow. "What's that?"

She heard herself speak as though it were someone else's voice. "That I did marry Ethan to stop you from taking me to court."

Zachary smiled. "I don't think you did. I think you married him because you saw in him everything you missed with Steve. I like that boy. I loved my son, but I didn't always *like* him."

Joanne now had both hands over her face.

"Neither did you, Jo," he said, slowly closing the few feet that separated them, the thump of his cane echoing in the big room. "How many times did you tell me he should make more time for Jason? You were willing to believe him about Beth because you were jealous of her, but you worried about Jason all the time. I think you wanted the boy just so you could make up to him what Steve didn't give him."

Joanne lowered her hands. Beth could see the lines that bitter disappointment had etched in her face.

"I wanted Steve to be better than he was," she said, her voice thin. "I told him Jason needed him. But he said...he said Beth wanted more."

"Jo, you knew that wasn't true." Zachary cupped his wife's cheek. "You wanted it to be true so you wouldn't have to blame him, but it wasn't. He became selfish and small. Admit it."

Joanne shook her head against the words, and Zachary pulled her into his arms. "He was such a cute little kid," he said to Beth, his own grief visible in his eyes. "It's hard to let go of that when they grow up and turn into someone else."

Tears welling in her eyes, Beth put a hand on Joanne's back. "Zachary, don't leave for Seattle like this. Why don't you spend the night and leave tomorrow? Come on, I'll walk you to your car."

Beth hugged Joanne before helping her into the Cadillac. "Steve and I had a good couple of years in the beginning. I like to remember that. I wish you would, too."

Joanne held her for a moment, then leaned back to look into her eyes. "You weren't ever as happy with him as you are with Ethan."

Beth was glad that had been phrased as a statement rather than a question, considering that Rush's grand unveiling had seriously endangered what she had with Ethan.

"I'll see you at home," she said.

Beth stood in the middle of the parking area that fronted the river and watched them drive away. She felt as though a heavy burden lay suspended in her chest. Much of it had been lifted by Zachary's words, but she'd come to care about her in-laws in the past few weeks more than she ever had when she'd been married to their son. She hated to think of them lonely and in pain.

Her worries had been relocated, not relieved.

She headed back toward the pier at a determined pace, scanning the crowd for Ethan or for Rush. She'd take on whomever she found first.

Then she stopped in her tracks. The pier was empty; the crowd was gone. Tables and booths had been abandoned. Where was everyone?

Then she heard shouts coming from the other side of the cannery. She followed them, picking up her pace until she was running. Had something terrible happened? It must have. What else would have made the artists leave their work unattended?

Then, as she rounded the corner of the building and saw the knot of about a hundred people gathered at the pier's railing, she realized that their shouts were cheers.

She stared in shock as Brodie and several other men hauled Ethan out of the water with a rope. Rush Weston's arms were wrapped around his neck.

Rush was peeled from Ethan's back and laid on the pier, coughing and spitting up water. Jan Billings knelt over him as the crowd gathered around.

Ethan, drenched and perched on the railing, swung his legs onto the pier and leaped nimbly down as Beth approached. Kelly threw a blanket around him. "Ambulance is on its way," she said. "Sorry about the musty smell. I keep it in the trunk of my car. Are you okay?"

"Fine," he replied tersely.

"Daddy!" Nikkie tried to embrace the bulk of him under the blanket.

He allowed her one moment, then kissed her temple and took a step back. "I'm okay, Nik. I don't want you to get wet."

"What happened?" Beth asked. Concern for him,

despite her anger and helpless frustration over the way this day had gone, made her voice and her manner sharp. "Did it make you feel better to throw Rush in the water?"

Ethan dried his face with a corner of the blanket. When he lowered the rough brown wool to look at her, she saw instantly that he wasn't at all hypothermic. A man couldn't be on the brink of freezing and still have eyes that hotly angry.

"Beth, he—" Brodie began, but Ethan silenced him with a look.

"When I can't speak for myself," he said, his tone deadly, "I'll let you know."

"My mistake." Brodie, probably also concerned about Ethan's dunking, snarled back at him. "Second one today. The first one was pulling you out of the water."

Ethan glared at his brother for a moment, then a smile curved his lips. "Did I forget to thank you for that? *My* mistake."

"I suggest everyone calm down," Kelly said diplomatically. "Here, Ethan. A vendor brought you this cup of coffee. Ah. There's the ambulance."

Kelly pulled Beth and Nikkie aside as Ethan moved over to Rush, who was now sitting up. Jan was rubbing circulation into his shoulders and arms.

Rush looked up as the crowd parted to let the EMTs through with their gurney. He focused on Ethan and even from a small distance Beth heard him say clearly, "Thanks. I'm not sure I'd have jumped in after *you*."

Ethan accepted that with a nod. "I just wanted to make sure you lived to serve your thirty days for swinging at me."

Beth heard the exchange with an awful sense of

having been impulsive and wrong once again. Oddly it made her feel more defensive than penitent. She put her fingertips to the throbbing that had begun at her right temple.

"Yes," Kelly said wryly, "stupidity does give you a headache, doesn't it? Rush was telling a group of guys that the model had been his lover. Ethan suggested he tell the truth. Rush swung at Ethan, not the other way around. Ethan dodged him and Rush landed in the river. He can't swim."

Rush was in the ambulance in a matter of minutes. The EMTs apparently tried to convince Ethan to go along to be checked over, but he refused.

The ambulance drove off. Jan Billings railed at Ethan about getting out of the cold air and into a hot shower and dry clothes even as she lent him the cell phone in her purse to call the office.

"I'm on my way home," he told Jan when he handed back the phone. "I appreciate your concern, but I'm fine. Beth!"

The note in his voice was authoritative. Considering Beth had intended to make the afternoon about taking charge of her own life, she didn't respond well to the sound of it. Now that she was sure he was all right, she became furious all over again for the way he'd reacted to the unveiling of Rush's bronze.

"Yes?" she asked frostily.

He whipped the blanket off, balled it in his hands and handed it to Kelly. "Thanks, Kelly," he said, then to Beth again, "You're coming with me. Nikkie, will you go back and watch her table?"

Beth tried to protest. "I can't just—"

Ethan ignored her and turned to his brother. "Will Bridges has Jason and Taylor at the carnival. He's bringing Jason back at two-thirty. Can you bring him home?"

"Sure."

"Nikkie is supposed to meet her friends at three at the taco booth," Beth informed him. "We can't just ignore her plans."

"That's all right," Kelly said traitorously. "At three o'clock, we'll move your table up against mine and I'll watch both of them. We'll get the kids home afterward, don't worry."

War was in the wind, and while Beth had been eager to confront it earlier, she'd felt completely in the right then. Now she was guilty of having accused Ethan of a petty act, when it had really been an heroic one. And she didn't want to walk into a fight at such a disadvantage.

"Joanne and Zachary are at home," she told him. "You go home and shower and I'll be along later."

Kelly pointed to the cannery. "Beth's old apartment is still there. It's tiny, but there is a shower and...you know, room to argue."

Ethan shook his head. "This is going to be a loud argument. We need privacy."

"You need the shower and dry clothes first," Jan insisted, her arms folded resolutely. "And I'm going to hang around until you do it, or I'll call the EMTs back and make them take you to the ER."

Brodie gave Ethan a push in the direction of the cannery. "Go shower. It'll take me five minutes to run home and get you a change of clothes."

Beth showed a stiff-backed Ethan to the shower in her small apartment. She handed him a towel, which he took with a terse thank-you and closed the door on her.

Fuming, she went back outside to help Nikkie as a crowd began to form around her table. It occurred to her that there was something to be said for notoriety.

True to his word, Brodie was back in a very short time with a bag, which he carried into the cannery. Ethan came out shortly afterward in a dark blue sweater and cords. He caught Beth's wrist in the middle of a transaction.

"Ethan, I was—"

But he interrupted her to speak to Nikkie. "Thanks, Nik. Uncle Brodie'll take you home."

"Where are you going?" Nikkie asked, wrapping a clay pot in newspaper. She looked worriedly from her father to Beth.

"We'll be home by dinner," he replied. Then he hauled Beth up the pier toward the parking lot.

Beth dragged her feet and pulled against him. "Ethan, my purse is—"

He threw an arm around her waist, anchored her to his side and kept walking. "You're not going to need your purse."

Beth pulled at the fingers biting into her side. "Every woman in this town is going to vote against you in the next election if you keep acting like a Neanderthal!"

The possibility apparently didn't concern him. He strode across the parking lot with her held close to his side. When he reached the Blazer, he put her in, then locked and closed her door.

He was behind the wheel in an instant and turned the key in the ignition. He switched off the radio, switched on the heater and whipped out of the parking lot and onto the fortunately empty highway with the speed of a competitor at Le Mans.

"You have a bad habit," she said coolly, "of letting your temper affect your driving."

"Don't worry about it," he replied. "I've had pursuit training. But it'd help me if you didn't distract me with conversation."

She leaned her head back against the headrest and closed her eyes. "Another one of those arguments where only *you* get to talk?"

"Yeah. Right. Whose voice are *you* hearing?"

Beth didn't respond, partly because he was right, and partly because she was trying to save her reserves of wit for what was coming. She was going to need them. He was a worthy if completely unreasonable adversary.

She had no idea where he was going. He followed the main road through town to the far end of the waterfront. There he turned off onto another road that led down a slope to a little cove sheltering a long-deserted yacht club. The old frame building had fallen into disrepair, and most of the windows were broken.

There wasn't a soul around.

The parking lot and boat ramp stood empty under a weakening afternoon sun. Clouds massed on the western horizon and began moving toward Cobbler's Crossing. The grass along the riverbank bent with the wind.

Beth looked away from the clouds as Ethan stopped in the middle of the parking lot, turned off the ignition with an angry jerk and rested his wrist on top of the steering wheel.

He stared angrily through the windshield, apparently collecting his thoughts for an attack on Rush's sculpture.

On the theory that the best defense was a good offense, Beth launched her own attack. She yanked off her seat belt and turned toward him.

"I'll save you the trouble, Ethan," she said, sad and disappointed that it had to turn out this way. "I've been through this with you once before, remember? I know exactly what you're about to say."

He turned to her, the anger in his eyes momentarily diluted by confusion.

"At the Appleby house," she said. "This is a slight variation on the theme. 'Do you have any idea,'" she said, her tone deepening as she mimicked his voice, "'what it's like to attend the unveiling of a nude statue in front of most of the town and discover that your wife posed for it?'"

She resumed her natural voice. "You were embarrassed, and like almost everyone else, you think that because someone models in the nude, there has to be lewd and lascivious behavior involved. That modeling was done in a sculpture class Rush was teaching in the presence of eighteen students, many of them other women. I had no idea Rush was planning me for the art association's front lawn, but I'm tired of defending myself to you. It's clear you're not going to have the tolerance for living with an artist that you claimed you would."

"The only thing that's clear," he returned, "is that *you're* the one who's completely misunderstood the situation. Sure, I was surprised to see that the sculpture was you, but I was not embarrassed. My initial anger was not that you'd posed nude for another artist, but that I dislike the man particularly, and I felt a very natural male inclination to kill him because he'd seen the very image I revere."

Her angry indignation severely dented, Beth tried hard to firm it up. "Because you thought—"

She'd been prepared to accuse him of presuming Rush had made sexual overtures, but Ethan interrupted her. "Don't tell me what I thought. You're not inside my head. In fact, I wonder if you've even been anywhere near me for the past month and a half if you can so misread me."

"Well, if you're not angry about Rush, what's the problem?"

"The problem is you," he said brutally. "I was raving inside that Weston had seen...you. But that was my gut reaction, and I was telling myself that I had to work on that, that what I was feeling wasn't reasonable and I had to get a grip on common sense and see that image of you for what it was—very...beautiful." His eyes grew turbulent and grave with that admission, then anger took over again. "Until you turned around to me and I saw you do it again."

"Do *what* again?"

"Mistake me for Steve." He said the words quietly, but the confines of the car amplified them and seemed to cause them to hang there long after they'd been said.

Beth opened her mouth to defend herself, but he went on, "Just like you presumed I threw Rush in the river. In the six weeks we've been together, I've proved Steve wrong about you over and over, but that still doesn't seem to separate me from him in your mind."

Beth watched the clouds move in over the water, heavy and dark and blotting out the sun. The interior of the car seemed suddenly darker, too.

"Maybe *you're* confusing *me* with Diana," she retorted. "I warned you once that we could never have what you had with Diana."

"I don't *want* what I had with Diana!" he roared. "It was great but that was *her!* I want *you!*"

"Then if you want me, you have to put up with a woman who poses for life-drawing classes! Or who might want to take a class herself! Do you want to go through this emotional struggle every time the subject arises or every time someone teases you because that's me on the front lawn of the art association's building?"

Ethan wondered how it was possible for a man to love a woman and want to murder her at the same time. But that was precisely how he felt.

"You know," he said, "I think you're the one who can't make the adjustment here. This isn't about modeling or not modeling. You're the one who still thinks you can't have your art and a relationship, too, but it isn't because of me. I think you've just decided it's easier to live day and night in your studio doing your thing and not having to worry about working someone else's needs into your life."

Somewhere deep down she recognized a grain of truth in that and closed it off. Assuming an air of feigned surprise was easier than assuming guilt.

"Gee," she said, "when I disagree with you, I end up in a jail cell. Do you think that notion could have anything to do with it?"

"No," he replied evenly. "I think your behaving like a brat has a lot to do with it. Did you really think you could take on another marriage—even one that was just intended for your own purposes—and never have to consult me on anything or explain yourself when necessary?"

She met his gaze, her own unflinching. "I didn't expect to have to do it at every turn. I guess I thought that at home you'd be my husband and not the sheriff."

The radio crackled. Then, "500, come in."

The voice was Ebbie's, and Ethan yanked the microphone off its hook. "500. Go ahead."

"Ethan, we have to transport a juvenile to Portland." Her voice sounded apologetic. "I know it's your day off, but there's no one else available."

The last thing Ethan wanted to do at that moment was transport a sullen juvenile a hundred miles and drive home in the dark on the winding highway.

Then he glanced at Beth, who looked cold and distant and even less appealing than the long drive in the dark.

"I'm on my way," he said, then replaced the mike on its hook and turned the key in the ignition. "We'll have to finish this later."

He expected a sharp retort, but she said nothing, folding her arms and leaning as far away from him as she could while he turned around and headed out of the parking lot.

CHAPTER SEVENTEEN

BETH STOOD for a long time under a lukewarm shower, trying hard to revive herself after a brief three hours of sleep. Ethan hadn't come home until just before midnight, and he'd never come upstairs.

She'd heard subtle sounds in the kitchen and lay tensely on her side of the bed, waiting for him to come up. By then her anger had abated somewhat and she'd been willing to have it out with him, to state her case again and listen to his.

But the opportunity never arose.

She'd finally fallen asleep shortly after four in the morning, and when she'd awakened at seven-thirty, he'd already left for the office.

She took that to mean he didn't want to talk. Maybe he no longer considered their relationship worth the argument required to keep it together.

Sadness weighted her limbs and burned in the pit of her stomach. She went downstairs, desperate for a cup of coffee, and found Jason and Nikkie whispering over breakfast cereal. They stopped guiltily when she walked into the room.

"Hi." She smiled from one to the other, trying to force cheer into her voice. The effort failed. "Didn't your uncle Brodie come over this morning?"

Nikkie studied her worriedly. "He isn't home. I made the coffee. How come Daddy left so early?"

Beth poured half a mug of the thick black brew and took a sip before answering. It was strong enough to generate sound when it hit her stomach. She withheld a wince. "I don't know, Nik. You'll have to ask him." She went to Jason, leaned over and kissed his cheek. "Guess you and I have to take a cab to school and to work."

"Cameron's coming to pick me up in his dad's van," Nikkie said. "The drama club's having a field trip today to the Coaster Theater in Cannon Beach. We can drop you and Jason on the way."

"Great." Beth headed for the basement stairs. "Do you think he'd have room for a few boxes, too?"

Nikkie looked surprised. "Boxes?"

"Yes. I have to take a few things back to the cannery."

ETHAN STARED at the coffee and pecan roll Ebbie had placed on his desk. After no sleep and enough caffeine to keep six people awake for forty-eight hours, he imagined that putting that much sugar into his system would be like dropping a match into a can of gasoline.

He felt too incendiary as it was. He pushed the roll away and tried to force himself to focus on the paperwork before him.

But Ebbie appeared in his office doorway looking uncharacteristically apprehensive. He felt himself tense.

"What?" he demanded.

She pointed vaguely in the direction of town. "There's a...a riot. On Ashley and Ninth."

He stared at her. "A riot. In Cobbler's Crossing."

"Yes."

"Well, aren't there two police units on this morning?"

She shifted her weight. "Yes. They're the ones who called for you."

"Curtis and Billings are patrolling."

"They're already there."

"God." Wishing now that he'd eaten the roll, Ethan ran out to his car and made Ashley and Ninth in just under four minutes. The sidewalk was choked with people, but not the type usually associated with a riot.

There were no professional agitators and no angry youths, just men in business suits standing in front of the bakery, older women with shopping bags, younger women with small children by the hand and pushing strollers. A pair of homeless men, one in a trench coat, one in a tattered paisley silk jogging suit, stood on a bench on the sidewalk across the street for a better look.

As Ethan left his car and pushed his way to the core of the crowd, he was grateful to see that there were no apparent injuries and the mood seemed more confused than hostile. Good. The situation was redeemable.

His thoughts on that changed when he finally reached the source of the disturbance and found every single member of his family involved and most of their friends.

He stared, unable to believe his eyes. Nikkie had Curtis by the arm and seemed to be giving him some elaborate explanation that had the vocal support of the entire drama club, whose members were gathered around her.

Zachary and Joanne were bending the ear of one of

two young police officers in the middle of the fray, while Brodie spoke to another.

Beth and Kelly and Portia Pintoretto had Billings cornered. Mrs. Pintoretto owned Gifts Galore, which Ethan noticed had a gaping hole where a display window had been. As he watched, Kelly and Mrs. Pintoretto grabbed each other's arms, apparently prepared to duke it out, but Billings stepped between them, looking desperate.

Just to add interest to the picture, a half-dozen medieval shields—the ones Beth had helped Nikkie and her friends make—were scattered about the sidewalk, two of them in the gift-shop window.

Trying to imagine how all this had come about, Ethan stepped intrepidly into the middle of it.

Jason was the first to notice his presence. "Dad!" he shouted, and raced toward him as though Ethan were God himself.

Ethan opened his arms and Jason flung himself into them. Nikkie was right behind him.

"Daddy, you've got to help us. It's all a big mistake, and...and..." She began to cry. "It's all my fault again, but Mrs. Pintoretto wants them to arrest Beth and Kelly, but they didn't really do it. Well, they did it, but they didn't do it on purpose!"

"Ethan!" Zachary joined them, leaning on his cane. "Thank God you're here. Please try to make them understand that Brodie says he can fix all of them without charge. I'll pay him of course, once he—"

"All what?" Ethan asked reluctantly, holding the children to him.

"The cars."

"What cars?"

"The ones I smashed into when I tried to stop the van."

"What van?"

"King Henry's van. You know. Cameron's."

Ethan remained quiet for a moment, trying to decide if it was him or the situation that simply refused to make sense. He searched his mind for a logical question.

"Why did you have to stop the van?"

"Because Beth was in it," Zachary said. "She was moving back to the cannery."

For an instant the sheriff in Ethan turned off, and the man in him felt a sudden and powerful onslaught of temper. She'd been leaving? While he was gone?

He looked for her face in the crowd, but couldn't find it. Billings had both arms out straight, holding Mrs. Pintoretto off with one hand and preventing a swinging Kelly from getting to her with the other.

"She *wasn't* leaving," Nikkie said, sobbing. "I told her Cameron would take her to work and Jason to school 'cause he was picking me up for our field trip—remember you signed the slip?" When he nodded, she went on, "Well, she asked me if there'd be room in the van for a couple of boxes, and when I asked her why, she said because she had to move some things back to the cannery. Jason and I thought she was moving her stuff back because you guys were gonna get a divorce. I know you had a big fight yesterday."

"So Nikkie called Kelly, and Uncle Brodie was there," Jason said. "And we thought they could come to the cannery and talk Mom out of leaving."

"But Grandma and Grandpa..." Nikkie began, then corrected herself. "I mean, Zachary and Joanne..."

Zachary smiled. "You were right the first time, Nikkie."

"Well, they overheard me telling Kelly on the phone, and they followed us and made Cameron stop the van so Mom couldn't leave until you got a chance to talk to her."

Ethan managed to assimilate all that, but he still had questions. "How did the window get broken?"

Joanne appeared. "Kelly did that," she said with a wide smile. "When Leadfoot Richards here got the van stopped—" she hooked a thumb at Zachary, who smiled proudly "—Kelly and Brodie were right behind us, and Kelly jumped out and started taking Beth's boxes out of the van, yelling that nobody was leaving anybody."

"Then Mom tried to get the boxes back," Jason said, his eyes shining with the excitement of the drama, "and they were fighting over them, and when Kelly pulled really hard, all the shields flew out and a couple of them went through that mean lady's window. Boy! They fly just like Frisbees!"

"The shields," Ethan asked, just to make sure he was keeping up, "were in the boxes?"

"Yeah," Nikkie said. "She wasn't moving out. She was just taking the shields to the cannery for storage until the Parents' Club auction."

Ethan felt such relief at that news that he gained a new confidence in himself and the situation. He looked around for Beth, but still couldn't spot her.

Billings was listening patiently while Mrs. Pintoretto chewed him out and Brodie was forcibly dragging Kelly away. He brought her toward Ethan and the group gathered around him.

"That woman needs a lobotomy!" Kelly declared,

yanking herself out of Brodie's hold. "And you didn't have to take her side!"

"I didn't take her side," Brodie argued. "I just thought you could have been a little more conciliatory about breaking her window."

"I tried. I explained to her that I'd have to repay her for her window in installments and she called me something rude in Italian."

"Do you speak Italian?"

"No."

"Then how do you know it was rude?"

"Because a universal gesture went with the word! And it's going to cost me everything I made at the fair and what's left of my savings, which I was going to use to buy a sign for the front of my studio."

Brodie looked smug. "No, it's not. I paid her."

Kelly's anger fell away and her expression softened. "You did?"

"I did. So you've got yourself a man who is more than a pretty face. Though I'm not a millionaire, I *am* able to take care of your damages."

She giggled and threw her arms around him. "My hero!" she exclaimed.

The drama club cheered. Joanne and Zachary nodded approvingly.

Curtis, Billings and the two police officers approached Ethan.

"Take Jason," Ethan directed Nikkie, "and see if you can find Beth."

"Right."

"Mrs. Pintoretto's willing to drop all charges," Billings said, "now that your brother's paid for the window."

"All right. And the owners of the cars?"

Curtis nodded. "Same. Damage isn't serious. A crunched bumper, a couple of lights and a bent mirror. Brodie says he can repair all of it. Believe it or not, everybody's happy."

"It's a miracle," one of the cops said. "When we walked into this, I thought we were going to have to call for hats and bats, just like in 'NYPD Blue.'"

The other cop grinned. "Fortunately for us, Drum, they're all your family. You think maybe you could put an electric fence around your house or something? Possibly post a warning when you guys are coming to town?"

"Hilarious, gentlemen." Ethan looked around at the dispersing crowd. "So we're finished here? No charges, no formal complaints, no tickets, no fines?"

"All clear. Except for you, who has to go home to this crime wave. Just to show you our hearts are in the right place, we'll sweep up the glass for you."

"Appreciate it."

"Daddy!" Ethan turned to find Nikkie and Jason looking concerned. The drama-club members were clustered around them, also worried. "Beth's in your car. In the cage."

He looked up and saw her seated in the back of his unit behind the metal screen that served to isolate the perpetrator. She had a hand to her forehead.

"You're not going to put her in jail again, are you?" Jason asked.

"No." He glanced up at Cameron. "How's your dad's van? Do you need to call him?"

Cameron shook his head. "Nope. It's cool. Not a scratch. We can still take Jason to school."

"I missed him when I went into the spin," Zachary called out. He and Joanne stood out of the way near a parking meter with Brodie and Kelly." "And got the car in front of me with my tail."

Joanne rolled her eyes. "Keep him out of the Grand Prix."

For the first time in about twenty-four hours, Ethan felt like laughing.

"Chinese food at Ming Ha's," he said to his newly adopted in-laws and to his brother and Kelly, who were picking up the shields. "Six-thirty? My treat."

"Sure," Brodie replied. "But why?"

Ethan couldn't think of a good reason, except that now that all their lives were interwoven, they didn't need one. "It's Monday. Family night."

He turned to the drama club, his daughter's eccentric but loyal support. "How about you guys? Chinese food tonight on me? Lots of old folks, though."

Heads nodded and their reply was unanimous. "Cool!"

"All right. See you tonight." He kissed Nikkie and Jason, then headed for his patrol car.

He opened the back door and leaned in to pull Beth out. She looked exhausted and upset and very fragile. "You need a lift somewhere?" he asked gently. "You can ride in the front."

Heavy-lidded blue eyes studied him suspiciously. "You mean we caused this whole—" she waved a hand at the barricades still up on the street, at the damaged cars just now being driven away, at the police sweeping glass off the street "—mess, and you're letting everybody off?"

God, he'd made quite an impression on her over the Appleby-house incident if she thought he could take this mini-riot, which was the result of everyone's love and concern for everyone else, and make them pay for it.

And then, because he felt guilty, he took off his hat and leaned down to kiss her slowly in apology. When he raised his head, he saw confusion in her eyes.

"What was that for?" she breathed.

"Because I'm sorry for ever bearing any resemblance to Steve, for not understanding instantly about the sculpture, for making you believe that anytime we disagreed about anything you were going to end up in jail."

The confusion in her eyes cleared and the love he'd grown used to seeing there shone brightly. She wrapped her arms around his waist and leaned into him with a little groan of contentment. "Oh, Ethan. I didn't think that. But what you said yesterday did make sense. When Steve died, I was so drunk with freedom that I did want to maintain it in a way, even after you married me. I was being selfish. So today I wanted to turn over a new leaf. I figured you'd have to take me in or something, and I was going to go quietly and wait for my chance to explain."

He walked her around the car and put her into the front seat. Then he got in behind the wheel. "You don't have to explain," he said. "Everyone's done it for you. The kids went nuts when they thought you were leaving. Zachary, Joanne, Kelly and Brodie were determined to stop you. And I think the drama club was just happy to be involved. They're all meeting us for dinner tonight, by the way. Chinese food."

She smiled. "How come?"

"Family night," he explained. "I'm taking you home. You're exhausted."

She looked at him across all the gear that sat between the two front seats, her expression disarmingly hopeful. "You don't have a coffee break coming or something, do you?"

"You hungry?"

She sighed. "Last night was horrid and I really really missed you."

Her words fell on him like a caress and made him curse the half mile between them and home.

He snatched the radio mike off its mounting even as he started the motor. "500," he said.

"500," Ebbie answered. "Go ahead."

"I'm code seven, Eb. For a couple of hours."

"It's early for lunch, Ethan."

"I'm not going to lunch, Ebbie. I'm taking Beth home."

"For two…? Oh. Oh! Right. Right. Two hours. Gotcha. Take your time. It's quiet, except for the riot you just cleaned up, and the rioters are all yours, aren't they? See you when I see you."

Ethan replaced the mike. All his. Despite the morning's events, he found great happiness in that knowledge.

"So how did it feel to arrive at the scene of a riot," Beth asked, laughter in her voice, "and discover that the rioters were your family?"

He laughed softly and accelerated. "Routine, my love. Routine."

...there's more to the story!

Superromance.
A *big* satisfying read about unforgettable characters. Each month we offer *six* very different stories that range from family drama to adventure and mystery, from highly emotional stories to romantic comedies—and much more! Stories about people you'll believe in and care about. Stories too compelling to put down....

Our authors are among today's *best* romance writers. You'll find familiar names and talented newcomers. Many of them are award winners— and you'll see why!

If you want the biggest and best in romance fiction, you'll get it from Superromance!

Emotional, Exciting, Unexpected...

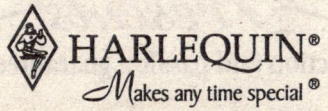

Visit us at www.eHarlequin.com

HSDIR1

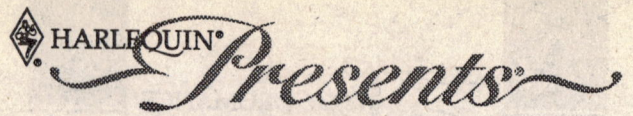

The world's bestselling romance series...
The series that brings you your favorite authors, month after month:

Helen Bianchin...Emma Darcy
Lynne Graham...Penny Jordan
Miranda Lee...Sandra Marton
Anne Mather...Carole Mortimer
Susan Napier...Michelle Reid

and many more uniquely talented authors!

Wealthy, powerful, gorgeous men...
Women who have feelings just like your own...
The stories you love, set in exotic, glamorous locations...

HARLEQUIN Presents

Seduction and passion guaranteed!

Visit us at www.eHarlequin.com

HPDIR1

HARLEQUIN® INTRIGUE

WE'LL LEAVE YOU BREATHLESS!

If you've been looking for thrilling tales of contemporary passion and sensuous love stories with taut, edge-of-the-seat suspense—then you'll love Harlequin Intrigue!

Every month, you'll meet four new heroes who are guaranteed to make your spine tingle and your pulse pound. With them you'll enter into the exciting world of Harlequin Intrigue— where your life is on the line and so is your heart!

THAT'S INTRIGUE— ROMANTIC SUSPENSE AT ITS BEST!

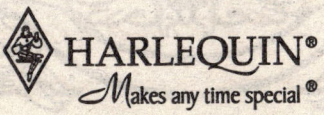

HARLEQUIN®
Makes any time special®

Visit us at www.eHarlequin.com

INTDIR1

Harlequin® Historical

From rugged lawmen and valiant knights to defiant heiresses and spirited frontierswomen, Harlequin Historicals will capture your imagination with their dramatic scope, passion and adventure.

Harlequin Historicals... they're too good to miss!

Visit us at www.eHarlequin.com

HHDIR1

Praise for Jasmine Cresswell

"Cresswell's woman-in-jeopardy plots are tightly woven with no loose ends."
—*Publishers Weekly*

"Ms. Cresswell masterfully creates a full, rich story...unwinding the tale piece by piece in such a way as to capture readers from the very first."
—*Romantic Times* on *The Refuge*

"Seat-of-the-pants tension and a surprising last-minute twist make this fast-paced story another winner."
—*Publishers Weekly* on *The Daughter*

Praise for Muriel Jensen

"The very talented Muriel Jensen has a definite skill for penning heartwarming, humorous tales destined to remain favorites."
—*Romantic Times*

"Ms. Jensen creates fully developed protagonists."
—*Affaire de Coeur*

"A well-practiced talent for blending humor and romance..."
—*Romantic Times*

JASMINE CRESSWELL

is a multitalented author of over forty novels. Her efforts have gained her numerous awards, including the RWA's Golden Rose Award and the Colorado Author's League award for best original paperback novel. Born in Wales and educated in England, Jasmine met her husband while working at the British Embassy in Rio de Janeiro. She has lived in Australia, Canada and six cities in the United States. Jasmine and her husband now make their home in Sarasota, Florida.

MURIEL JENSEN

is the award-winning author of over sixty books that tug at readers' hearts. She has won a Reviewer's Choice Award and a Career Achievement Award for Love and Laughter from *Romantic Times,* as well as a sales award from Waldenbooks. Muriel is best loved for her books about family, a subject she knows well, as she has three children and eight grandchildren. A native of Massachusetts, Muriel now lives with her husband in Oregon.